BURIED
LIES

KRISTINA OHLSSON is a political scientist and has held the position of Counter-Terrorism Officer at OSCE. She has worked at the Swedish Security Service, the Ministry for Foreign Affairs and the Swedish National Defence, where she was a junior expert on the Middle East conflict and the foreign policy of the European Union. Her debut novel, *Unwanted* was published in Sweden in 2009 to terrific critical acclaim and all her novels have since been bestsellers. Kristina lives in Stockholm.

Also by Kristina Ohlsson

Unwanted
Silenced
The Disappeared
Hostage
The Chosen

KRISTINA OHLSSON

BURIED LIES

Translated by Neil Smith

SIMON &
SCHUSTER

London · New York · Sydney · Toronto · New Delhi

A CBS COMPANY

First published in Sweden by Piratförlaget under the title *Lotus Blues*, 2014
First published in Great Britain by Simon & Schuster UK Ltd, 2017
A CBS COMPANY

Copyright © Kristina Ohlsson, 2014
Published by arrangement with the Salomonsson Agency
English translation copyright © Neil Smith, 2016

The right of Kristina Ohlsson to be identified as author
of this work has been asserted in accordance with sections
77 and 78 of the Copyright, Designs and Patents Act, 1988.

Paperback ISBN: 978-1-4711-4883-5
Trade Paperback ISBN: 978-1-4711-4882-8
eBook ISBN: 978-1-4711-4884-2

This book is a work of fiction. Names, characters, places and
incidents are either a product of the author's imagination or are
used fictitiously. Any resemblance to actual people living
or dead, events or locales is entirely coincidental.

Typeset in Sabon by M Rules
Printed and bound by CPI Group (UK) Ltd, Croydon, CR0 4YY

MIX
Paper from
responsible sources
FSC
www.fsc.org   FSC® C020471

Simon & Schuster UK Ltd are committed to sourcing paper
that is made from wood grown in sustainable forests and support the Forest
Stewardship Council, the leading international forest certification organisation.
Our books displaying the FSC logo are printed on FSC certified paper.

BURIED
LIES

PART I

'It's about my sister'

**TRANSCRIPT OF INTERVIEW WITH
MARTIN BENNER (MB).**

INTERVIEWER: FREDRIK OHLANDER (FO),
freelance journalist.

LOCATION:
Room 714, Grand Hôtel, Stockholm.

MB: This story I'm about to tell you, I can
promise you now: you're not going to
believe me. Okay? But do you know what? I
don't care. Because I have to explain what
happened to me. From start to finish. I
need to get it out.

FO: Okay, I'll listen. That's what I get paid
to do. I'm not a police officer, and I'm
not a judge. I'll just keep quiet and
listen.

MB: I hope so. It's important that you listen,
and even more important that you write it
down. So that my story is recorded, saved
for posterity. Otherwise this conversation
is a waste of time. Got that?

FO: Of course. That's why I'm here. To hear
your version of events.

MB: You're not going to be hearing my version.

FO: Sorry?

MB: You said you were here to listen to my
version of events. That implies that
there are other versions. Mine, and at
least one other person's. And that's not
the case.

FO: Okay.

MB: I can see what you're thinking. That I'm
either stupid, or batshit crazy. But I can
tell you, I'm not.

FO: Maybe we should take it from the beginning
and not bother discussing what I think
or don't think. So, you claim that you're
the victim of a conspiracy? That you've
been accused of committing crimes of which
you're innocent?

MB: You're going too fast.

FO: Am I?

MB: You said we should start at the beginning.
But you didn't. Because when this story
started, I wasn't the one sitting in the
dock.

FO: Sorry, you're right, of course. So, why
don't you tell me? So this conversation
goes the way you imagined.

MB: You'll have to forgive me for being
pedantic about the details. But what you
write after we've finished this conversation

is the most important thing you'll write in
your whole life.

FO: I don't doubt it.

(Silence)

MB: There's one more thing you need to know
before we get down to it.

FO: Oh?

MB: This is the most clichéd fucking story
you're ever going to hear.

FO: Really?

MB: Definitely. It's got all the stereotypical
elements. Unsolved murders. A big drugs
baron. A successful lawyer who's addicted
to sex. And – drum roll – a sweet little
child. A perfect film script, in other
words. If it wasn't for one important
detail.

FO: Which is?

MB: That it isn't a film. That it really
happened. Here and now. Right under the
noses of all the ordinary people who were
too stupid to notice. And nothing – nothing
at all – turned out to be the way it looked
at the start.

1

Bobby brought the stormy weather with him. Rain isn't exactly unusual in Stockholm. But I clearly remember that before Bobby came into my life, we used to have sunshine.

Whatever the case, it was raining now. I didn't have much to do, and I didn't want much to do either. It was summer, and I was about to shut up shop for the holidays. Lucy and I were going to be heading for Nice, to swim and sunbathe. Drink cocktails and smear each other in suntan oil. Belle was going to stay with her grandparents. And sure as hell, that wasn't the best time for someone to ring the doorbell. But they did. Helmer, our assistant, let him in and showed him to my room. He stopped in the doorway.

I know a problem case when I see one. The moment I set eyes on Bobby for the first time, I had a bad feeling. It wasn't the way he was dressed. Nor the fact that he smelled like an old cigarette factory. No, it was the look in his eyes that gave him away. His eyes were like two pieces of old lead shot. Pitch black.

'What's this about?' I said, without bothering to take my feet off the desk. 'I'm about to finish for the day.'

'Not until you've spoken to me,' the man said, and walked into the room.

I raised my eyebrows.

'I didn't hear myself say "Come in",' I said.

'That's funny,' the man said. 'I did.'

So I took my feet off my desk and sat up properly.

The man held out a hand across the desk.

'Bobby T.,' he said.

I laughed in his face. It wasn't a nice laugh.

'Bobby T.?' I said, shaking his hand. 'How interesting.'

How fucking ridiculous, was what I actually wanted to say. Who the hell calls himself Bobby T. in Stockholm? It sounded like a corny name for a corny gangster in a corny American film.

'There were two Bobbies in my class when I was little,' the man said. 'So they called us Bobby L. and Bobby T.'

'Really?' I said. 'Two Bobbies? Unusual.'

Probably not just unusual but unique. I tried to stifle my laughter.

Bobby stood in silence in front of my desk. I looked him up and down.

'Well, there were,' he said. 'But if you don't want to call me Bobby T., you don't have to. Bobby works, too.'

My mind was drawn to the world of American cinema again. There, Bobby would have been a big, black man with a mama with curlers in her hair and a dad who was a bank-robber. And Bobby T. would be the eldest of fourteen kids, and would try to pull girls by telling them how he walked his little brothers and sisters to school while his mother got drunk. Why do women always fall for that crap? Men they feel sorry for.

But back to the real Bobby. He was fair-skinned. Skinny and unkempt. His hair was curly with grease and his skin shiny. What did he want?

'You'd better get to the point,' I said, already starting to tire of my visitor. 'You see, I wasn't lying when I said I was about to finish for the day. I've got a hot date this evening and I want time to shower and change clothes before I meet her. I'm sure you understand.'

I don't think he understood at all. Lucy and I sometimes play a game, trying to guess when people had last had sex. Bobby looked like he hadn't had any for years. I wasn't even sure if he used to wank regularly. Lucy's much better at that sort of thing than me. She says you can tell if men wank a lot by looking at the lower part of their palms.

'I'm not here on my own behalf,' Bobby said.

'No?' I sighed. 'Who are you here about, then? Your dad? Your mum?'

Or a mate who didn't mean to hit the woman he mugged last week?

Not that I said that.

I've learned to keep my mouth shut when I have to.

'It's about my sister,' Bobby said.

He squirmed and the look in his eyes softened for the first time. I clasped my hands on the desk and waited, trying to look patient.

'I'll give you ten minutes, Bobby T.,' I said.

To stop him thinking I had all the time in the world.

Bobby nodded several times. Then he sat down, uninvited, on one of the visitor's chairs.

'I'll tell you,' he said, as if I'd expressed interest in his story. 'I want you to help her. My sister, I mean. I want to get her off.'

How many times have I heard that before as a defence lawyer? People get themselves into all sorts of dodgy situations, then want help to get out of them. That's not how it works. My role as a lawyer isn't to help people get to heaven instead of hell. My task is to make sure the people making the decision do a decent job. And usually they do.

'You're saying she's been accused of committing a crime?' I said.

'Not one. Several.'

'Okay, she's been accused of committing several crimes. Hasn't she already got a defence lawyer?'

'She had one. But he didn't do his job.'

I rubbed my chin.

'So now she wants a new lawyer?'

Bobby shook his head.

'She doesn't,' he said. 'I do.'

'Sorry, I don't follow. You want a lawyer for yourself? Or you think she ought to have a new one?'

'The latter.'

'Why do you want that if your sister disagrees?' I said. 'You should be careful about telling people what they want. Most of them can look after themselves.'

Bobby swallowed and the look in his eyes hardened again.

'Not my sister,' he said. 'She could never look after herself. I was always the one who did that.'

So he was the responsible brother. How lovely. There are far too few of them in the world. Or not.

'Okay, listen. Unless your sister is a minor, you have no authority to wade in and make decisions about her defence.

You're actually doing her a disservice. It's better for her to make those decisions for herself.'

Bobby leaned forward and rested his elbows on my desk. I couldn't bear his breath and pulled back.

'You're not listening to what I'm saying,' he said. 'I said my sister could never take care of herself. Past tense.'

I waited, unsure of what was coming next.

'She's dead,' Bobby T. said. 'She died six months ago.'

I'm very rarely, if ever, taken by surprise. But on this occasion I was. Because I couldn't dismiss Bobby T. as either drunk or high.

'Your sister's dead?' I said slowly.

Bobby T. nodded, evidently pleased that I'd finally understood.

'Then you'd better explain what you're doing here,' I said. 'Because dead people don't need defence lawyers.'

'My sister does,' Bobby said, his voice trembling. 'Because some bastard ruined her life with false accusations, and I want your help to prove it.'

It was my turn to shake my head.

I chose my words carefully.

'Bobby, you need to go to the police. I'm a lawyer, I don't do criminal investigations. I . . .'

Bobby banged his fist on the desk and I jumped involuntarily.

'I don't give a shit what you do,' he said. 'Because right now you're going to listen to me. I know you're going to want to help my sister. That's why I'm here. Because I heard you say so. On the radio.'

I was taken aback.

'You heard me say on the radio that I wanted to help your sister?'

'That's exactly what you said. That it was every lawyer's dream to defend someone like her.'

It slowly dawned on me what he was talking about. And who his sister was.

'You're Sara Texas's brother,' I said.

'Tell! Her name was Tell!'

The anger in his voice made me flinch. He quickly changed his tone.

'You said you wanted to help her,' he repeated. 'You said so, on the radio. So you must have meant it.'

Oh fuck.

'That was an interview about current cases,' I said, now making an effort to sound friendly. 'I didn't express myself very clearly. That was foolish of me. Your sister's case was extremely unusual. That's why I said she was a lawyer's dream client.'

I could hardly believe it was true.

In front of me sat the brother of a woman who had confessed to no fewer than five murders before she escaped from a supervised outing and killed herself the day before her trial was due to start.

'I know what you said,' Bobby said. 'I've listened to the interview over and over again. It's available online. And I've done my research about you. You're smart.'

Flattery can get you a long way.

He said I was smart.

And obviously I thought he was right.

But I wasn't so smart that I could bring the dead back to life.

'I'm afraid you're going to have to accept the facts,' I said. 'Your sister was accused of some very serious crimes. And she confessed, Bobby. She looked the lead interviewer and the prosecutor right in the eye and said that she'd murdered all those people. First she murdered two people in the US when she was an au pair in Texas. Then she murdered another three here in Stockholm. The weight of evidence was – and is – compelling. There's nothing you can do for her now.'

He sat in complete silence for a while, just looking at me, before he finally spoke.

'She was lying. She didn't kill them. And I can prove it.'

I threw my hands up in resignation. Then I came up with what I should have said right at the start: 'If you've got information which suggests that your sister was innocent, then you need to go to the police. Immediately. Because that means someone else is the murderer, and that person needs to be apprehended.'

When I get angry or wound up, my nostrils flare. Like a horse. That was one of the first things Lucy told me when we first met, and if she could have seen me now she would have laughed.

'Do you understand what I'm saying, Bobby? You have to go to the police.'

The wretched rain was hammering at the window behind me with such frenzy that I thought the glass would break.

Bobby looked wound up as well.

'I've already been. They wouldn't listen to me. Not when Sara was still alive, and not afterwards either.'

'Then you'll have to go again.'

'They won't care.'

'It might look that way, but believe me, they'll listen. If they choose not to take what you tell them any further, it's because they regard it as being of no interest. And you'd have to accept that.'

Bobby got up so abruptly that his chair fell over. His previously pale face was now bright red.

'I'll never accept what they did to Sara. Never!'

I stood up too.

'In that case, I don't honestly know what you should do,' I said. 'Because I can't help you.'

For a moment I thought he was going to punch me, but then he seemed to swallow the worst of his anger. Instead he opened his jacket and took a folded sheet of paper from his inside pocket.

'Here,' he said, holding it out towards me.

I took it, somewhat reluctantly, and unfolded it.

'So?' I said when I'd read what it said.

'Proof,' Bobby said. 'Proof that she was innocent.'

I read it again.

It looked like a bus or train ticket. The writing was in English.

Houston to San Antonio
5:30 p.m.
Friday 8 October, 2007

I had to make a real effort not to get annoyed. I didn't have time for this sort of nonsense.

'A bus ticket someone bought to travel from Houston to San Antonio at half past five on the afternoon of Friday 8 October, 2007. Is this your proof that your sister was innocent?'

'It's a train ticket, not a bus ticket,' Bobby said angrily, like there was a big difference between the two. 'You don't know my sister's case yet, I can tell. On Friday 8 October, 2007, the first murder that Sara was accused of was committed.

The victim died at eight o'clock that evening. In a city called Galveston in Texas. But my sister can't have been the murderer, because at the time she was on a train heading for San Antonio. That's her ticket you're holding.'

I didn't know where to start. A ticket proved nothing, of course. She could just as easily not have caught the train. Always assuming that the ticket was hers to start with.

'Where did you get this?' I said, waving the sheet of paper.

'From Sara's friend, Jenny. She was an au pair as well. In the same city as Sara. She took the ticket to the Texas police but they didn't want it. She ended up sending it to me by courier, and I took it to my sister's useless lawyer.'

What could I say?

It was true, I didn't know the details of Sara Tell's case, but I'd read enough to have a broad idea. The evidence against her was solid. The prosecutor had plenty of material. The ticket didn't prove a damn thing.

But I realised Bobby wasn't going to leave my office unless I gave him something to take away with him. Hope. That's what everyone who walks through my door wants.

So I did what I usually do when there are no other options. I lied.

'Okay, Bobby,' I said. 'How about this? You leave the ticket and a phone number with me, and I promise I'll look into it. I'll call you at the end of the week, let's say Sunday, to tell you if I want to carry on working on your sister's case. And if I decide I don't want to, you need to accept that. Agreed?'

I held out my hand.

He hesitated for several long moments before shaking it.

His hand was cool and dry.

'Agreed.'

He wrote his phone number down on a scrap of paper. Then he disappeared from my office at last. Leaving me sitting there with an old train ticket in my hand. Like hell was Sara Texas innocent. But it didn't matter if she was, seeing as she was already dead and buried.

I opened the top drawer of my desk and dropped the ticket in it.

In an hour's time I was going to be seeing Lucy, and there was no way she was going to have sex with me unless I had showered first. I had to get home.

Then I heard the door to the office open again, and Bobby was soon back inside my room.

'Two more things,' he said. 'One: like I said, Sara had a lawyer. But he didn't do his job. You'll realise that when you look at the case. That he let her down.'

'And what makes you think he let her down?'

'He knew things, but he never said anything to anyone. He knew about the ticket I just gave you. And, like I say, other things.'

I hate people who speak in riddles. I hate games. The only person I play games with is Belle. She's four years old, and still believes in Father Christmas.

'What do you think he knew?'

'Talk to him. Then you'll understand. I'm not saying more than that.'

His rhetorical posturing irritated me, but I couldn't be bothered to carry on the discussion.

'And the second point? You said there were two more things?'

Bobby swallowed.

'My nephew, Mio. He disappeared the day my sister killed herself. I want you to find him.'

Sara Texas had been the single mother of a small boy. The police suspected that Sara had killed him and hidden his body. As far as I was aware, their investigation hadn't generated a single theory about what had happened to the child.

'I need to make a very clear distinction here,' I said. 'This is a law firm, not a charity that looks for missing people. Sorry. I've promised to take a look at your sister's case, but I'm afraid I can't help you find out what happened to her son.'

'It's all connected,' Bobby said. 'You'll see. It's all part of the same story.'

Then he turned round and walked out. This time he didn't come back.

2

'I'm not going to have sex with you tonight, just so you know.'
Why do women say that? We'd barely had time to sit
down and order our first drinks before Lucy felt she had to
ruin our date.

'Listen, sex was the last thing on my mind when I came
here,' I said.

'Oh, Martin.'

'What? It's true.'

Our cocktails arrived and I took a small sip of the bitter
drink. G&T, a timeless classic.

Obviously Lucy didn't buy my transparent lie. She knows
me. She knows *men*, knows we're always thinking about sex.
It's biological, there's nothing we can do about it.

'If you weren't thinking about sex, what were you thinking
about?'

'Sara Texas.'

Lucy shuddered and almost spilled her drink. She always
starts with a Cosmopolitan before moving on to wine.

'Okay, that's a good one.'

I could feel her relax as her smile grew warmer. Maybe I'd get to have sex with her after all. In which case I'd be sure to thank Bobby properly next time I saw him.

The thought of seeing Bobby again was enough to dampen my mood. I took a thirsty gulp of my G&T and felt Lucy's hand on my shoulder.

'Has something happened?'

'We had a visitor at the office after you left,' I said.

I told Lucy about Bobby, and she listened, wide-eyed.

'But that's crazy,' she said when I'd finished. 'So, Sara Texas had a brother who thinks she was innocent?'

'That's usually the case, though, isn't it?' I said. 'There's nothing unusual about criminals having relatives who want to believe they haven't done anything wrong. But . . .'

Lucy waited.

'What?'

'Bloody hell, Lucy, there was something weird about the bloke. Apart from the fact that he was Sara Texas's brother. He was so pushy. So certain.'

'That Sara was innocent?'

'Yes, partly that, but also that I would agree to take her case on.'

Lucy frowned.

'But Sara Texas is dead, isn't she?'

'Of course she is. And has been for several months now.'

The newspapers had been full of articles about her. About her growing up in the Stockholm suburb of Bandhagen, and her alcoholic dad who used to sell her to his friends. Her teachers had spoken out, revealing what a tragic childhood she had. And they cried, too, saying they regretted not telling Social Services earlier.

'I don't really remember the story,' Lucy said. 'What was it again, how did she end up in Texas?'

'She was an au pair.'

'Bloody hell, who'd employ someone like her as an au pair?'

'What do you mean, "someone like her"? Surely anyone can look good on paper? The question is really, how can anyone employ girls who've only just left home as au pairs? I mean, it's hardly the age-group we encourage to become parents.'

Lucy took a sip of her cocktail.

'It must have been such a relief for her. Getting away from her crazy family.'

'I'm sure it was,' I said, seeing as the same thought had occurred to me. 'A shame she didn't do anything more creative with her new-found freedom than murder a load of people.'

Lucy grinned.

'You're the salt of the earth, Martin.'

'You too, baby. That's why you can't do without me.'

I put one arm round her back and she didn't brush it off.

We were a couple, once upon a time. I don't think I've ever been smugger than I was then. I, Martin Benner, had managed to catch the hottest lawyer babe in the whole of Stockholm, possibly the whole of Sweden. Lucia 'Lucy' Miller. It didn't get better than that.

Maybe not, but it didn't last particularly long. And obviously that was my fault. As usual, I panicked and started sleeping with other people. A tiny part of me thinks I can't help it. Everyone has their bad habits. Some people burp when they eat, others are incapable of being monogamous.

'Where's Belle this evening?' Lucy asked.

'With the au pair,' I said curtly.

'Speaking of handing responsibility for raising your child to someone else.'

'Someone else who isn't a child herself. Signe's fifty-five, the perfect age for an au pair.'

'Bollocks, the only reason you employed an older au pair was so you wouldn't be tempted to sleep with her.'

I finished the rest of my drink and pretended I hadn't heard her.

'Another one, please,' I said to the bartender.

'You still don't think Belle should come to Nice with us?' Lucy said.

'Belle is definitely not coming to Nice with us. She's going to stay with her grandparents. That'll be perfect.'

Most people who meet me don't think I've got any children. I haven't, either. At least, no biological children. And certainly none that were planned. Belle is, or was, my sister's daughter. My sister and her husband died in a plane crash just over three years ago. Belle was nine months old at the time. No one, me included, imagined that Belle would end up living with me. Everyone thought she'd go to her father's sister and her family. But her aunt, the bitch, didn't think she could look after her niece. She already had two children, so it would be unfair on the others to take another child into the family. Her husband agreed with her, said they didn't have the time or money to raise another young child. An abandoned baby didn't suit their idyllic lifestyle. The house wasn't big enough, the car was too small.

But Lucy hit the nail on the head: the only thing that wasn't big enough was their hearts.

So Belle was going to go to a foster family. In Skövde, of all places.

I can still remember the way my pulse-rate went up when I heard that. I don't know how I got to the Social Services office, but all of a sudden I was sitting there.

'But we've already discussed this,' the social worker said. 'Belle's aunt doesn't want to look after her. And nor do you. And as for your mother, Belle's grandmother, she's too old. The same goes for her father's parents. Which means that someone else will have to take care of her.'

She gave me an encouraging smile. 'The family has a long tradition of fostering. They live on a lovely farm with lots of animals. It will be a good environment for Belle to recover in.'

I could see it clearly before me. Belle would end up living with a load of hicks out in the middle of nowhere and learn to milk cows by hand. And there was no way on earth I was going to let it end like that.

'I've changed my mind,' I heard myself say. 'I want her to come and live with me.'

I cried that night. For the first time in many, many years. I hadn't even cried at my sister's funeral. Once I'd finished crying I went into my study and moved all the furniture out. I painted the walls yellow and had the floor revarnished. Belle moved in four days later. Before that I'd never changed a single nappy in my entire life. I'd never warmed a bottle of formula. I'd actually never felt the weight of such a tiny person in my arms.

I still have nightmares about how much Belle used to scream back at the start. If it hadn't been for Lucy and my mother, I'd never have got through that first year. But afterwards I thought it had been worth it. Sometimes it's good to do the right thing.

Lucy ordered a glass of wine.

'It'll be good to get away,' she said.

'Couldn't agree more,' I said.

I pulled her closer, inhaling the scent of her hair. It was okay if she didn't want to have sex with me, as long as she didn't have sex with anyone else.

'So what are you going to do?'

'About what?'

'About Sara Texas and her brother.'

'What am I going to do? Nothing, obviously. I mean, what's there to do? The woman's dead. She confessed, Lucy. That's it. It's over, nothing more to say.'

'And that ticket?'

'What about it? It's a train ticket, that's all. It doesn't prove anything. Anyway, it's not my job to sort out that sort of detail. That's up to the police.'

Lucy said nothing. She knew I was right. The only surprising thing was that she thought it worth discussing.

'What are you thinking?' I said.

'Nothing. I'm just being silly. Of course she wasn't innocent. And even if she was, you're right – it's the police's job to deal with that.'

She took a sip of her wine.

I was looking at a woman at the other end of the room. Attractive, and obviously bored by her company. She was holding her wine-glass with both hands. No ring. I could have her in less than half an hour.

Lucy followed my gaze.

'You're fucking incredible, Martin.'

'Stop it, I'm just looking.'

I gave her a kiss on the cheek.

'It doesn't do any harm, does it?'

Lucy looked annoyed.

'Finish your drink,' she said.

'Do you want to go home?'

'Yes, and you're coming with me. I've changed my mind. Of course I want to have sex with you tonight.'

3

Remember: the oldest trick in the book is the one that works best. It was enough for me to glance at another woman for Lucy to decide to have sex with me. As I lay naked beside her on the floor of her flat an hour or so later, I was amazed at how easy it was to get what you wanted the whole time. She'd started the evening saying no, and ended up saying yes.

Same old story.

My mobile rang.

'Martin, you've got to come over. The cellar's flooded.'

Perfect.

My mum only rings to ask if she can look after Belle, or because she wants my help with something. I have a standard response to requests for help.

'You know I'd help you if I could, Marianne. But I'm afraid I simply haven't got time. A client needs me, and I can't leave her in the lurch. Call someone else and I'll take care of the bill later.'

The idea that being rich doesn't make you happier is

rubbish. Money means you can buy time, and time lets you buy freedom. And a person who is free is also happy.

I've never actually called my mum 'Mum'. Her name is Marianne, and there's no good reason not to call her that.

When I hung up I saw that Lucy was looking at me.

'That wasn't very nice.'

'It's getting late. I need to go home and relieve the babysitter.' I got up from the floor and stretched.

'You know, I could go home with you,' Lucy said. 'Stay the night and take Belle to preschool tomorrow.'

I pulled on my pants and trousers.

'Baby, that's probably not a good idea.'

We both knew why. So that Belle didn't see us together too often. Because I didn't want her to think that we were a proper couple.

'Another time, okay?'

Lucy went into the bathroom and closed the door. I heard her turn the tap in the basin. So I wouldn't hear her pee. Ridiculous.

But what was even more ridiculous was that I was still thinking about Sara Texas. And Bobby.

She had confessed to five murders. This case had never been some trashy reality show. There was evidence. Sara had been able to account for specific times and dates. She'd said where the murder weapons were, insofar as there were any. And she had described other details that no one but the murderer could have known about.

Even so, doubts were starting to grow inside my head like a vague itch.

That damn ticket. That didn't prove anything, did it? It wasn't even an individual ticket, there was no name on it to say who had used it.

Bobby said he got it from his sister's friend Jenny. Bobby. That was a really stupid name, too. A problem name. In Sweden, anyway. I remembered photographs I'd seen in the papers. She wasn't at all like her brother. Which didn't matter, of course. I wasn't much like my sister. We had different fathers. Mine was black and came from the USA. From Texas, in fact. My sister was as white as Mum. Her father came from Sälen. Actually from Sälen, the ski resort. I never imagined anyone really lived there.

I smiled at the thought of how different my sister and I used to look. The first time I dropped Belle off at preschool the staff were astonished. I could see it very clearly even though they didn't say anything. How could such a tall black man have such a fair little child?

Sara Texas. Obviously her name was Tell, not Texas, as her brother had pointed out. Texas was what the newspapers called her. Because that was where she claimed her first victims. Like a hunter.

I sighed. I wasn't going to be able to resist, I knew that. I was going to sit down and read through all the articles I could find about Sara Texas, I'd stay up all night if necessary. When dawn came I'd rub my eyes and fall asleep at my desk. The spell would be broken the moment Belle woke up. Irritable and dishevelled, I'd drive her to preschool and wait for Sunday, when I would call Bobby and explain things to him. That his sister's case was interesting, but not for me.

Seeing as she was dead.

Seeing as I wasn't a private detective.

Bobby had said a single sentence that I couldn't shake off quite as lightly. That Sara's lawyer hadn't done his job. That he had 'known things'.

Lucy came out of the bathroom. Naked and beautiful. It was hard to believe that she had once been mine.

'Do you remember who defended Sara Texas?' I said.

Lucy laughed and picked her briefs off the floor.

'I knew you wouldn't be able to let it go.'

'Stop it, I'm just curious.'

'I can understand that. Tor Gustavsson was in charge of her case.'

I let out a whistle. Of course, old Gustavsson, I'd completely forgotten that.

'Didn't he retire fairly recently?' I said.

'December last year, just after Sara died,' Lucy said. 'You missed his leaving do because you and Belle were in Copenhagen that weekend.'

I found myself smiling when Lucy reminded me of that trip to Copenhagen. It had been a great success. Just Belle and me. We flew there for the second weekend of Advent and stayed in one of the hotels along the coast. That was probably the first time I properly understood that children change over time. That they grow gradually. For some stupid reason I was surprised that Belle ate so nicely when we went to restaurants. She could say what she liked and what she didn't like. I drank wine and she drank fizzy pop. When we went back to the hotel, she walked all the way. No pushchair, no carrying. Not that it was particularly far, but I was still proud of her. And incredibly sad. About the fact my sister had died when Belle was so small. And that the person looking after Belle – me, in other words – didn't even know that she could feed herself.

After that I promised myself that I would be more present in her life. And I've kept that promise.

The memory went from warming to painful and I had to blink a few times.

'It was boring as fuck,' Lucy said. 'Gustavsson made the longest speech ever, going on and on about all the great things he'd done in his career.'

'Did he mention Sara Texas?'

'No, and that was seriously bloody weird. Because I don't think he actually ever worked on a bigger case than that. But I dare say he saw that one as a failure. Seeing as she died.'

That was true. I remember being surprised when I saw Gustavsson being quoted in the papers. Why had Sara picked one of the best lawyers to defend her when she'd decided to admit everything and then commit suicide before the trial?

'Shall I call for a taxi?' Lucy said.

I tucked my shirt in my trousers.

I looked out of the window and saw the rain. Was that how it was going to be from now on? Rainy and wet.

'Yes please,' I said.

Shortly afterwards I was sitting in the taxi. I called my mother to ask what was happening with the flooded cellar. A plumber was on his way.

4

The au pair, or whatever you wanted to call Signe in light of her advanced age, was sitting drinking coffee in the kitchen when I got home.

'Have you had a quiet evening?' I said.

She smiled.

'Absolutely, no problems.'

Signe does all the things that I don't have time for as a single man with a full-time job. I drop Belle off at preschool and she picks her up. She does the shopping and cooking. When Belle starts school she'll help with her homework too. She doesn't have to do the cleaning and ironing. The cleaner does that.

Like I said. Money buys time and gives you freedom. And it's that freedom that makes people happy.

Once the au pair had gone I took a look into Belle's room. Belle was lying on her back with her mouth open. The pink duvet seemed too big; she looked like she was disappearing beneath it. I crept over quietly and pulled it down a little. Much better. I leaned over and kissed her softly on her forehead.

Then I went back to the kitchen and took out the bottle of

whisky. My grandfather taught me to drink whisky. Always single malt, and never cold. You're only allowed ice with blended whiskies.

The wooden floor creaked beneath my feet as I walked into the library and closed the door behind me. There's no better guard-dog than an old floor. When Belle had been with me for a year, I bought the next-door neighbour's flat and knocked through from mine. We needed space, me and the little girl.

I turned the computer on as I sipped the whisky.

Sara Texas.

I was just going to check a few things before going to bed. If Bobby wanted a private detective, he'd have to ask someone else.

I found myself thinking about Tor Gustavsson. The lawyer who hadn't done his job. Who 'knew things'.

I'll start with that, I thought. I'll call old Gustavsson in the morning, then I'll call Bobby and tell him I don't want to get involved.

The fan in the computer whirred quietly.

My fingers flew over the keyboard.

Sara Texas Tell.

What secrets had she taken with her to the grave?

Twenty-six. That was how old Sara Tell had been when she confessed to the murders of five people. Three women and two men. In the field of criminology she was regarded as unique. After she was arrested and remanded in custody, there had been a big debate as to whether or not she was a serial killer. I couldn't really understand that. Of course she was a serial killer. If she hadn't been an attractive young woman, that discussion would never have taken place.

People are very reluctant to believe things that fall outside the realm of what they expect. Sara Tell wasn't beautiful, but she was attractive. Her features were so finely chiselled that her face looked like a doll's. She was taller than most women, almost one metre eighty. If she hadn't been, the case would have felt even more peculiar. Because then it would have been pretty much impossible to understand how she could have committed her crimes.

She never gave any explanation for the murders. Not that I could see in the papers, anyway.

It was past midnight and the air in the library was starting to feel stuffy. The whisky looked cloudy and my back was stiff.

I remembered the radio interview that Bobby heard me do. The interviewer was a sensation-seeking reporter who wanted to know what I thought about Sara's chances of being found not guilty. I sometimes get asked that sort of thing about high-profile cases, partly because I spent a very short period of my life in the police force. And in the States, no less. As far as Sara was concerned, I said that the chances of her being found not guilty were non-existent, but that I thought everyone – no matter what they had done – had the right to a defence lawyer during court proceedings. To the question of whether I could imagine defending Sara, I replied just as Bobby had said: that Sara's was a dream case. That I would have been happy to help her.

With what? I wondered, as I sat at the computer reading article after article about the horrific crimes she had committed. Sara Texas didn't strike me as a woman in extremis. On the contrary. She seemed to have been perfectly capable of taking care of herself. In the pictures from the trial she looked very focused. Straight-backed, attractive. For some reason I was struck by the fact that she wore glasses. A serial killer with a pretty face, glasses and a nice jacket. It didn't make sense. And not because I have any prejudices about the sort of people who commit crimes in our world. Sara Texas was a paradox. And that was what made her interesting. And that was why I would have liked to have met her.

Almost unconsciously I reached for a pen and sheet of paper. I quickly sketched out some of the basic facts. She had committed her first murder when she was twenty-one years old. She stabbed a young woman in Galveston, Texas. The following year she murdered a man in Houston. After that she moved back to Sweden. She had just become a mother when she committed her third murder. Before her son was three she had notched up numbers four and five.

It took the police in Texas five years to figure out that she was responsible for the murders of the woman in Galveston and the man in Houston. A coincidence helped unlock the case and led them to request her extradition from Sweden to the USA. The Swedish authorities said no, obviously. We don't hand people over to countries where they run the risk of receiving the death penalty. But we are able to try people for crimes even if they were committed abroad. And that was what the prosecutor decided to do.

Only then did they work out that Sara had murdered three other people too. The cases had been languishing unsolved by the police until then. And would probably have remained like that if Sara herself hadn't mentioned them.

Why on earth would anyone do a thing like that?

Confessing to three murders that no one would have thought to ask about. It was beyond me.

Ignoring the fact that using newspaper articles as source material was rather frivolous, I thought I had identified several more things that were hard to understand.

No fingerprints.

No DNA in the form of blood, saliva or hair.

No items left at the crime scenes.

No witnesses to the crimes.

But, on the other hand, she had known or at least met all the victims while they were alive. That sort of detail had to be regarded as compromising, given the circumstances. Seeing as there were no fewer than five victims, murdered on two continents, it was hard to ignore that particular fact. But they were hardly close friends of Sara's. One of the victims worked at a hotel she had stayed in. Another one was a taxi driver who gave her a ride. The sort of connections that could never be described as close.

All in all, there was really only one conclusion: in a Swedish court she would have been found not guilty on all charges if she hadn't confessed and presented her own evidence.

I shook my head slowly.

Why would anyone do that? Guilty conscience? Because they felt a need to tell someone?

But Sara never expressed any regret. She never asked anyone's forgiveness or explained her crimes. Christ knows what her motivations were.

I was feeling tired, my eyes were stinging. I turned the desk-lamp off and went to bed.

There was something odd lurking in the case of Sara Texas. Something I didn't know how to find.

That annoyed me.

Really fucking annoyed me.

5

It was raining again. Drops of water the size of blueberries were falling from the sky, spoiling both my hairstyle and my jacket.

Lucy smiled as I walked through the door.

'Don't you look lovely?' she said.

She gave me a quick kiss.

'Thanks for last night, by the way.'

'Thank you,' I said. 'As always, very enjoyable.'

Lucy and I set up the law practice almost ten years ago. We were both relative newcomers in the business, and equally ambitious. I know I thought of her as a kindred spirit. She was incredibly driven in everything she did, and still is to this day. We used to talk about how successful we were going to be, and how many employees we'd have. That bit never happened. We were comfortable, just the two of us, and never felt like letting anyone else in. Apart from our assistant, Helmer.

A friend once asked me how I could bear to work so closely with a woman I was in love with. I didn't understand the question. I still don't. Being close to Lucy wasn't and isn't a problem. Quite the contrary; I'd go to pieces if she packed up and left.

'You look tired, did you stay up late?'

'No, not really,' I said, stifling a yawn.

'Really? You look like a panda with those rings round your eyes. Admit it – you lay awake reading about Sara Texas.'

'Not at all,' I said drily. 'But I did *sit* up reading. It's pretty interesting, actually.'

'I can imagine,' Lucy said. 'Good-looking girl, after all.'

I went into my room and barely had time to close the door before it opened again. Helmer, our assistant, came in.

'A plumber called. He wanted to check where to send his invoice for sorting out a flooded basement. I told him we didn't have a basement and to send his fake invoices to someone else.'

'Then you'll have to call him back and apologise,' I said. 'Of course we've got a basement, and it flooded yesterday.'

Helmer looked totally flummoxed. He does that rather too often for my liking, but Lucy's fond of him.

'I don't understand.'

'You're not supposed to. Please, call him back. The invoice will be paid through the business.'

Helmer disappeared, closing the door behind him.

It took me less than five minutes to find a home number for retired lawyer Tor Gustavsson. He was a legend in his day. Slightly undeserving, perhaps, but even so. He once defended a very successful businessman who was accused of murdering his wife. How Gustavsson managed to get the guy off was a mystery, but evidently both the District Court and Court of Appeal had found him not guilty in no time at all. After that everyone wanted to work with Gustavsson.

But now he was retired. Sara Texas had been his last big case. I hoped he wasn't going to get grouchy because I called. Grouchy old men are a pet hate of mine.

The phone rang and rang. No answer. I was just about to hang up when someone answered in a high voice and said: 'Hello?'

I cleared my throat, a habit I'd picked up when I was surprised.

'Martin Benner,' I said. 'I'm calling from the law firm Benner & Miller. I'm trying to reach Tor Gustavsson.'

There was a moment's silence.

'I'm terribly sorry,' the voice eventually said. 'Tor isn't up to taking any calls at the moment.'

I was speaking to a woman. If she'd been here in front of me, I dare say I could have got Gustavsson on the phone.

'I'm sorry to hear that,' I said. 'I'm calling about a fairly important matter.'

'Are you a journalist?'

The question took me by surprise.

'What? No, certainly not. I'm a lawyer, like I said. Sorry, can I ask who I'm speaking to?'

'Gunilla Gustavsson, Tor's daughter-in-law. What's this about?'

I hesitated. Something told me that Sara Texas's name was unlikely to open any doors.

'An old case,' I said. 'One Tor worked on . . . some time ago.'

I heard a sigh at the other end of the line.

'Is this about Sara Texas?'

Fuck.

'Yes,' I had to admit.

'That case almost broke my father-in-law. I'd rather you didn't discuss it with him.'

'Perhaps I could call back when he's feeling better?' I said.

'I don't think so. You see, Tor suffered a severe stroke a while back. And last week he had a heart attack. As if that wasn't enough, he came down with a lung infection two days later. He quite literally has to devote all his energy to getting better. Otherwise we don't know if he'll make it.'

Her voice was clear and composed, but I could detect a definite undertone of anxiety. Hardly surprising, given what she'd just told me.

'Of course,' I said. 'Send him my best wishes. I hope everything works out.'

I'd only met Tor Gustavsson a handful of times, but there was a chance he'd remember me.

'Thanks,' the daughter-in-law said. 'I'll tell him you called. You could always try calling Eivor instead.'

'Eivor?'

'His assistant. She should be able to answer any questions about Sara Texas.'

I was instantly curious.

'How do I get hold of Eivor?'

'She retired at the same time as Tor. She lives in a small flat in Gamla stan.'

Tor's daughter-in-law read out a phone number.

'Tell her I gave you her number,' she said. 'Eivor's practically one of the family. She is very fond of my father-in-law.'

I could imagine. It's always the same. Behind every successful man is a woman with a gentle smile, pointing out that his trousers are too short. In Tor Gustavsson's case, the woman's name was Eivor. In mine she didn't yet have a name. It certainly wasn't Lucy, at any rate.

Before I dialled Eivor's number I called Belle's preschool.

She had been upset when I dropped her off that morning. I wanted to make sure everything was okay.

'She's fine now,' the woman who answered said. 'Don't forget that she needs a packed lunch tomorrow. We're going on an outing.'

Outing and packed lunch. Always something to remember. As soon as I'd hung up I called the au pair.

'Belle needs to take food to school tomorrow.'

'You mean a packed lunch? And preschool, not school.'

'Exactly. You can sort something simple out this afternoon, can't you?'

'Martin, it's only a matter of making a few sandwiches and buying a drink.'

'You mean I ought to do it myself?'

The au pair fell silent.

'Buy some sort of drink and I'll sort out the sandwiches,' I said.

Then I ended the call and concentrated on more important things than a few manky sandwiches.

Eivor. Tor Gustavsson's old assistant. Would she be able to help me?

She would. And – even more importantly – she was willing to. We met in her flat. A small but magical home. Like something out of a magazine. She must have put her soul into refining these meagre square metres in which she had chosen to live.

She showed me into the kitchen and nudged me onto a chair at a triangular table. We were evidently going to drink coffee.

'I assume you've got a lot to do, so I won't stay long,' I said.

Meaning, of course, that I had a hell of a lot to do that was more important than drinking coffee with a complete stranger. But that sort of subtle message seemed to pass Eivor by.

'You can stay as long as you like,' she said. 'I've got all the time in the world.'

God didn't give me many talents to work with, but He did give me a unique ability to manipulate women of all ages and cultures. Eivor wasn't a hard nut to crack. I made myself more comfortable at the table and listened attentively as Eivor explained how badly things had gone for Tor Gustavsson, and how sad it was.

'You should have seen him at work,' she said. 'I swear – time used to stand still in court when he made his closing statements.'

I came very close to laughing but managed to make it sound like a cough.

'I've heard a lot of good things about Tor,' I said. 'He was a true upholder of the law, he certainly was.'

'He's not dead yet,' Eivor said.

'Tor *is* a true upholder of the law.'

It was obvious that they'd had an affair. Maybe lasting decades. Eivor talked warmly about the many years she spent as Gustavsson's assistant. With a bit of skilful manipulation I managed to hurry the story along until finally we reached Tor's last big case: Sara Texas.

'She confessed, of course,' Eivor said. 'Tor tried to reason with her, I know that. But she refused. Justice needed to be done.'

'Did Tor ever doubt that she was telling the truth?'

'No, why would he have done? The evidence was

unambiguous. Everything the girl said could be proved. So what was he supposed to do? He gave her the support she needed, made sure she wasn't treated badly during the time she was in custody. And . . . well, then it turned out the way it did.'

'She committed suicide.'

Eivor nodded slowly.

'Yes, she did. Tor was so upset when he heard. But it wasn't his fault. I told him that plenty of times.'

An old grandfather clock was ticking in the corner of the room. Rain was beating at the window and I wondered what I thought I was doing. Sitting and drinking coffee with a garrulous old lady. What did I actually imagine I could get out of her? A revolutionary revelation that she and Gustavsson had kept quiet about for months?

I was chasing ghosts.

Because an idiot calling himself Bobby T. had marched into my office and messed things up.

'Do you know if Tor was in contact with Sara Tell's brother?'

Eivor started.

'You mean Bobby? Oh, yes. He was so angry with Tor, you know. Screamed and shouted at him in the office.'

'What for?'

'Because he'd got it into his head that his sister was innocent.'

'Did he have any proof of that?'

'I remember him coming to the office once waving a ticket about. But Tor wouldn't listen to his nonsense. Nor would Sara. She forbade Tor to speak to her brother, and after that Bobby stopped coming to the office.'

This was interesting. So Sara had pushed her brother away when he tried to help her.

'Why do you think it was so important for Sara that she be convicted of the murders?' I said.

'So that she could be at peace,' Eivor said with a distant look in her eyes.

She toyed with her coffee-cup.

'That's what we all want, I suppose,' she said. 'Peace.'

Peace. That was probably the most ridiculous thing I'd ever heard.

The kitchen suddenly felt cold and bare. The coffee tasted of horse-piss and I wanted to get back to the office. Maybe I'd have reason to return to Eivor, but for the time being I clearly wasn't getting anywhere.

'Well, thanks for letting me take up your time,' I said, putting the cup down in the tiny sink.

'I should be thanking you,' Eivor said. 'It was good of you to come.'

As if I'd come for her sake.

She followed me out into the hall and watched as I put my shoes on. We really ought to stop that in Sweden. Forcing people to walk around in their socks. It's so humiliating.

'I've actually got a few things in the attic that you might want to look at,' Eivor said.

I looked up, curious.

'From the Sara Texas case, I mean,' she clarified. 'Only one box. Do you want to take a look?'

I hesitated. Was I seriously contemplating wasting even more time on this dead loss of a case?

What the hell, seeing as I'd already started poking about in it I might as well see it through to the end.

'I'd be happy to take a look,' I said.

As if in response to what I'd just said, I heard a rumble of thunder roll across the rooftops.

'I'll just nip up to the attic and get it,' Eivor said, pulling on a cardigan. 'You wait here.'

I took the opportunity to reply to a few emails while she was gone. It felt uncomfortable being alone in her flat.

She was soon back.

'Right, let's see.'

She was breathing hard as she put the box on the floor and crouched down beside it. It looked like she'd taken the stairs all the way up to the attic.

Her hands were shaking slightly as she opened the cardboard box.

I stood behind her, peering over her shoulder.

Papers and files and what looked like notebooks.

Far too much for me to go through there and then.

'I'd be happy to take the box away with me,' I said firmly.

She stood up.

'I'd rather you didn't,' she said.

'I haven't got time to make a decent evaluation of so much material here and now,' I said, then added in an authoritative voice: 'There wouldn't be any problem with me taking it with me, would there? There can't be any secrets in there that the police don't know about, surely?'

Eivor went pale.

'Of course not.'

'In that case,' I said, bending down to pick the box up. 'I'll borrow this for a while.'

6

'Okay, Sherlock, what are we going to do with all this?'
Lucy was kneeling beside the box I had brought back from Eivor's.

'No idea. We can take a look at it tomorrow. Now I've got a meeting with another client, and then I'm picking Belle up from preschool.'

Sometimes I collect Belle myself. To salve my guilty conscience or because I want an excuse to get away from the office. And sometimes just because I'm missing her. But on that particular day it was because I wanted to get out of the office.

'Another client?' Lucy said without looking at me. 'So you've got more than one at the moment?'

I stood still.

No, I hadn't. I only had one client, the one I was about to go and see in prison. Unless I was seriously considering getting involved in the case of Sara Texas?

I was on the point of getting in over my head, I was all too aware of that. But at the same time I couldn't escape. People think us lawyers have an exciting job that constantly keeps the adrenalin pumping. We haven't. There aren't many interesting cases. The exceptions are so rare that you basically never even get to hear about them before they've been allocated to someone else. Which was why Bobby's visit got me going. Whether or not I wanted it to.

'Let's talk tomorrow,' I said.

I pushed aside all thoughts about the box I'd brought from Eivor's. Everything was happening too fast. Way too fast. I had one thing I was supposed to be concentrating on, and that was the client I was going to see in prison.

'Are we meeting up this evening?' Lucy said.

That was unusual. We basically never saw each other two nights in a row. That would only confuse us. If we got horny between our dates we had to have sex with other people.

'No,' I said. 'I've got to work.'

That was a lie, and Lucy knew it. But I didn't feel like seeing her. We were going to Nice soon, that would have to do. Once, Marianne, my mother, had asked me to explain my relationship with Lucy. I couldn't. It is what it is. Marianne implied that she felt sorry for Lucy. That made me cross, because feeling sorry for Lucy was to seriously undervalue Lucy. And that was something I had never done.

I drove the car from the office to the prison. It was a distance of less than one and a half kilometres, but the weather was bloody awful. Our office is by Sankt Eriksbron, in one of the tall towers at the end of the bridge. Nice view, high rent.

At the time I was driving a Porsche 911. Because I wanted to, and because I could.

'Faster!' Belle would sometimes say when we were out driving.

She knew how fast it could go, and loved it when I put my foot down. Things are going to turn out okay for Belle; she knows what the important things in life are.

I parked illegally on Bergsgatan and ran through the entrance to the prison with the speed of someone on the run.

The prison guard grinned.

'Ran all the way, then?'

'Do pigs fly?'

The guard grinned again and let me into the room where my client was waiting.

'He's been looking forward to seeing you all day,' the guard said.

'Great,' I said, brushing some of the rain from my shoulders. The door slammed behind me.

My client looked relieved when he caught sight of me. We shook hands and sat down.

At the start we had agreed that Lucy would take care of this joker, but then we figured out that he was better suited to me. He had no previous convictions, but had admitted the assault of another guy on Kungsgatan almost a week ago. It had been a vicious attack. My client had offered no better explanation than to say he had been drunk.

I had been told that much by the guy's previous lawyer. I usually hated to get second bite of the apple, but I'd made an exception in this instance. His first lawyer was a friend of mine, and needed to hand the case on for so-called personal reasons. His teenage daughter had tried to commit suicide and he'd taken some time off work to, as he put it, sort his life out again. Terrible business. I'm dreading the day when Belle becomes a real person with real problems. Real problems that I can't buy my way out of.

'I know your story,' I said. 'But I'd like to hear it again from you.'

My client started to talk. His words came easily, as if he had been waiting a long time for the chance to tell someone about how he'd messed up.

He'd been out drinking with some friends. They were celebrating their first summer since graduating from high-school, and the fact that they had all managed to find work. My client had applied and been accepted to be a floor-layer's apprentice. His eyes positively shone when he talked about the possibilities a job like that could offer.

'You can make loads of money,' he said. 'One day I might be able to set up my own business.'

'What's going to happen with that now?' I said. 'I mean, you're going to be convicted of assault, seeing as you've confessed and there are witnesses.'

The guy looked deflated.

'Well, nothing good's going to happen now, of course.'

He swallowed hard and picked at one of his cuticles.

'Do you think I'll be sent to prison?'

His voice was a whisper, barely audible.

He was absolutely terrified.

I'd seen it plenty of times before. Façades crumbling from the most hardened young criminals. Their voices breaking as soon as there was any talk of being locked up.

But this guy was different. Very different, even.

There was something wrong with his story.

'Tell me again,' I urged him. 'You and your friends came out of the bar. You were drunk. And then a guy showed up and was a bit of a nuisance, and you felt you had to beat him up.'

My client went pale.

'He wasn't just a nuisance. He was provoking us.'

'In what way?'

'He said things.'

'Like what?'

'I can't remember.'

'You can't remember? But you do remember punching him?'

'Yes.'

A whisper again.

'Okay, so tell me. How did you hit him?'

'With my fist clenched. Across the cheek. On his temple. So he fell backwards and hit his head.'

That was what made it so bad. The fact that the guy had fallen and hit his head. He'd been in hospital ever since and would have to learn to live with epilepsy. It was a pretty tragic story for all involved.

I glanced at the documents I had taken with me.

'There are four witnesses to what happened,' I said. 'Five if we count the victim, but his injuries have left him with memory loss. The first witness is an old man who couldn't see properly, but who thinks the person who assaulted the victim was wearing a red jacket. Which you weren't. The second and third witnesses are your friends. Both claim not to remember a single moment of what happened. They don't remember what was said, and they don't remember you hitting anyone. And the fourth witness . . .'

My client squirmed on his chair.

'Are you feeling okay?' I asked, even though it was a stupid question.

'I'm fine.'

'Good, then I'll go on. The fourth witness is your friend

Rasmus, and he, unlike all the others, does remember what he saw and heard. And his story matches yours exactly.'

I put my papers down.

'He must be one of your very best friends,' I said in a voice dripping with irony. 'The sort who stands by you through thick and thin. Even helps you get caught for a serious crime that could have far-reaching consequences for the rest of your life. Nice guy.'

I tilted my head, and saw tears welling up in my client's eyes.

'Come on, now,' I said. 'Tell me what happened.'

Before he had time to start, I interrupted.

'Actually, don't bother. Just tell me why you lied.'

He opened his mouth to reply, but I interrupted again.

'And, just to be clear – don't bother telling me you're not lying. Because you are. Badly, at that.'

My client looked tired. He sat in silence for a long time before he started to talk. When he opened his mouth I thought I'd won. That he'd stop messing about and tell me what was going on. But he didn't.

'I'm not lying,' he said.

It was as if he physically grew as he spoke those clearly untrue words.

'I'm not lying,' he repeated, louder this time. 'I hit the other guy. It was an accident that he ended up getting hurt as badly as he did.'

Silence settled on the room.

'Then I don't know how I can help you,' I said, throwing my hands out.

The young man looked at me obstinately.

'It doesn't matter,' he said. 'I was the one who did it, after all. Now I'll have to take my punishment.'

He blinked, and before he looked down at the table I had time to see the fear in his eyes.

It wasn't the kind of fear I'd been expecting. Not the sort exuded by people afraid of an impending punishment. No, this was something else. A fear that had nothing to do with the assault.

Slowly I packed my things away.

'I'll be back,' I said.

The young man sat without speaking as I left the room.

The fear in his eyes haunted me.

Help me, they whispered. Help me.

7

I'd promised Bobby that I'd get in touch by Sunday evening that week, at the latest. I don't know why I said Sunday evening specifically, because it's hardly a time when I'm usually working.

Whatever. I had a decision to make.

When I finished work on Friday I tucked the box I'd got from Eivor under my arm and went home.

'Are you going to be working this weekend?' Lucy asked when she saw me carrying the box.

'Well, I haven't had as much time to look at it this week as I planned.'

That was actually true. The client who had confessed to the assault, the one I was convinced was innocent, had taken up all my time. In vain I'd ploughed my way through all the available material in an attempt to find an explanation as to why he was acting the way he was. The guy was going to remain a mystery until he decided to change that. Hopefully it wouldn't take too long.

I had consciously been avoiding Eivor's box. I get carried

away far too easily. Think too little and act too quickly. That doesn't work if you want to do a thorough job. So I'd left the box alone. To get a bit of distance from the whole thing. Now a few days had passed and I could still feel the same tension inside me. There was something worth digging into when it came to Sara Texas. That train ticket, for instance. The question was: what was the justification for spending time on her? Bobby was hardly likely to pay for my services, and the state certainly wasn't going to.

'Give me a call if you feel like doing anything?' Lucy said.

'Sure, baby.'

It was raining again. Fucking shitty weather. Thinking about Nice no longer provided the same sort of comfort. Sara Texas's story had made me restless and distracted. I couldn't carry on like this.

Belle let out a squeal when I got home.

If only I'd known how much love such tiny people have to offer. To offer, and simultaneously crave. She was overflowing with joy as she clung to my neck and kicked her legs to wrap them round my waist.

'Friday!' she trilled. 'Friday!'

We couldn't get rid of Signe quickly enough. As soon as she had gone we put on some loud music and relaxed for a bit before it was time to eat. I had a whisky and Belle played with a doll. Belle is like other four-year-olds, not much good at doing anything. But we're working on that. Being able to relax is important. Belle's mum was pretty crap at it. She thought that hard work and no play paid off. A lot of women seem to believe that. That's why they get overtaken by men like me. Men who realise that the best strategy is to be in a state of permanent repose, so that you can exert yourself like an absolute demon on the very rare occasions when you get the chance to make a real difference to your life.

I wanted Belle to understand that. I didn't want her to be the sort that people like me could just sideline.

'Where shall we have brunch on Sunday?' I said.

Children need routines. Adults probably do as well, but children need them even more. So I came up with some when Belle moved in with me. One of the first I established was the routine of going somewhere nice for brunch every Sunday. Right from when she was a baby. I'm a fussy person, and Belle is rapidly turning into one. So the next routine fell into place naturally as soon as she learned to talk: we discuss where to go on Sunday on Friday evening. Which, incidentally, leads me to a third routine: Belle and I always spend Friday evenings relaxing and having a cosy time together. We each do our own thing on Saturday. I see my friends, and Belle visits her grandparents or – in emergencies – the au pair.

At least that was the way our routines looked before everything fell apart.

Anyway, Belle was concentrating so hard on the doll in her lap that she didn't hear me at first. I repeated my question.

'Not Berns,' she said.

I agreed with her. Berns, that den of iniquity, was cool twenty years ago. But not now. And things like that are important to trend-conscious people like Belle and me.

'How about the Grand Hôtel?' I said.

'How about Haga?' Belle said. 'Then we can go to the park.'

Her face lit up when she said that. I felt a warm glow spread through my chest. You could see her starting to come up with her own excellent suggestions, and I liked that. The way she celebrated her own brilliance.

'Haga Forum is a good suggestion,' I said. 'Right, I'm going to start cooking.'

I headed off to the kitchen with the whisky in my hand.

Belle followed me, clutching the doll in her arms.

'What's that box?' she said, pointing at the cardboard box I'd taken home with me.

'Nothing special,' I said.

I wasn't planning to open it until Belle was asleep. I don't believe in prettifying the world for little children, but there are limits to the horrors you can share with them. Belle left the box alone and pulled a chair over to the stove. She likes watching when I or the au pair make food.

'Steak and chips,' I said. 'I got the meat from Östermalmshallen. Not bad, eh?'

Belle smiled. She learned at an early age that you don't eat your steak well-done, and that sauce made from powder is disgusting.

'Is Lucy coming?' she asked.

I stiffened.

'She might be coming on Sunday. Or tomorrow.'

'Is she coming to brunch too?'

I looked at her seriously.

'Belle, when we have brunch it's always just you and me. Same as always.'

Belle nodded, then turned serious as well.

'Just you and me,' she said, putting her hand on my arm.

When I woke up I was lying on my front in a bed that was far too small. Belle's of course. This tradition of reading bedtime stories is a bloody silly idea. It's bad for parents. You can't help failing. This time I'd only managed to read half a story before falling asleep. Now it was just past midnight and I had no idea if I was going to be able to get to sleep again.

I slid carefully off the bed. It didn't work, and Belle woke up. She sleepily mumbled something and I adjusted the covers before walking out of her bedroom.

I felt fragile and alone. Night has that effect on me. Maybe I should call Lucy?

No, I wasn't going to do that. For her sake as well as mine.

I went out into the kitchen and switched the light on. The remains of our dinner were still on the kitchen table. The food had dried onto the plates and the bin smelled. I ran my hand through my hair. It would have to wait, I didn't feel up to dealing with it just then.

I was about to turn the light out when I caught sight of the cardboard box.

Eivor's treasure chest.

Well, why not? Who said I had to wait for daylight before starting to go through whatever was inside the box?

I quickly cleared the plates from the table and lifted the box up. It weighed no more than a few kilos. The thought of what Eivor had hidden in it made me smile. She must miss her old life, her work, terribly. Why else would she have stored a load of old rubbish up in her attic?

At the top of the box was a half-full folder.

'Loose ends,' someone had written on a note on the front of the folder.

I felt worried. Loose ends? I hoped it wasn't police material that Eivor had tucked aside. If that was the case, I'd really rather have nothing to do with it.

The folder turned out to contain a number of sheets of handwritten notes. I let out a sigh as I began to read. It was going to take time to read and attempt to understand everything.

'*Sara indicated the size of the golf club she used to kill the man in Houston. She couldn't say exactly what sort or which brand it had been.*'

One of many charming details. Sara was supposed to have knocked her second victim unconscious with a golf club, then smashed his head in with the same implement. No fingerprints were found on the club. They'd been wiped off.

I carried on reading:

'*Afterwards she put the club back in the bag. Note: probably a 3-iron, made by Ping. Owned by the victim. Cover missing. Sara says she doesn't remember if she removed it, but the forensic evidence shows it was missing. Why doesn't she want to say where it is?*'

I put the file down with a feeling of unease.

That sort of detail, whether the cover of the golf club had been removed after the attack, was a typical control question that anyone confessing to a murder must be able to answer. But Sara had said that she 'didn't remember'. Not good. Not good at all.

Further down in the box I found a bundle of Post-it notes held together by a paperclip. Why on earth had Eivor saved those?

'*Buy cake,*' the top one said.

'*Roses for Märit,*' another one said.

Märit was Tor Gustavsson's wife. So he had his secretary, with whom he had been having an affair, buy flowers for his wife. Charming.

It wasn't until I got to the last note that I reacted to anything on them.

'*Contact Sheriff Stiller, Houston. Who's Jenny's boyfriend?*'

I frowned. Jenny wasn't a name that had appeared in any of the newspaper articles I'd read. But I still recognised the name from somewhere.

The ticket.

Bobby had said he got the train ticket from Sara's friend Jenny. Could this be the same Jenny? In which case, why had Gustavsson been interested in her boyfriend?

I'd have to have another talk with Eivor, that much was obvious.

I poked about curiously through the rest of the box's contents. My fingers closed around a hard-covered notebook. Someone had put an elastic band round it, and had written on a Post-it note: '*Sara's diary?*' Astonished, I removed the elastic band and opened the book. Why did Eivor have Sara's diary? That should have been with the police.

Whoever had written it was evidently keen to keep things brief. There weren't many lines per day. Most weeks the diary's author didn't seem to have written on more than two or three days. I had a list of which dates the various murders had taken place. None of those dates appeared in the diary.

I put the notebook down on the table and picked up the folder again.

I took another look at old Gustavsson's notes.

The more I read, the more worked up I got. Because Gustavsson had obviously reacted to a number of inconsistencies in Sara's story without actually following up any of them. The missing golf club cover was just one of several things. What had he done with his doubts? Had he spoken to the prosecutor? With Eivor, maybe?

I felt my determination grow as I stood there with the folder in my hand. Bobby was probably right. His sister's lawyer hadn't done his job. And he had 'known things'.

Resolutely I tossed everything back in the box and took it into my room with me. I knew I wasn't going to be able to keep my fingers off the diary. I'd end up reading it until I fell asleep.

So Saturday would be devoted to work rather than pleasure. Because, like I said, I had a decision to make.

Would I really consider representing a dead client?

8

When I woke up on Saturday morning I found myself lying on my back with Sara Texas's diary on my chest. Belle was standing silently beside the bed. She does that sometimes when she wakes up. Creeps in to my room and stands and stares at me until I open my eyes. It's actually very unpleasant; I can never get used to the fact that she does that.

'I'm hungry,' she said.

'And good morning to you as well,' I said, putting the book to one side.

I felt fired up again the moment my fingers touched the book's stiff covers. It had afforded me a good deal of interesting reading before I fell asleep. It seemed completely incomprehensible that it hadn't attracted the attention of the police.

'Rudey nudey,' Belle said as I got out of bed.

'Speak for yourself,' I said.

'But I've got pyjamas on.'

She tugged at her pyjamas top.

'Don't do that, you'll make it bigger,' I said.

Belle shrugged her shoulders.

'But I'm getting bigger too.'

I pulled on my clothes and sloped off to the kitchen.

'Eurgh,' Belle said when she saw the previous day's washing-up.

I had to agree. We'd have to eat breakfast in front of the television. Belle watched some children's programmes while I read the last pages of Sara's diary. If it was actually Sara's diary. That was one of the things I wanted to clear up over the course of the day.

'Right, let's put some clothes on so we can get going. I'm afraid I've got to do some work today.'

'Where am I going to be, then?' Belle said.

I smiled.

'At Grandma's.'

We were there barely an hour later.

'What's that noise?' Belle said when we were standing in the hall at my mother's.

'It's the fan in the cellar, sweetheart,' Marianne said. 'You see, there was such a bad flood the other day that some nice men had to come and pull the floor up. Now they've put a dehumidifier in there to dry everything out.'

'That'll be covered by your home insurance, won't it?' I said, remembering the invoice they had phoned about.

'Probably,' Marianne said. 'I mean yes, it is.'

She helped Belle take her coat off.

'What are we going to do today?' the child asked.

'I thought you could do some baking,' Marianne said.

It was probably good for Belle to spend time with her grandmother. I basically never bake anything. Nor does the au pair. Lucy reckoned it counted as baking when she made waffles, but I didn't buy that. Nor did Belle, frankly.

'When are you picking her up?' Marianne asked me.

'Five o'clock,' I said.

That would give me plenty of time to do what I'd got planned.

'Do you want to eat here this evening?' Marianne said.

I hadn't thought about that. I suppose I'd vaguely considered letting Lucy come and see Belle and me, but nothing more than that.

'I don't think we can,' I said.

Marianne looked disappointed.

'We don't see enough of each other, Martin.'

I didn't agree with that either.

'Thanks for having Belle,' I said, and left the house.

As I got in the car I could see Belle and Marianne standing in the window watching me. But Belle was the only one who waved as I started the car and drove off.

Just as I suspected, it wasn't hard to arrange another meeting with Eivor. I implied that the contents of the cardboard box had provoked some questions, and she agreed to see me like a shot.

'Will you bring the box back?' she said.

'I need to keep it a bit longer,' I said.

Not the answer she wanted.

'You look very different today,' she said when she opened the door.

She looked at my green polo shirt and brown trousers. She was quite right, I hadn't looked like that the last time we met.

'It's Saturday today,' I said. 'This is what I look like when I'm not at work.'

We sat down at her little kitchen table again.

I got straight to the point, keen not to waste any time.

'Last time I asked you if you ever thought Sara Tell was innocent. Your answer was no.'

Eivor's expression became serious.

'Naturally,' she said.

'Naturally,' I repeated. 'But despite that I found a folder marked "Loose ends" in the box you gave me. When you read Gustavsson's notes, it's clear that he reacted to a number of things in Sara's version of events. Things she ought to have known about but couldn't account for. Such as what had happened to the cover of the golf club used in the murder in Houston.'

The silences that arise when the person you're talking to has nothing sensible to say speak volumes. Eivor considered what response to give for a while. A small part of me felt sorry for her. It wasn't her job to defend Gustavsson's work. If she wanted to she could tell me to go to hell. But she didn't, because she was far too loyal to her old boss.

'I didn't know that folder was in the box,' she said. 'That was silly. Of course not everything Sara said was as detailed as one might have wished. But . . . it was enough. Who remembers every single detail of individual events several years later?'

That was true, of course, but we weren't talking about any old events here, rather a series of premeditated murders. In which case it felt like the memory ought to work rather differently.

'There was a notebook in the box, too,' I said. 'Which you or someone else had marked "Sara's diary?". How did you get hold of that?'

'We got it from a friend of Sara's. Or rather from Bobby, who got it from the friend.'

'Jenny?'

Eivor lit up.

'You know about her?'

I shook my head.

'Just a guess. Because a Jenny cropped up in the case. Someone who claimed to have a ticket that proved Sara couldn't have murdered the woman in Galveston.'

Eivor's face gave nothing away. I was wondering why Bobby hadn't mentioned the diary as well.

'So Jenny gave Bobby both a diary and a ticket,' I said slowly. 'What did the two of you make of those items?'

Eivor shrugged.

'There wasn't much we could think, according to Tor. The ticket itself proved nothing, Jenny could have got hold of that from anywhere. And the diary ... Sara refused to acknowledge it. Or the ticket, come to that. Have you read the notebook?'

I had.

'Whoever wrote that diary seems to have been a fairly fragmented character,' I said. 'The entries are short, and practically episodic. Most of them aren't dated. Looking at the handwriting, I get the feeling that the same person wrote all the entries. Did you get anyone to analyse the handwriting?'

Eivor got annoyed.

'Why would we have done that? Completely unnecessary; she said the book was nothing to do with her.'

'True, but considering what was written in it, I think I would have it checked out anyway.'

Eivor hadn't read the diary, that much was very clear. We'd reached a point where we were skirting round each other, and that wasn't good. She was defensive, didn't want to entertain the possibility that they had done anything wrong or could have done anything differently. And all I wanted was to have a straight conversation.

'Amongst other things, the person writing the diary had a very troublesome ex-boyfriend who acted in a very threatening manner,' I said. 'One who scared the writer of the diary. Even though he seems to have been living in Sweden while she was in Houston. And there's someone called Lucifer who appears several times. He seems to have travelled all the way to the USA to cause trouble for her. Unless he was American and was already there – that isn't entirely clear.'

The legs of Eivor's chair scraped the floor as she stood up.

'I know Tor mentioned that,' she said. 'But, again, what did it prove? Nothing at all. I mean, "Lucifer"? You can't take things like that too seriously. Sara just snorted at those entries. And so did we. Anyway, you can't help wondering what Jenny would have been doing with Sara's diary.'

It was an important question. I didn't have a good answer to that one.

'Were Jenny and Sara good friends?'

'If you ask Jenny, the answer is yes. If you asked Sara, the answer was no. The two girls were both au pairs in the same part of Houston. The Heights, that was what it was called. According to Sara, Jenny was more interested in their friendship than she was.'

'Where's Jenny now?'

'She stayed in Texas. Ended up getting married to some businessman. She's got children of her own now, and her own au pair.'

There was something condescending in Eivor's voice that I had trouble accepting, but I let it pass. To my mind it seemed like Jenny had done best out of the two girls.

'Let's see if I've understood this right,' I said. 'Sara and Jenny knew each other in Texas six years ago. Last year Sara went on trial for five murders, and suddenly Jenny races across the Atlantic with an old train ticket and a diary that both prove that Sara could be innocent.'

'She didn't race across the Atlantic,' Eivor said. 'She phoned. And then sent those things over by courier. To Bobby, who brought them to us.'

'But you and Tor showed the diary and ticket to the police?' Eivor squirmed.

'Of course we did. But they weren't interested.'

But I was. Bobby may have been onto something after all. There were certainly loose ends to follow up in Sara's case. Threads the police appeared to have ignored entirely. There were several things mentioned in the diary that ought to have been picked up.

'One last question,' I said, pulling the Post-it note I'd found the previous evening out of my pocket. 'Why were you going to call the sheriff in Houston about Jenny's boyfriend?'

Eivor reached for the note and looked at it with the same concentration as archaeologists do when they find old bits of stone that could be remnants of something interesting from a fuck of a long time ago. The problem for Eivor was that this wasn't an old piece of stone, but a piece of paper with her own writing on it.

'Ye-e-es,' she said hesitantly. 'Why were we going to call Esteban about that?'

'Esteban?'

'Esteban Stiller, the sheriff in Houston. A very nice man, always answered all our questions.'

Clearly a very obliging guy, this Esteban, I thought.

'What did he have to say about Jenny's boyfriend?'

Eivor went on staring at the scrap of paper.

'Now I remember!' she said eventually. 'You see, Tor found an article in an American newspaper saying that Jenny's ex-boyfriend had spent some time in custody for the Houston murder, but was released on lack of evidence. Tor wanted to find out why he'd been picked up in the first place.'

'And what did Esteban have to say about that?'

'That they'd made an embarrassing mistake. But he didn't say what they actually had on him.'

'You said ex-boyfriend, even though it says boyfriend on the note. So this isn't the guy Jenny's married to these days?'

Eivor snorted.

'I hardly think so. Jenny is a very smart young lady, you know. She'd never have married a negro.'

Negro. There aren't many words in the world that I can't stand, but negro is one of them. Couldn't she see she was talking to a black man?

'So the guy who was first in custody for the murder was an Afro-American?' I said, stressing the last word.

Eivor blinked.

'Afro? No, he was from China, if I remember rightly. You know how untrustworthy they can be there. But I don't think he was a murderer.'

No, and evidently not a negro either. A Chinese negro, that was a new one. Ignorant bitch.

I stood up abruptly and thanked her for letting me visit.

'When can I have my box back?' she said, sounding anxious.

I turned round in the doorway.

'When I've finished my investigation,' I said.

And knew that I'd made my mind up. I'd give it a go. I was going to help Sara Tell to get justice.

Fuck knew how that was going to work.

PART II

'So fucking ... innocent'

FO: I don't know what to say about what I've
heard so far. You probably said it best
yourself. Christ, what a clichéd story.

MB: Isn't it? And believe me, it's going to get
even worse.

FO: Is that possible?

MB: I'm afraid so. Take the weather, for
instance. Do you remember how much it
rained back at the start of the summer?
Remember how wet and horrible it was?
Sometimes I wonder if all that wetness
made a difference somehow. That life sort
of turned into slippery soap, and that's
why I lost my grip on it.

FO: You mean you had control of your life

before . . . well, before all that
happened?

MB: I did. I'm very conscientious. I know,
it doesn't look like it, but I am. Before
all hell broke loose I was in control.
Of everything. And now . . . everything's
different. Everything.

(Silence)

MB: But we were going to take everything from
the start, wasn't that what you said?

FO: That's right.

MB: It started with the rain. I think it's fair
to say that. If it hadn't been for the
rain, I don't think I would have embarked
upon the whole project the way I did.

FO: The project?

MB: Trying to get Sara pardoned posthumously.
I can't explain why it became so important
to me. I mean, she was already dead, after
all. Which, in a way, is also partly how
this all started. With Sara dying. If only
she'd been alive. Then I could have gone
directly to her instead. But of course that
wasn't possible now.

FO: Do you regret it?

MB: Do I regret what?

FO: Deciding to help her.

(Silence)

MB: What am I supposed to say to that? On the one hand there's only one answer to that question, which is of course I fucking do. But on the other hand . . . is there anything more pointless? Than regret? I don't really think there is. That was then and this is now.

FO: That's very poetic.

MB (Laughing quietly): Poetic but true. It all feels so distant now. Even the rain has gone.

FO: So what happened? You called Bobby T. and said you were going to help him?

MB: I called him. Then we had another meeting. And by then . . .

FO: By then?

MB (Whispering): By then, without even knowing it, I'd already started to dig my own grave.

9

Brunch with Belle. A sacred element in an otherwise relatively unstructured day. It was Sunday, and I needed to meet Bobby to tell him what I wanted to do with his sister's case. I called him that morning and said I wanted to see him.

'So you'll help Sara?'

As if she were still alive.

His voice was even, gave no hint of either happiness or excitement. Bobby T. was like a glass of lager that had gone flat.

'I'll explain when we meet,' I said. 'Come to my office at four o'clock this afternoon.'

Then I called Lucy and asked if Belle could stay with her while I met Bobby. She agreed.

Belle chose her dress for our brunch with care. I've nurtured that in her, encouraging her to develop a feminine side. God knows the number of times I've been condemned for that. Defining certain things as feminine and others as masculine is evidently wrong. But not to me. And there the discussion stops, because I'm the one raising Belle, no one else.

'What are you going to wear?' Belle said, creeping into the bathroom where I was standing shaving.

She was dressed in just her black pants.

'I thought I'd wear my black chinos with a blue shirt,' I said.

I made sure I sounded serious, so she'd understand that the business of clothes was important, and not the sort of thing you decided on a whim.

'What are you going to wear?'

She tilted her head to one side.

'The pink London dress.'

I smiled. The London dress had actually been bought in Copenhagen, but from a British boutique.

'That's lovely,' I said. 'Yes, wear that.'

Belle ran out of the bathroom. I heard her rummaging about in her bedroom, then she came back a little while later.

'Help me,' she said, pointing behind her head with her hand.

I put the razor down and buttoned her dress.

'Do you want me to tie your hair up?' I said.

She shook her head.

'No, thanks, it should be long.'

'You mean loose.'

'No, long. Are we going now?'

'Soon.'

A short while later we walked out of the house, hand in hand. We took a taxi to Haga Forum, with Belle commenting excitedly about all the things she saw along the way.

'Are you going to a party?' the taxi driver said.

'We're going out for brunch,' Belle said.

Some people say children can't sit still. Others say they aren't interested in food. But I say it's just a question of

planning and having realistic expectations. I'm not expecting her to sit and spend two hours eating brunch like an
adult. There's not enough room in her body for that much
food, and besides, she doesn't understand the value of eating
slowly. So I let her eat as quickly as she likes, and then she
can sit and draw or listen to stories on my phone. Watching
films is out of the question. Not in a restaurant, that just
isn't on.

I myself eat slowly, and I eat a lot. Then I read a number
of magazines that I've carefully selected to take with me.
Sometimes Belle tries to get my attention, and I let myself be
interrupted. Otherwise I let her look after herself on the other
side of the table.

On that particular Sunday I was unable to concentrate
on my magazines. My impending meeting with Bobby was
monopolising my thoughts. I felt naked and unprepared. I
knew I ought to talk the matter through with someone before
I went into action. Why should I spend my time trying to clear
the name of a dead woman? No one would thank me for it.
No one would pay me.

Yet there was still something about the notorious case that
exerted an almost magnetic power over me. It felt like I was
staring into a dark pond where someone had hidden some
treasure.

'Dive in!' a ghostly voice whispered inside my head. 'Dive
right in, for fuck's sake!'

Of course I was going to dive in.

How could I resist?

Stockholm is a seductive city. It's the water that elevates it. The
water lying like an immense mirror at the feet of the buildings.

Venice can fuck right off. It's Stockholm that shows how to make a city look good with water.

Lucy's flat was in a narrow street in Birkastan. There was no sign of either water or greenery there. Belle held my hand tight as we walked away from the car.

'Why does she have to live where it's so dark?' she said.

I often wondered the same thing.

'You'll have to ask her,' I said.

Lucy looked worried when I dropped Belle off.

'Martin, what are you thinking of saying to him?'

It was much harder to cut off Lucy than it was Marianne.

'Can we talk about it when I come back?' I said, already halfway out into the stairwell.

'I think we should talk now,' Lucy said.

I sighed and slid back inside the flat.

'I'm going to say that I can't bring the dead back to life, but that I might be able to grant her a bit of peace.'

Lucy looked like she wasn't sure if she should laugh or cry.

'I knew you wouldn't be able to say no,' she said.

I squirmed. Felt like a schoolboy.

'It's too good, Lucy. It's just too good.'

'What's he offering you in return?'

'Nothing. Not money, anyway.'

'I don't like this,' Lucy said. 'You barely know who this Bobby is.'

'Stop it,' I said, and laughed. 'Okay, I'm going now, see you later.'

I opened the front door again. Belle had already run off into the flat and was nowhere in sight.

'I'm serious, Martin. People are going to think you're doing the bidding of a madman.'

I wondered for a moment if there was something in that. I didn't think there was. Who was really going to care if I had a bit of a poke about in an old police investigation? I wasn't exactly thinking of going to the media with my dilemma.

'I'll be back soon to pick up Belle,' I said.

'Promise you'll call if anything happens.'

'Sure,' I said.

When I walked into the office I wondered what she'd meant. If 'anything happened', it was likely to be an emergency, and then Lucy would be the last person I turned to. A couple of solidly built cops would feel more reassuring.

Or Boris, I thought.

Boris was a man who had once come to my office to ask for help. A man with not one but both feet on the wrong side of the law. Boris was the sort of man who couldn't handle daylight. A man of darkness who had to stick to the realm of shadows so he didn't get spotted by the police or other sworn enemies. We both knew that he couldn't have got the sort of help he'd had from me from many other places. Not that I'd done anything criminal. I'd never do that. But you could say that I'd done all I could for him. Partly out of curiosity, but also out of fear. I wasn't sure how safe I'd feel if I turned down a guy like Boris. So I helped him. Which meant that we were connected by an unspecified bond of gratitude. His number was still in my phone. It made me feel safe.

I was ten minutes early. I got up from my desk twice to adjust the lighting in the room. It was evidently summer outside, but you wouldn't know it from the light. It was as dark as November.

I ought to have done something else with those ten minutes

instead of playing with the lamps. I ought to have thought through my decision one more time, re-examined it really thoroughly. Too much eagerness, too little reflection.

He showed up right on time. His jeans came from a bygone age, his t-shirt was filthy. If anything, he smelled even more strongly of cigarette smoke than before.

This time I stood up when Bobby came into the room. I shook his hand and invited him to sit down on one of the visitor's chairs. Black wooden chairs that I'd had upholstered with zebra-skin. A souvenir from Tanzania.

'Have you made up your mind?' Bobby asked before his grubby denim backside landed on the zebra for the second time in a week.

'I have,' I said.

I left a theatrical pause. It's important to keep the upper hand in negotiations and ordinary conversations alike. Otherwise you never get anywhere.

Bobby shuffled uncomfortably and I started to worry that the studs in his jeans would spoil my lovely chair. Maybe it would be best to get to the point.

'I've decided to help your sister,' I said.

Bobby's expression didn't change.

I waited.

Bobby still didn't say anything.

Hadn't he heard what I said?

'I'll see what I can do,' I said. 'I mean, I can't promise you anything. Not a damn thing, actually. But I've got a bit of spare time, and it looks like you were right about Sara's defence not being handled particularly well.'

Bobby nodded slowly.

'Good,' he said, without showing any trace of the enthusiasm

I'd been expecting. 'I think I understand what you're saying. You'll look into the case, but you're not promising anything. I'll buy that. When do you start?'

I felt slightly confused, affronted even, by his reaction. Why wasn't he more excited? A bit of gratitude wouldn't have done any harm.

'I suppose I've already started,' I said. 'I'm going to try to get hold of the report of the preliminary police investigation tomorrow, and I'll see if I can get any help from the original detectives.'

'Texas,' Bobby said.

'Sorry?'

'You ought to go to Texas.'

I was astonished.

'I'm sorry, but I don't think that's going to happen.'

Texas. Was he mad? What would I do there?

'Then you won't be able to help Sara,' Bobby said simply.

I swallowed. This was getting out of control before it had even started.

'It's important that you have realistic expectations of what I can achieve,' I said brusquely. 'This is something I'm going to have to do in my spare time, when I haven't got other work to be getting on with. Believe me, I'm upset about what happened to your sister, I really am, but the fact is that she's no longer alive, and ... well, that can make it hard to motivate people to cooperate in getting her name cleared. And as for going to Texas ... I don't think that's anywhere near the agenda.'

I'd been to Texas twice. I saw my father on both occasions. I preferred not to think about him. He used to live in Houston. The same city where Sara had been an au pair.

Bobby looked at me with his dark eyes. Eyes I suspected had seen far too much crap to belong to such a young person.

'Naturally, I'll pay you,' he said.

I looked at him sceptically. With what? it was tempting to wonder. Bobby didn't strike me as the sort of person who had much in the bank.

'I had an inheritance,' he said. 'Money from my grandmother. So I can pay. If you have expenses. Like when you go to Texas, for instance.'

I leaned across the desk. Clasped my hands together and tilted my head to one side.

'Bobby, read my lips. There's not going to be any Texas trip.'

Was I imagining things, or was he smirking at me?

'We'll see,' he murmured.

We sat without speaking for a while. I glanced at my watch. Damn fine watch, come to that. A 2010 Breitling Bentley. It had been something of a bargain, I got it in Switzerland, last one in the shop, 85,000 kronor.

'Either way,' I said, trying to wrest back the initiative in our conversation. 'I'll work at the pace I've got time for, and I'll contact you when I've got anything I want to share with you. Or, of course, if I need your help.'

I forced myself to smile.

'Does that sound okay?'

Bobby shook his head.

'You seem to think that this is just a game,' he said. 'It isn't. Not for me. And not for Sara. If you aren't going to take this seriously, then . . .'

He stopped himself and I seized the opportunity to take over.

'Tell me, Bobby,' I said gently. 'If I don't take this as

seriously as you, what are you going to do? Go to another law firm? Please, be my guest. Because you see, this isn't a case I feel I have to take on. In fact, it doesn't even feel like a case at all. Not remotely. So shall I explain it to you one last time? Your sister confessed to murdering five people. She helped the police find enough evidence for five murder convictions. Then she escaped the day before the trial was due to start. In all likelihood, she found and abducted her son, Mio. Then she killed first her son, then herself. That, my friend, isn't a case. It's a tragic fucking mess.'

As I spoke those last words I raised my voice and sounded properly angry.

Bobby responded with all guns blazing.

'But you still can't keep away from it,' he said. 'Can you? Because you know I'm right. You know Sara didn't carry out those murders. And you want to be the one who uncovers the miscarriage of justice. The guy who shows where the line between right and wrong runs.'

He nodded to himself.

'I know your sort,' he said. 'That's why I'm here. Because I know you can't turn it down.'

I'm very, very good at showdowns. I almost always win. Apart from the odd occasion when I have a bust-up with Lucy or Belle. I didn't know if I dared go up against Bobby. Earlier on I'd already picked up a definite sense that he was one step ahead of me, that he knew something I didn't. Something decisive. Maybe he was keeping it to himself because this was a test. He wanted to see how quickly I could find the information on my own. Or else he was playing a game that I didn't understand. In which case I could be on shaky ground.

I rubbed my chin.

There was one thing he needed to be very fucking clear about. If he thought I was interested in playing some ridiculous game, he could find another lawyer. As a player I really only have one fundamental principle, and I never break it: I only play games where the rules are known and agreed in advance.

'Listen, Bobby,' I said. 'I think you've misunderstood one rather important detail.'

He looked at me attentively, almost curiously.

'This,' I said, sweeping my right hand through the air. 'This is an office. Not a film studio in Hollywood. And what you and I are doing right now, this is a perfectly ordinary meeting. Not some Italian sit-down where everyone gathers round and starts by putting their guns on the table. If you want to find someone to play with, you're going to have to go elsewhere, because there's no one else like you in this room. No one remotely like you. Is that understood?'

Lucy would have been furious if she'd heard me. She hates it when I start acting all superior towards people at a disadvantage. She says it's because I haven't dealt with my shitty childhood. That I can't stand anyone who reminds of the people around me when I was growing up. She could be right. Either way, Bobby seemed to understand what I was getting at.

'I get it,' he said. 'I just want to reassure myself that you're going to do a good job. A *proper* job. That's why I want to pay you. So that I know we've got an agreement.'

'I don't want to be rude, but do you realise how much I cost to employ? I don't know how much you inherited from your grandmother, but . . .'

Bobby interrupted me there: 'No, you don't. But I do. I

inherited enough. You'll get your money. As long as you do what I've asked you to.'

I was forced to think. What had he actually asked me to do? I was supposed to get justice for his sister. Demonstrate that she was innocent of the murders she had confessed to. And then he had asked me for one other thing.

'The boy,' I said. 'Mio. Your nephew. I'm afraid I have to repeat what I said to you last time we met. I'm not going to find him, because I'm not actually going to look for him, I'm afraid. Not as long as I don't have good reason to think that his death has anything to do with the five murders. And as things stand, I don't.'

Bobby swallowed, hard. He ran one hand through his filthy hair.

'Okay, you can say that. But you'll change your mind. Because like I said, it's all connected.'

I decided not to continue the discussion. I'd said what I needed to, and I knew he'd understood. That would have to do.

For the first time, Bobby looked uncertain.

'So what happens now? How do you start?'

'I start the way I mentioned a short while ago,' I said. 'I'll contact the police and go through their material. Talk to the officers who conducted the interviews if possible.'

'Good,' Bobby said, mostly for the sake of saying something. 'Good.'

I thought of something else. 'You haven't made any inquiries of your own? If you have, it would be a good idea to tell me what you found out. To save any duplication of effort.'

Bobby looked at me through almost closed eyes. It was impossible to read what was going through his mind just then.

'Obviously I've had a bit of a look,' he said. 'Spoken to a few people. There was one guy I got quite interested in.'

'A guy?'

'A boyfriend. My sister had a bloke she used to spend a lot of time with, but she dumped him when she went off to Texas. He never got over it, apparently. I think he went all the way to Houston to get her back.'

This was interesting. A problematic ex appeared in the diary. But it also gave me an idea of what I was facing. I'd already told anyone who was prepared to listen that I wasn't thinking of doing the police's job for them. Even so, that seemed to be the direction I was moving inexorably towards.

'What was his name?' I said, reaching for a pen.

'Ed, I think.'

'Surname?'

'No idea.'

I raised my eyebrows.

'You never met him?'

'No.'

I thought for a moment, something about what he had said was nagging at me.

'Were you and Sara close?'

His eyes glazed over.

'Yes,' he said in a hoarse voice.

'How come she expressly told you to drop any attempt at getting her off? Because I know that's what she did.'

Bobby's face closed up.

'She didn't know any better,' he said. 'And she was frightened. Of something.'

'Had she been threatened?'

He shrugged.

'I wasn't allowed to see her, so I don't know.'

I looked at my notepad. All I'd written was one word: Ed.

'It would be useful if I could have the names of some of Sara's friends,' I said. 'If she had any. So I can get somewhere with this story.'

Bobby looked thoughtful.

'Okay,' he said slowly. 'I'll see what I can come up with.'

I thought of something else I wanted to mention.

'There's something you forgot to tell me about last time we met,' I said. 'Sara's diary. The one Jenny sent over by courier. Eivor had it. Don't miss out things like that in future – if I'm going to make any progress, I need all the information I can get.'

'I didn't think the diary was that important,' Bobby said hesitantly. 'And there was so much else to think about when I was last here.'

'Well, we'll see how important it is,' I said. 'There are events and people mentioned in the diary that I want to follow up. Do you know who Lucifer is?'

Bobby grinned.

'Lucifer? That's Dad. Bastard. Although ...'

I was so surprised that I didn't notice at first that he'd stopped himself. But then I accepted it. Lucifer seemed a reasonable name for a father who sold his own daughter.

'Yes?' I said 'Although ... ?'

'Well, Lucifer. That was what Dad's friends called him when they were drunk. I didn't know Sara used that nickname as well.'

'Are you sure Lucifer couldn't be anyone else? If I understood the diary correctly, he seems to have done the same thing as Ed: got on a plane to Houston to cause trouble for Sara.'

'He may have done,' Bobby said. 'I don't really remember.' He looked down.

'Either way, I don't know anyone else who's called, or who's ever been called, Lucifer.'

It troubled me that he was so uninformed. He had clearly been very fond of his sister. Even so, he didn't seem to know a flying fuck about her everyday life.

I started to feel that I wanted the meeting to end. It was time for Bobby to go home.

'Fine,' I said. 'I'll be in touch when I've made some progress.'

Bobby stood up.

'What do you think, then?' he said. 'About Sara's case?'

'I don't think anything,' I said brusquely. 'Look, I've barely scraped the surface, but just like you, I think there's something dodgy about your sister's confession. What I need to do to prove that is turn the problem around and ask the following question: why did she take the blame for five murders she didn't commit? What could motivate someone to do something so utterly insane?'

Bobby clenched his jaw tight.

'That's what I want to know,' he said. 'How could she get it into her head to confess to five murders? And how did she know all the things she said when the police questioned her? About the murder weapons and God knows what else?'

That was what I was wondering too.

10

Rörstrandsgatan is the mecca that the affluent middle-classes of Vasastan make their pilgrimage towards. A ridiculous number of overpaid people in their thirties and forties hang out there. The street stretches from Sankt Eriksplan up towards Karlberg, which means that it's very close to the building where Lucy and I rent our office, and an excellent place to find a choice of restaurants after work. And, for some inexplicable reason, Lucy also chooses to live in Birkastan. And if we're heading back to hers afterwards, that's another reason to crash-land in Rörstrandsgatan.

So that's where we ended up after I'd concluded my meeting with Bobby and went to collect Belle.

'How did the meeting go?' Lucy said, helping Belle put her things in her rucksack.

'Brilliantly,' I said.

'Seriously?'

'What do you think? The guy's a bit weird, but he does care about his sister.'

'And what do you care about, exactly?' Lucy said.

I shrugged my shoulders.

'I don't know. There's something smouldering away there.'

Lucy sighed.

'So he wasn't threatening?'

'Not in the slightest.'

'You're sure? Remember what I said; you could have called me.'

I let out a laugh.

'Come off it, Lucy. No one in their right mind would call you if they needed a bodyguard. I might just have called Boris, though.'

Now it was Lucy's turn to laugh. At last.

'Boris? Bloody hell, I'd almost forgotten him.'

'Christ, I'll have to tell him that next time I speak to him.'

Apparently there are lots of people who don't swear in front of their children. I'm not one of them.

Lucy suggested that we go out and get something to eat. Belle grinned and took my hand.

'I want to do that too,' she said.

I looked at her. I tried to imagine what Belle would have been like if my sister hadn't died. She certainly wouldn't have had brunch at Haga Forum and then Sunday dinner in a restaurant, that much was obvious. The thought made me feel dizzy, and I hoped there was no life after death. Because just then I really wasn't sure I wanted to have to answer to Belle's mother and father after I died.

I'm doing as well as I can, I thought. She gets fed, gets to see new things, and she has a comfy bed to sleep in every night. She was pretty much the first child in preschool out of nappies, and it's only a matter of time until she can wipe her own backside. So on the whole I reckoned I was doing pretty okay.

'Let's head down to Bebe,' I said, referring to a place that started out serving Indian food, then turned into something else serving generally decent food.

'I'll just put some lipstick on,' Lucy said, slipping into the bathroom.

Belle watched her go with interest.

I was more concerned about my meeting with Bobby and his unfathomable relationship to his dead sister. Sara had expressly forbidden her lawyer from having anything to do with her brother. But he still cared. Because they'd once been the best of friends.

'No other similarities, but it sounds a bit like you and your brother,' I said to Lucy when we were sitting in Bebe. 'You're also close to each other.'

'So far, I haven't murdered a load of people,' Lucy said.

'I said no other similarities.'

Lucy said nothing, just looked hard at the menu.

'What would you like?' I asked Belle. 'There's ...'

'I want a hamburger and a milkshake.'

All three of us ended up ordering the same thing. The milkshakes at Bebe were like a drug. Lucy and I asked to have ours spiked with bourbon.

Belle sat and did some drawing while we waited for the food.

'You don't like me digging about in Sara Texas's case,' I said eventually, to break the silence.

'No,' Lucy said. 'You're right, I don't.'

'Why not?'

'Because I can't get away from the feeling that you're being exploited.'

'By Bobby?'

'By both of them,' Lucy said, pulling a face.

'Come on, Sara's dead.'

'But all the same, she's still manipulating her brother,' Lucy said. 'From beyond the grave. She's got him in a neck-lock he doesn't seem to be able to get out of. It's been six months since she died, Martin. Why hasn't he moved on?'

'He misses his sister. Not to mention her son Mio, presumed dead. There's nothing odd about that, is there?'

Lucy drummed her long fingernails lightly on the table. Blood-red nails. Nice. They'd look good with her black bikini when we got to Nice.

Our milkshakes arrived. Belle started drinking right away. I couldn't be bothered to point out that if she drank too much before the food arrived she wouldn't want her hamburger.

'You think Sara committed the murders?' I said.

'Without a shadow of a doubt.'

'Why haven't you said so before?'

'I did. After your first meeting with Bobby. But I haven't reminded you since then, that's true. I naïvely assumed that you'd reach the same conclusion.'

She sighed and drank some of her milkshake.

'Maybe I will,' I said. 'But there are actually a few loose ends I'd like to look into before I'm prepared to let go of it.'

'Maybe you could wait until you've been through the police file? What look like "loose ends" from this distance might in fact be properly investigated and dismissed lines of inquiry.'

'I know that,' I said. 'But I still need to hear it. I want to hear it directly from the detectives who investigated her ex-boyfriend and father; I want to know that there aren't any other possible perpetrators who have got off unpunished just because the police thought it would be fun if the pretty girl was guilty.'

Lucy looked up at the ceiling.

'Yeah, because that's how it works,' she said. 'The police choose someone they think is guilty, according to the size of the suspect's breasts.'

'Baby, that's not quite what I said. Not remotely.'

'But it's what you meant.'

I couldn't help smiling. It's tricky when the people around you know you well. Tricky, but nice.

The food arrived and Belle threw herself at her hamburger while Lucy and I carefully began to rearrange our plates. More salt, more pepper, less bread and definitely no disgusting pickled gherkins. Why do we never remember to say we don't want them?

'So how are you thinking of making any progress with this mess?' Lucy said after a few bites.

'Now you sound like Bobby,' I said.

'Who's Bobby?' Belle said.

'The brother of a real nutcase,' Lucy said, and burst out laughing.

'Can't I have a brother too?' Belle said, and I swear, my laughter caught so far down in my throat that it actually hurt.

Lucy smiled happily.

'Well, that sounds like an excellent idea,' she said. 'What do you think, Martin?'

'Belle, that's a bit complicated. A brother isn't the sort of thing you get, just like that,' I said.

'Please, tell us in more detail,' Lucy said, putting her cutlery down.

Bloody tease.

'What are you up to?' I said. 'I didn't know you wanted kids. Sorry if I've been insensitive.'

For a moment, time stood still. Before Lucy managed to rearrange her face so that she looked cool again, I caught a glimpse of sadness. It was the first time I understood that she probably hadn't finished with the whole issue of whether or not she wanted children.

'We live in an unfair world,' I said, mostly for the sake of saying something. 'I can be a dad until I'm ninety years old, whereas you women can barely reach half that age before it's too late.'

It felt like it was my fault that things were the way they were. As if I were God and had waved my magic wand to make women lose their fertility before they were fifty. When Lucy didn't say anything it felt as if I had to carry on talking.

'Mind you, I read about that clinic in Italy. They've helped women in their late sixties to get pregnant. Probably something that dirty old git Berlusconi set up. The Hugh Heffner of European politics.'

When I get nervous I start to laugh at my own jokes. There's no excuse for it, but that's how it is. I tried to stifle my enthusiasm for my own remarks by drinking some more milkshake. The only result was that I ended up with milky bourbon in my nose. It stung like hell.

'You don't look terribly well,' Lucy said wearily as drops of white sludge fell onto my plate from my nose. 'Hugh Heffner.'

And then she started to laugh, against her own instincts. Belle joined in, and for a brief moment I caught myself thinking:

This is it.

This is the family I never had when I was growing up.

This is the family I don't deserve.

I grew serious and wiped my mouth. Belle and Lucy carried

on messing about, while I lost myself in thoughts of Sara Texas. Who at some point while she was growing up was supposed to have ended up so crazy that she turned into a murderer. The sort of person who snatched people's lives from them without a moment's regret.

Lucy thought she was guilty, but I wasn't so sure. Bobby had said I'd find out that everything was connected. That the disappearance of Sara's son was linked to the murders. I didn't understand what he meant by that. Regardless of whether or not Sara had committed those five murders, it seemed somehow cruelly logical that she had chosen to take her son's life along with her own. The only question was what she had done with the body. Her social network had been thoroughly investigated, there was no way she could have given him to any member of her family without the police knowing about it. Which meant the boy was dead. But why had she laid him to rest somewhere else? That didn't make any sense to me.

I realised that there were big gaps in my knowledge. There were two questions that I was particularly keen to find answers to:

What did Sara get up to during her last hours of liberty?

And who was the father of her son, Mio?

11

A new working week began. Now it was properly summer. The rain was pouring down and our assistant Helmer had gone off on holiday. It was just under two weeks until we went to Nice. But the longing for sun and cocktails that had obsessed me a week ago was now out of reach. Instead I was driven by a feverish desire to understand Sara Texas's fate.

I could sit at my desk in silence for long periods at a time, just staring at a photograph of her. I looked at her long, wavy hair, at the alert yet somehow sad eyes gazing into the camera. The photograph had been in Eivor's box, and was marked 'taken by Bobby, 2010'. Back then she still had a life, an identity other than that of a feared criminal.

Did I have any idea, back then when I was sitting there with the photograph in my hand, of where I was heading? Of course not. If I had known – or even suspected – then obviously I would have backed out while there was still time. But as it was, I was distressingly unaware of what lay ahead of me, and therefore carried on digging my own grave. With a sturdy grip of the spade, I drove it into the ground time after time.

Each time just as convinced that I was getting a step closer to solving the mystery.

There was one thing I was clear about, however, when I arrived at work that first Monday after deciding to give poor, dead Sara a chance: I had to stop playing at being a master detective and take a more professional approach to the case. No more coffee round at Eivor's, no more guessing games. Now I wanted facts, and I wanted them fast. So I turned to the police.

It took me a few minutes to find out who had been in charge of the investigation. I have plenty of good contacts within the force. The fact that I myself was an officer once upon a time, if only for less than twelve months, obviously helps. To my immense satisfaction it turned out that I knew the officer personally, Detective Superintendent Didrik Stihl. A seriously good guy.

'Martin Benner, it's been a while,' he said when he heard who was calling.

Yes, it had been. A very long while, in fact. At least a year, I quickly calculated.

We exchanged the usual masculine pleasantries. Was I still sleeping with Lucy? Yes. Was he still sleeping with the same woman – in other words, his wife? Yes.

'Are you really calling after all this time just to find out about my sex life?' Didrik eventually said.

He laughed as he said it. And coughed. Didrik was a man who had smoked far too many Marlboro Lights before he came to his senses.

'No,' I said. 'I'm phoning about something else entirely. Sara Texas. You were in charge of that case, weren't you?'

Didrik fell silent.

'Yes, I was,' he said eventually. 'Why are you calling about that?'

I hesitated. Should I tell him the truth? That her peculiar brother had contacted me. That he was willing to pay me to give his dead sister justice. Life has taught me a few fundamental rules. One of them is that the truth is in principle always the best option. Even when it hurts or is a bit embarrassing.

So I told him what had happened, and what I had spent the past week doing.

Didrik sighed down the phone when I'd finished.

'Martin, let me give you some good advice. Leave all that crap well alone.'

'Why?'

'Because it's old. Because it's done and dusted. Because it was a unique and miserable business. Sara Tell is dead. The investigation's been shut down. There's no way you can start digging about in this without looking like an idiot. Is that really what you want?'

Over the years, Didrik has been one of the few people I've listened to. But not this time. He had his duties as a police officer, and I had different duties as a lawyer. I reached out towards the photograph of Ronald Reagan that I keep on my desk. You have to pick your role models with care. The guy who armed the Russians to destruction is one of mine.

'I'm afraid I can't let it go,' I said. 'I promised Bobby I'd give it a try. Besides, I'm seriously bloody curious.'

Didrik groaned down the phone.

'Listen to yourself,' he said. '"Promised Bobby" – what does that mean? And since when have you cared about what you've promised or not promised? Look, if you insist on going ahead with this, you'll have to do it without my help. I don't have much time for that Bobby. Even his sister didn't want anything to do with him.'

Without my help, he said. That didn't sound good.

'A beer,' I said.

'Sorry?'

'Let me get you a beer. And you can tell me honestly what you remember and answer a few questions. After that I'll manage on my own.'

Didrik muttered something I couldn't hear.

'What do you say?' I said.

'I say you're an idiot,' Didrik said, louder. 'But sure, I'll let you get me a beer.'

'Thanks,' I said. 'Thanks very much indeed. This evening, at the Press Club? Six o'clock?'

The only reason I picked the Press Club was that they had a ridiculously wide range of beers.

'The Press Club, six o'clock sounds good. See you then.'

I put the phone down and tried to settle down to work. I had important business to attend to. Above all, I had to pay another visit to the prison to see the guy who looked like he was going down for assault. This time I had to get him to talk. Properly.

Before I did anything I called Signe and made sure it would be okay if I got home a bit late. I remembered a time when I used to be free. A time when I came and went as I pleased in my own home, when I had complete control over my time. Children change all of that. I realise that I've bought myself a degree of freedom by having an au pair, but in truth – the reality I live in now is considerably different to the one I had just a few years ago.

As usual, Signe was cooperative. She didn't have a problem staying two extra hours. If she'd said no it wouldn't have been a problem either. Belle could have come to the Press Club with me.

The piles of papers on my desk weren't large. Much the same as usual for the time of year. Nice and calm. I pulled out the file of the guy in custody. To my own surprise I realised that it irritated me. I didn't have time for that sort of nonsense. I'd rather have devoted my energy to Sara Texas's case.

There was a knock on my door and Lucy walked in. Anything that seems too good to be true is usually just that: too good to be true. At first I thought she was carrying five small bottles of drink. Then I saw that it was sun-cream. She dropped them on my desk and sat down on the edge of it.

'What I want to know is, are you aware of how strong the sun is in Nice in the summer?'

I stared at the sun-cream.

'How am I supposed to know that?' I said.

Lucy rifled among the bottles of lotion. Her skin shone white under the thick watchstrap that adorned her left wrist. That was one of the things I loved about Lucy. That her pale, freckly skin and red hair complemented my dark colouring so perfectly.

'You do want to go, don't you?' she said.

She didn't sound worried, but asked in a neutral voice.

'Of course I do,' I said.

'You seem very distracted.'

She stroked my cheek and ran her hand down my chest. She kissed me very gently.

'Are you worrying about something?'

'No,' I said. 'No, nothing at all.'

She pulled away but put her hand on my arm.

'You're not letting this Sara Texas business get out of proportion, are you?'

She meant well, but I still felt annoyed. I already had one mother; I didn't need another one.

'Of course I'm not,' I said curtly, and stood up. 'You'll have to excuse me, but I've got to get to the prison. We can talk about sun-cream later.'

Lucy stayed on my desk while I put my papers in the briefcase I always had with me.

'Will I see you tonight?' she said.

'I'm having a beer with an old friend in the police.'

'About Sara Texas?'

'It's just a beer.'

She stood up as I began to walk towards the door.

'It's been several days since we last met up.'

'We met up yesterday.'

'You know what I mean, Martin.'

I'd reached the front door now.

'You mean it's been a while since we had sex.'

She was smiling when I turned to look at her.

'Something like that.'

I gave her a crooked grin.

'That's because I'm saving up for Nice. See you later.'

'See you.'

I closed the door unnecessarily hard behind me. Agitation turned into frustration. Lucy had made her choice, and now she had to live with it. She'd said we shouldn't be a couple, that she couldn't be in a relationship with someone who was as unreliable as me.

You make your choice, I thought. And then you live with the consequences.

12

Someone who clearly had the same difficulty as Lucy in dealing with the consequences of his life-choices was the young man I was meeting for the second time inside Kronoberg Prison. It was abundantly clear that he wasn't doing well. Like most people who have extra restrictions placed on them while they're in custody. Swedish custodial legislation is vicious, beyond anything found in any of the world's other democracies. All lawyers know that, as do all police officers. Unfortunately the country's politicians also know it but choose not to do anything about it. I find that utterly incomprehensible.

The guy looked wretched. I wondered what he'd been doing. Had he been rubbing his clothes against the walls of his cell?

'Are you eating properly?' I said.

He'd lost weight and had deep shadows under his eyes.

'Yeah,' he said.

Christ, people who don't know how to lie really shouldn't try.

'I don't want you to eat for my sake, but yours,' I said.

I slung my briefcase up onto the table, opened it and took out the papers I'd brought with me.

'I'd like us to go through what happened one more time,' I said. 'Because your story really doesn't make sense, you know.'

Once again he reacted by getting cocky, which looked ridiculous when he had so little energy to try to act cocky with.

'I told you what happened. You're just going to have to fucking believe me. You're my lawyer.'

I stifled a sigh.

'Yes,' I said. 'I know I am. That's pretty much the only reason I'm here. And I'm really trying to do a good job. But it would be a lot easier if you helped me to do it even better.'

The young man lowered his eyes and scratched his arm with intense concentration. He was his usual self again now. Scared and fragile. It gave me an obvious way-in.

'Come on,' I said. 'I've read the witness statements your friends gave. The ones who say they don't remember anything. They're obviously talking shit. Neither of them had drunk enough for that whole memory loss thing to be believable. Your parents have also expressed their surprise. They can't understand why your best friends aren't standing up for you and saying what really happened. That you never hit that guy.'

I saw that he was listening, but he was still refusing to look at me.

'I get the impression that they're scared,' I said in a calm voice. 'Just like you.'

His frenetic scratching stopped, but he remained silent.

'You'll go to prison for this,' I said. 'Do you understand what that means? Do you know what it does to a person, being locked up? Not being allowed to come and go as you like, do what you like?'

Now he looked at me, and tears welled up in his eyes.

I shook my head.

'Don't do that to yourself. Not if you can avoid it.'

Then, at last, he started to talk.

'I can't,' he said.

'You can't what?'

He sobbed quietly with his head lowered.

'I can't tell you what happened.'

'Why not?'

'Because that would make everything much worse.'

'Sorry, but what? It could get worse? Worse than ending up in prison? Worse than losing your apprenticeship?'

My client nodded as tears ran down his thin cheeks.

'So tell me about it,' I said. 'Tell me what could be worse than all that.'

I sat patiently, waiting for the young man on the other side of the table.

'Maja,' he whispered eventually.

'Who?'

'Maja. My sister. She's fifteen, she's got Down's Syndrome.'

I did my best to understand. Was he going to tell me that it was his sister with learning difficulties who hit the other guy?

'Okay, Maja. Was she in the bar with you?'

He shook his head.

'No, it's not that.'

He flashed me a look that was burning with fear.

'He'll sell her.'

I felt myself stiffen.

'Who'll sell her?'

'Rasmus. He'll sell her to his mates if I don't say it was me. Do you get it now? Do you see why I have to say it was me?'

I got it. Rasmus was the only witness who thought he remembered the evening when the assault took place.

My heart was turning somersaults in my chest.

I understood so much more than he could imagine.

My client looked at me as I lost myself in my own thoughts.

'You mustn't tell anyone,' he said, as if to get my attention. 'Not unless you can save Maja as well.'

I blinked and forced myself back to the present.

'It'll work out somehow,' I said, hoping I didn't sound too distracted.

Unfortunately I did.

'I knew I shouldn't have said anything,' my client said, rubbing his forehead with the back of his hand. 'Fucking hell, how could I be so fucking stupid?'

His rage and anxiety made me pull myself together.

'Stop that,' I said sternly. 'I promise I'll help you find the best possible solution to this. Believe me, once your friend ends up in here, he won't be able to hurt your sister.'

My client shook his head hard.

'He'll get out again,' he said. 'Twice as bad as before. Then he'll get me and Maja. Anyway, he's got friends. Loads of friends who'd do anything he wanted them to while he's inside.'

I sighed.

'Come on. Believe me, there are very few people who actually go along with that sort of mafia behaviour when it comes down to it. Do you seriously believe that he's got "loads of friends" who would be prepared to kidnap a fifteen-year-old girl with learning difficulties and sell her to dirty old men? Forget it.'

I could see I was getting through to him. My client calmed down, but looked just as frightened as he had before.

'Okay, this is what we do,' I said. 'I'll go to the police with this information, and they'll sort this all out. Do you think those friends of yours who couldn't remember anything when they were questioned might remember your version if we ask them? Or does your so-called friend Rasmus have a hold over them as well?'

'I don't know,' my client said.

I didn't believe he did. If that were the case, they'd already have given a false testimony, just as the perpetrator himself had.

'You won't forget Maja, will you?' my client said. 'She's the person this is all about. You do get that, don't you?'

'Absolutely,' I said.

I got ready to leave. All's well that ends well. I couldn't imagine that the police would fail to offer his sister protection. It was both their job and their duty. But I didn't actually agree with him. This wasn't about his sister Maja at all. It was about a young man who had been beaten up for God knew what reason, and whose injuries had left him with epilepsy.

My client remained seated with his head bowed as I stood up. He was a bit like Bobby. The same gangly body, the same battered appearance.

Yet still very unlike him. This guy had every chance of having a good life. And, being brutally honest, that didn't seem to be the case for Bobby.

I patted my client on the shoulder.

'This will all get sorted out before too much longer,' I said. 'Try to eat something, and get some sleep, and I'll be in touch again soon.'

He watched me in silence as I left the room. I felt something resembling relief. Now that I had this case behind me I could devote more of my time to Sara Texas.

My client had actually helped me understand something I'd been thinking about a lot in the previous week. Why certain people in certain situations confessed to crimes they hadn't committed.

They did so to help someone else, or because they were being threatened.

And sometimes they did so for both reasons at the same time.

Anyone hoping to ride to Sara Texas's defence didn't need to find an alternative murderer. It would be more than enough, as I'd said from the outset, to find a plausible explanation for why she had confessed to murders she hadn't committed. For instance, that she was being threatened. Or that she was protecting someone else whom she didn't want to see punished.

If this second explanation was why she acted the way she did, I had to admit that I was worried. Because I'd never met anyone I liked so much that I'd be prepared to help them if they'd killed a handful of people. Still less shoulder responsibility for their crimes.

Getting my client to start talking had been relatively easy. But Sara Texas was dead; I wasn't going to get a peep out of her. So I had to ask myself: if my client hadn't decided to tell me about the threat to his sister Maja, how could I have found out about it?

13

The Press Club isn't half as intellectual as the name implies. Like I said, I only go there because of their fantastic range of beers. Why a police officer like Didrik goes there, I have no idea. I suppose he must like the beer as well.

'Either you haven't got enough work on, or something else has made you take on such an idiotic commission,' Didrik said.

'I don't know if I'd call it a commission,' I said, drinking straight from the bottle.

'That only makes it worse.'

Didrik looked like he'd been born with a brown beer bottle in his hand. The perfect accessory to his expensive jeans and bespoke jacket.

'Do you still buy all your clothes in Italy?' I asked wearily.

Wearily because I was envious.

'Of course,' Didrik said. 'Where else am I going to shop? Dressmann?'

We burst out laughing at the same time.

A young woman sitting over in one corner with what looked

like a really boring guy was looking at me. I looked back, and raised my bottle in a discreet greeting. She nodded and smiled shyly.

'You sod, nice to see you haven't changed,' Didrik said, following my eyes.

'I'm just looking,' I said.

'Right. How's Lucy?'

'Fine, thanks. We're off to Nice in a couple of weeks.'

'Just the two of you?'

'Yep.'

'And Belle?'

'She's going to stay with her grandparents.'

Didrik shook his head.

'It's a bit silly, trying to pretend that you and Lucy aren't a couple, don't you think?'

I shrugged and tried to get eye contact with the girl I'd raised my drink to. She looked back unflinchingly. The hunter in me woke up in less than two seconds. She was prey, and I didn't even have to catch her. She was already lying there waiting for me, if I could just be bothered to pull my bow.

Didrik grinned.

'You're being childish, Martin. You're going to have sex with that girl just to prove that you aren't together with Lucy.'

I cleared my throat and put my bottle down. It was time to shift the focus of the conversation, even if he was basically right. Of course I'd end up having sex with the girl I'd spotted. But that had nothing to do with Lucy. No, I fucked because I was horny. If there were other underlying reasons, I wasn't remotely interested in analysing them. Life's complicated enough as it is.

'Sara Texas,' I said.

'I'd rather talk about your sex life,' Didrik said. 'You're such an inspiration.'

'It never occurred to you that she might actually have been innocent?'

Didrik became serious.

'Come off it,' he said. 'A little part of me honestly thought we were going to meet up for a beer because you were bored.'

I raised one eyebrow and he relented.

'Okay, fine, we'll do it your way. No, I never thought she was innocent. Because, as you've doubtless realised, she was extremely cooperative.'

'Precisely,' I said. 'And since when do murderers behave like that?'

For some reason my keenness annoyed Didrik.

'Okay, you need to calm down,' he said sharply. 'You're talking rubbish, Martin. You've been badly informed, and it doesn't suit you. It wasn't the case – let me emphasise that, it *wasn't* the case – that sweet little Sara started talking the moment we brought her in for her first interview.'

I stopped myself and waited for him to go on.

'It all started when the police in Texas got in touch with a request for help. Obviously there was never any question of extraditing someone who might end up on death row, but we were more than prepared to bring her in to question her ourselves. The Yanks sent us what they had, and the prosecutor agreed to set up a preliminary investigation. We found her pretty much immediately, I seem to recall. And got nowhere. The cops in Texas had done a good job of linking her to the murders in Galveston and Houston, but it wasn't enough. There was no forensic evidence.'

A waitress appeared and asked if we wanted any food to go with our beers. I ordered a bowl of nuts.

'Please, go on,' I said to Didrik. 'You were saying that there was no forensic evidence?'

He ignored my unmistakably ironic tone.

'So we brought her in for questioning. Have you seen pictures of her? She didn't look older than fifteen or so. So damn ... innocent. None of us believed she was guilty. I felt like starting by apologising for bothering her and calling a halt to the whole stupid thing there and then. But obviously I couldn't do that, so we went ahead as planned. And do you know what she did then?'

'No.'

'She became defensive. Wouldn't admit a thing.'

This was new to me.

'She didn't confess to any of the murders?'

'Nope. Not that we thought that was strange. We certainly didn't have enough to hold her, so we had to let her go. A colleague who was on his way home from work saw her leave Police Headquarters. He said she was crying like a baby.'

'Doesn't sound all that strange,' I said.

'Of course not,' Didrik said. 'But then the Yanks got in touch again. They'd received an anonymous email that we helped them to trace. The IP address led us to Sara.'

I waited for him to go on. The fact that the Americans had received an anonymous email didn't feel all that exciting. The girl with Mr Charisma looked at me and smiled broadly when her date dropped his fork and leaned over to pick it up. I smiled back quickly. Sorted: I wanted her, she wanted me. Now all we had to do was arrange the practicalities.

'An email,' I said, to let Didrik know I was listening.

'An email,' he repeated. 'Sent from Sara's computer. Can you guess what it contained?'

'No idea.'

'A description of where the police could find the knife used in the Galveston murder.'

'Let me guess,' I interrupted. 'It was in a shoebox that had been hidden in a swamp in Florida.'

'Nice try, but wrong. It was in a plastic bag.'

'Plastic bag, shoebox – who cares?'

'In Sara Texas's storage locker up in the attic.'

So there was compelling evidence pointing to Sara's guilt. Of course I'd known that all along, but it still felt dispiriting to have it confirmed. That's what happens to those of us who are always looking for the ultimate high. We often end up disappointed.

For a moment I had to check my own motives for getting involved in a dead woman's eventual culpability for five murders. Could it simply be that I was bored? God knows, I'd done some pretty peculiar things in the past to liven up everyday life. And even though several years had passed, I was still in shock at the way my life had changed since Belle came to live with me.

But this time it was different, I told myself. I wasn't just bored and out for an adrenalin kick. There were a lot of things about Sara's case that appealed to me. It had been the same when she was still alive, too. I hadn't been lying on the radio when I said that I would have liked to be her defence lawyer. The simple fact that the case had such a clear connection to Texas made my pulse-rate increase. I could still remember all the smells and colours I associated with my time in the state. I remembered the countless hours I spent in my car, driving all over the rugged landscape in an effort to see as much of it as possible. I had the car radio on at full blast, and I learned to love country music. That was my farewell tour, my farewell to the USA. And to my dad. There are some parental betrayals that we learn to live with, and there are those that we never get over. My dad's was the latter sort.

'I don't know what I could have done differently,' he had said as I stood and packed the car.

That was the first time I hit another person. Bang, right in the jaw, and he slumped to the ground. Then I slammed the boot shut and drove away. I left him lying in a cloud of sand and exhaust fumes. Once upon a time he had left my mum on her own with a small child. And he claimed he didn't know what he could have done differently.

He died six months later. Neither Marianne nor I attended his funeral.

'I can see I've managed to sow a few doubts,' Didrik said, interrupting my thoughts.

I took a few deep swigs of my beer.

'Not at all,' I said. 'It was obvious that you had evidence against her. It's a bit odd that she brought the murder weapon home from the US, though.'

'I'm not sure the word "odd" really has any place in this context. I mean, we're talking about a serial killer here.'

I laughed. Didrik could be quite funny, in spite of his strict adherence to the facts.

He went on: 'Martin, she knew all the victims. Can you explain a coincidence like that to me?'

'I don't have to. Let's talk about that email instead. What was your theory? That Sara was suddenly struck by such terrible remorse that she emailed the police in Texas after she'd been called in for questioning that first time?'

'We're never going to get an answer to that, and to be honest I don't really care,' Didrik said firmly. 'The email came from a laptop we seized in her flat. The knife was in her storage-space in the attic, no one else had access to it. An attic that turned out to be an absolute goldmine when we went through it more systematically in conjunction with the full search of her home.'

'Really?'

'Really. We found the belt that was used in the third murder, her first one here in Sweden. You remember, she strangled an ICA-supermarket cashier. And we also found traces of arsenic.'

I frowned.

'Which victim was she supposed to have poisoned?'

'The fifth.'

I put my beer bottle down.

'I'd like the whole of the report from the preliminary investigation.'

'No problem, it's in the public domain seeing as the charges were actually filed.'

'I'd like to see the slops as well.'

Didrik's face clouded over.

'Of course.'

His mobile rang and he quickly pulled it out of his jacket pocket. I made use of the break by getting eye contact with the girl I'd been cruising. She got up from her chair and smiled apologetically at her date. It was a polite but strained smile. Nothing like the one she fired off at me as she passed our table on the way to the ladies' room.

I saw Didrik chuckle as I slid out of my chair and followed

her. She looked surprised but happy when I opened the door
to the ladies' bathroom and walked in.

'Well, hello, you're not allowed to be in here,' said another
woman who was washing her hands in the basin.

'I'm not, am I?' I said. 'Why don't you go into the men's
room and say the same thing to the women using the toilets
in there.'

Now, I hadn't actually been inside the men's room first,
so I didn't honestly know if there were any women in there.
But there usually were, and I thought that was justification
enough for what I said. Not that I cared. The idea of separate toilet facilities for men and women feels ridiculously
old-fashioned.

The woman washing her hands didn't answer. She just finished up as quickly as possible and left the room.

'Alone at last,' I said to my prey, as if I'd been waiting all
evening for this.

She giggled.

'We aren't,' she said.

'Sorry, we aren't what?'

'Alone.'

She gestured with her foot towards the row of toilets. They
were all occupied. She was wearing extremely expensive shoes
with very high heels. And she knew how to walk properly in
them.

'I've already got a date,' she said.

Sorry, love, it's too late to play hard to get, I thought.

'He doesn't seem to be terribly entertaining,' I said.

She laughed loudly. Brilliant white teeth and eyes that were
clouded with alcohol. The fact that she could still walk in
those shoes was impressive.

'True,' she said. 'I'd go so far as to say he's pretty boring. I work with him, he asked me out.'

I took a few steps forward, standing shamelessly close to her. She didn't move.

'You deserve better,' I whispered in her ear as I heard someone flush one of the toilets.

I put one hand gently on her backside.

'Do you want to go home alone, or would you like company?' I said.

14

There must be at least a million books about the noble art of picking up women. I can't really see why. I mean, it's so easy, as long as you go for the right women. One minute later I was back with Didrik. He shook his head.

'I don't know how you find the time and energy,' he said.

'Watch and learn. You've got potential, after all.'

'Why, thank you, very good of you to say so.'

Neither of us felt much like hanging around. We'd already done what we needed to, and I assumed that Didrik would be heading home to his wife. I called home to make sure that the au pair was able to stay until ten. She could. I had a word with Belle and said goodnight. I felt a pang of conscience in my chest as I put my phone away. I hoped Belle never had to understand the way I lived. Never ran into a man with the same lifestyle as me.

'Before we leave, give me an idea of what you've got in mind,' Didrik said once I'd tucked my bank card next to the bill. 'If Sara Texas was innocent, then who killed all those people?'

'It's the police's responsibility to answer that question,' I said. 'As far as I'm concerned, the question is more: if Sara Texas was innocent, why did she lie and say she was the murderer?'

Didrik sighed.

'Because she was mentally ill?'

'Wrong. Because she was frightened, or because she was protecting someone. Or both.'

'You think someone was threatening her? Ridiculous. Absurd.'

I remembered what my client told me in prison that afternoon.

You won't forget Maja, will you? She's the person this is all about. You do get that, don't you?

My client's words merged with what Sara's brother Bobby told me when I made it clear I wasn't going to try to find Sara's son, Mio.

It's all connected. You'll see. It's all part of the same story.

Those words caught in my mouth as I formulated my next question.

'Didrik, what happened to the little boy? What happened to Mio?'

Didrik looked at me intently.

'We don't know, but I'm afraid we believe his mother killed him before she committed suicide.'

'So why haven't you found him?' I said. 'Why wasn't he with her when she died?'

'I can't answer that. What are you insinuating? That someone else took the boy?'

I didn't know what to say, so I kept quiet. My thoughts weren't ready yet, my conclusions not yet formulated. But I was beginning to suspect that Bobby was right. There was a risk that Mio had been to Sara what my client's sister was for him. A hostage.

'Where was the boy while Sara was in custody?'

'With foster parents.'

'Who was his father?'

'Don't know. No one had acknowledged paternity, anyway. Sara claimed he was a stranger she'd met in a bar.'

'How did she die?'

'Sara? That was in the papers. She pulled a real classic. She jumped off Västerbron.'

Naturally, I'd read that in the papers. But I liked forcing Didrik to tell me.

'Were there witnesses?'

I hadn't read anything about that in the papers.

'An elderly man on a bike saw her throw herself over the railing. If you're wondering if she was murdered, the answer is no. The old boy said she was alone. So she didn't have the boy with her.'

The waitress came back with the receipt and my card. My recently recruited date glanced attentively at me. *Are you leaving?* she seemed to be asking. I nodded imperceptibly. She'd have to find some way of ditching her tedious date, because I didn't fancy a three-way.

'Bastard,' Didrik said.

'You're just jealous.'

'I suppose so.'

We gathered our things and made our way towards the door.

'Did you follow up any other leads?' I said. 'She seems to have had both a very persistent boyfriend and a father who didn't want to let go of her.'

'You've got that from Bobby, of course. Well, we certainly looked into it. But believe me, we didn't find a damn thing.'

'What about those things her friend Jenny sent over? The diary and train ticket?'

'No value as evidence. Sara could prove she was in Galveston at the time of the murder there. She never acknowledged the diary.'

We parted on the pavement with the usual pleasantries about having to meet up again soon.

'Get in touch if you need any more information,' Didrik said. 'I'd be happy to help you stick to the facts in this case. It's easy to get lost when you start looking into Sara Tell's past. If you keep a cool head, you'll find that this case dies of natural causes quicker than it takes you to make that bird come.'

I laughed.

'This evening, then. Well, so far you haven't managed to convince me that Sara was guilty.'

Didrik looked genuinely concerned. From the corner of my eye I saw the young woman walk out with her date. He gave her a feeble hug and then walked away. A real loser. Tragic.

She was standing a short distance away, waiting for me.

'One last thing,' I said. 'If Sara did actually murder all those people, and if it was so important to her that the police realised that she was the perpetrator, why did she kill herself before the trial?'

Didrik threw his arms out.

'There could be a thousand reasons for that. Maybe she was ashamed?'

'Ashamed?'

'Guilty, then. I don't bloody know. But I can tell you, I sleep soundly at night. Seriously. I don't feel I let Sara Tell down, nor the families of the murder victims.'

I took a step towards my new friend.

'And how do you know she only killed five people? Maybe there were ten victims?'

'I have to admit that I've spent a lot more time thinking about that. But we didn't manage to link her to any crimes beyond those five, so I presume that was all of them.'

I raised my hand in a final farewell. I had almost reached the young woman now. She looked happy.

'It was good to see you,' I said to Didrik. 'Let's speak soon!' Didrik nodded briefly.

'Look after yourself. See you!'

He headed across Vasagatan and set off towards the Central Station.

I watched him go, then turned my attention to the young woman standing in front of me.

I held out my hand in an exaggerated gesture: 'Martin.'

She took it, and squeezed it surprisingly hard. 'Veronica.'

'Is it okay if we go back to yours?' I said. 'My place is a right mess. I've a water leak in the basement.'

15

'Shall we meet up again?'

She was lying with her head on my chest, and her long hair was tickling me. No dark roots on show. She was that unusual thing, a genuine blonde.

The sex had been good. Very good. I realised I'd been in greater need of relieving the pressure than I'd imagined. All those thoughts that Sara Texas had triggered. It couldn't be healthy.

I stroked her arm gently. It was probably quarter to ten, something like that, I ought to leap out of bed and throw myself in a taxi.

'I don't honestly know,' I said. 'I've got a lot of things going on in my life right now.'

She raised her head.

'Are you seeing someone else?'

Why do women always think it's so important to know? I never ask that question.

'No.'

She tried to hide it, but I could tell she was relieved.

Her head sank back down again.

'Not that it matters,' she said quickly. 'I mean, it's not like we've made any promises to each other. I'm very happy with what's happened this evening. I don't need a relationship. I really don't. I hope that's not what you're thinking? That I'm like that?'

She raised her head again. Pleading.

Oh no. Always the same old tune.

'Not at all, don't worry,' I said, and started to move. 'I don't think anything. I realised from the start that you weren't after anything serious.'

I flashed her an encouraging smile, perfectly aware that I hadn't said what she'd been hoping to hear.

'Good,' she said.

I pulled my clothes on in silence.

She didn't move from the bed.

'You're okay about me not staying, aren't you?' I said. 'I need to get home and sort out that bloody pipe. The plumber says they're probably going to have to put some fans in.'

She nodded.

'I know,' she said. 'My parents had a water-leak in their house a few years ago. Those fans were there for weeks.'

'God, what a nuisance,' I said, checking my trouser pockets to make sure I'd got everything.

Time to leave while things were still nice and calm. There might even be the potential for a rematch.

'Funny,' she said. 'I didn't think you were the sort of guy who lived in a house with a cellar.'

'I'm the sort of guy who needs a lot of freedom and plenty of space,' I said with a smile. 'Look after yourself, and thanks for a really great evening.'

I leaned over and kissed her. She followed me out into the hall naked. When I took her bra off an hour earlier I thought her breasts were two of the most perfect I'd ever seen. Sadly they didn't stand up to closer examination. I only needed the slightest of touches to know. You can tell at once if they're real or not. These, sad to say, weren't. I had no idea what they'd looked like before, but I guessed that they were perfectly okay. So why fix something that wasn't broken?

I gave her a quick hug before I opened the door and left.

'You're welcome to call me sometime if you're bored,' she said.

'I might very well do that,' I said. 'Take care.'

Five minutes later I was on my way home in a taxi. I was going to be about quarter of an hour late. I hoped the au pair wasn't going to spoil the evening by being grumpy.

I got home to a silent flat. Signe was waiting in the kitchen. She was sitting reading the paper.

'Have you had a good evening?' she said.

I tossed my keys onto the worktop and sank onto one of the kitchen chairs.

'Very good. How have things been here?'

'Fine. Belle told me about all the fun you had over the weekend.'

There was warmth in her smile as she looked at me. For some inexplicable reason that made me blush. I wasn't sure I deserved that sort of warmth. Not when I place higher priority on a decent fuck than the chance to put Belle to bed.

As if she could read my mind, Signe stroked my back as she got up from the table to go home.

'You want the best for her, Martin. I don't think anyone could ask for more.'

Was she right?

Maybe, maybe not.

Signe went home, leaving me alone with Belle. I remained seated at the kitchen table. I was finding it difficult to sum up the day. Good or bad, that was the question.

My meeting with Didrik hadn't given me what I'd been hoping for. I'd felt something shift when I met my client in prison, when I began to see similarities between his situation and Sara Tell's. Rather naïvely, I had been hoping that feeling would get stronger when I met Didrik. It didn't. I poured myself a glass of water and went and sat in the library. I pulled my notes from my case. Didrik had confirmed a lot of what I'd already read, and had added several new details. It didn't help. Because Didrik hadn't wavered one iota from his original conclusions. Which, of course, was both logical and only to be expected. If he'd started to wobble on the question of guilt, then he really ought to set up a new preliminary investigation to look for the real murderer pretty damn quick. Or murderers. Because who said there was only one perpetrator behind all the killings?

If you stood back and looked at all five murders more generally, it soon became abundantly clear that there wasn't much to link them together. Nothing beyond the troublesome detail that Sara Tell had known, or at least met, all of the victims. A detail which, I had to admit, was hard to ignore. Regardless of the whole question of guilt, Sara must have been part of everything that had happened. Somehow or other.

Fucking hell. If only I'd been on the pitch when the match started. I told myself I could have got her to talk. Just like my client today. It was noble but stupid of him to lie to protect his disabled sister. He'd been prepared to sacrifice a sizeable chunk of his future for his sister's welfare. I really don't like that sort of reasoning. Martyrdom has no place in the modern world. I hate self-sacrificial people. Women who abandon their careers for their children's sake – as if children never grew up – or people who always put the wishes and needs of others above their own. Pathetic. I can't stand it.

At least not in large doses. After all, I'd just been sitting at the kitchen table wondering if I was paying enough attention to Belle's needs. But that was an entirely different matter. It wasn't about making sacrifices, but about right and wrong. That made it harder.

I scratched my head, rubbing my fingers through my very short hair. I couldn't make much sense of anything, personal or professional. Tomorrow I'd be able to read the report of the preliminary investigation, which would give me a much better idea of what had been done and what was missing. Maybe I'd also have to rethink my decision to go into battle for Sara's sake.

My notes stared up at me from my desk.

Was I on the point of making a fool of myself? What if it got out that Martin Benner was chasing ghosts and evil spirits? That wouldn't look good. Not unless I was certain I'd be able to come up with anything useful at the end of it.

I had to take another look at the sparse pages of notes I'd made over the previous few days to remind myself what had sparked my interest.

The diary and the train ticket. Was there anything worth a closer look there? I thought there probably was. The diary was Sara's; trying to claim anything else was just absurd. But the entries in it needed to be interpreted by someone who knew Sara better than me. Ideally, I needed to get hold of Jenny, her friend in Houston. I wanted to get an idea of who she was, why she was interested in Sara even though Sara didn't want her help. The train ticket was just as interesting as the diary. Didrik had said that Sara had been able to prove she was in Galveston when the murder there took place. I wanted to see that evidence.

Something else that bothered me was that there were obviously other suspects. At least in Texas. Jenny's ex-boyfriend, the Chinese negro, had been a suspect. These were important facts, but they felt hard to get hold of.

I shuffled on my chair. It wasn't that I thought it unlikely I'd come to the conclusion that Sara was definitely a killer. To put it bluntly: if she *wasn't*, then someone had done a brilliant job of framing her. They'd crossed oceans to kill people in her name.

Who has enemies like that? I asked myself.

Not me, at any rate.

But Sara Texas did. Well, it looked like it, anyway. What I had to do now was find someone who could tell me more about her life. Preferably in Stockholm, because I had no plans to go to Texas.

Or did I?

The thought made my mouth dry. I'd promised myself I'd never go back to the States. Besides, I didn't feel particularly inclined to do what Bobby wanted, even though he had a point when he said that a trip to Texas would be inevitable.

I sighed. Even if I put all the objections to one side, one big problem remained: how could I persuade Lucy to swap Nice for Texas?

16

'You can't be serious.'

Lucy was looking at me as if I'd lost my mind. It occurred to me that maybe I had. Was I seriously standing there suggesting that we go to Texas instead of Nice?

'I mean, it must be about a hundred degrees there in the summer,' she said.

Ah, an opening. If the temperature was her only objection, I'd soon be able to deal with that. But it wasn't quite as simple as that, as it turned out.

'Baby, we'd stay in the best hotels, drive the most comfortable cars. You wouldn't even notice the heat.'

'How lovely. Might as well stay at home, then.'

Not a chance. I was going abroad if it was the last thing I did. That endless Swedish rain was already way too much for me.

'You win,' I said. 'We'll go to Nice.'

Lucy looked at me incredulously.

'Martin, you do know what you're doing, don't you?' she said. 'What did Didrik manage to get into your head yesterday? Did he think it was a good idea to carry on looking into Sara's case?'

'Not exactly.'

I didn't like her mentioning the previous evening. Even if we weren't a couple, it would be unfortunate if she managed to find out what I got up to before I went home. As if she suspected that something was wrong, she went on breezily: 'I tried to call you, actually. Yesterday evening. But you didn't answer.'

'I wanted to spend some time concentrating on the material,' I said. 'You know, I got quite a bit more from Didrik. Sorry, I had my phone on silent.'

Lucy flashed me a teasing smile.

'A date with Sara Texas, then. Lovely.'

If only she knew the thoughts she triggered by using the word date. I managed to force a stiff smile.

'Do you fancy lunch later?' Lucy said when I didn't respond to her joke.

'Sure,' I said. 'How about Texas Longhorn on Fleminggatan? It's been ages since I had one of their burgers.'

'But we had hamburgers at Bebe on Sunday.'

'That's not the same thing at all. Bebe is Bebe. Texas is completely different.'

'Wow. Lots of Texas today.'

Lucy didn't look at all enthusiastic, but agreed to the suggestion. Regarding hamburgers. Definitely not the trip to Texas.

The doorbell rang and I went and answered it.

A young guy in jeans and a tennis shirt was standing in the stairwell.

'Martin Benner?'

'Yep.'

'Delivery for you.'

He carried a number of cardboard boxes into the hall and asked me to sign for them.

It was the records from the preliminary investigation into the case against Sara.

At first Lucy didn't want anything to do with the material. But once she'd stuck her beautiful hands in the shit it was like she'd been struck by the same curse as me.

We sat on the floor like a couple of teenagers, reading document after document. The interviews with Sara basically contained little more than her unambiguous confession and her description of where they could find the evidence. With the exception of the first session, the one conducted because the Americans had asked for help. I read it through once, then a second time.

'Look at this,' I said, handing Lucy the sheaf of papers. 'Then compare it with the others.'

Lucy read through it while I made coffee. I don't remember if it was raining. But it certainly wasn't nice weather.

'Strange,' Lucy said when she'd finished reading. 'You almost wouldn't think they were talking to the same person.'

'Exactly,' I said, remembering what Didrik had said. First they take her in for questioning and get nothing. She doesn't know what they're talking about and says clearly that she's upset at having been brought in by the police. She says she's never heard of the murders in Galveston and Houston. Or at least she doesn't remember anything about them. Then a few weeks pass. The Yanks receive an anonymous email and that leads to further questioning and a search. The second time round there's a completely different atmosphere. Suddenly she's talking both more and less at the same time.

I was talking so much, and so quickly, that I forgot I had a cup of coffee in each hand. Lucy relieved me of one of them and took a sip.

'It's bloody weird. But we can't be the only ones to think that, about the fact that she changes her story all of a sudden and for some reason starts saying stuff that's every policeman's wet dream.'

'It obviously took them by surprise,' I said. 'But ... in the end the story held together. They made some pretty remarkable discoveries in her attic, and when she started to talk, everything made sense. I presume they must have checked her phone records for the weeks between the interviews. And if they couldn't find any sign of an accomplice, they probably found themselves in a position where they had to buy her story.'

Lucy rummaged through the documents.

'I'm not giving up that easily, though,' she said. 'Just so you don't start to think I'm on your side. The woman was guilty – the question is whether or not she was mentally ill. She almost must have been. What did the psychiatric evaluation say?'

'They didn't have time to do one.'

Lucy stopped looking.

'Then I think we can agree that she was ill.'

'Does that make it feel better?'

'Yes.'

Lucy looked at the heaps of paper which by now were covering most of the floor.

'We've got our work cut out for the whole summer, if we want it,' she said.

She ran her finger across the heap closest to her. The same nail-varnish she had on Sunday. Bright red. I felt the all too familiar desire come to life again. I wanted her. Ideally immediately.

But Lucy's radar was far too sophisticated for me to be able to mount any sort of surprise attack.

I didn't manage to get any further than putting one hand on her thigh before she was on her feet.

'I'm hungry,' she said. 'Let's go and have that hamburger.'

'Are you going to play hard to get again?' I said.

'Damn right I am.'

She went into her office to fetch her handbag. My mobile rang. It was Marianne, wanting to talk about the leak in her cellar.

'Those fans, do they have to be on at full blast?'

'How the fuck am I supposed to know?'

'Martin, don't swear like that.'

I don't understand this idea of saying some words are rude and others aren't. Words are just words. And I've been swearing ever since I first learned to talk.

'It's lunchtime now,' I said. 'Lucy and I are heading out for something to eat. I'll have to call you later.'

We ended the call and I put my mobile away.

'We need to work through the murders systematically,' Lucy said. 'I haven't really got much of an idea about the three she committed here in Sweden.'

'You mean the three she was charged with but never convicted of? The three she confessed to without actually committing?'

Lucy held the door open for me.

'Exactly,' she said wearily.

We emerged onto the street and headed down Sankt

Eriksgatan. The leaden clouds hung heavily in the sky. I realised that I was walking slightly hunched over, as if I thought they were going to fall. We swung into Fleminggatan. The most boring street in the whole of Stockholm. There wasn't a single building I could imagine living in. You almost feel like closing your eyes when you're walking down it.

We passed a succession of plate-glass windows. I watched our reflections in the dirty glass. She was in high heels, sand-coloured trousers and a white blouse, with red hair that could make even Julia Roberts scream with envy. I was wearing my favourite chinos and a blue shirt. We looked bloody good. I put my arm round Lucy's shoulders.

'What are you thinking of doing next?' Lucy said. 'You go through everything from the preliminary investigation, and then what?'

'I need to start talking to people.'

'Such as?'

'I've already had the pleasure of meeting Sara's brother, but it would be good to talk to her mother as well. It would make things easier if I could get in touch with other people who knew her, friends and so on. I'd really like to have had a conversation with that friend of hers in Houston, Jenny. And if she's got any other relatives left in Stockholm. Sara, I mean.'

Lucy nodded to herself.

'Sounds a lot like police work,' she said.

'Come on, it's just a way of getting my bearings.'

I didn't really believe that myself. Once a police officer, always a police officer. Who was it who said that? One of my colleagues in Texas, maybe? As usual, thinking about Texas dredged up memories of my dad. Who ran away but still didn't understand what he could have done differently.

I held Lucy tighter. She felt the change and slipped her arm round my waist.

'Is there a reason why you don't want to talk to Sara Texas's sister?' Lucy said.

I stopped dead on the pavement. We were less than a block from Texas Longhorn.

'Sorry?'

'Her sister. There was a brief mention of her in one of the articles I read.'

So Sara had had a sister too. A sister I had missed when I did my research, which was sloppy of me. But it was even weirder that my good friend Bobby hadn't said a word about her.

I decided there and then to talk to her as well.

If I could find her.

17

Before I could start arranging any meetings I needed to do more research. Much more. Otherwise I risked making a complete fool of myself. There was no good reason to sit in the office going through all the material, so Lucy and I put the boxes we wanted to look at in the car and drove back to mine as soon as we'd finished lunch.

We settled down in the study. I was confident I would make a big breakthrough once I'd looked at everything in detail. That wasn't what happened.

The hamburger left me in a post-lunch coma and I wasn't the slightest bit horny any more. Nor was Lucy. But we did work hard to get a better idea of the timeline, and understand the crimes more clearly. I didn't even ask if Lucy wanted to help; somehow I had taken it for granted that she was reluctantly complicit in what I was doing.

'This isn't a pretty story,' Lucy said once we started to get a clearer idea of the chain of events that had led to Sara's arrest. The fact that she was let out on licence seemed incredible.

That had been one of the big scandals of the case. That Sara

Texas, suspected of having murdered five people, was allowed out from the prison where she was being held under specific conditions. Her father, ironically, had been the victim of a violent mugging while Sara was being held in custody. He was still unconscious in hospital when she was charged, and the doctors were saying it would take a miracle for him to survive. So Sara was let out for an afternoon, and was escorted to the hospital by armed guards. To say goodbye to a man who used to sell her body to his friends, who went all the way to Houston to cause trouble for her, and was known as Lucifer.

It wasn't easy to understand how she had escaped, but somehow she managed to disappear. Later the police reluctantly admitted that she had asked for five minutes alone with her dad, and that was evidently all she needed to make her escape through the window. On the fifth floor.

'She's the most famous criminal in Sweden right now,' the lead detective said in a television interview. 'She's not going to get far.'

A ring of steel was set up around Stockholm. Surveillance at airports, railway stations and harbours was stepped up. Completely unnecessarily. Sara appeared to have gone straight to her son's preschool and picked him up. That was another scandal. None of the staff had been able to explain how it had happened. The boy, Mio, was only four years old. At the time he went missing the children were all playing outside. One moment he was there, the next he was gone.

The police had believed she would be easier to find when she had the boy with her. With that, they probably broke some sort of record in the number of wrong judgements made in a single day. Because it looked like Sara never had any interest in leaving Stockholm, and wasn't planning to travel any great distance. That evening she jumped off Västerbron. Her body was picked up by the coastguard. The boy's body was never found. As Didrik had confirmed the previous evening, the witness who saw her jump said she was alone.

I found the name of the witness. Magnus Krusberg.

'Gooseberry?' Lucy said.

'Krusberg,' I said.

'Pretty unusual name.'

'This whole story feels pretty unusual.'

'I don't understand why she had to take her son with her,' Lucy said.

I thought about that. If for some reason I had no choice but to commit suicide, would I take Belle with me? Not a chance.

'Perhaps she wasn't the one who took him,' I said.

Lucy lowered the sheet she was reading and looked at me in surprise.

'So who was it, then?'

'I don't know. All I know is that I can't get this story to fit together. Nothing makes sense.'

I couldn't escape the similarities I had seen earlier with the client I had visited in prison, the one whose sister with learning disabilities had been threatened by the real perpetrator. I thought through it all again.

Why would anyone accept responsibility for a crime they hadn't committed?

Because they were being threatened, or to protect someone they loved.

Perhaps not just loved, but someone they also felt a degree of responsibility towards. Non-negotiable loyalty. The sort you might have with a brother or sister. Or, even more so, with your own offspring.

'She accepted responsibility for the murders to protect her son,' I said slowly. 'Then she escaped for the same reason.'

'To protect Mio?'

'Yes.'

'From what, or whom?'

'From whoever it was who was threatening to harm the boy.'

Lucy shook her head.

'That doesn't make sense, Martin. It just doesn't.'

She tossed her papers down and turned towards me. I interrupted her before she had time to start.

'The police in Texas contacted their colleagues in Sweden and asked them to take her in for questioning,' I said. 'This they did, and – as we both agree – the first interview is different in every respect from those that followed. When they picked Sara up two weeks later, all of a sudden she's a different person. She gives up and serves the police what they want on a silver platter. What could explain such a complete transformation? Why didn't she confess during the first interview?'

'Because she thought she could get away with it,' Lucy said. 'The weight of evidence was completely different the second time they took her in.'

'Yes, and how come? Well, because Sara herself had emailed the police in Texas and told them where to find the weapon used in the Galveston murder. Now why the hell would she do that? Why not just tell the whole story to the police in Stockholm?'

'Because she thought she could stick it out? And when she realised she couldn't, she shopped herself in an anonymous email. You've got to stop pretending this woman was normal. She murdered five people. End of story.'

I felt so restless I had to stand up. I went over to the open window and breathed in the fresh, cool air.

'There's another explanation,' I persisted. 'That during the first interview she didn't have a clue about any of the murders. Once the police started sniffing about, the real perpetrator got worried. In all likelihood someone who was already in Sara's immediate vicinity. He – or she – paid Sara a visit and frightened her into confessing not only to the murders in Texas, but also the three in Stockholm.'

'I'm just wondering who this person is,' Lucy said. 'Someone so powerful that Sara didn't think there was any point going to the police for help. I mean, think about what was at stake here. Five cases of premeditated murder. It would have been decades before she got out.'

'Maybe she panicked,' I said. 'Maybe she would have tried to escape even if her dad hadn't got ill. Don't forget, she escaped through a fifth-floor window. If you do that, you're desperate.'

'Or cold.'

'Or both. Either way, she made her way to her son's pre-school and tried to save him.'

The window blew open and almost knocked a plant over. I put the pot on the floor and opened the window wide.

'But she didn't save him, did she? In all probability she killed him.'

'We don't know the slightest thing about that,' I said. 'Anyway, what if the threat against the boy was so terrible that killing him felt like a mercy?'

I didn't honestly believe that myself, but it was the only thing I could think of.

'Unless you were right when you said that someone else took Mio,' Lucy said. 'Maybe she was working with someone.'

'Maybe,' I said.

I'm really shit at guessing games. I did my best to stick to the facts, but it still went wrong. Sara escaped at two o'clock in the afternoon. Six hours later she was dead. The boy disappeared from preschool at four o'clock. What could she have done with him in such a short space of time?

'The murders,' Lucy said. 'Let's concentrate on the murders instead. We're not getting anywhere with the rest of it.'

She started to sort the documents on my desk.

'I need a whisky,' I said. 'Shall I get you one as well?'

The first murder was committed in Galveston during the autumn of 2007. Galveston is a dump in the south of Texas, a seaside resort on the Gulf of Mexico. Once upon a time it was the largest city in Texas, a place where a lot of migrants settled. Then a hurricane struck and destroyed the whole city, and it never really recovered.

Shit happens.

The victim's name was Jane Becker, and she worked at the Carlton Hotel down by the beach. The family for whom Sara Tell was an au pair used to stay in that particular hotel when they visited Galveston for weekends or during the holidays. Sara was with them on several visits. The police investigation conducted when Jane Becker died discovered that she had been selling sex to guests at the hotel outside her working hours. Persistent rumours in Houston suggested that Sara Tell made extra money the same way, both in Houston and Galveston. There was, however, no evidence to support the claim.

One theory was that Jane was murdered because she realised that Sara was competing for clients and threatened to expose her to her host family. Another was that the murder was an accident, that Sara killed her by chance. Sara herself refused to talk about the motive. Either way, the murder was described as brutal. The victim was stabbed more than ten times in the chest.

The second murder took place in Houston in the spring of 2008. A taxi driver was beaten to death with a golf club that had been in the back of his car. Sara was seen getting out of his car outside a nightclub, yelling 'Fucking pig!'. An hour later he was dead. The police were working on the theory that Sara was molested in the car and then went to find the driver to take her revenge. The man was found dead beside his car. The boot was open, which at first led the police to suspect he was the victim of a robbery. But they never identified a suspect and the investigation was going nowhere until they caught sight of Sara.

'I don't see how they ended up investigating Sara,' Lucy said.

'Coincidence,' I said, seeing as I had recently found the answer to that question in the background information relating to the request sent from the police in Texas to their counterparts in Stockholm. A detective who was working in Galveston at the time of the first murder moved to Houston in February 2012. At that time the murder of the taxi driver was still an open case, even if it was pretty cold. The detective's first task was to shake some life into it. Someone had taken a picture of Sara as she got out of the taxi in front of the nightclub, and that picture had been sitting among the rest of the material relating to the case. Sara had never contacted the police herself, but the detective recognised her from a previous occasion. Lucy looked at me.

'What previous occasion was that, then? How the hell could

he have recognised her in 2012? That was several years after she left the US.'

I read the document again. I couldn't actually understand the notes.

The detective who had moved from Galveston to Houston claimed he recognised Sara from another murder investigation.

Slowly my pulse started to speed up.

'Hang on a moment,' I said.

Lucy tried to take the document from me, but I clung onto the desiccated sheet of paper tightly.

'He recognised her from the investigation into the hotel murder in Galveston,' I said. 'After all, Sara had stayed at that hotel several times. And the victim was murdered in the backyard of the hotel.'

'So? What difference did that make? Did the police talk to everyone who'd ever set foot in that particular hotel?'

I shook my head.

'Of course they didn't. But there was indisputable evidence that Sara really was in Galveston when the first murder was committed.'

'Shit!'

It was as if someone had burst a large balloon in the room, then walked out. A balloon which had belonged to me, and which I was far too fond of.

Furious, I threw the document down.

Evidently that train ticket Bobby had given me was the joke of the century. Unless the police in Galveston had made up the fact that they questioned Sara in connection to the murder there, and I thought we could safely rule that out.

She had been there.

Sara had been at the hotel in Galveston when the first

murder was committed. And not on a train heading towards San Antonio.

'Okay, I think we drop this now,' Lucy said when I didn't say anything for a while. 'Or do you want to try some more angles first? Maybe talk to Sara's sister?'

'No, definitely not. No point.'

I could feel anger throbbing inside me. Bloody hell. I'd discussed the train ticket with both Eivor and Didrik, and they just let me go on. Would it have done any harm to say, nice and quietly, 'Look, just let that go. There's evidence that proves where Sara was when the murder was committed'?

'But they did,' Lucy retorted when I tried to explain why I was so angry, even if I was probably more embarrassed. 'Both of them tried to get you to understand that there was evidence – genuine evidence – but you didn't listen.'

I read through the account of the Texas police again, but it was impossible to reach any other conclusion than the one I'd already come to.

The detective had recognised her.

Because she had featured in another murder investigation, in Galveston.

How he was able to remember and recognise her several years later was beyond me, but on the other hand that wasn't my problem. Maybe he'd taken a liking to her, had a bit of a crush on her.

It didn't matter.

The train ticket was worthless, and I felt like I'd made a right fool of myself. Didrik and Eivor had punished my naivety by letting me pointlessly work my way through an entire police investigation.

'But we've still got the diary,' Lucy said, in an obvious

attempt to console me. 'And Gustavsson's list of things that he wasn't sure about.'

But that sort of talk wasn't going to wash with me. I had to accept facts: there was no great miscarriage of justice to uncover. Sara Tell had confessed to five murders, and she had done so emphatically. What difference did a few unclear details make? Taken as a whole, the evidence against Sara was so overwhelming that any objections to her confession felt pathetic.

'Fucking hell,' I said. 'Okay, that's enough. We'll get rid of these boxes of material tomorrow, and in less than two weeks from now you and I can piss off to Nice.'

My career as the representative of the dead was over before it began. Sara Texas's whispers from beyond the grave had fallen silent.

Or so I thought.

PART III

'Do you believe me now?'

TRANSCRIPT OF INTERVIEW WITH
MARTIN BENNER (MB).

INTERVIEWER: FREDRIK OHLANDER (FO),
freelance journalist.

LOCATION:
Room 714, Grand Hôtel, Stockholm.

FO: Okay. So you had a chance to back out?

MB: Yes, and I didn't take it. Well, I'm not
sure it was that much of a chance, really —
I was already lost. The case died that
afternoon, right in front of my eyes. The
train ticket was a bluff, and everything
else collapsed along with it.

FO: But that was fairly predictable, wasn't it?
I mean, the train ticket was just a false
trail, a diversion.

MB: You might think so. If it weren't for
the fact that a conclusion of that sort
breaks rule number one in this case.
Which is that nothing was what it seemed
at first.

FO: Oh, so the ticket turned out to be of some use to you after all?

MB: We haven't got to that part yet. One thing at a time.

FO: Wasn't it annoying that Lucy thought differently to you all the way through?

MB: I don't really understand the question. That was – is – the basis of our collaboration. That we're so different, and can therefore act as the perfect sparring partner for each other.

FO: For an outsider it's kind of difficult to understand your relationship. It seems to be, or at least have been, fairly turbulent?

MB: Only when we were in a relationship, and when we broke up. Since then the nature of our friendship has been very clear.

FO: You're allowed to be with whoever you want, while she stays at home waiting for you?

MB: If that's your summary of what I've told you so far, then you're a very poor listener. Lucy's my equal. She can sleep with whoever she wants to. If she wants to.

FO: Of course. Sorry, I've said several stupid things in a row now.

MB (Sighs): I'm not sure there's any need for you to apologise. On some level I realise that what Lucy and I had must have looked like a peculiar relationship to other people.

And it didn't get any less strange during
the course of the summer.

FO: What about Nice? It doesn't really feel
like that holiday ever actually happened,
or did it?

MB: No, it didn't.

FO: I see. So you stayed at home instead?

(Silence)

MB: Not exactly. Because one day the office
doorbell rang again, and then everything
started up again.

18

They say persistence is a virtue, but I've always doubted that. The world is full of good characteristics for a person to have, but persistence? No, I don't think so. Most people around me know that about me, and respect it. Not Belle, though. With the straightforwardness of a four-year-old she keeps trying to get my attention, and doesn't realise that she's playing with fire when she asks the same question over and over again, or breaks the same rule time and time again. That was one of the things I had to work hardest at when she first came to live with me. Not to give in to the urge to open the window and chuck her out when she became too much of a nuisance.

After we discovered that the train ticket wasn't the exciting piece of the puzzle that I'd been trying to turn it into, we didn't talk much about Sara Texas. Someone more zealous than me would probably have rowed to shore seeing as he was already sitting in the boat, but that's not my style. Nothing is more important to success than choosing your battles.

In fact, everything returned to normal as early as the

following day. Lucy and I resumed our aimless wait for our holiday, and could barely summon up the enthusiasm to answer the phone. Lucy went on talking about which sun-cream she was going to take to Nice, with me only half-listening. Later I called Veronica, the woman I'd met at the Press Club.

'Would you like to meet up again? I could come round to yours with a bottle of wine and some different cheeses?' I said.

'That would be great. I'd love to see you again!' she said.

Just a little too enthusiastic. What I lack in patience I compensate for by being a mean strategist. After decades as an addict of the sort of kick that only really good sex can give you, I'd developed my dating technique to perfection. It's all about fucking with style. A lot of women can envisage having no-strings sex with a guy – more than once, even – but not if he treats them like shit. That ought to be obvious, really, but a lot of guys make the mistake of thinking that if they show respect for the woman they want, she'll think the relationship is serious and get upset – and become a problem – when she realises that this isn't the case. But that rarely happens to me now. I was extremely confident that it wasn't going to happen with Veronica.

Veronica wanted to see me on Friday, but obviously that was impossible because Belle and I always have our cosy evening together then.

'How about Saturday?'

'Thursday,' I said. 'Tomorrow.'

Partly because I didn't want to have to wait, and partly because she wasn't worth a Saturday evening. Lucy might want to do something then.

I barely had time to put the phone down before the door of

my office was thrown open. Lucy was standing in the door-way dressed in just her bikini.

'If you can't be bothered to care about my sun-cream, maybe you'd care to think about what I should wear?'

How many times can a man get turned on by the same woman? It's questions like that that keep me awake at night.

'Nothing,' I said hoarsely.

'Oh, Martin,' she said.

Yep, everything was back to normal. Lucy and I played silly games and made paper aeroplanes out of old case notes. I carefully put the material from the preliminary investigation into Sara Texas's case back in its boxes and carried them down into the basement. I'd drive the whole lot to the tip another day, but at that moment, with the disappointment still fresh, I just wanted it out of the flat.

I managed to do just one sensible thing during the days that followed, and that was to reassure myself that things were going okay for my client, the one in prison who was worried about his sister Maja. His so-called friend was taken into custody both for the assault and for making unlawful threats, and my client was allowed to go home. Without anyone asking me, or expecting me to be there, I sat in on the meetings my client had with the police about the future protection of his family. The police conducted a thorough investigation of the friend's network, and concluded that the level of threat faced by my client and his sister could only be regarded as low.

'Only as long as he's locked up,' my client said.

The police had a plan for that too. Supplementary measures would be put in place when the piece of shit got out. For my part, I felt relieved. As did my client, eventually.

Everything was nice and peaceful. Sometimes we even got a

hint of sun between the showers. We had so little to do in the office that I let Belle stay and play there two afternoons in a row when she should really have been at preschool.

I'd have been happy for things to go on like that. Nothing but tranquillity, sun and a child playing. But there was one little detail that had completely passed me by: the fact that some people were a hell of a lot more persistent than me. Not only more persistent, but also more stubborn.

Friday afternoon came, and I was sitting in my office writing an email. I'd met up with Veronica the previous evening, and I'd made plans for the weekend. It was, by and large, a very good day. Then the doorbell rang, and I remember thinking: 'What now?' We weren't expecting any deliveries, and Lucy had finished for the day. It crossed my mind that it might be Bobby. I swore to myself, I needed to phone him and tell him I'd abandoned the case.

But when the door opened it wasn't Bobby. It was a woman.

'Are you Martin Benner?' she said.

There isn't much to say about her appearance. She looked ordinary. Not pretty, not ugly, just ordinary. I like that. I like people who don't try too hard.

'Yes,' I said. 'I'm Martin. Can I help you with something?'

She stepped hesitantly into the hallway.

'I think so,' she said. 'At least, this is where Eivor sent me.'

Eivor. I'd almost forgotten about her. I needed to return the box of treasure from her attic. Because I had no use for it any more. Obviously it was kind of her to refer new clients to me now that Gustavsson was no longer active. The thought made me stand slightly taller. Gustavsson was a legend, and now people were coming to me instead. Not a bad development at all.

Unfortunately it turned out that the woman standing in front of me wasn't a new client at all.

She held out her hand and I shook it.

'Jenny Woods,' she said. 'I was friends with Sara Tell in Houston. I contacted Eivor a couple of days ago about a few things I sent over before the trial. I understand that you're taking another look at her case?'

There are hundreds of ways to get rid of someone, but I only know two. The nice one and the nasty one. All the ones in between – like the kind one, the diplomatic one, the violent one – are beyond me.

With Jenny I started off with the nice one.

Without asking her into the office, I gave it to her straight out in the hall. No, I wasn't taking another look at Sara Tell's case. I conceded that Eivor may have had reason to believe that, but on close inspection I had come to the conclusion that it was unnecessary.

Jenny brushed the hair from her face and tucked it behind her ears. She looked nothing like I'd imagined. I'd seen pictures of Sara, of course, and assumed that Jenny would have roughly the same style. Judging by the photographs it looked like Sara pretty much lived in jeans and chequered shirts, and that she preferred trainers to anything else. Apart from when she was in court during the custody proceedings, when she had worn a jacket and skirt.

If Sara was the girl who went around in big shirts and jeans, Jenny was the girl in knee-length office skirts and pearl necklaces. An unusual style for someone who wasn't yet thirty.

'I don't understand,' she said. 'Are you working on Sara's case or not?'

What was so unclear about it?

'Not,' I said, now in a harder tone of voice.

'But you were?'

'No. What I did do was take a look at it. There was no need to do more than that.'

Jenny looked at me.

'Can I ask how you reached that conclusion so quickly? If I understood Eivor correctly, it's only been a week or so since you went to see her, and at that time you'd only just started your work.'

I took a deep breath and did my best not to sound as irritated as I was. Besides, I was reluctantly beginning to feel curious. Had Jenny flown back from the USA after talking to Eivor?

'I checked a number of issues that I thought the police might have missed,' I said. 'When it turned out that those issues didn't affect the case, I decided not to pursue the matter, seeing as I had nothing more to go on.'

Jenny nodded slowly.

'Okay, now I get it,' she said. 'Eivor told me you had the train ticket I sent Bobby, along with the diary. Are you counting that as one of – how did you put it? – the issues that you looked into?'

Her way of expressing herself suggested that she came from a different background to Sara who had a brother by the name of Bobby.

'Yes,' I said. 'And when I realised it was irrelevant I decided not to expend any more energy on it.'

I looked pointedly at the time.

'I'm sorry, but I can't help you. Regardless of what Eivor might have said. So if there wasn't anything else, I'm going to have to ask you to leave.'

Jenny laughed.

'It's not me you need to help. It's Sara.'

Not another one. I almost joined in with her laughter.

'Listen,' I said. 'It's like this: Sara's dead. It was stupid of me to start poking about in this mess, and even more stupid that I didn't say as much the first time I met Bobby. If you want to grant Sara peace, you should turn to a priest instead. Because I'm afraid I can't help you.'

Jenny became serious.

'Just tell me how you came to the conclusion that the train ticket had no value as evidence.'

I was more than happy to do that. In a few short sentences I explained what Lucy and I had figured out.

'Sara was staying in the hotel in Galveston the night the first victim died. Which makes it impossible for her to have been on a train from Houston to San Antonio at the same time,' I summarised.

'And you took the claim that Sara was staying in that hotel on that particular night from the detective's account of how he recognised her during the investigation into the Houston murder?'

'Exactly.'

'But you probably haven't seen any transcript of an interview in Galveston?'

I grew uncertain. No, I couldn't say that I had.

Jenny interpreted my silence to mean that I wasn't contradicting her.

'You haven't seen a transcript of an interview in Galveston because there isn't one,' she said.

I folded my arms in front of my chest.

'So how did the detective recognise her?'

'Because he tried to pick her up in a bar in Galveston when she was there with her au pair family on another occasion. And Sara gave him the brush-off. But he could hardly say that to his colleagues, could he?'

How many times in our lives are there moments when we make genuinely fateful decisions? Not many. And we rarely realise just how important those moments are until much later.

'I'm not lying,' Jenny said. 'If you don't mind, I'd be happy to prove it.'

I stood there in silence, just looking at Jenny.

She wasn't like Bobby. She wasn't the sort of person who screamed trouble. Which made her more credible. But all the same – I'd dropped the case. Was I about to pick it up again?

I thought about the boxes containing the material covering the investigation. They hadn't got as far as the tip yet. The distance to the starting line wouldn't be far at all if I wanted to give my private investigation another go.

I don't know if I was driven by curiosity or boredom.

But eventually I said: 'I'd be happy to hear what you have to say. Shall we go out and get a coffee?'

19

There's a café at Sankt Eriksplan called Xoko. It was Lucy who first took me. Now I was there with Jenny Woods who had been friends with Sara in Houston. I was feeling pretty sceptical as we sat down at one of the window tables. The café appeared to have been invaded by women with pushchairs. I hate this whole baby culture that's developed in Sweden. I certainly never took part in it. I sent Belle to preschool when she was ten months old and – as far as I can tell – it hasn't done her any harm. Why would it? She got everything she needed, and more besides.

I ordered two coffees which were brought to our table.

'I'll give you half an hour, not a second more,' I told Jenny.

'Ten minutes will do,' Jenny said.

She was calm and composed. I saw her looking at the pushchairs but couldn't read what she was thinking.

'Do you have children?' I said.

I had a vague memory that Eivor had said she did, but it didn't hurt to try to be nice.

'Are we really going to waste time talking about me when you're in such a hurry?' Jenny said drily.

I retreated instantly. Obviously I didn't give a damn whether or not she had a family.

'You're right, that was silly of me. So, tell me,' I said.

'Where do you want me to start?'

'Pick up where we were when we left the office.'

'You just want to talk about the train ticket?'

'If you've got anything else to say, go ahead. But yes, the train ticket is of particular interest.'

Jenny didn't touch her coffee. She just sat there staring down into the cup as if she didn't understand what was in it.

Then she turned her attention to me.

'Sara and I got to know each other in Houston in January 2007. We'd both just started work as au pairs with families living in the same neighbourhood in the Heights. That's a residential area about seven kilometres from downtown Houston. I don't really know what we were expecting. Houston's a huge but pretty soulless city.'

'I know it,' I said neutrally.

'You've been there?'

I'd lived there. In an earlier life. But I didn't tell her that.

'A few years ago,' I said.

'Then you know what it's like,' she said. 'The city is kept afloat by oil, and the people who live there are either surfing on it or drowning in it. Neither Sara nor I were particularly happy to start with. But then we found each other and started spending time together. We were very different, but we still managed to have a surprisingly good time together. I could see that Sara was damaged, that she'd had a hard time growing up. Life in Houston seemed to suit her. She could be anonymous there. She liked that.'

I was making an effort not to show how restless I was.

The train ticket, I thought. Tell me about the damn train ticket!

'Her au pair family was better than mine. They travelled quite a lot and she always got to go with them. Plenty of people in Houston like to get out of the city at weekends and during holidays. Galveston's about an hour's drive south, and Sara's family went there whenever they could. They always stayed at the same hotel. The Carlton. It's right on the seafront. Sara loved being there. She was obsessed with the sea, did you know that?'

I shook my head. No, I hadn't known.

Jenny's face broke into a smile and I found myself thinking about something my mum used to say to me and my sister when we were growing up. That people are always more attractive when they look happy. It was true. Especially with someone like Jenny who looked pretty plain otherwise. But not when she smiled.

'The au pair family didn't need Sara much when they were travelling,' she went on. 'She had a room to herself and could do her own thing. If I was free I'd take the car and drive down to hang out with her. I used to stay in her room without telling anyone. In the evenings and at night we used to go out clubbing or drinking. That was how she met Larry.'

Larry? I perked up instantly and raised my eyebrow questioningly.

'Larry was the policeman who later moved to Houston and got it into his head that Sara was a double murderer.'

'Ah.'

'He was out with some friends and came over and hit on Sara. Several times. It was late summer, before the first murder took place in Galveston. Three weeks before the killing Sara was there with her family to look after the children while the parents went to a wedding. The next day she went out to get coffee. And he came up to her again, this time in uniform.'

'So he hit on her while he was on duty?'

'Yep. Probably wanted to impress his partner, something like that. Sara was very attractive, after all.'

From what I'd seen in pictures of her, I could only agree.

'So he was persistent, this Larry?'

'God, yes. But Sara kept saying no. That time with the coffee she said no rather more clearly. She threw it right in his face.'

I started to laugh.

'Seriously? She threw coffee in the face of a uniformed police officer?'

'As you can probably imagine, he got very upset. But after that she didn't have any more trouble from him. Not until last year, when he got a new job in Houston and tried to breathe new life into the case of the taxi driver's murder.'

I became serious. We'd reached a more complicated part of her story, and it was important that I follow her reasoning.

'If I understand you right,' I said, 'then this detective, Larry, simply made up the claim that he had interviewed Sara in Galveston about the first murder?'

'Exactly,' Jenny said. 'I suppose he was just sitting there in Houston, new at his job, keen to look good. Then suddenly up pops Sara, who had left such a memorable impression, in the middle of a murder investigation. He recognised her in that picture someone took and gave to the police later. The one of her getting out the taxi and swearing at the driver who was later found dead.'

'I've seen it,' I said. 'It was published in the papers, too, wasn't it?'

'Of course,' Jenny said. 'I remember seeing it because there was so much coverage of the taxi driver's murder. The police wanted to contact the woman in the picture, but Sara never got in touch. She'd had bad experiences with the police when she was younger.'

'So the two of you talked about it? You knew it was her in the picture?'

Jenny shook her head.

'Not until afterwards. I didn't recognise her when the picture was published in the papers. You know what pictures like that look like, taken in the dark while people are moving. A bit fuzzy, not very focused. It wasn't until the autumn, when Sara called me after the first police interview, that I took a closer look and saw it was her.'

Up till then I hadn't had terribly high expectations of my conversation with Jenny. But now I straightened up, pushed my empty coffee cup away and listened attentively.

Jenny lowered her voice, as if she were afraid that one of all those pushchair-wielding mothers was listening.

'To give Larry the policeman the benefit of the doubt, his thinking wasn't entirely unreasonable,' she said. 'He recognised Sara in the photograph, and realised that she hadn't got in touch with the police. And he knew she usually stayed in the hotel in Galveston where another murder had been committed. So he went to his boss in Houston and said he recognised Sara from an exploratory interview in Galveston, seeing as she had been staying in the hotel the night the murder happened. But that was just something he made up because he was too embarrassed to admit where he really knew her from. And no one seems to have bothered to check it. Because he said he was the one who had questioned her, presumably they didn't feel any need to dig out a transcript of the interview. Anyway, according to Larry she hadn't said anything of interest to the police.'

But that wasn't enough for me.

'You're saying he invented an occasion when they had met, which just happened to make her a double murderer?' I said. 'That sounds crazy. And he was taking a hell of risk. If the case had gone to trial in the US, or even if charges had been pressed, he'd have had to come up with documentary evidence to back up his story, even if Sara had confessed. Same thing if the case had actually gone to trial in Sweden.'

I stopped myself. I couldn't remember seeing any mention of this in the preliminary investigation. Had that line of inquiry been dropped once they'd found the murder weapon, the knife, in Sara's attic?

'If I've got this right,' Jenny said, 'Larry said he'd conducted such a large number of interviews the night the woman died in Galveston. And, to his own embarrassment, he hadn't documented them all. But he was able to produce a list of people who had been staying in the hotel that night, and Sara's name was on it. It doesn't seem to have been a very difficult thing to manipulate.'

'How do you know all this?'

'Let's just say I have my contacts.'

'In the police?'

'Yes.'

I was having trouble buying what she was telling me. It

was way too much of a coincidence. Would a Houston police officer really link Sara to a crime scene just for the hell of it, so he could claim to recognise her and paint her in an unfavourable light? That would be a pretty screwed-up strategy.

'What about Sara's au pair family?' I said. 'Were they on that list too?'

'No, he couldn't stretch his lie that far, and that was part of the problem for Sara,' Jenny said. 'Because Sara had the weekend off when the Galveston murder took place, and went to San Antonio to meet up with a guy she'd just started seeing. But she didn't want to tell anyone that, so she lied. If anyone had asked the au pair family where Sara was that weekend, they'd have said Galveston, because that's where Sara said she was going, but that she was going to stay at a different hotel, seeing as the Carlton was way too expensive when she was travelling on her own.'

'Fuck,' I said.

'You see how it all fits together?' Jenny said. 'The train ticket you've got is genuine. It really was Sara's, and I could have testified to that in court, if I'd been given the chance. Because I was with her in San Antonio. That's why I had the tickets. I kept them afterwards, as a souvenir. It was on that trip that I met my husband. Sara wasn't as careful about holding on to things as me, and she could be a bit careless. That's why I had her ticket while we were there – so she wouldn't lose it – and that's why she didn't want it afterwards.'

She fell silent.

'Do you believe me now?' she said.

'Yes,' I said.

I needed to absorb what I'd heard. Jenny excused herself and went to the bathroom. I sat at the table thinking. So Sara had an alibi for at least one of the murders. What that said about the police officer who had identified her was something I would have to think about later. The first time she was taken in for questioning, the police were interested in just the two American murders. It was only later that the investigation expanded to encompass the three Swedish murders. Lucy and I had both reacted to the fact that Sara had gone from trying to defend herself against the accusations during that first interview, to confessing to not just two but five murders during the second one.

Jenny came back.

'You said she called you,' I said.

'After the first interview she called me and asked for help. She said she wanted both the train ticket and an old diary she'd left in Houston because it contained a load of miserable stuff she didn't want to drag back home to Sweden with her. She gave it to me at the airport when she left. To be honest, she asked me to burn it, but I tucked it away in a box. I suppose I thought there might come a time when she'd regret it, and of course that's what happened.'

'And she knew that? That you'd kept it?'

'She guessed as much. God, I was so surprised when she called. We hadn't been in touch for years. She was hysterical, desperate. Then I called her about a week later, because the ticket and diary had been returned to me. I'd been so wound up when I sent them that I put the wrong postage on them. After that I decided not to send anything by post, and had them couriered over instead. But all of a sudden Sara no longer wanted either the ticket or the diary. She said things were all sorted out and that I could throw them away. Obviously, I didn't. Then I read in the online papers that she'd confessed to a load of murders, and couldn't help wondering if she'd gone mad. I mean, I knew she hadn't killed anyone in Galveston. I went to the police, but they weren't interested. So in the end I had the parcel sent over to Sara's brother Bobby. I'd never met him, but he seemed very engaged in Sara's problems. But that evidently didn't do a blind bit of good.'

'No, evidently not,' I said.

My mind was racing at the speed of light. There were so many things I wanted to talk to Jenny about. About Sara's ex, and her dad. About the rumours of prostitution.

'Sara's ex and her dad seem to have caused a lot of trouble for Sara, even in the US,' I said, as a start.

Jenny frowned.

'I know her ex showed up in Houston, she talked about it. That was actually something we had in common. I had an ex who decided to go to the States after I'd moved there.'

'Er . . .' I began.

But Jenny waved her hand dismissively.

'Don't forget, the USA is one of the biggest tourist destinations in the world. Loads of young people go there. I don't know about Sara, but now that I've got a bit of distance to that first year in Texas, I think I might have blown the problem of my ex out of proportion. At the time – when I was in the middle of it all – it felt exhausting and oppressive. But now, who knows what he was thinking, why he acted the way he did? He never threatened me, just wanted to see me. But I thought even that was too much.'

I have to confess that I wasn't really that interested in Jenny's old boyfriends. I was completely focused on Sara Tell and her messy past. So I hurried the conversation on. Stupid of me, but I didn't know that at the time.

'What did you make of Sara's father?'

She looked at me blankly.

'Nothing. What do you mean?'

'I read it in the diary,' I said. 'That he showed up in Houston as well, causing trouble.'

Jenny shook her head slowly.

'No, I think you must have misunderstood that,' she said. 'Sara's dad was never in the US.'

It was my turn to look surprised.

'But he's mentioned several times,' I said. 'Lucifer.'

I swear I saw Jenny stiffen. And go pale.

'Lucifer?' she said, fumbling with her coffee cup. 'I don't recognise the name. Are you sure it refers to her dad?'

I wasn't. But I was sure that Jenny was lying. She knew who Lucifer was. And was refusing to say.

My mobile rang and I took it out of my pocket to reject the call. It was Belle's preschool.

Damn. You don't reject calls like that.

A breathless preschool teacher started to talk way too fast at the other end.

Belle had fallen over.

Hit her head.

'It's not good, Martin. We've called an ambulance, it'll be here in a few minutes. Can you meet us at the Astrid Lindgren Children's Hospital?'

I admit that there are times I choose to see Belle as a lodger, as someone who isn't going to be in my life forever. But there are other, far longer times when I know that she's mine, that I'm the only parent she knows and has left. This was one of those times. There's nothing – *nothing* – that terrifies me as much as the thought that Belle is like everyone else. Mortal.

If anything were to happen to her, I'd be finished. Because the moment I stood in Social Services and said I wanted her, I entered into an indissoluble contract with my dead sister.

Belle is my responsibility. Every day, and every night. Even when we aren't together.

'I'll be there in ten minutes,' I said, my heart pounding so hard I thought it was going to burst.

I put the phone in my pocket and stood up.

'I've got to go,' I told Jenny. 'But I'll call you. How long are you in Stockholm?'

'I'm flying back to Houston on Sunday. There are other things we ought to discuss. Sara didn't commit those murders. And she didn't kill herself, or her son. At least not of her own accord. I'm convinced of that.'

'We can talk about that later,' I said. 'I've got to run.'

'One last thing: are you sure it was Bobby who came to your office asking for help on Sara's behalf?'

'Yes.'

'Strange,' Jenny said. 'Very strange. But we can talk about that next time.'

We exchanged phone numbers.

'I'll be in touch before Sunday,' I said.

I turned away and walked out, leaving Jenny at the table.

That was the last time I saw her.

20

If it weren't for the constantly overhanging threat of death, we wouldn't know what it means to be alive. When I arrived in A&E at the Astrid Lindgren Children's Hospital it was as if the rest of the world had ceased to exist. I couldn't see anything apart from Belle. She was lying on a trolley. Her face was ashen and her hands were clenched as if she were cramping. Almost in passing I registered the spatter of blood reaching up the wall, halfway to the ceiling.

'We had a bit of trouble getting her to lie still,' one of the nurses said as she saw me glance at the blood. 'But she's calm now.'

'I see,' I said, even though I didn't see at all.

Belle's eyes were as empty as my grandfather's were when he died, before they had to close them. What the hell had they given her?

I leaned over so that my face was level with hers.

Gently I put my hand on the top of her head.

'I'm here now,' I whispered. 'Everything's going to be okay. You'll soon be as good as new.'

Only then did she react and start to cry. To my immense surprise, so did I.

'It looks worse than it is,' a doctor told me. 'The cut on her forehead is long, but not very deep. Her arm is broken in two places – you can see here – and she's got concussion. But we'll take care of all that for you.'

I looked at Belle's little arm. It was buckled, as if someone had driven over it in a car.

'She fell from the climbing frame,' a voice said behind me. 'It was an accident.'

I turned my head and only then did I catch sight of one of Belle's preschool teachers. For a brief moment I thought about going over and punching the idiot woman.

There's no such thing as accidents, I wanted to shout. People allow them to happen. Belle hasn't been hurt one single fucking time while I've been looking after her.

But for some reason I can't explain, you never shout when you really think you're going to. You choose to focus on something else instead. In this instance my primary task was to keep Belle calm. But I'm fairly sure the woman felt my derision when I turned away from her.

'You can go now,' I said. 'We don't need you any more.'

'Accidents happen so easily,' the doctor said.

'I'm terribly sorry,' the teacher said.

From the corner of my eye I saw her leave the room. One of the nurses followed her.

I stayed with Belle. Her wounds were treated by different doctors and by the time evening fell she was lying in a hospital bed with a bandage over her forehead and her arm in plaster. If it hadn't been for the concussion we could have gone home, but I was actually relieved and grateful that we were able to stay. In just a few hours the hospital had become a source of support that I didn't know how to manage without.

At seven o'clock that evening I finally called Lucy and asked her to come to the hospital to pick up the key to my flat, then go and pack an overnight bag for me.

Lucy arrived less than half an hour later, absolutely furious.

'Why the hell didn't you call me earlier?' she said in a voice shaking with emotion.

She went over to Belle, who was asleep, and sat down on the edge of the bed.

I was so tired that I couldn't get up from the visitor's chair.

'We've had our hands full,' I said quietly.

Then we sat like that for a long time. Lucy with Belle, and me beside them. If anyone had come into the room, they'd have thought we belonged together.

That we were a proper family.

Some of my acquaintances claim to be able to sleep anywhere, and under any circumstances. I've always assumed they were lying. I can sleep if I'm lying in a silent, cool room in a comfortable bed. None of these requirements was met by Belle's room at the hospital.

I lay there tossing and turning between stiff sheets, feeling the sweat on my back stick my t-shirt to my skin. I usually sleep naked but assumed that would be too much for the hospital staff. At half past eleven I got up and opened the window, but the night nurse came in and closed it, saying it wasn't good for the ventilation system.

As if there actually was one.

Belle woke up twice, upset. Both times I went and lay down

beside her. We were lucky enough to have a separate room. Thank God.

There were no curtains in the window and I lay awake looking at the dark blue sky that refused to turn black when night came. Just after three o'clock the sun started to rise again. So I did the same. Belle was fast asleep in her bed. I felt so worked up that I could barely manage to breathe properly.

Out.

I needed to get out. Just for a little while.

With an agility that actually surprised me, I crept out into the silent hospital corridor. There was no one in sight. Good. I was only going to stretch my legs.

I carried on through the glass doors and down the stairs to the ground floor. It was like I couldn't stop myself, I just had to breathe some fresh air.

Once I was outside I never wanted to go back in again. I sat down quietly on a bench beside the entrance. I remember not thinking about anything special; I just sat there enjoying the cool night air. Until the door slid open behind me and a security guard made his presence known.

'Can I help you? This entrance is closed now, I'll have to ask you to use the door in A&E.'

I stood up quickly.

'My daughter's in here,' I said. 'I just wanted to stretch my legs.'

The guard looked at me.

'Next time it would be a good idea to tell the staff first. Otherwise you won't get back in again.'

I hurried back up to Belle. There weren't going to be any further nocturnal outings. Belle was going to be discharged later that morning, and it would be a very long time before we set foot in a hospital again.

When I lay down again I fell asleep instantly, only to be woken by a nurse opening the door to our room at six o'clock. In hospital patients are expected to get better even if they aren't allowed more than a few hours' sleep per night.

At ten o'clock we were discharged.

Belle barely said a word all day. She followed me like a little dog, refusing to be on her own. When she finally did start to talk, it was only about things that had happened in the hospital. Lucy came over and I managed to get some time to myself, which I used for nothing better than going to the toilet.

It was afternoon before I realised that I should call Jenny. There was no answer, so I left a message. I tried again an hour later.

'Who are you calling?' Lucy asked.

'No one,' I said, and went out into the kitchen to prepare an early dinner.

At eight o'clock, after Belle had fallen asleep, I called Jenny again. Her phone was switched off this time, and I reached her voicemail straight away.

I couldn't help feeling annoyed. Didn't she realise that I'd had to leave Xoko because there'd been an accident? If I remembered rightly, she'd said she was going back to the US on Sunday. I had no idea if that was morning or evening, but either way Sunday was no more than a few hours away.

Lucy came into the kitchen.

'Is everything okay?'

'Sure.'

'Who do you keep trying to get hold of?'

I hesitated. She'd think I was mad if I told her the truth – that

Sara Texas's case had aroused my curiosity again, this time because her friend had turned up at our office.

Bobby and Jenny.

Sara didn't appear to have any other allies. Wearily I squeezed the phone in my hand.

'Is it Bobby?' Lucy said, with fresh sharpness in her voice. She was close, but I didn't have to admit that.

'No.'

Lucy crept up behind me and put her long, thin arms round my waist. I stroked her pale skin and wondered seriously what I would have done if I hadn't had her in my life.

'You're so fucking mean, Martin,' Lucy had said the night we broke up. 'Not once can you bring yourself to tell me you need me. Or that you even like me.'

There seems to be a bit of an inner-city trend going on in Stockholm for getting yourself a therapist. I did it too, back then. I wanted to know if there was something wrong with me.

'No,' the therapist said. 'You're just a person who doesn't like being demonstrative about closeness. Lots of people are like that. Whether or not it's a problem is up to you to decide.'

Thanks a lot. I never went back, and I haven't been in a relationship since then. Nothing serious, anyway. But sure, there were days when I wondered if Lucy and I hadn't got lost in the no-man's-land that stretches out to the east of 'I don't want to be your girlfriend any more'.

On that particular evening everything felt so fragile that I didn't feel up to a discussion about Sara Texas. I knew exactly where I stood. I was back in the match, with renewed hunger. The boxes containing the preliminary investigation were as enticing as a mirage in the desert, and there was nothing I wanted more than to throw myself at them. But they'd have to wait. Other urges took the upper hand.

It would be stupid to claim that it was any sort of sacrifice, having sex with Lucy. No chance. But it was impractical. Afterwards I realised that I could hardly ask her to go home. So I lay awake in the darkness, waiting for her to fall asleep. Then I got out of bed and put on the clothes I'd tossed on the floor.

It didn't matter that it was late and that I was tired after my adventure at the hospital with Belle. I couldn't wait, I was drawn to those cardboard boxes in the basement as if they possessed some magical enchantment. My mobile was on the desk in the library. No missed calls. I don't know if it was because I was tired or just an attack of thoughtlessness, but I tried calling Jenny again. Her phone was still switched off and I hung up. It would be unfortunate if I failed to get hold of her. I had a lot of questions I wanted to get answers to. And I was curious to know what had brought her back to Stockholm. Because she would hardly have travelled all the way from Houston just to talk to me, surely?

It didn't take me long to fetch the boxes from the basement. With my eyes stinging with tiredness I started to read document after document. Belle woke up just after midnight, anxious. I gave her a paracetamol because she said her arm was hurting, then tried to help her find a comfortable position where the plaster-cast wasn't in the way. I didn't lie down beside her because I knew I'd never get up again.

I went back to the study once she'd settled down. I don't know what time it was when I fell asleep. But that night I slept at my desk. And that was where Lucy found me the next morning when the doorbell rang at eight o'clock and she had to get up and answer it because I didn't hear it ringing.

'Martin,' she said, shaking me. 'You need to wake up. The police are here. They want to talk to you. They say it's important.'

21

Lucy and I don't always agree on what counts as important. She thinks that sun-cream is important, for instance. I don't. But this time we were in full agreement. Because the police not only wanted to talk to me, they also wanted me to go to the station with them.

My first impulse was to laugh.

'Sorry, but shouldn't you be chasing real crooks?'

My joke fell flat when one of them replied, 'My colleague and I are of the opinion that someone who might be involved in a murder is a real crook. So if you wouldn't mind getting dressed instead of standing here arguing?'

'Murder?'

The echo came from Lucy.

'What's this about?' I said, having lost any urge to play games.

I felt like I did the time I was sitting in front of a doctor who said he thought I might have HIV, which it turned out I didn't. HIV isn't the sort of thing you want. Nor is being told that you're suspected of murder.

'Come with us and you'll find out.'

So I went with them, whilst making it very clear that I wasn't going to say a word until my lawyer was present.

'I'll come with you,' Lucy said, heading towards the bedroom.

'Great idea,' I said. 'We can just leave Belle here on her own.'

Lucy stopped.

'I'll call your mother,' she said. 'I'll come to the station as soon as she gets here.'

You always think there are some experiences you'll be spared. Or those at the very least which are highly unlikely ever to happen. But this was happening to me. The police had come to my home to get me so that they could question me about a murder I hadn't committed. I got dressed and then glanced into Belle's room. She was sleeping on her back with her plastered arm across her stomach.

For a moment I was seized by an inexplicable panic. What would happen to Belle if I didn't come back? After all, stranger things had happened than people being convicted of crimes they didn't commit. Sara Tell had succeeded in getting herself charged with no fewer than five murders she hadn't committed.

Lucy's warm hand on my shoulder prompted me to let go of the door-frame and go with the police.

'It's just a misunderstanding,' she said. 'Go with them and get it sorted out. We'll have breakfast when you get back.'

I didn't say a word as we were driving to the police station.

When we were almost there my mobile rang.

It was Didrik.

'Hi, Martin, I'm sorry to call so early. Where are you?'

If it was a joke, it wasn't funny.

'I'm sitting in a car having a little ride with two of your colleagues. Nice lads, they were very keen to give me a lift to Police Headquarters.'

I heard Didrik groan down the phone.

'Oh, for God's sake,' he said. 'I'm really sorry about this. One of my colleagues took the decision, and I don't agree with it. Listen, I'm sure we can sort this out in no time. It's just that . . .' – he lowered his voice – 'your name has cropped up in a new murder investigation and we're curious to find out why. Even if I suspect I have a pretty good idea already.'

I don't even want to think about how many rules Didrik was breaking when he made that call. But I have to admit that I was and still am very grateful that he did. Because after that I was able to relax slightly and contemplate what was happening to me more generally. Perhaps it might even be beneficial to be suspected of involvement in a crime, to see the process from the other side, so to speak.

If only it had happened some other day.

It annoyed me immensely that they had decided to invade my home on a morning when I really needed to be with Belle. On the other hand, I presumed that taking things like that into account was out of the question in a murder investigation. And once I had got that far with my thoughts, it occurred to me that I still didn't know who had died.

'Jenny Woods,' Didrik said. 'Do you know anyone of that name?'

As soon as he said her name I felt the last of my anxiety dissipate. Dissipate and be replaced by plenty of other feelings, foremost among them surprise.

So it was Sara's friend Jenny who had died. On the night between Friday and Saturday, when I was in hospital with Belle, I was told.

Excellent timing, seeing as I had a verifiable alibi for my whereabouts at the time of the murder. But simultaneously bad. Partly because I had liked her when we met, and partly because her death meant – to be horribly blunt – that I was going to be left with a whole load of unanswered questions.

I explained all that I could to Didrik and the other officer who was sitting in on the interview or whatever it was. It didn't take long.

Jenny had turned up at my office, just as Bobby had done a week or so before.

She had also come about the same case.

She had mentioned speaking to Eivor.

We went out for coffee and she confirmed what I had suspected all along – that Sara Tell was innocent of at least one of the murders in Texas.

'Then I received a call from Belle's preschool saying that she'd been hurt,' I concluded. 'So I left at once and we ended up staying in hospital overnight. We were at home all day yesterday. All night too, for that matter.'

Didrik's expression didn't change until I said that Belle had been in hospital. Then his police mask slipped for a moment.

'How is she now?' he asked.

'Hard to know when I'm sitting here,' I said.

A silence followed.

'Now it's your turn to talk,' I said. 'What happened?'

Didrik rubbed his forehead. He had clearly also been woken too early, even if I suspected that he hadn't spent the night sleeping at his desk, unlike me.

'Well, Jenny Woods died shortly after 1:30, two blocks from her hotel. She was killed in a hit and run on a pedestrian crossing. There are witnesses who say that the car – a Porsche 911, by the way, like yours – was driving fast, and sped up when she stepped into the street. She didn't stand a chance. After she was hit the car carried on without stopping.'

I didn't know in what order to react to what I had just heard.

'You say she died at half past one,' I said. 'It wasn't completely dark, but it wasn't exactly light either. There's no reason to think that whoever was driving mistook her for someone else?'

Didrik threw his hands out.

'Who knows?' he said.

'I mean, Jenny Woods left Sweden in 2007. Who knew she was in Stockholm?'

'You mean apart from you?' Didrik's colleague snapped.

He was clearly convinced that I was the murderer.

Didrik flashed him a stern glance.

'I can't answer that right now,' he said. 'We'll have to see what the investigation throws up.'

He slid down his chair so that he was half-lying behind his desk. We were sitting in his office rather than one of the interview rooms. We wouldn't have been doing that if their suspicions against me had been anything but shaky.

'Where's your car at the moment?' he said.

'Locked away in the garage,' I said. 'At least I hope it is. I took a taxi to and from the hospital.'

'We'll have to check that,' Didrik said.

The thought that my car might have been stolen was enough to make me feel stressed. Not so much because I loved my car, but because it was a deeply unsettling thought that someone had gone to the effort of making it look like I drove around at night running people down.

'Was the car the reason I was brought in for this delightful morning meeting?'

Didrik laughed.

'Come off it, cowboy,' he said. 'Of course it wasn't.'

'My mobile,' I said.

'Exactly. You did call her a number of times.'

'After she'd died,' I pointed out.

Didrik got to his feet.

'Thanks for coming,' he said, making it sound like I'd come voluntarily. He held out his hand. 'Well, we can't spare you any more time right now. We've got a murder investigation to be getting on with.'

I stood up as well.

'You've got several murder investigations waiting for you,' I said, without trying to hide the irritation in my voice.

Didrik stiffened.

'What do you mean?'

'I mean that it's laughable that you haven't said a word about the fact that I just told you Sara had an alibi for the murder in Galveston. She didn't commit a single one of those five murders. When are you going to realise that and do your duty, and actually find the real killer?'

Didrik's hand was dry and warm when I shook it.

'Be careful what conclusions you come to,' he said. 'It's easy to come along six months behind everyone else and tell them they're wrong.'

'It's my sworn duty to point out that you're wrong,' I said. 'And if you're going to carry on working with blinkers on, you won't find the person who killed Jenny Woods either.'

Didrik's face turned red with suppressed rage.

'Well, I think you should go home now and check that your car's in the garage,' he said.

Without further conversation I left Didrik's office and marched out of the police station. I ran straight into Lucy.

'Are you finished already?' she said. 'What's going on?'

'Let's get in the car and I'll tell you on the way home,' I said. 'Or did you take a taxi?'

'No, I used the Porsche. Hope you don't mind.'

Relief can take so many forms.

'Definitely not,' I said, taking my mobile out and calling Didrik.

He answered immediately.

'Okay, you obstinate sod, come down and take a look at the Porsche straight away. Lucy's driven it here.'

'God, it'll be good to get away to Nice,' Lucy said as we waited on the pavement.

I looked from Lucy to the Porsche.

'We're not going to Nice,' I said. 'At least, I'm not.'

Lucy swallowed.

'You'd rather stay at home with Belle?'

'No,' I said.

A far too chilly summer breeze blew past, making Lucy's hair dance.

'So where do you want to go, then?' she said.

I was just about to reply when I noticed it. The dent in the car. On the bonnet.

Slowly I walked over to the car. If you imagined that the dent had been caused by someone being run down, it could only be described as modest.

'Oh shit,' Lucy said. 'Martin, I swear, I didn't do that. It must have been there when I got the car out to come here.'

'You can be quite sure it was,' I said, without taking my eyes off the dent.

The door of the police station opened and Didrik and one of his gorillas came out.

'Ready and waiting, I see,' Didrik said in a voice dripping with sarcasm.

He fell silent when he saw the bonnet of the Porsche.

Without a word I gave him the car-keys.

'Come on,' I said to Lucy. 'We'll have to get a taxi home.'

We walked away, hand in hand. The dent was the police's problem. I had an alibi for the time of the murder, and that was all that mattered.

'Are you going to explain what's going on?' she said when we were a short distance away.

I was, absolutely. The problem was that at that moment I didn't actually know what sort of game I had been dragged into. And – most importantly of all – I hadn't realised that I wasn't one of the players.

I was just one of many pieces on the board.

22

'You need to get yourself out of this, Martin. Can't you see that?'

Lucy's eyes flashed with anxiety.

We were sitting in the bar of the Hotel Amaranten drinking coffee. I hate the Amaranten. The bedrooms are the size of shoeboxes and the lobby reeks of cigarette smoke. But it was close to Police Headquarters and we needed coffee.

I was livid. And worried. I can't pretend otherwise. Someone was trying to frame me for premeditated murder. It was impossible to take it in, on any level.

Lucy grabbed my arm hard.

'It's sheer luck that you happen to have such a good alibi, Martin,' she said. 'It's rotten for Belle, but bloody lucky for you. Take this as a warning. Pack up and get out while you can.'

'Pack up and get out? What exactly are you suggesting? That I flee the country? Ask Mafia-Boris for a new passport and take off for Costa Rica?'

Lucy sighed and let go of me.

'I didn't mean literally,' she said quietly. 'But that bit about calling Boris . . . maybe that isn't such a bad idea.'

I could see how scared she was. So scared that she was advising me to get in touch with a mafia boss who owed me. As for me, I just felt pretty numb after everything that had happened in the past twenty-four hours: Belle's accident and my encounter with Jenny and now this.

Jenny's murder confirmed what I'd always suspected. That there was another murderer on the loose, free as a bird. As long as detectives like Didrik insisted that Sara Texas had committed all those murders, the real perpetrator could feel perfectly safe.

The fact that Jenny had to be got rid of was, in a bizarre way, logical.

What about me? What did I have to do with all this?

It also felt odd that I would be got rid of by being sent to prison for a crime I hadn't committed. That sort of thing was hardly going to make me shut up. The logical option would have been to murder me as well.

I slid restlessly down from my barstool.

'Baby, I need to get home and shower, and think through all this,' I said. 'Can we talk later?'

Lucy looked at me as if I'd gone mad.

'Sorry? You're just going to go now?'

'What's the alternative? Sit here and hang out until the sun goes down?'

She put her coffee cup down hard.

'You're a fucking useless team player, Martin. We're a team, you and me. This isn't just about you. It involves me too. And Belle.'

I had plenty of objections.

Sara Texas's case was mine, not Lucy's.

Belle was my daughter, not hers.

I was the one who was the subject of a conspiracy, not her.

But I didn't manage to get a single word out. I was far too tired to argue. Without saying a thing I reached out one arm and drew Lucy to me. I felt her breath against my chest and held her even tighter.

'I didn't know we were a team in this particular case,' I said with my face in her hair. 'Sorry.'

'You need to be careful,' she whispered. 'Promise you will be.'

I promised. With the same degree of conviction as when I promised my mother that I wouldn't jump off the balcony with an umbrella (I did, of course, and broke my leg), and in the same firm voice as I once promised Lucy I wouldn't lie to her (which I never actually did – I answered honestly the very first time she asked me if I was sleeping with other women).

'There's something going on,' I said. 'I can't just let it go. If I do, I'll be the one who gets hit next time I try to cross the road.'

It wasn't before the words left my mouth that I realised that they could very well be true. The question was: what was the best way of securing my long-term survival? Was it by uncovering the tangle of events that had led to Sara's ludicrous confession? Or was it by doing as Lucy said – to regard the attempt to frame me as a warning and back away from the whole mess?

Someone was evidently watching me, from an uncomfortably close range. Someone who thought I had already found out too much. But what information did I have that could be regarded as sensitive? None. Not until I met Jenny Woods, anyway. My pulse sped up. There was no longer any doubt in my mind that what she had told me had been correct.

My mind was still racing.

'I need to get out of here,' I said.

Lucy picked up her handbag and left with me. The cool morning air blended with exhaust fumes. Summer Stockholm in its essence.

We walked down Kungsholmsgatan towards the city centre. As we passed Oscar's Theatre I hailed a taxi.

'Lucy, I really am extremely grateful for all your help, yesterday and today,' I began.

She shut me up by putting her index finger to my lips.

'Don't you dare try to get rid of me,' she said. 'I'm coming home with you.'

She opened one of the back doors and got in.

'Come on, now,' she told me.

With a sigh I did as she said. I evidently wasn't going to get shot of her.

The taxi rolled off towards Östermalm. I stared hard through the windscreen. Of all the questions churning in my head, two felt like they needed answers more urgently than the others: who had known Jenny was in Stockholm and that she was planning to see me? And how did that person know what she had to tell me?

In books and films, lawyers solve puzzles. They uncover great conspiracies and they fight day and night for their clients. In real life none of that is true. The jigsaw has already been solved, and we're rarely missing any important pieces. Unfortunately. It would be much more exciting if that weren't the case, but it is.

I realised that I wouldn't have been much good as Sara Texas's defence lawyer. Not if she wanted, and needed, to be found guilty of the crimes to which she had confessed. I'd have got frustrated. Massively fucking frustrated. I would have questioned her strategy, called her an idiot. And sooner or later I would have started to do what I was doing now: follow up the loose ends that had been neglected by the police.

If everything fitted together the way I suspected, that would have been the point where Sara would have fired me. When she realised that I was going to do a better job than Didrik and his colleagues. Because there was no doubt that Sara had wanted to be believed when she confessed. If I hadn't been convinced of my own theory before, I was now. Sara had been threatened. And the threat had been so terrifying that decades locked away in prison seemed a more enticing prospect than denying the charges and keeping her freedom.

Unless she had known all along that she wouldn't end up in prison because she was going to die before that? Had she been happy knowing that she wouldn't have to rot in a cell? We would never know. The only thing that was clear was that she couldn't have foreseen that her father would end up at death's door, thus providing her with a possibility of an escorted excursion from custody.

Coincidences and apparently random events came together to form a picture that I couldn't quite make sense of. I shuffled restlessly in the back seat of the taxi. The threat that had made Sara Texas confess to five murders appeared to be heading in a different direction now.

Towards me.

Like hell was I going to give in without a fight!

As if I'd just woken from a long trance, I turned to look at Lucy. She looked back at me with a sombre expression.

'I've got to get hold of Bobby. He must have talked to someone. He's the one who set all this crap in motion, and he's the one who's going to have to put a stop to it.'

Lucy shook her head slowly.

'You're crazy,' she said. 'You're not going to let this go, are you?'

'What did you expect?' I said irritably.

The taxi pulled up outside my door. I tugged my wallet from my inside pocket. Before I handed the driver my American Express card I fixed my eyes on Lucy.

'Okay, listen up. If you want to be on my team, you're going to have to accept that we do this my way. I'm the one who's being threatened here, not you. And it's my future that's on the line, not yours. And I'm the one with a child to provide for, not you.'

When I said that last sentence she started. Once again I saw that sorrow cross her face. A sorrow I didn't understand.

'If you insist on coming up to the flat and helping me get to the bottom of this crap, you're more than welcome. But I repeat: we're doing this my way. If you can't accept that, I suggest that we ask this nice gentleman to drive you home.'

I waved my credit card.

'The meter's running, Lucy. What do you want to do?'

She raised her chin defiantly.

'You're not just mean,' she said. 'You've also got a lousy memory. You wouldn't have got half as far in life if you hadn't had me.'

She unfastened her seatbelt.

'I'll come up with you,' she said simply. 'Anything else is out of the question.'

Belle was awake, and worried, when we got home. She hugged me tight and wrapped her plastered arm round my neck. Sometimes I think no one has ever loved me so unconditionally. I try not to wonder if she has felt the same love from me.

'Grandma said you'd probably be gone a really long time,' she said.

I flashed an angry glare at Marianne.

'Now you know that's not true,' I said. 'I always come back, don't I?'

Belle had had to get used to the idea that I went away from her at an early age. I went away and came back. Business trips, holidays. That morning I had only been gone a matter of hours. It scared me to realise that she had already had time to miss me.

'You're sure you don't need any more help?' Marianne said as she stood in the hall.

To be honest, I needed all the help I could get. I would have liked her to take Belle with her when she left. But there was no way that was going to happen. Belle needed time to recover from her trauma in her home environment. Lucy could look after her when I didn't have time.

'Thanks for coming,' I said, opening the door.

Marianne looked sad as she left.

'This thing you keep doing,' she said. 'Calling me in as a babysitter every five minutes but never letting me be part of your family or your life. It hurts, you know.' She touched her chest. 'In here,' she said. 'This is where it hurts.'

It was the wrong day for that sort of conversation. I had

neither the inclination nor the time. But I could have put my hand to my chest and talked about things that hurt. Such as when I was seven and had to go to school in trousers that were too short because my mother had spent the last of her money on cigarettes. Or when I was fourteen and didn't dare go out with my friends because I thought my mother would choke on her own drunken vomit if I didn't watch over her.

Marianne is a different person these days. The sort of person who looks after herself. I know she wants to be told how clever she's been for dealing with so much crap. And I do let her know, just not with words. I let her look after Belle, the best thing in my life. But I have rather more difficulty slotting cosy days *en famille* into my calendar. We aren't there yet, the two of us. Why is that so hard to understand?

'I'll be in touch,' I said brusquely.

Marianne left the flat and I shut the door firmly behind her, then turned both locks. I felt like washing my hands with disinfectant after touching the door. That was where the police arrived to pick me up for interrogation. The thought of it made me feel sick.

I went into the kitchen. Lucy was sitting there reading with Belle. I didn't like the fact that Belle's usually bright eyes looked dull with fever and tiredness.

'Is it normal to run a temperature when you break your arm?' I said.

'How should I know? Call the healthcare helpline,' Lucy said, stroking Belle's hair.

So I did. But first I called Bobby. No answer. I tried again. Still no answer. So I sent a text: 'Call me. Important. Best, Martin Benner.'

While I was waiting for my call to the helpline to be

answered I got out my laptop. Lucy watched me as I sat down at the kitchen table and opened it.

'What are you looking for? Can I help?'

I shook my head. She was already doing what she could to relieve me by having Belle on her lap.

In my head a list was starting to take shape. Time was racing away from me. I had to decide who I wanted to meet to find out more about Sara Texas. When Lucy and I were eating hamburgers at Texas Longhorn, I had said that Sara's sister was the top priority. I still thought that, but seeing as I couldn't get hold of Bobby it seemed more logical to start with someone else. I needed to speak to his and Sara's mother.

Her name had cropped up at several points in the preliminary investigation. Jeanette Roos. Someone with such an unusual name shouldn't be too hard to track down on the internet.

I was right. I didn't manage to find a telephone number, but it was easy enough to find her in the electoral register. She still lived out in Bandhagen, where Sara had grown up.

As I was writing down the address my call finally got through. An older-sounding woman gave brief answers to my questions. No, there was no need to worry about a high temperature. No, it probably wasn't anything to do with the accident. Thank you and goodbye.

'An unusually uncomplicated person,' I said to Lucy when the call was over.

In my experience, people who give medical advice about children tend to be a bit retarded. I couldn't believe my eyes not long after Belle was born and my sister was sitting in my office breastfeeding her. Blood was running from her nipples, tears down her cheeks.

'They say you mustn't stop breastfeeding,' she said. 'They say it can harm the baby.'

It turned out that loads of things that seem perfectly inno-cuous at first glance can be lethal: dummies, baby formula, regulated feeding and sleep. Anything that could make life simpler was forbidden. When Belle was mine and I was the one taking her to the clinic instead of my sister, you could say that things were rather different.

I was told all sorts of drivel.

Belle wasn't 'hitting her weight percentiles'.

Belle wasn't crawling.

And of course I knew that Belle mustn't under any circum-stances come into contact with anything containing sugar?

In the end I pushed the baby-clinic fascist up against the wall and roared at the top of my voice that if she trotted out one more piece of brain-dead advice, I'd ram a sugar-coated percentile up her fat arse. I can wholeheartedly recommend that to every parent. From that day on I never had any more problems with the clinic. Probably because Marianne or the au pair usually take Belle to those ridiculous check-ups now.

I suspected that threats involving sugar-coated percentiles and backsides would have limited, if any, effect on whoever was trying to frame me for murder. I was at a massive dis-advantage, and it was pissing me off. It doesn't matter what currency you gamble with, the person with access to the most information will always leave the table victorious. In other words, I needed to get hold of more definite information to work with.

Lucy glanced at the note where I'd written down Bobby and Sara's mother's address. Jeanette Roos. I presumed the name Tell came from the children's father.

'What are you thinking of doing?' Lucy said.

'Heading out to Bandhagen to pay a visit to Sara and Bobby's mother. Ask her if she knows where her son's got to. Find out about Sara's relationship with her and her father. And ask about the sister.'

Lucy looked at me warily.

'Her father? What, you're not thinking he committed all those murders?'

'I'm not thinking anything. But I've got to start somewhere. Otherwise I'm not going to get anywhere.'

Belle was drawing flowers on a sheet of white paper. The bandage on her forehead looked ridiculously large. I stroked her hair gently.

'Can you stay with Lucy for a little while?' I said. 'I need to go and see an old lady.'

'You will come back, though, won't you?' Belle said anxiously.

My throat felt tight when I replied.

'I'd never leave you,' I said. 'Never.'

23

The building was five storeys high and two hundred kilometres long. Or at least it felt like it. I didn't care about the fact that it was Sunday. I was a hunted man who needed to get a dangerous situation under control fast. I stood outside the locked main door and rang the entry phone. My journey to Bandhagen had taken an unexpectedly long time. First it took forever to get hold of a decent hire car. Then I had to get the bastard satnav to work. If Jeanette Roos wasn't home, I was planning to park nearby and wait. I had expended far too much effort on this just to give up.

But I didn't have to wait. Jeanette Roos answered in less than a minute. Her voice bore testament to years of smoking and drinking. Marianne could have ended up sounding like that if she hadn't got a grip on things.

'What do you want?' she said over the speaker.

'I'd like to talk to you,' I said, after introducing myself. 'About your daughter, Sara. And your son, Bobby.'

'So you're a journalist? Sorry, I don't talk to the press.'

For a moment I was worried that she had hung up, but her laboured breathing gave her away.

'I'm a lawyer, like I just said,' I said. 'It's important that we talk.'

'What for? Sara's dead and buried. If you cared, you could have come sooner.'

It started to pour with rain. Vicious little drops hit the back of my neck. They reminded me that I still hadn't got round to having a shower.

'Sadly I didn't have the honour of representing your daughter,' I said, making a real effort not to yell at her. 'But Bobby showed up at my office a week or so ago and asked me to take a look at her case. Since then a number of things have happened which are making me wonder if Sara made all those confessions of her own volition. I won't need to stay long. But there are several questions I'd really like to get answers to.'

I couldn't hear a sound from the entry phone.

'Hello?' I eventually said.

'You said Bobby came to see you?' Jeanette Roos said. 'Bobby, Sara's brother?'

'Yes,' I said.

Another silence.

Then the lock clicked.

'Come up,' Jeanette Roos said.

If Eivor, Tor Gustavsson's former secretary, appeared to live in a doll's house, Jeanette seemed to inhabit an old crack den. Someone had made a valiant attempt to liven it up with some half-dead geraniums and sun-bleached embroidered pictures in crooked frames.

My mentor at university, an old professor who refused to

retire, taught me early on never to lie more than was absolutely necessary. People notice when you do, and they get upset. So I didn't say 'What a lovely home!' or anything like that, just followed Jeanette into the kitchen where she evidently wanted the meeting to take place. She lit a cigarette with trembling hands, then went and stood next to the extractor fan. A tiny part of me wanted to point out that if she wasn't going to switch the fan on, she may as well stand wherever the hell she wanted. But I held back on the sarcasm.

'Tell me about Bobby,' she said.

In a few short sentences I gave her an account of our meetings. About the ticket he had given me, and what we had agreed.

'He'd heard me on the radio,' I said. 'He knew I was interested in Sara's case. At first I was sceptical, but now that I've acquainted myself with the material I can understand that you and the rest of her family must have felt incredibly frustrated. It's upsetting to see how badly the police did their job.'

I paused and waited while she stubbed the cigarette out in the drainer. I couldn't figure out if she was drunk, or under the influence of some other shit. Her tics and shakes could just as easily have been a sign of nerves, or some sort of illness. But her eyes told a different story. They were clear and steady.

She looked at me with something that felt like sympathy.

'I have a pretty good idea of where someone like you comes from,' she said, looking me up and down. 'You don't have to tell me what you think about this part of Stockholm, or my flat. I can see that well enough. But I can also tell that you mean what you say. You seem to be genuinely interested in Sara and the hell she went through.'

I nodded in confirmation.

'I am.'

'Tell me,' she said. 'Do you really think Sara was lying when she confessed to those five murders?'

'Yes.'

Her tone surprised me. It sounded as if she was less convinced of her daughter's innocence.

'Interesting,' she said. 'So I assume you also have a good explanation of why she lied?'

I didn't like the fact that I was sitting down while Jeanette was standing.

'I suspect that she was being threatened,' I said. 'I'm not sure how, but I believe the threat was also aimed at her son.'

Jeanette's expression didn't change.

'What do you think happened to your grandson, Mio? Is what the police are saying true? That Sara took his life as well as her own?'

Jeanette's shaking hands fumbled for the cigarette packet again, and she managed to pull another one out.

'I don't know what to think,' she said hoarsely. 'I don't know if you've got children, but I find it impossible to get my head round the idea. That my daughter would have killed her own kid.'

She got the lighter to work and lit the cigarette. Soon the kitchen was filled with even more smoke. I was going to smell like a crematorium when I left.

'Why do you think she killed herself?' I said. 'Why jump off Västerbron instead of trying to escape?'

Jeanette shook her head wearily.

'Who knows?' she said. 'Who knows?'

Unless I was mistaken, she had softened up. So I went on feeding her questions.

'As I understand it, Sara had problems with her father?' I said.

'Who didn't?' Jeanette said with a dry laugh.

The laugh turned into a muffled cough that echoed deep in her lungs.

'He was a real sadist,' she said when she finished coughing. 'A domestic tyrant of the first order.'

'I've heard that he used to sell Sara to his friends. Is that true?'

Jeanette sucked greedily on the cigarette.

'That's private,' she said curtly. 'But yes, it's true.'

And what did you do about that as her mother? I wanted to scream.

But I sat there in silence. God knows what battles had been fought in that flat.

'What was it like when she moved to the States?' I said. 'Did he carry on causing trouble for her then?'

'Hardly,' Jeanette said. 'Well, let me put it like this: as long as that man was alive he caused trouble. For anyone and everyone. But the trouble varied over time. Soon after Sara moved he suffered his first stroke. After that he only left the flat on a handful of occasions. The last time he went out he got mugged and knocked down.'

So Jenny had been right about that too. Sara's father hadn't caused trouble in Texas. So who was Lucifer?

I asked Jeanette, but she just looked back at me inscrutably.

'Oh, so that's what you're getting at? His friends did sometimes call him Lucifer. But he never went to the USA.'

I changed track. But my heart was still racing. Something told me that identifying the Lucifer in the diary was important.

'How about Sara's ex?' I said. 'Ed, that was his name, wasn't it?'

Jeanette rested her head against the inactive extractor fan.

'He was quite a piece of work. A guy who spent the last of his money on a plane ticket so he could be close to her and make her life a misery. But I assume you're asking about him because you want to know if he could be the real murderer. And to that question I'd have to say no. There's no way on earth that Ed could have come up with such an intricate plan, killing a handful of people and then finding a way to get away with it.'

A smile played across her face. It struck me that she had probably been very attractive once upon a time. Before life stripped her of all energy and sparkle.

But I wasn't ready to accept her evaluation of her erstwhile prospective son-in-law's abilities. I needed to get someone else's verdict as well. Not that I knew how that was going to happen.

'What was Ed's surname?' I said.

'Svensson,' Jeanette said. 'And his name's Edvard, not Ed.'

She was starting to look restless. Maybe it was withdrawal kicking in, maybe just a general lack of patience. I'd have to hurry to get to the end before she threw me out.

I glanced at my watch.

'I'm taking up too much of your time,' I said. 'I'll leave you alone. Just a few quick questions. Bobby made quite an effort to help Sara. Do you know why she wouldn't accept that help?'

'Presumably because she was so intent on claiming responsibility for those murders,' Jeanette said, and for the first time her voice sounded shaky. 'If not, I don't know why she acted the way she did.'

'Were she and Bobby close?'

'Very.'

I recalled Bobby's demeanour the first time he showed up in my office. The fact that anyone could be close to someone like that was beyond me.

'Do you know where Bobby is now?' I said. 'I don't want to worry you without cause, but I think it might be important that I get hold of him.'

I left out the story about Jenny Woods being killed in a hit and run. That would have been too much for anyone to hear.

Jeanette coughed again. Mucus moved up and down her throat.

'You say Bobby came to see you and begged on Sara's behalf?'

I nodded. Jeanette was the second person in a short time who had questioned that particular part of my story. Jenny had done the same thing.

'Very, very strange,' she said. 'Because Bobby doesn't actually live in Sweden these days.'

I looked up in surprise.

'Where does he live, then?'

'Switzerland. He's probably the only Swede to emigrate there and become a lorry driver.'

I tilted my head.

'Maybe he's on holiday,' I said. 'Why would it be so unlikely for him to be in Sweden? Switzerland isn't that far away, after all.'

Jeanette quietly put her cigarette down.

'Bobby isn't like his sister,' she said. 'Even though we don't see each other he gets in touch every so often. And when he hasn't got time, his girlfriend contacts me. Believe me – he hasn't spent a single day outside Switzerland in the past few weeks.'

She looked at me through narrow eyes.

'It looks like someone's messing with you. Because you certainly haven't met my Bobby, I can assure you of that.'

When I didn't respond she went out into the hall.

'Come with me,' she said.

We stopped in front of a photograph on top of a chest.

'This is Bobby,' Jeanette said. 'Was this the man who came to your office?'

I couldn't take my eyes off the picture.

Because the man gazing out from the photograph bore no resemblance to the man who had appeared in my office and introduced himself as Bobby Tell.

24

If I could, I would obviously have dropped the job the moment I saw the picture of Bobby. But I was already caught up in it. My own liberty and future were in the balance. So I had to figure out what sort of crap I'd got mixed up in.

It was pouring with rain as I got ready to drive back into the city. The hire car smelled of plastic and I was starting to smell of sweat. Sweat and cigarette smoke. The last thing I got out of Jeanette was how to contact Sara's hitherto anonymous big sister. Marion. I called her from the car.

'Mum's already phoned to warn me that you'd be getting in touch,' she said. 'I'm afraid I don't think I can help you.'

'I'd still very much like to see you,' I said.

'Sorry,' the sister said. 'I don't want to get involved.'

There was a click, and she was gone.

I wasn't going to let her get away that easily. I took me less than two minutes to find her address. To my surprise, she lived in a flat on Kungsholmen, two hundred metres from the City Hall.

Her mother had sounded rather cryptic when she gave me her daughter's telephone number.

'She's too grand for the rest of us,' she had said. 'But she'll probably like you.'

So her name was Marion. You had to give Jeanette a bit of credit for giving her children imaginative names, at least by Swedish standards. Bobby and Marion. Only Sara had ended up with a normal name.

It was half past three when I pulled up outside the block where Marion lived. I left the car immediately beneath a 'No Parking' sign and ran over to the entry phone. There was no answer when I rang her flat.

I still wasn't going to give up. I was a man with a lot of questions, and I was damn well going to get answers. Heaven help the poor fool who tried to get in my way.

I rang one of Marion's neighbours instead. I had more luck there. In a matter of seconds I was standing in the stairwell. Being able to say that you're a lawyer on urgent business is as effective a way of introducing yourself as being a police officer with a drawn gun. People never hold out for long; they soon give in.

The stairwell was being renovated. Plastic and paper and tubs of paint stood along the walls. Painters don't work on Sundays. Spurning the lift, I jogged up to the third floor where Marion lived. 'M. Tell', it said on her door. I don't remember how many times I rang the bell. Three or four, maybe. Not a sound from the flat. Eventually a neighbour opened his door and peered out. An elderly man who looked cross.

'She's not home,' he said. 'Haven't you grasped that?'

It wasn't the person who had let me in through the front door.

'Sorry,' I said. 'I didn't mean to disturb you. You don't happen to know where she is? It's urgent.'

The old man squinted at me through smeared glasses.

'What do you want with her?' he said.

For various reasons I wasn't at all sure this man was going to be as easily impressed by my status as a lawyer. But I tried anyway.

'I'm a lawyer,' I said. 'I'm working for Marion's family. It's extremely important that I get hold of her.'

The elderly man laughed.

'Marion's family are employing a lawyer? Splendid. You'll have to tell them that Marion still doesn't want anything to do with them. Please, just leave her alone.'

If I hadn't understood before, I did now: the old man knew Marion. Well enough to be aware of her background and her shaky relationship with her family. I decided to change both the subject and my own attitude.

I took a cautious step towards him.

'I can see how this must look,' I said in a subdued voice. 'But you have to believe me when I say that it's in Marion's best interests to talk to me.'

The man frowned.

'She's not in any trouble?' he said.

I hurried to shake my head. Even the suggestion that it would be in Marion's best interests to see me was stretching the truth.

'Not as far as I'm aware,' I said. 'Not yet.'

But, I thought to myself, there's a storm brewing among the dead of her family. And if a total stranger like myself could get caught up in the mess there was no guarantee that a woman who was Sara's sister would remain untouched by it.

'Where is she?' I said.

It's horrible watching people make mistakes. Considering how much the old man knew about Marion's past, he ought to have appreciated that she might be sought by people who wished her harm. How was he to know who I was? A tall man in scruffy but expensive clothes, mounting a concerted offensive against the door of her flat. Obviously the old man shouldn't have trusted me. Obviously he shouldn't have given me any information about Marion's whereabouts. But he did. Because that's how we work. We're so keen to do the right thing that we don't even notice when we get it wrong.

'She's gone to the country,' the old man said. 'She gives me a spare key to her flat when she's away. That's how I know where she is.'

'When are you expecting her back?'

'Later this evening.'

I held my hand out. The old man took it, hesitantly.

'Thanks,' I said. 'Thank you. You've been a great help.'

He snatched his hand back. His face bore clear signs of sadness. Probably lived alone, which would explain why he cared so much about his young neighbour's welfare.

'She's been through some rough times, Marion,' he said. 'Really rough. But she's a decent person. Please, don't ruin things for her.'

I promised not to. If I had been asked there and then to explain why it was important for me to see Marion, I wouldn't have been able to give a sensible answer. All I knew was that I had to meet the few people who had been close to Sara Texas whose names I knew. Because one of them surely had to be able to give me some explanation or clue regarding the question that was now troubling me more than any of the others:

who was the man who had come to my office claiming to be Bobby?

I had asked to see pictures of Sara's ex-boyfriend Ed, so I now knew it wasn't him. A shame, because otherwise he would have been my first guess.

The situation confronting me now made me feel even more shaky. Someone had assumed a false identity to involve me in the hunt for the truth about Sara Texas, while someone else was trying to frame me for a murder I hadn't committed. Were they one and the same person?

The thought made me feel giddy. At the very least, I had considerably bigger problems than I had realised at first.

My legs felt weak as I left Marion's building. I'd have to return later. If I felt up to it. Otherwise I'd try again the next day.

The hire car was waiting where I had left it. There was no sign of a parking ticket. One reason to be cheerful, anyway.

Lucy called my mobile as I was heading along Hantverkargatan.

'When are you thinking of coming home?' she said in a worried voice.

I looked out across the water of Riddarfjärden as I passed the City Hall. The rain had stopped, but Stockholm was being slowly asphyxiated under heavy clouds. The air in the car seemed to run out and I opened the window.

'I'll be home soon. Very soon.'

People say that the big changes in life happen very quickly. Life changes direction overnight, in the blink of an eye. Like the way Belle was left without parents because of a plane crash. That wasn't something the rest of us had ever imagined.

Not even in our worst nightmares had we conjured up a scenario like that.

But it wasn't like that with Sara Tell's case. In hindsight, I can't really draw a clear dividing line between Before and After. Maybe it's actually very simple: my life changed the moment I let the man calling himself Bobby into my office.

'What I don't understand at all is how I fit into this whole thing.'

Lucy and I were sitting on my roof terrace. Half of it is covered. It's fairly spacious, I suppose you could say. And I've got a nice view as well.

'Can you see all the way to Mariannelund?' Belle asked when she had a big thing about the extremely tedious Emil from Lönneberga in the book by Astrid Lindgren.

'Better than that,' I said. 'You can see the whole of Stureplan.'

Not that Stureplan was actually much to look at. Decadent trust-fund idiots who were probably going to die young from syphilis. But the location was perfect. I like living in the centre of the city. And Stureplan is very central.

'I don't understand how you fit in either,' Lucy said. 'I think this is seriously bloody unsettling, Martin.'

It wasn't that I disagreed with her. I just didn't have anything to say. I looked out through the rain, past Stureplan and over towards the two towers on Kungsgatan.

'You have to talk to the police. Have you done that yet?'

I shook my head.

'Not yet. I've only just got home, after all.'

Belle was asleep. She didn't usually have a nap this late in the afternoon, but the accident seemed have left her more tired than normal. Nothing funny about that. On the contrary, I was happy to get some time on my own with Lucy.

I'd tried calling the fake Bobby several more times. No answer. Maybe it was stupid to go on chasing him, but I had too many questions to be able to stop myself.

'He came to our office,' I said quietly. 'That's pretty cocky, you have to admit. He could have called or emailed, but he chose to come in person. What would he have done if I'd seen through him? How could he be so confident that I didn't know what Bobby looked like?'

Lucy brushed some hair from her face.

'Because Bobby never really appeared in any of the papers. You weren't involved in the police investigation and you weren't Sara's lawyer. So there was no way you'd have known what Bobby looked like.'

I considered what Lucy had said. She'd just put her finger on something very important that neither of us had thought of.

'Why not?' I said. 'Why didn't Bobby appear in any of the papers? If he was so keen to clear his sister's name? Not once did he turn to the press. He could easily have sold the story of how his sister's case hadn't been properly investigated by the police.'

'I'd say that's just one of a whole load of weird things,' she said. 'Another one is how the man who came to see you could have got hold of that ticket.'

That hadn't occurred to me before.

'Could he have got it from Bobby?'

'You mean that he's acting as some sort of front? Bobby daren't visit you himself so he sends someone else? Maybe.'

She shivered.

'You ought to have some blankets out here,' she said. 'The wind's really cold when you're so high up.'

She was talking as if I lived at the top of a skyscraper.

'You can sit on my lap,' I said, holding out my arms.

'Dream on,' Lucy said. 'I'm not going to sit on your lap, and not on your face either.'

I started to laugh, wearily and without much enthusiasm.

'Harsh,' I said.

'I'm just being honest,' Lucy said. 'You should try it.'

I threw my hands out.

'I'm honesty personified,' I said humbly. 'Ask me a question and I'll give you an honest answer.'

Lucy smiled.

'Who's Veronica?'

I wondered the same thing. It took me almost half a minute before I remembered the woman I had slept with from the Press Club. Fuck. Had she managed to get hold of my home number? Because she hadn't called me on my mobile.

'She called when Belle and I were making lunch,' Lucy said in response to my unspoken question.

'Oh,' I said.

'So who is she?'

I sighed. How many games is it possible to play at the same time? Not many. Not if one of the games involved people you've met starting to die.

'We fucked. Once. No, sorry, twice. I'm not planning to see her again.'

Lucy fell silent.

Far too silent.

'Are you okay, baby?' I said.

She didn't look at me when she replied. Her eyes were fixed on a point that appeared to be just to the south of Stureplan.

'I'm fine,' she said. 'I always am.'

25

There was a time when I thought you had to love your family. Now I know that that isn't the case. I choose to see that as both a blessing and a potential threat. A blessing because it means that I don't have to see my mother more than is necessary. And a threat because it could mean that Belle will leave me as soon as she gets the chance. In spite of my limited parenting skills, the fact remains: I have no fucking idea what would be left of me if anyone or anything took Belle away from me.

I went back to see Marion Tell a few hours later. She was home, just as the old neighbour had said. Marion didn't look like anyone else in her family. With her dazzling white teeth and perfect bob, she looked like the complete antithesis of everything her mother's appearance suggested. Jeanette had said that her daughter was too grand to want to see her and Bobby. I'd say she was too smart. Few things create deeper divisions than an uneven distribution of intelligence and talent.

It was obvious that the neighbour had talked to her. She

didn't look happy when I rang the bell and she opened the door.

'I thought I made it clear to you that I didn't want to answer any questions,' she said.

She was attractive, in that way that only women who work in the arts are. Cool and slender. For some reason I found myself getting annoyed by her arrogance. The fact that I was so ridiculously tired probably helped. My short but memorable discussion with Lucy on the terrace hadn't improved matters. It irritated me that she knew about Veronica. Even though we had both agreed on the rules of the game, I had a feeling that they only applied with certain reservations. We were allowed to have sex with other people, but only if the other person never found out. Because we still had expectations of each other, regardless. I of Lucy, and she of me. And in my current situation I couldn't afford to lose her.

I took a step closer to Marion.

'I think you should listen very carefully to what I've got to say,' I said. 'A couple of weeks ago a man came to my office. He said his name was Bobby, and he said he was Sara Tell's brother. He had with him a train ticket that he said proved his sister had an alibi for at least one of the five murders she confessed to. On Friday someone else came to see me. Sara's friend Jenny. She told me the story behind the train ticket, thereby confirming her sister's alibi.'

'Fascinating,' Marion said.

'Shut up, I'm not finished,' I said. 'The night before last Jenny was murdered. She was run down outside her hotel. By my car.'

If I hadn't had Marion's attention before that, I did now.

She looked at me without saying anything.

'The problem for the person who stole – or perhaps I should

say borrowed – my car was that I spent the entire night in hospital. It would be hard to find a better alibi, don't you think? Well, I'm afraid that's not enough for me. Someone is so upset by my investigation into your sister's case that the person in question is trying to frame me for a murder I didn't commit. It's only a matter of time before they realise that I'm not going to be locked up or charged with that crime.'

'And you think the murderer will make another attempt to get at you?' Marion said slowly.

'I don't know what to think,' I said. 'All I know is that someone is going to a lot of fucking effort to cover up whatever it was that made your sister confess to five murders she hadn't committed. Even if you've distanced yourself from your family, and even if Sara is dead, I think you have a duty to do whatever you can to see that she gets justice.'

Everything I was saying was obvious. At least to my mind. Rhetoric is best when you keep it simple.

Marion reacted furiously.

'Who are you to come to my home and lecture me about my family?' she said, her eyes flaring with anger and something that looked like grief. 'I was sixteen years old when I left home. Otherwise I'd have died there. Do you get that? Died! Sara and Bobby chose to stay. The weak, pathetic idiots.'

She paused for breath.

I took the chance to invite myself in.

'Are we really going to have this conversation on the doorstep?' I said.

There was a risk that she'd respond by slamming the door in my face. But she didn't.

'Come in,' she said.

I stepped inside and closed the door behind me. We stood

there in the hall. Evidently that was as far as she was going to allow me. I looked at her as she stood there with her arms folded. Her neighbour had said that she'd spent the day in the country. With her long white trousers and dark blue blouse she looked more like she'd been to a gallery or a smart wine-bar.

'You think your brother and sister got what they deserved?' I said. 'Because they weren't strong enough to break away at the same age you did?'

Marion shook her head.

'They were like two baby birds, waiting desperately for me to go back and take them away from there. How would that have worked? Neither of them was disciplined enough to hold down a job. Not to mention education. While I was working my arse off to get perfect grades, Sara and Bobby did all they could to sabotage their own futures.'

'You're the eldest?'

'Yes.'

'That usually entails a degree of responsibility.'

'Sure. But that responsibility doesn't extend beyond helping people to help themselves.'

I realised that in many ways, Marion was a copy of me. Just like I had, she had done all she could to turn out different to her parents, and had realised that would only happen if she made different choices in life. Trying hard at school was one such choice.

Knowledge is power. Power is freedom. Freedom is everything.

Our eyes met in tacit understanding. I could see she had recognised that we were the same sort, she and I.

'How do you think I can help?' she said.

'Bobby tried to get his sister off with the police and her lawyers. What were your thoughts about that?'

'You mean did I think she was innocent?'

'Yes.'

'No.'

Her reply came quickly. I blinked in surprise.

'No?'

'No.'

Silence.

'You think Sara murdered five people?' I said.

'I'm not a lawyer,' Marion said. 'And I'm not a police officer. But I knew Sara. If you ask me if I think she was sufficiently damaged and crazy to kill other people, I'm afraid I have to say yes to that question. But as to what the actual evidence says about the matter of guilt, you'll have to ask someone else.'

Shaken, I tried to find the words to express what I wanted to say.

'As I understand it, Bobby believed the exact opposite on both of the matters you've just indirectly referred to,' I said. 'He didn't think Sara was capable of murder, and he thought the evidence was too weak.'

'But she confessed.'

Marion shrugged her shoulders.

'People sometimes take responsibility for crimes they haven't committed,' I said.

'A lot of things happen,' Marion said. 'And they all happened to Sara.'

'I haven't been able to find any indication that Sara was charged with any violent offences before,' I said.

'Because she never was,' Marion said. 'Sara got away with an awful lot of things.'

'Did you say that to the police?' I said.

'That Sara had been physically violent before? No, I didn't.'

I couldn't help feeling sceptical about what she was saying. Up to that moment I had been prepared to see Sara Tell as a victim: a victim of a conspiracy and of threats that were so unpleasant that she was prepared to shoulder Job's yoke without the slightest resistance.

'I can't get this to make sense,' I said. 'You say you left your childhood home when you were sixteen. You abandoned your brother and sister. But you still think you know them pretty well.'

Marion's hall was gloomy. I didn't like the fact that I couldn't see her face properly. I couldn't see her reaction to what I'd said.

'Families are like chewing gum,' she said. 'You can go as far away as you like, but once it's stuck to your shoe you can never get rid of it. We saw each other from time to time, obviously. When Sara finally started to talk about moving away from Stockholm I felt happy for her. She made one attempt to leave home after she finished school, but that went wrong. She was subletting a flat but didn't keep up with the rent. She had something like five jobs in the space of a year, but she kept getting fired. How anyone could have employed her as an au pair is beyond me. She was the least together person on the planet.'

Marion sighed. I was close to doing the same. Exhaustion hit me like a hammer-blow in the back. I had to go home and get to bed. Two sleepless nights were too much for anyone.

'Who was Sara violent towards?' I said.

Marion looked away. It's odd – family betrayal always hurts, even long after the relationships that held things together have broken.

'A lot of people,' Marion said. 'Before she moved to the States, anyway. She took a wrong turn, so to speak. Started hanging out with a gang of real hooligans who used to get their kicks beating people up. I know drugs were involved as well. I never understood how Sara never got caught. The others in the gang did, one after the other. But Sara and Ed seemed to be made of Teflon. Nothing ever stuck to them.'

This was new. I thought back to the pictures of Sara I had seen in the papers. The murderer with the pretty face and academic glasses. Actually rather similar to her big sister, I realised now that I was looking at Marion. But how could no one have known? How could Sara's past as a gangster have gone completely unnoticed by police and media?

'So Sara's ex, Ed, was an active member of the same gang?' I said.

'I'm pretty sure that was how they met,' Marion said.

'Did you ever meet him? Ed?'

'Only once. He seemed genuinely sick. A truly disturbed individual. Used to beat Sara black and blue. Which was kind of good in a way. It was his fists that gave her the push she needed to take off to the States.'

I couldn't really accept the point of Marion's argument. There was nothing positive about a girl being abused by her boyfriend and running all the way to Texas.

'Was Ed smart too, or just sick?'

I was reluctant to use the same expression as Marion, but did so anyway. You have to be careful about saying people are mentally ill.

Marion laughed.

'I wouldn't say he was smart. More lazy and lethargic.'

'When Sara moved back home from Texas, do you know if she still had trouble with him then?'

'Not that I'm aware of. But we had very sporadic contact

at the time, me and Sara. Especially after I found out she was pregnant.'

'You didn't think she should be a mother?'

'Are you kidding? I thought it was terrible. I don't know how many times I stood with the phone in my hand, thinking about phoning Social Services.'

She fell silent, as if she felt she had said too much.

'Who was Mio's father?' I said.

'I don't know.'

'Ed?'

'I said I don't know.'

'But Mio was living with foster parents while Sara was in custody?'

'Yes.'

My chest muscles stiffened as I held my breath. For a fraction of a second I was transported three years back in time. I could see myself standing with the phone in my hand, being told the news. That Belle would be placed in a foster home in Skövde. My throat stung as I breathed out.

You can let down your adult siblings. But little children? No, you can't abandon them. Not if you have the chance to do the right thing. And I thought I could see that Marion had had the chance.

'You never considered looking after Mio yourself?' I said.

'Not for a moment. I don't take responsibility for other people's mistakes. Especially not if they last a lifetime.'

Human beings can be so incredibly different.

The air in the whitewashed hall ran out. I needed to get out of there, fast.

'Thanks for your time,' I said, reaching for the door handle. 'By the way, you haven't heard from Bobby recently?'

'No, and I can't say I'm sorry.'

I was starting to get seriously tired of the unembarrassed way she kept marking the distance between her and her family. The door opened and cool air from the stairwell slipped into the hall.

'Can you think of any good explanation as to why Bobby never turned to the media for help with Sara's case?' I said. 'He went to the police and her lawyer, but never to the papers.'

'Because Sara asked him not to. He came and asked if I could present the family's case to the mass media. Probably because I was the only one of us who looked remotely present-able. But I refused, of course. Later on he texted to say that it didn't matter anyway. Sara had forbidden him from carrying on his campaign to get her exonerated.'

I supposed that would do as an explanation. With a short nod I thanked her again and left the flat.

Marion followed me.

'I can tell you think I'm a bad person,' she said. 'But I'm not. I'm just the sort of person who tries to do the right thing for myself.'

I was already halfway down the stairs.

'Sometimes the best thing you can do is to try to do the right thing for other people,' I said.

Then I turned and walked away.

26

It had gone nine o'clock by the time I got home. Lucy had put Belle to bed and was sitting on the terrace with a glass of wine.

'Did it go okay?' she said.

'I don't know how to answer that,' I said.

My legs felt like they were made of soft toffee. I sat down, exhausted. Going in to get a wineglass felt like as much of a challenge as carrying a grand piano up the stairs.

I reached distractedly for Lucy's glass.

'How was she?' she said, letting go of the glass without protest.

'Peculiar.'

'Did you fuck?'

I swallowed the wine and it caught in my throat. It stung like fire when I coughed.

'For fuck's sake, Lucy.'

'You usually call me Baby.'

I rediscovered my legs and went in to get a glass of water. I heard noises from Belle's room and hurried to take a look.

She had got tangled up in the covers and was bumping the plaster-cast against the wall as she tried to pull free.

'Shhh,' I said, and helped her untangle herself.

I held my hand to her forehead and waited until she fell back to sleep. Then I padded gently out of her room. Lucy was still sitting where I had left her.

Without responding to her tawdry question I told her what I had found out from Marion. Lucy listened quietly but attentively.

'You need to watch out,' she said when I had finished. 'You're in a situation where you're getting information from all sides, but with no way of evaluating it. Who knows what a bitter sister might blurt out? How can you be sure she isn't making up all that stuff about Sara's violent past?'

I drank some wine. From the street came the muffled sound of traffic, and the evening sky was heavy with the same clouds that had hung there all day. We ought to forget the whole thing and go to Nice like we'd planned. That would have been the right choice, the only rational option.

'I don't think she was lying, seeing as she was almost pathetically honest about everything else.'

'You mean the nephew she let Social Services look after?'

'Amongst other things.'

Lucy took her wineglass back.

'Do you need me tonight or is it okay if I go home to sleep?' she said.

I was seized by an irrational fear that if I let her leave the flat she'd never come back. I wouldn't be able to live with that. No way.

As usual when I got scared, I adopted a defensive attitude. Because I knew what she was trying to say, indirectly.

'You were the one who broke up with me.'

She stood up abruptly.

'Don't start with all that crap again,' she said. 'I'm not going to take that.'

I was on my feet just as quickly.

'But it's true. You said you weren't prepared to give me another chance, but that you wanted to keep seeing me. Without any conditions or expectations. That's exactly what you said.'

I sounded like a five-year-old trying to renegotiate an agreement that had been wrong from the outset without bursting into tears.

'And here we are anyway,' Lucy said quietly. 'Full of expectations and weighed down with obligations. Not because we're a couple but because we're friends, Martin.'

I lowered my head wearily.

'I didn't mean to hurt you,' I said. 'Sometimes I see other people, that's just the way it is. I didn't think of it as wrong. I thought that's how you wanted it. I've always assumed that you sleep with other people when you feel like it. And I don't really have a problem with us doing that.'

I looked up cautiously.

Lucy was running a hand through her wild red hair. The way I loved curling it round my fingers.

'In theory it's a great agreement,' she said. 'But in practice ...' She fell silent.

I waited as long as I could bear to.

Then I asked, 'What do you want, Lucy?'

She looked tense.

'I don't know,' she said. 'Right now everything feels pretty crap. This whole Sara Texas mess. It's taken up so much time and energy. We're not going to get to Nice, I think we both know that.'

She shook her head.

'Bloody hell, Martin. Someone's trying to frame you for murder. Someone who's already run down and killed a woman in your car. Aren't you scared?'

Her green eyes were wide with worry.

If I was scared? Yes, I was. But I was also determined not to let whoever was after me win. There aren't many battles for our peace of mind, and we can't afford to lose them.

'Of course I'm scared,' I said. 'But the threat won't get any smaller if we just ignore it. That's starting to look very obvious now.'

'So what are you going to do?'

'First of all, sleep. Tomorrow I'm going to call Didrik at National Crime and tell him what's happened. It's important that the police have everything documented. Then we need to try to figure out who came to the office pretending to be Bobby Tell. I'll let Didrik have the mobile number I've been in touch with, maybe he can trace it back to someone. And I think we ought to consider the idea of going to Texas. It could be a bad mistake to think we can sort this out without leaving Stockholm.'

I realised that the thought had been there all along. I couldn't tackle five different murders, and would never have time to do so. But I didn't have to. Sara's time as a suspected murderer had started in the USA, and there were only two murders there. If I could get her cleared of the two Texas murders, the Swedish ones would follow.

I said as much to Lucy.

'Texas is so far away,' she said. 'And the Swedish murders are in our own backyard.'

'But that breaks the chronology,' I said. 'It seems pointless to ignore the murders that first brought her to the attention of the police.'

Lucy shook her head slowly.

'I think she did commit those murders, Martin. All of them.'

'Still? You still think Sara Tell murdered five people? In spite of everything that's happened in the past few days?'

She shrugged.

'The evidence,' she said. 'The weight of evidence is overwhelming.'

'Only if we fail to get to the bottom of this,' I said. 'I think that'll show all the so-called evidence in a completely different light.'

An unnecessarily chill evening wind was making me shiver. We walked quietly back into the flat.

'We,' Lucy said. 'You said we need to find out who came to the office and asked you to help Sara. That we ought to go to Texas.'

I stroked her back.

'If you want to,' I said.

'Do you need me, then?' she said.

The question was incomprehensible, no matter how simple it sounded.

'More than ever,' I whispered.

She hugged me harder than I deserved.

'Prove it, then,' she said. 'Prove it.'

Sleep does something to us. Something good. When I woke up the following morning I had slept for over ten hours. My head was heavy when I lifted it from the pillow. From the kitchen I could hear muffled sounds from Lucy and Belle.

Lucy had stayed the night, of course. She had asked me to prove how much I needed her. So I did. The only way I knew how. I made love to her until I quite literally passed out. That sort of effort ought to have earned me a few points.

'Am I going to preschool today?' Belle said when I walked into the kitchen.

Lucy stared at my naked body.

'You forgot your underwear, Martin.'

Without a word I went back to the bedroom. I'm man enough to admit when I've made a mistake, and to put it right.

I returned to the kitchen, this time wearing not only pants but jeans and a t-shirt.

Belle giggled and I kissed her on the head.

'You're not going to preschool today. Signe's going to come and look after you.'

Lucy smiled playfully as I poured a cup of coffee. My hand was shaking slightly.

'What about us?' she said. 'Are we staying at home with Signe as well?'

I drank the hot coffee, felt it run down my throat and warm me from the inside in the summer chill. Rested and relatively recently fucked, I felt ready for any battle.

'We're going to work,' I said. 'And we're going to call the police.'

Which was one of the first things I did when we got to the office. Everything was the same as usual there, which was the contrast I needed to understand how much my life had changed over the course of the weekend.

Someone had stolen my car and run down and killed another person.

That sort of thing doesn't pass without leaving its mark.

People say that the police are always drinking coffee. It's true. During my short time as a police officer in Texas I had more coffee breaks than at any other time of my life. And from what I'd heard, things were no different in Sweden.

When I finally managed to get hold of Didrik I was pretty sure he was in the middle of a coffee break. Not that I said as much when he took the call.

'Bloody hell, are you sitting there having a wank at work? I've been calling and calling, but you don't seem to have had a spare hand to answer with.'

I thought it was very funny. A cop who needed two hands for a wank had to be pretty special.

Didrik didn't appear to share my opinion.

'Martin, did you want anything in particular?'

You could say that.

I began with the most important point.

'When can I have my car back? I hate hire cars. It feels like I'm cruising round in a Batmobile for pensioners.'

Didrik muttered something inaudible to someone who was evidently standing nearby.

'I'm afraid I can't answer that at this moment in time,' he said.

Can't answer that at this moment in time?

'Sorry, all due respect to the forensic examination, but how long is it going to take?'

'I don't know. Anyway, it's only been twenty-four hours.'

He was right there, of course, but I was keen to get my life back to normal again. Ideally as soon as possible.

The line fell silent.

'Anything else?' Didrik said. 'If not, there's something I'd like to talk to you about.'

Maybe that should have set my alarm bells ringing. But it didn't. Unless they were ringing too quietly for me to hear.

'I've got more to tell you,' I said in a slightly louder voice.

'Okay,' Didrik said.

His dismissive attitude was unsettling me.

'I've been doing some research,' I said. 'Amongst other things, I went to see Sara Tell's mother.'

I heard Didrik sigh.

'Didn't I tell you to leave that shit alone?'

I ignored him. Again.

'The man who came to my office wasn't Bobby,' I said. 'Jeanette showed me a picture of her son. It wasn't the guy who claimed he wanted to clear his sister's name.'

Another silence on the line.

'So who was it, then?' Didrik said.

'No idea. But I'm pretty pissed off that I didn't ask the guy to show me some ID.'

I sighed as I said that. How could I have been so naïve that I didn't even ask the man calling himself Bobby to show me his driving licence?

'I can imagine,' Didrik said.

His dry tone of voice brought me up short. Then, and only then, did I hear the alarm bells.

'I've got a phone number, too,' I said, reading out the fake Bobby's mobile number. 'If you've got time, it would be great if you could help me check it out. See if it's cropped up in other cases, that sort of thing.'

'I might be able to do that. Anything else?'

I hesitated. In the end I decided to tell him the rest of what I'd found out.

'So you met Marion?' Didrik said. 'Interesting woman.

Good that you seem to have taken in what she told you. You can't deny that it reinforces the suspicion that Sara was guilty, can you?'

I raised my eyebrows in surprise.

'Sorry, but did you know Sara used to be in a gang that beat people up? If you did, why wasn't there anything about that in the preliminary investigation?'

'The information we had was very hard to substantiate,' Didrik said. 'And we didn't need it. As you know, we had plenty of other evidence.'

I didn't agree.

Didrik went on before I had time to say anything.

'It's a coincidence that you've called, because we were about to try to get hold of you,' he said. 'We need to talk to you again. Would you mind coming down here?'

In spite of the polite phrasing, I could detect an order in his tone. That worried me.

'Sure,' I said slowly. 'What's this about?'

'We can talk about that when you get here.'

'Talk about what? Didrik, if . . .'

'Save your questions and get down here. Preferably right away.'

I felt a familiar stubbornness flare up.

'What happens if I don't come? I've got a few other things to be getting on with.'

Didrik cleared his throat.

'If you don't come voluntarily in the next half an hour, I'm afraid I shall send someone to pick you up. Which would you prefer?'

27

Good lawyers are a rarity. Those that *are* good tend to be busy and are therefore difficult to get hold of when you need them. Lucy was both accessible and good. She's more than good. Brilliant, you could say.

She reminded me of the most important points on the way to Police Headquarters.

'Don't answer any questions he doesn't ask.'

'We don't even know what he wants.'

'Yes, we do. You're suspected of committing a crime. Otherwise he wouldn't have threatened to come and get you.'

My gut feeling told me she was right, but the thought was so difficult to take in that I chose to avoid it.

We were marching quickly down Sankt Eriksgatan. At the junction with Fleminggatan we turned left and walked for the second time in a matter of days past those dull buildings. When we reached the crossing with Polhemsgatan we had to wait for the lights.

'Couldn't he have said what this was about on the phone?' Lucy said.

Her dark glasses covered half her face, but I could still see the tension in her features. Sadly I had no consolation to offer. I was far too worried myself.

'Hopefully it's all a misunderstanding,' I said. 'You'll see, we'll be out of there as fast as we arrived.'

A police officer came down and fetched us from reception. We were escorted to a floor I'd never visited before and shown into an interview room. There we had to wait for quarter of an hour before Didrik and one of his colleagues appeared. It was the same man I'd met on Sunday morning. On that occasion we had sat in Didrik's office. It felt a long time ago.

We greeted each other politely. As if we were no more than fleeting acquaintances who hadn't seen each other for a very long time.

'Thank you for coming so promptly,' Didrik said. 'I'm sorry to be late getting here. Something came up that I had to deal with.'

I made a generous gesture with my hands.

'That sort of thing happens to the best of us,' I said.

Lucy gave me a long glance, but said nothing. Wise of her.

Didrik stared intently at some documents he had brought with him. Eventually he lifted his eyes from them.

'Can you tell me what you were doing between one o'clock and three o'clock in the night between Friday and Saturday?' he said.

'I was at the Astrid Lindgren Children's Hospital. With Belle.'

'I can vouch for that,' Lucy said.

Didrik looked surprised.

'I see, so you slept at the hospital as well?'

'No, I left around nine o'clock.'

'So how do you know where Martin was at two o'clock?' Lucy retreated.

'Obviously I don't know. But Martin was already in bed when I left.'

It made me sound like a child who had been put to bed in a cot I couldn't get out of. 'He was already in bed. With a nice big nappy over his backside.'

'I see,' Didrik said. 'But unless you chained him to the bed, I presume we can agree that he could have left when you weren't there?'

Lucy blushed and gave a brief nod.

'I could have left, but I didn't,' I said firmly.

I was starting to get fed up of Didrik's games. The clock was ticking and I could think of a thousand things that were more important than sitting in Police Headquarters fooling around.

'You didn't leave Belle's room at all that night?'

'No.'

'And there were just the two of you in the room?'

'Yes.'

'Do you recall if you slept soundly?'

'What do you think? Of course I didn't. I was shaken up by what had happened. And it was hot in the room, and I wasn't allowed to open the window.'

That was when I remembered that I had actually gone outside.

'Hang on,' I said. 'Sorry, there's been so much going on in the past few days. I did go outside.'

'So what are you actually saying?' Didrik's colleague said sourly.

Lucy looked at me in surprise.

'I went outside the hospital briefly to get some fresh air. I couldn't sleep properly and, like I said, it was too hot.'

'So you walked out of the hospital in just your pyjamas?'

'No, I pulled on a pair of trousers and a top.'

'And when was this?'

I tried to remember the exact time.

'Sometime around three, maybe. I don't remember more exactly than that.'

Didrik thumbed a sheet of paper he had in front of him.

'I thought the hospital was locked at night,' he said.

'It was,' I said. 'When I went back inside I had to ask a guard to open the door for me.'

Only then did I realise where the interview was going.

I stifled a deep sigh.

'But of course you already know that,' I said. 'You've spoken to the guard and you know I went outside the hospital that night.'

Didrik's face hardened.

'Correct,' he said. 'The guard confirmed what you just said. That he let you in just after three o'clock. What we now need to know is what time you went outside?'

Time stood still. The room was so quiet that I could hear myself breathe.

In and out.

In and out.

'Didrik, I was outside no longer than twenty minutes at the most.'

'Who can confirm that?'

I ran my hand across the table top.

'No one.'

'You didn't see a single person when you went out?'

I thought for several long moments.

'No,' I eventually said. 'Sadly not.'

Didrik looked dejected.

'You have to understand how this looks,' he said. 'A young woman was knocked down and killed on a pedestrian crossing. From what we've been able to see from the damage to your car, she could have been killed by your Porsche. You yourself can't provide a firm alibi for the time of the murder. We've turned your car inside out. There's nothing to suggest that anyone has tampered with it. We've also taken the liberty of inspecting your garage. According to the owner of the property, it's been two years since you last had a break-in.'

I forced myself to stay calm. The conversation had taken a turn that I couldn't have foreseen even in my wildest fantasies.

'You say Jenny could have been killed by my Porsche,' I said. 'Could have been. You're not certain?'

'How certain do we need to be?' Didrik said. 'None of us seriously believes that Jenny came into contact with more than one Porsche-owner during her stay in the city.'

'Now hang on a minute,' I began.

Didrik slammed his hand down on the table, making me jump.

'If you have anything to tell us, this is your best opportunity to do so!'

Lucy squirmed and I ran my hands over my head.

'This is crazy,' I said.

'At least we agree on that,' Didrik said.

I tried to take it from the beginning.

'I was the one who came to you,' I said. 'I called and told you that Bobby had been to see me. He contacted me, not the other way round. Same thing with Jenny Woods. I have no idea what's going on, but you have to agree that it looks like I've walked into a pretty elaborate trap?'

I was out on thin ice and I knew it. I was pleading, and that's never good. But on the other hand, I had just pointed out something important, and Didrik knew it.

'Sure,' Didrik said. 'If it is a trap, it's astonishingly well planned. I'm the first to admit that was my initial reaction when this whole circus started. But now I have to take this new information into account.'

He had done a good job. I had to give him that. Even so, my heart was racing in my chest. Because I couldn't explain how someone could have taken my car without leaving the slightest trace behind them. Not even Lucy had keys to the car and garage.

'You haven't let the keys out of your sight at all?' Didrik said.

'No.'

'Never?'

I reflected.

'Yes,' I said. 'Once. You had them. You borrowed the Porsche for a friend's stag party.'

An awkward silence filled the room.

'I'd like to go further back in the story,' Didrik said. 'You said just now that it was Bobby who came to see you, not the other way round.'

I nodded, relieved not to have to discuss the Porsche, which seemed to have developed a life of its own.

'But when you called me half an hour or so ago, you said it wasn't Bobby who came to your office. Which is it?'

I groaned out loud. This was going badly wrong.

'Excuse me,' Lucy said. 'But what does Bobby have to

do with this? The fact that he has only just found out that
it wasn't Bobby who came to our office ought to support
Martin's account.'

Didrik focused his attention on Lucy.

'Have you met him as well?'

'No.'

'Spoken to him on the phone?'

'No. Once again – how is this relevant?'

Didrik pulled a picture from the pile of papers in front
of him. He put it on the table. I looked at it. It was the man
Jeanette had shown me a photograph of and said it was Bobby.

'I can see that you recognise him,' Didrik said.

'That looks like the guy in the photograph Jeanette Roos
showed me.'

'You mean he looks like Bobby?'

'Yes. If that's what Bobby looks like.'

'It is,' Didrik said. 'And he's dead.'

I jerked back involuntarily.

'Dead?'

'He was also run down and killed on Friday night. Without
any witnesses, unfortunately, which is why it's taken longer
to ascertain the cause of death. It also took a while to get
confirmation of his identity.'

My mouth was dry as dust.

'Some water?' Didrik's colleague said.

I accepted a glass in silence.

'The pathologist has been able to determine a fairly precise
time of death. Sometime between two and three o'clock that
night. Need I say that we find this troubling? That someone
else you can be linked to was run down and killed on the
same night?'

I put the glass down hard. Once again I forced myself to breathe as slowly as I could. I didn't succeed terribly well this time. Lucy put a hand on my arm but I pulled away.

'You think I murdered these two people? Are you mad?'

I shouted the last three words.

Lucy tried to calm me down while Didrik and his colleague sat impassive on the other side of the table.

'According to Jeanette Roos, Bobby wasn't even in Stockholm. She said he was in Switzerland,' I said.

'Then she was lying,' Didrik said. 'Or else just badly informed. We've been in touch with Bobby's girlfriend. He does live in Switzerland but he's been in Stockholm for at least the past three weeks.'

I didn't know what to say. All I wanted was to stand up and walk out of there.

'Can you look me in the eye and tell me you've never seen this man?' Didrik said slowly, holding the picture up.

I looked into his grey eyes.

'I've never met him,' I said in a firm voice.

'This isn't the man who came to your office?'

'No.'

Didrik read the sheet of paper at the top of the pile. He rattled off a phone number and asked if I recognised it. I said I didn't memorise the contact details of people I knew.

'Whose number is it?' I said.

'Bobby was carrying a phone with that number,' Didrik said.

I shrugged my shoulders.

'Then it makes perfect sense that I don't recognise it,' I said.

Didrik smiled.

'I know we can all suffer from a poor memory, but I thought you might have recognised that particular number.'

'Because?'

Didrik looked genuinely troubled.

'Because it's the number you yourself read out to me less than an hour ago and asked me to help trace.'

PART IV

'Lotus?'

INTERVIEWER: FREDRIK OHLANDER (FO),
freelance journalist.

LOCATION:
Room 714, Grand Hôtel, Stockholm.

FO: Okay, let's see if I've understood this
correctly. At this point you still didn't
know who came to see you and got you
interested in Sara Texas's case?

MB: That's right.

FO: But the real Bobby Tell was dead? Like
Sara's friend from Houston, Jenny Woods?

MB: Correct.

FO: And the police thought you'd murdered them?

MB: That was where the evidence was pointing.

FO: You must have been seriously freaked out.

MB: Also correct.

(Silence)

FO: You haven't explained why you wanted to meet here at the Grand Hôtel. In this particular room. Something tells me that isn't just coincidence.

MB: You're doing it again. Getting ahead of events.

FO: So there is a reason why we're meeting in this particular location?

MB: There is. But we're not there yet.

FO: So what happened with the police? They didn't remand you in custody?

MB: The evidence wasn't strong enough. And they didn't have a credible motive. Asking for me to be held in custody would only have made things harder for them. But after we left Police Headquarters that day we both assumed we were being watched. Physically and electronically.

FO: What sort of surveillance are we talking about here? Phone-tapping?

MB: Phone-tapping, internet monitoring, physical surveillance. The whole lot. Twenty-four hours a day.

FO: Presumably they imposed official restrictions as well?

MB: They asked me to stay in Stockholm. So I could be available for subsequent interviews.

FO: And did you do that?

MB: No.

28

The plane tickets cost fifty-five thousand kronor. We were going to be flying the day after the interview with the police, Lucy and I. Business class. If you're going down, you may as well do it in style. My fate had merged with Sara's. My only chance of clearing my name was to find the person who had earlier framed Sara. That was the conclusion I drew from everything that had happened.

'Don't do anything stupid now, Martin,' was the last thing Didrik said to me when we parted.

His remark was almost comical. The concept of 'stupid' had shifted from defined to fluid in the space of an hour. I had been wrongly accused of the murders of two people. One of whom I had never even met. It was a stroke of sheer luck for the real murderer that I had been out to get some air the night I spent at the hospital with Belle. If I hadn't done that my alibi would have been unimpeachable.

The dilemma for the police was that all their information was too vague, not strong enough to have me remanded in custody. They believed my car was the one involved in both hit and runs, but they couldn't prove it. They believed they could dismantle my alibi, but they weren't sure. And they lacked any suggestion of a motive. The question they were struggling with was obvious: why would I have killed Bobby Tell and Jenny Woods? I was terrified of the moment they thought they had an answer to that question, because then I'd be finished. For good.

I didn't have the slightest doubt that the person who had gone to such trouble to frame me was going to help the police to understand my motivation. So I was in a hell of a hurry to put a stop to this madness. It was only a matter of days, or perhaps a week or so, before I would find myself remanded in custody without bail.

Lucy didn't hesitate about coming to Texas with me. But we spent hours debating whether or not we should take Belle. To me it was a question of her physical safety.

'This isn't a family holiday,' Lucy said. 'Taking her would be a huge risk. If Didrik finds out that you've left the country and also taken your daughter with you, he'll think you've gone on the run.'

'So what do you suggest I do? Leave Belle in Stockholm?'

'No, with her paternal grandparents at their cottage in the archipelago. After all, she's been looking forward to going to see them. She'll be safe there, out in the country with them.'

Naturally. She was right about everything.

Belle was actually my biggest worry. If anything happened to me, if I died or ended up in prison, she would be back to square one. Without parents, and without a safety net. And there'd be no one to save her from growing up with foster parents in Skövde. Just thinking about it was physically painful. And I felt a rage so intense that it frightened me. Belle and

I had come a hell of a long way together. I simply couldn't accept that someone was trying to take what we'd built up away from us.

Not without a fight.

Not without one hell of a battle.

Belle was the last thing I would give up. That was all there was to it.

So I found myself calling her grandparents and explaining as briefly as I could that I needed their help. I didn't tell them exactly what had happened, but they could hear from my voice that it was important for them to be there for me.

'I see you're calling from a phone with a hidden number,' Belle's grandfather said. 'Is that something new you've started doing?'

'It's only temporary,' I said. 'I'll let you have a new number you can reach me on.'

The first thing Lucy and I did when we got back to the office after seeing the police was to switch off our mobiles and remove the batteries. We tucked them away in a cupboard and Lucy, whom we assumed they wouldn't be tailing physically, popped out to get new ones. Just in case she was being followed – by the police or our as yet unknown antagonist – she went to a lot of effort to shake anyone off. She changed underground trains four or five times. She walked right round a number of shops before finally buying what she wanted. She paid in cash, then came back to the office. The police weren't stupid, of course. They'd try to pick up the signals from our new phones, so we had to be very restrictive in our use of them. If the police got hold of the new numbers they'd be no good to us. For that reason Lucy had bought eight phones, and the same number of SIM cards.

We went to similar lengths to minimise the risk of our internet use being monitored. And we daren't take any risks when it came to the possible bugging of the office. Anything sensitive was communicated in writing, on sheets of paper that we then burned. When we needed to have longer conversations we went out into the stairwell.

I was reluctant to go home that day. But in the end I had no choice.

Belle had had a lovely day with Signe. But children have a razor-sharp ability to read social situations. Belle figured out that something was wrong immediately.

I picked her up in my arms and tried to joke my own anxiety away. It didn't work.

'You're going to go and stay with Grandma and Granddad,' I said. 'Tomorrow.'

'Tomorrow?'

I explained that some things had happened. So-called grown-up things. Nothing to worry about, nothing nasty, but it would be best if Lucy and I could be on our own for a little while.

'How long?' Belle said.

'A week,' I said. 'Then we'll be home again.'

That was what I hoped, anyway, that it would take a week to shed some light on the conspiracy I had evidently been dragged into.

Belle slept in my bed that night. It was impossible to get her to sleep in her own. I lay on my back for ages waiting for her to settle down. Then I crept out of the bedroom and started to pack. There are no curtains in the flat, but I've got blinds. I lowered them all. Belle and Signe had been at home all day and there hadn't been any visitors. So the flat hadn't been searched, and it hadn't been bugged. Presumably they were waiting for an opportunity when the flat was empty. That made me feel a little safer, even if it was only a modest relief. I no longer knew what inner peace was. The fact that I had been looking forward to a trip to the Riviera as recently as a week ago seemed quite incomprehensible.

Logistics. There's nothing more vital in any emergency situation. I don't know how many times I ran through our plan before we set off. I would drive Belle out to her grandparents the next morning. Then I would pick Lucy up and together we would make our way to Arlanda. The hire car would have to sit in the long-stay car-park. That was going to be a seriously expensive car.

I made the most important phone call of the day once my bags were packed. He answered on the third ring. My friend Boris. Well, not my friend. Acquaintance. And a dubious one at that. I was pleased I had such a choice of mobiles. Because it really wouldn't be great if the police noticed that particular contact just then.

'It's been a while,' Boris said when he answered.

His voice sounded the same, even though I hadn't heard it for several years. Smoky and hoarse. Well-used, as Lucy once described it.

'It has,' I said. 'Far too long. Sorry about that.'

Boris laughed.

'Don't worry, my friend,' he said. 'You're not the only one to blame. I have – how can I put it? – been busy, not easy to get hold of. I was on the point of ditching the number you just called, so you're lucky to get hold of me.'

I thanked my lucky stars that he had answered. It wouldn't

have felt good to leave Sweden without talking to Boris first. Not good at all.

'I'm very pleased you answered,' I said.

He fell silent. I heard a noise in the background. Possibly a chair scraping the floor.

'What's happened?' he said.

He knew I wouldn't have called him otherwise. We weren't friends in the sense that we met up regularly over a cup of coffee.

'I can't go into detail,' I said. 'The short version is that I'm in the shit. Seriously in the fucking shit, even. Someone's trying to frame me for a double murder.'

'What?'

'Don't interrupt, I haven't got time to explain. Lucy and I are going away for a week, to try to get to the bottom of this whole mess. I need . . .'

'Hang on a moment.'

My heart-rate increased as I squeezed the phone. I didn't have time to wait, and no time to listen.

'You said I could call you if I ever needed help,' I said. 'I'll never need help more than I do right now.'

'Okay, I can hear it in your voice. You don't have to tell me how badly you need help, I've worked that out. What I'm wondering is something else you said. That you and Lucy are – how did you put it? – going to get to the bottom of this. Are you crazy? I mean, you don't know how to play a game where someone else's opening gambit is a double murder, do you?'

I ran my hand along the cool kitchen worktop. The kitchen smelled faintly of food. My stomach started to rumble and I found myself wondering if I'd ever come back to the flat.

'I refuse to see this as a game,' I said. 'I see it as an

investigation that needs to be conducted, and I'm pretty good at that. But . . .'

'But you need protection?'

'Not me. Belle.'

Silence once more.

'Martin, listen to me,' Boris said quietly. 'I know what you did for me. I'll never forget that. Believe me, I'd be dead if it weren't for you. So I'm prepared to do pretty much anything you ask me for. But looking after Belle. Christ, you can't be serious? Do you really want to entrust that lovely little kid to an old ogre like me?'

For the first time that day I burst out laughing.

It almost felt as if Boris was repaying his debt by spreading a little happiness in my life.

'We ought to meet up more often so we get better at understanding each other,' I said, turning serious again. 'I don't want her to stay with you, I want you to keep a watchful eye on her while I'm gone. If you can't watch her yourself, I want you to ask someone you trust to do it. I can pay handsomely if need be. Money isn't a problem, as long as I know I can rely on the person concerned.'

'That makes more sense,' Boris said, sounding relieved. 'Where's she going to be while you're gone?'

The thought of leaving Belle with Boris for a week was still making me smile. She'd never have recovered from a trauma like that.

'She's going to be staying with her father's parents out in the archipelago.'

I described where, and Boris asked a few more questions.

'I'll put my best men on it,' he said. 'Don't worry about payment, it's on me, no question.'

If he hadn't owed me a favour I'd never have accepted an arrangement like that, but I was happy to now. When it comes to guys like Boris, mafia bosses with contacts all over the world, from China to Russia to South America, you have to stay in credit. Because his debt-collectors don't function like the rest of us.

I felt relief spread through my body. Thank God, at least Belle was okay now.

'I have to admit that I don't know if she's under any kind of real threat,' I said. 'But I've got reason to believe that whoever started all this crap has harmed a child the same age as her before.'

My thoughts went to Mio, who vanished the day his mother Sara died.

'Say no more,' Boris said. 'I'm genuinely pleased you called. It's bothered me for years that I haven't had a chance to repay you.'

Exactly what I had done for Boris only he and I knew. Lucy knew of his existence, and had met him once. She avoided asking anything about him, and I was grateful for that. She had only asked me one question: 'Why did he come to you, of all people?'

I didn't have a good answer to that. Nor did Boris. The situation with Boris was a bit like Bobby, really; for some reason I attract the strangest people with the hardest problems. And deep down I'm probably rather pleased about that.

After I finished my call to Boris I phoned Lucy one last time.

'All ready for tomorrow?' she said.

'All ready,' I said.

'Good, see you then,' she said.

I hung up with a guilty feeling in my chest. I hadn't only

got myself caught in the shit, I'd also got it smeared all over the only people I've ever loved. Shit's like that, it sticks to whoever's standing closest.

The problem with this particular dirt was that I didn't know how to get rid of it. My usual solution, to buy myself free, wasn't going to work. It didn't matter if I had all the damn money in the world – I didn't even know who I ought to give it to.

I had to try to unwind and get a few hours' sleep. Otherwise everything would go to hell before I'd even got to the airport.

Out of all the things I had to think about, my anonymous enemy troubled me least. Who was the man who had come to my office to plead for help on his sister's behalf?

He wasn't Bobby, as he had claimed.

Nor was he Sara Texas's ex-boyfriend Ed – I'd seen a picture of him in Sara's mother's flat.

So who the hell was he, and what were his motives?

And, maybe even more importantly: had he come to see me of his own volition, or was he working for someone else?

29

Two murders, not five. I tried to turn that into a mantra rolling round my head of its own accord. To stop us thinking about the fact that Sara had been accused of five murders and concentrate on the two she was supposed to have committed in the USA. In the end it worked pretty well. Maybe even for Lucy, who hadn't said anything on the subject of guilt since our chat on the roof terrace.

Our flight to New York took off at quarter to eleven in the morning. I had no trouble leaving the country. Whether that was through sloppiness or naivety I don't know, but either way, the police hadn't bothered to seize my passport or block it. We would have a four-hour wait for the connection to Texas. Lucy and I sat in our throne-like seats eating nuts.

'If the circumstances were different, this could have been a really nice trip,' Lucy said.

I didn't reply. The memory of how it had felt to hand Belle over to her grandparents was still far too painful. If I hadn't known that Boris would be keeping an eye on her, she would have had to come with us to the US. I'd never have left her without being convinced she was safe. I didn't expect any help from the police.

'Where are you going?' Belle's grandfather had asked when we met at the little harbour where he'd left the motorboat that would take them out to the island.

'USA,' I said.

'How do I reach you?'

'On the number I gave you yesterday. Or by email.'

He nodded. Out of all Belle's relatives on her father's side, her grandfather was the one I liked best. A thoughtful older man who didn't ask too many questions and who seemed to think it best if people could keep things to themselves.

'Good luck,' he said, and shook my hand.

He could see that something had happened, but had the sense not to ask more questions.

'Thanks,' I said. 'And thank you for looking after Belle.'

He rested a hand on her head.

'You never have to thank us for that. We should be thanking you. Again. For sorting everything back then. That time . . .'

We had talked about it, he and I. He agreed with me. It was a disgrace that Belle's aunt, his daughter, wouldn't take her. It would have been great for Belle to grow up with children the same age and two parents. Now she had me instead. Which wasn't too bad, on the whole, but it could have been better.

Lucy stroked my arm and brought me back to the present.

'Are you okay, Martin?'

'No.'

I closed my eyes and leaned back against the headrest. My body had been running on adrenalin, and it had exhausted me. I hadn't set foot in the USA in over two years. I'd sworn never to go back. Yet there I was, sitting in a plane that was roaring across the Atlantic. God alone knew what demons and ghosts from the past the trip was going to wake up.

While a lot of people knew that I had once been a police officer in the USA, not many of them knew how I had ended up there. Not that it was a particularly remarkable story. That was where my dad was from. The man who had once abandoned me and never come back. After high school I took my lovely grades and headed off to Texas to meet him. Maybe I thought he would be able to answer some of my many questions. He had a new family, I found out. He didn't want to be reminded of crap from the past, and asked me to leave him in peace.

I didn't. Because I thought that if he was given a bit of time he would regret pushing me away. I was born in the USA, so have American citizenship. My parents met while my dad was an exchange student in Stockholm. When they realised Marianne was pregnant they went to the USA and lived there for two years. All so that I would have the same citizenship as my dad, and to give Marianne a chance to get to know her husband's home environment.

When I was one year old they decided to move back to Sweden. Marianne set off first with me and all the luggage. My dad was going to follow along later. But he never did. He called Marianne and said he'd changed his mind. He didn't want her, or me. According to Marianne that's when her problems started. The drinking and smoking. Everything got better when she met the guy from Sälen who became my sister's father, but when he walked out as well things fell apart again.

I remember the astonishment I felt when I first arrived in the USA. I had expected to feel at home, to discover that I was much more American than Swedish. That didn't happen. At first I thought it was because there was something wrong with Houston, where my dad lived. So I tried living in Dallas for a while instead. That didn't work either, so I went back to Houston. I can't really remember the details of how I ended up in the police force. It certainly wasn't something I'd ever thought about back home in Sweden. But suddenly the opportunity presented itself, and I had nothing better planned. The training was only a year and a half, and then I got my first job. I lasted a year before resigning and returning to Sweden after another tragic encounter with my so-called dad.

Twelve years passed before I went back, this time as a well-paid lawyer. My father wasn't impressed. And that was the last time I saw him. I didn't miss him before he died, and I haven't missed him since.

It took less than half an hour for me to fall asleep in my seat on the plane. I slept until we started to come down to land.

Houston was insanely hot. We landed in the afternoon and the sun was frying the tarmac until it went soft. Lucy watched the bags while I sorted out a hire car. You can say what you like about Americans, but they're good at cars.

'Did you have to get such a big car?' Lucy said as we slung our cases in the back.

'There wasn't anything else,' I said.

'Really?' Lucy said, getting into the passenger seat of the Lincoln I had hired.

I took several deep breaths of the hot air before getting behind the wheel. It felt very odd to be back. I had always felt that I didn't just have a problem with my dad but with the USA as a whole. The two of them had blurred to become one and the same thing. Simply by getting on a plane and crossing the Atlantic it felt like I had escalated the conflict.

The engine purred as I drove out of the airport. Motorways as wide as Swedish potato fields opened out as I followed the instructions of the satnav.

We were going to be staying at the Hilton in downtown Houston. Houston is a huge city. The city centre is fairly compact, but if you want to move around you need a car, or you have to use an awful lot of taxis. I could remember exactly where my dad lived but had no intention of going anywhere near that district unless I had to. His wife probably still lived in the house. Where the children were – my half-siblings – I had no idea. The years had passed and they would be grown up now. I had never felt anything for them, and they had never tried to contact me. Like fuck was blood thicker than water.

'Do you think the police know we've left yet?' Lucy said.

I had switched my old mobile back on. It was important that the police could contact me, so it didn't look like I was trying to hide.

'Don't know,' I said. 'But I did my best to shake off anyone watching me before we left, so they ought to be wondering where we've got to by now, if nothing else.'

I was keen to avoid a situation in which the Swedish police contacted their American counterparts to warn them. I wanted to talk to the police in both Houston and Galveston, and it was important that those conversations were not spoiled by the fact that I had become the subject of a murder investigation.

The Hilton Hotel looked just like the pictures. Cold and sterile. Professional staff, just the right amount of smarminess.

A bottle of chilled champagne and a bowl of fruit were waiting on the coffee table of our mini-suite.

'Nice,' Lucy said, picking up the bottle.

I had earned most of my money from shares, stock options, derivatives and God knows what else. As a lawyer I am well paid, and believe it is therefore my duty to make my assets grow. Lucy doesn't feel the same way, and thus has less money than me. She hates stocks and shares, and always thinks she's being taken for a ride before any deal has been reached. She doesn't listen to me, and nor should she. I'd never want to take responsibility for any losses that might ensue.

Nothing makes you feel shittier than flying. We tore our clothes off and went and stood in the shower. I had sex with Lucy against a cold tiled wall. It wasn't one of our better fucks, but probably one of the most needed. I had suggested having sex on the flight from New York to Houston, but Lucy said no.

'You can get fined for that,' she said.

'If that's your only objection, I think we should go to the toilet right now,' I said, unbuckling my seatbelt.

Lucy sighed and didn't move a muscle. And I decided not to raise the subject again.

After the shower, when Lucy was drying her hair, my mobile rang.

I froze in the middle of what I was doing.

The police, of course. Already.

Bloody hell.

'Martin Benner,' I said when I answered.

First there was silence, then, sure enough, I heard Didrik Stihl's voice.

'Didrik here, how are things?'

I never answer that sort of question.

He waited for a moment before he went on.

'Okay, I was just calling to say you can come and get your car.'

Bonus points to the police. They had lost track of me and were therefore offering me the chance to get my dearest possession back again. They must have broken into a cold sweat when they couldn't trace either me or my mobile.

'Thanks,' I said. 'That's good of you.'

'When will you be picking it up? Just so I let the guys in the garage know.'

I laughed.

'I'll call in sometime next week.'

I could hear how upset Didrik was from his breathing.

'Martin, for God's sake, what are you up to now?'

'Nothing for you to worry about. Just let me know if you want me to come in for more questioning. I can be there within twenty-four hours.'

Didrik let out a low groan.

'You're in the States, aren't you?'

I didn't answer.

Lucy came out from the bathroom naked. She looked at me anxiously.

'Thanks for calling, Didrik. Speak to you soon.'

'You fucking lunatic, you're in Texas, aren't you?'

'Why are you asking questions I know you can get the answers to from your marvellous surveillance technology? Look after yourself now, I'm going out to get something to eat with Lucy.'

Didrik sighed.

'I hope you know what you're doing,' he said.

Then, and not before, anger flared up inside me. Who was Didrik to say something like that to a man in my position? If he'd done his job properly in the first place, this whole story would have been very different.

I realised that I had new problems to deal with, much sooner than I had hoped. There was a distinct risk that it would now be much harder for Lucy and I to talk to the detectives the way we'd planned. So I broke one of my own cardinal rules. I lied. To gain time and to keep Didrik's pulse down at a level I could handle.

'You're right,' I said, managing to make my voice tremble. 'I'm in Texas. To bury my brother. Okay?'

Lucy stared at me as if I'd lost my mind.

'I'm sorry,' Didrik said when he had recovered. 'I didn't know you had a brother. But ... I presume he's your father's son? Or was?'

'That's right,' I said, with my heart thudding so hard with shame that it must have been visible through my chest. 'Dad's youngest. It's not easy to have a relationship with a brother who grew up on the other side of the Atlantic, but I did my best. And now he's not here any more. Don't worry, as soon as he's in the ground Lucy and I will head back to Stockholm.'

I could see Didrik before me, the way he nodded thoughtfully when he hears something that makes sense.

'That's good, Martin. The fact that you answered your phone really tells me all I needed to know. That you haven't gone on the run. Sorry to bother you. We'll speak soon.'

I ended the call and put the phone down, then met Lucy's gaze.

'Problems?' she said.

'Nothing I can't handle,' I said.

We didn't speak as we dressed. That very evening we were due to meet the sheriff Eivor had spoken about in such glowing terms. Sheriff Esteban Stiller. I'd managed to get hold of him and had spoken to him over the phone. Even though I was cagey about the details, it hadn't taken long for him to agree to a meeting.

The appointment to see the sheriff was like an oasis in the desert. God help him if he couldn't provide us with some useful information. Because time was running out for me much faster than I could ever have imagined.

30

The Old River Café was located on the edge of the Heights, the part of Houston where Sara Tell had worked as an au pair. I had never been there before, but Sheriff Esteban Stiller had. It was his suggestion that we meet there.

Eivor had described Esteban as a very nice man. After just five minutes I was inclined to agree with her. I didn't even have to ask what Lucy thought. She looked almost turned on.

'Naturally I had you checked out,' Stiller said once we had our coffees. 'You didn't last long in the force.'

'True,' I said. 'It wasn't really for me.'

'According to one of your bosses who's still here, you had a lot of potential.'

I looked down and stirred my coffee. I didn't deserve any praise for my efforts with the Houston Police Department.

Esteban leaned back in his chair.

'What about you?' he said to Lucy. 'Did you start out as a police officer as well?'

She shook her head, making her curls dance on her shoulders.

'No, I'm just a lawyer.'

Just a lawyer. As if my police training made such a difference.

'I see,' Stiller said in the inimitable way that only Americans can say those words.

I see.

Really?

'So now you're here to find out more about Sara Tell's adventures.'

The turn in the conversation came without warning and felt liberating. None of us had time to sit there talking rubbish.

'That's right,' I said. 'We're interested in anything you can tell us.'

'But you must have done a bit of reading in advance?'

'We've read pretty much everything,' Lucy said.

'Then I don't see how I can help you.'

He glanced at the time and took a sip of the beer he had ordered to go with his coffee. An incomprehensible combination, in my opinion.

'We'd like to know, for instance, if you had any other suspects for the murders in Houston and Galveston,' I said.

'What I'd like to know is why the two of you have flown all the way to Houston just to poke about in this old crap.'

He put his beer glass down hard, and the look in his eyes was no longer so friendly.

'I thought we'd already said?' I said.

'You said Sara's brother showed up in your office asking for help,' Stiller said. 'Six months after she died. And then you said you'd just started to look into the case when Bobby was suddenly murdered.'

True enough, that was what I had said. I didn't think it

would help our trip if I said it wasn't Bobby who had come to see me. Just as little as it would help my credibility to explain that I myself was now suspected of killing him.

'Do they know who was responsible for his murder?' Stiller said, as if on command.

'Not yet,' I said. 'But they're working on it.'

I pulled out the train ticket I had been given by fake Bobby, and which with Jenny Woods's testimony gave Sara Tell an alibi for the murder in Galveston. I passed it to Stiller.

'This ticket,' I said. 'Do you recognise it?'

He took it.

'Sure I do. Sara's friend brought it to us. What was her name again?'

'Jenny,' I said. 'Woods. She's also dead.'

Stiller put the ticket down slowly.

'How did she die?'

'Same way as Bobby. They were both run down within the space of an hour.'

I outlined the sequence of events as briefly as I could, still without mentioning my own supposed involvement. It suddenly struck me that it was odd for both Bobby and Jenny to be out and about so late. Where had they been going?

'Well, I'll be damned,' Stiller said.

That was the reaction I had hoped to get from Didrik.

I took the ticket back and put it in the inside pocket of my jacket.

'Makes you wonder who's got good reason to silence the two of them after such a long time,' Stiller said.

'Isn't it obvious?' Lucy said with a sharpness in her voice that I rarely heard. 'There's only one person who had any reason to want them dead: the real murderer.'

Said by the woman who, deep down, seemed convinced that
Sara, and no one else, was our culprit.

Stiller said nothing, just looked out of the big window where
we were sitting. Slowly he watched the cars driving past.

'Let's take a walk,' he eventually said, and got to his feet.

We left our cups and beer on the table. I know we never
paid for any of it.

'You think we were sloppy,' Stiller said when we had turned
into a quieter street.

Large Southern States villas decorated with flags lay
scattered on lawns that breathed of eternal summer and
inadequate rainfall. This was the kind of area my dad had
lived in.

'You think we ignored alternative culprits, and that we
didn't follow up the loose ends. But we did. We looked
under every goddamn rock. We brought Jenny's ex in for
questioning, because he'd threatened taxi drivers on several occasions when he was drunk. They tipped us off that
he might be involved. But unlike Sara he had an alibi for
every single second of that evening. He'd been in another
fight and was in a police cell pretty much the whole night
through. All very embarrassing, of course, but the officer
who arrested him hadn't done the paperwork properly and
it was all a mess.'

Stiller shrugged his shoulders as if he didn't think it was a
big deal that someone could be locked up for a whole night
without it appearing anywhere in police records.

'What about the others?' I said.

'What others?'

That made me think. Sara's father had evidently never been

in Texas. But her ex-boyfriend Ed had been. And whoever was known by the name Lucifer.

I mentioned both of these to Stiller.

He stopped mid-stride.

'You can forget Ed,' he said. 'He wasn't in the US when either of the murders took place. But Lucifer . . . How do you know that name?'

'I didn't know it was a name,' I said.

A different sort of anger flared up. They genuinely hadn't read Sara's diary.

'Just answer the question,' Stiller said sharply.

'I found out about someone called Lucifer from Sara's diary. You know, the book Jenny tried to get you and your colleagues to take an interest in?'

Stiller wiped the sweat from his brow. It was far too warm an evening to be out for a stroll.

'If it's the Lucifer I'm thinking of, he didn't have anything to do with the murders,' Stiller said, and started walking again.

'Who is he?' I said.

'Okay, we're moving away from the murder investigations that Sara was caught up in, just to make that clear.'

We nodded. We understood.

'Lucifer was the head of the biggest drug network we've ever cracked here in Texas,' Stiller said. 'I was never part of the investigation, but a lot of my colleagues were. They got away with it for years, but eventually we managed to bring them down. We arrested over fifty people in one night, at several different locations in Texas. Twice that number of illegal immigrants were caught and deported from the country. It was quite a clear-out, if I can put it like that.'

There was no mistaking his pride in his colleagues. I tried

to imagine something similar in a Swedish context. It was impossible. No one would dare to boast about deporting a hundred unregistered individuals over the course of one night.

But regardless of the boasting, he was unwilling to contemplate any link between Sara and the big mafia boss.

'Was Sara involved in drugs?' I said.

'Sara was involved in everything,' Stiller said. 'Drugs, prostitution, murder. That was clear from what we found out about her activities in Galveston. The idea that someone else stalked her across two continents and committed no fewer than five murders in her name is so stupid that it defies belief. You can forget about Lucifer. She didn't know him. She must have been referring to someone else in that diary.'

Our opinions on that matter differed, but I didn't say so out loud. I had spent days trying to imagine what Sara's enemy, the person who had framed her for five murders, had looked like. For the first time I thought I could see a hint of an answer to that question.

I forced myself to carry on walking when I would rather have stopped to catch my breath.

Drugs and prostitution and murder.

And then a single mother in glasses and a smart jacket.

I tried to use that contrast to come up with an argument in Sara's favour. But Stiller didn't buy it.

'We're talking about a damaged girl who had been on the wrong side of the law since her early teenage years,' he said. 'Someone who was sold by her own father. So you can't just look at the last years of her life and say, "What an exemplary member of society!" That's not a serious argument. When

Sara committed her first murder in Galveston she was already up to her ears in shit.'

'But how could she have been in Galveston if her friend Jenny can prove that she was in San Antonio?'

'Could,' Lucy said quietly.

'What?'

'You said she can prove that Sara had an alibi. I changed it to could.'

'Good point,' I said. 'You can't get this to make sense, Stiller. Sara didn't commit those murders. Not the one in Galveston, and not the one in Houston either. And certainly not the three she confessed to in Sweden.'

Stiller stopped again.

'I'm going to tell you something,' he said. 'Something very few people are aware of, but which unfortunately I think you need to know to stop you spending the rest of your lives chasing shadows. Can I trust you to keep what I'm about to say to yourselves?'

We were standing in the shadow of a huge cork oak. Lucy discreetly lifted the hair that was making her back hot. A pattern of sweat was visible on the fabric of her blouse.

'You can trust us,' I said, and realised that I meant it. 'We won't mention it to anyone else.'

Stiller seemed to weigh things up for a while. In the end he said, 'Okay. I might regret this, but right now I believe you need to know how I can be so certain that Sara committed the murder here in Houston.'

We waited. A dog was barking in one of the gardens and a man drove past in a big jeep. I could have been a child here. God knows what would have become of me then.

'There was a witness,' Stiller said in a low voice.

'A witness?' I repeated.

He nodded.

'A witness to what?'

My heart was racing as I waited for him to reply.

'To the murder of the taxi driver.'

31

I let out a laugh.

'A witness,' I said. 'Who doesn't appear anywhere in the file covering the preliminary investigation. A very mysterious witness.'

'Not mysterious, but deserving of protection,' Stiller said with a pointed look.

I frowned. I hoped I had misunderstood him.

'I can see you've made the connection,' Stiller said. 'At first we only had the photograph someone took of Sara when she was getting out of the taxi. After we released it to the press we got hold of an individual who had seen something. Someone who had been there, and who hid in terror behind a rubbish bin as a woman beat the taxi driver to death with a golf club. The most perfect, useless witness I've ever come across in my whole life. Because the person in question had been a witness in a high-profile drug trial in California two years earlier, and had then been given witness protection – a new identity, in other words – by the FBI.'

'So you couldn't use the information you'd been given?' I said.

'No, not in writing, and not verbally either. Inside the police only I and a handful of others knew about it. The FBI gave us an oral presentation of what the witness had said.'

A number of objections were fighting for space in my throat.

'So you never met the witness?'

'No.'

The silence that followed was as oppressive as the heat.

'Bloody hell,' I whispered.

Stiller sighed and put his hands in his trouser pockets.

'The funny thing is that we didn't know who Sara was,' he said. 'If we had, we would have brought her in at once. Instead it took us several years to get hold of her. Via the FBI we showed the witness another picture of her. And were told once again that she was the murderer.'

I ran my hands over my face.

'I don't get it,' I said. 'She was seen getting out of the taxi and going into a nightclub. So how did she find the taxi driver later?'

'Sara was on her own in the nightclub that evening,' Stiller said. 'Our theory was that she went to sell either drugs or herself, seeing as both activities went on in the basement of the club. There were witnesses who saw her leave the club just an hour later. We believe she managed to get picked up by the same driver. Maybe he tried to pay her for sex, we don't know. But for some reason he drove her into a dark alleyway and got out of the car.'

'Maybe he tried to rape her?' Lucy murmured.

'Maybe,' Stiller said. 'Either way, I regard the witness's identification of her as one hundred per cent reliable. So this talk of her being innocent – you might as well drop that.'

When he saw the look on my face he hurried to add,

'Obviously I can't say anything about the murders in Sweden. To be honest, I was extremely surprised when I found out she was a serial killer.'

I folded my arms across my chest. In spite of the wretched heat I was shivering.

'Why?' I said. 'Why was that surprising if none of the rest of it was?'

Stiller peered at me, then stared at a cat as it ran across the road.

'The murders in Galveston and Houston both showed signs of rage, an impulsiveness that suggested that they weren't premeditated. In both instances we concluded that they were a consequence of rapidly escalating conflicts. The fact that Sara used drugs probably played its part. Of course it's well known that drug-users often get irrational and paranoid. But from the little I know about the murders in Stockholm, they were different. Better planned, less violent. If you can ever say that a murder is more or less violent.'

That made sense. It all did, really. Because Sara wasn't an addict in her later years. She'd been clean. Having a son must have persuaded her to pull herself together. She looked after things, took care of her son as well as herself. So it was possible that her changed circumstances would have affected how she carried out the murders.

If that was what she had actually done.

In spite of the evidence I was being told, I couldn't get things to fit together. The decision to come to Texas suddenly seemed overwhelmingly the right thing to have done. This was where something had gone wrong, this was where Sara's chances of having a normal future had been wrecked, once and for all.

As Stiller himself pointed out, there was a very clear

dividing line between the murders in Stockholm and those in Texas. The decision to focus on the American murders had been the right one. But that didn't mean I wasn't faced with reluctantly having to admit that it looked like Sara had in fact committed one of the murders. The one in Houston. The one that was usually called 'her second murder', but which was probably her only one.

But how could all of this have happened?

And how had I, of all people, been dragged into the aftershocks of this drama?

'I'm not giving up,' I said, and felt Lucy look at me with a mixture of sympathy and exhaustion. 'Sara wasn't in Galveston the night the woman was murdered at the hotel. She was in San Antonio with Jenny Woods. And Jenny was run down and killed after telling me what she knew.'

Another car drove past. A huge Chrysler. Where would the Americans be without their massive cars? Was there anyone who ever took the bus from time to time?

'I don't think we're going to get any further,' Stiller said. 'You think one thing, I think another. So Jenny said Sara wasn't in Galveston? Interesting. Because I've got a colleague, Larry Benson, who's certain he interviewed her in Galveston after the murder because she'd been staying at the hotel where the murder took place.'

'I presume you know that Larry Benson made repeated attempts to get Sara into bed during her stay in Galveston?' I said. 'And that Sara was so unimpressed that she ended up throwing hot coffee in his face?'

For the first time I thought I was about to see Stiller laugh.

'For Pete's sake,' he said. 'You think he tried to frame Sara for murder because she spurned his advances?'

He shook his head and left the protective shade of the oak tree.

'So you know about that?' I repeated.

'No,' Stiller said. 'I'm actually pretty shocked that you believe something like that. And I don't mean the bit about Larry trying to hit on Sara, because that could well be true. But the fact that he might have lost it completely because she threw coffee at him . . .'

'Never mind the coffee,' I said. 'What I'm trying to say is that he made up the bit about her staying at the hotel because he didn't want to explain what had really happened, and how he happened to recognise an addict he hadn't seen for several years.'

Stiller became serious again.

'You never saw a transcript of the interview, did you?' I said.

'No, but she was on the list of witnesses who'd been questioned.'

I didn't know whether to laugh or cry.

'Call the hotel,' I said. 'Ask them to check their records. I swear, she wasn't there that weekend.'

But Stiller just shook his head. He suddenly stopped in front of one of the houses.

'Do you know who lives here?' he said.

Lucy and I stared stupidly at the house.

'No.'

'Sara's au pair family. If you want to get hold of them, this is where they live.'

Esteban Stiller slowly turned towards us and gave a short bow.

'And this marks the end of the tour,' he said. 'I'm going

back to the café to get my car. I can't spare you any more time. But it was a pleasure to meet you. It's always nice to meet Scandinavian idealists who refuse to see the world for the wretched place it is.'

He shook hands with Lucy, then me.

'Don't call me again,' he said, and I knew I wasn't going to defy him unless my life depended on it.

I swallowed hard. I still wasn't happy.

'Lucifer,' I said. 'I want to know more about Lucifer.'

Stiller's grip of my hand grew harder and he pulled me so close that I could smell the tobacco on his breath.

'Listen very fucking carefully to me, now. I'm giving you a final warning, and I'm doing that because I like you. Stay away from that man. You won't survive a confrontation with him. And for the last time: Sara had nothing to do with him.'

I held my ground. Stubborn and desperate for new leads.

'You have to admit it's odd that he appears in Sara's diary,' I said, pulling free.

'If she was referring to the same Lucifer, then yes. It's odd. But not unthinkable. Sara was involved in drugs and prostitution. Who knows, maybe she was on the periphery of his network? We may have missed her when we investigated him. It goes without saying that it's hard to find everyone involved in a network of that size.'

I shook my head.

'The diary gives the impression that she knew him personally.'

Stiller burst out laughing.

'Out of the question,' he said. 'A piece of advice: drop any leads that point towards Lucifer. You don't want anything to do with him.'

'I wasn't thinking of getting in touch with him in prison,' I said. 'I'd just like to talk to one of the detectives who was involved in mapping his network and activities.'

Stiller's face darkened.

'Lucifer isn't in prison,' he said.

'But you said . . .'

'I said we cracked his network. But we didn't manage to get Lucifer convicted of anything more than assault. He spent less than a year inside. Again – stop poking about in this shit. Stay away from Lucifer, and stay away from my colleagues. Because you won't find anyone who's willing to talk about him. No one at all.'

With that Stiller turned and set off down the road.

We watched him until he turned off towards the café.

It was as if he had vanished into thin air.

32

The wine in the hotel bar tasted like soap.

'Disgusting,' Lucy said, pushing the glass away.

'Who cares?' I said, gulping down the bitter liquid.

If I could have taken alcohol intravenously I'd have accepted gratefully.

'She murdered the taxi driver,' I said.

'I know,' Lucy said.

'But she wasn't in Galveston that night.'

Lucy said nothing.

I nudged her with my elbow.

'Lucy, look at me. She wasn't. Jenny was trustworthy. And she had the ticket.'

Lucy still said nothing.

'I know you think the ticket could have belonged to anyone, but I know it was Sara's.'

Only then did I notice that Lucy was on the brink of tears.

'What is it, baby?'

Pink patches appeared in her cheeks.

'What *is* it?'

She was almost shouting, and several people in the bar turned round.

I tried to get her to talk quieter but it was impossible.

'Martin, we left Stockholm in the middle of an on-going police investigation in which you're suspected of a double murder. The only witness we had who could make Sara look innocent has been killed. No matter which way we look at it, we haven't made any progress. You're still a murder suspect, we still don't know who came to the office pretending to be Bobby, and darling, we still don't have any serious evidence which proves that Sara was innocent. Quite the reverse, in fact.'

She lowered her voice.

'How can you be so certain that Jenny Woods was telling the truth? How do you know she didn't take drugs and wasn't involved in prostitution too? You've got to face the facts. Sara Tell came from a bad place, and she took bad decisions.'

I let her words hang in the air between us for a while. Our dilemma was obvious. We didn't know which of us was right. And – even worse – we didn't know how we could find out either.

'Don't you even agree that the American murders are different to the Swedish ones?' I eventually said.

Lucy toyed with her wine-glass.

'Yes,' she said. 'But I'm not sure that matters. Maybe the first two murders taught her something. That she had to be less impulsive, less careless.'

I didn't have the energy to argue. I didn't have the energy to come up with a counter-argument.

'Sod this. Let's go to bed,' I said.

Lucy took my hand as we left the bar.

'You do know I'm on your side, don't you?'

I nodded.

I did know. That was one of the few things in life I could be properly sure of.

Inside my exhausted head a plan was starting to take shape. First I wanted to meet Sara's au pair family. Not because I thought they had any vital information, but to get a better picture of Sara's time in the USA.

And then there was the guy who was known as Lucifer. I wanted to contact one of the detectives who knew about him and his network. Sheriff Stiller had said Sara had nothing to do with him, but her diary said otherwise. And if it was true that Sara was involved in drugs and prostitution, it seemed unlikely that the Lucifer mentioned in the diary could be anyone other than the drugs baron that the Texas police had caught.

But most of all I wanted to meet Larry, the policeman who had identified Sara from a photograph and who claimed to have met her in Galveston on the night of the murder there. He was the last person I thought about before I fell asleep. To my mind he was one of the key characters. He was the only person linking Sara to the scene of the murder in Galveston. If I could persuade him to change his story, Sara's alibi would look viable.

But that didn't change what Esteban Stiller had told Lucy and me, which had shaken me more than I cared to admit: that there was strong evidence indicating that Sara had murdered the taxi driver in Houston.

It must have been self-defence, I thought. It must have been a mistake.

*

When the sun rose the following morning I was lying awake, peering at the window. We had forgotten to close the curtains and now the room was bathed in sunlight. Jetlag's a bastard. If you fly west you slip into the sleep pattern of a baby, fall asleep early and wake up even earlier. If you fly east you're fucked. You never catch up. When we flew to Texas we'd been moving west. I had no idea if I was rested when I woke up at five o'clock in the morning. I just wanted the day to start so that we could get going.

I knew I was starting to lose my internal compass. I no longer knew who or what I was chasing. The truth, I had thought. But the more I found out, the more uncomfortable it was getting. Because again and again I was being confronted by details I couldn't ignore.

Such as the fact that Sara Texas's own sister believed that Sara was capable of committing five murders because she had once amused herself by beating up people on the streets of Stockholm.

And the fact that there was a witness who claimed to have seen Sara kill the taxi driver with a golf club.

And the fact that the things that had been troubling me in her account of the murders could easily be explained by her having committed at least two of the murders under the influence of serious drugs.

It wasn't looking good. Not for Sara, and not for me. It was the thought that brought me back down to earth again. Because this was no longer just about Sara Texas. Not for Lucy and me. It was also about me and why I had been dragged into this mess of bizarre events.

Lucy woke up a quarter of an hour after me.

'How early can we visit the au pair family without scaring them?' I said.

Lucy stretched.

'If we want to catch them before they go to work, we should probably be there by seven o'clock. But on the other hand that does seem like a weird time to go and see people we don't know. Shouldn't we wait until this evening?'

I didn't think so. The au pair family were too important for me to want to postpone meeting them. At twenty to seven we drove away from the Hilton to the house that Sheriff Stiller had shown us in the Heights the previous evening.

Lucy had been right. Seven o'clock was almost too late.

We found the Browns on their driveway, about to get into their respective cars. The husband drove a gigantic Hummer, the wife a slightly smaller vehicle. A Ford, a model I wasn't familiar with. There are loads of things women need to stop doing. Driving smaller cars than their husbands is one of them. Never mind the environment – this is about money and power.

They looked at us in surprise as I pulled up in front of their house and we both leapt out of the car the moment it stopped. We hadn't called to warn them that we wanted to see them – fear of rejection had been too great.

The Browns' surprise didn't exactly diminish when we introduced ourselves and explained why we were there.

'You're journalists?' the woman who had been Sara's au pair mother said.

'Lawyers,' I said.

I didn't give them the whole background story. Partly because it would have taken too long, and partly because it wouldn't increase the likelihood of their trusting us. They were in a hurry, and evidently not interested in talking about Sara.

'We've put that whole business behind us,' the man said curtly. 'We've said all we have to say to the police.'

The air was already warming up. I could feel sweat trickle down my back as I stood on the Browns' drive. I caught a glimpse of a child of about ten in one of their windows. A girl.

'You didn't have any doubts before employing Sara?' I said.

'Why do you ask?' the woman said.

I shrugged.

'I've got a four-year-old daughter myself. I'd find it very hard to entrust her to a twenty-year-old drug addict involved in prostitution, who was also a member of a gang who got their kicks attacking people in the street.'

The woman's jaw dropped and the man took a step towards me. I resisted the urge to back away.

'Who are you to come here and judge us?' he roared. 'We didn't do anything that hundreds of other families in this neighbourhood don't. Employing a stranger to look after our kids so we can both keep our careers alive. Do you suppose Sara wrote about her past and her lifestyle when she applied for the job? Hardly, because then she wouldn't have got it. We only found all that out much later.'

Much later. How could that be true? How could you not notice that you had a drug addict in your home?

'What I'm actually wondering is how come you didn't realise what Sara was like when she arrived,' I said calmly. 'I get that she didn't mention the drugs and prostitution in her application. But how did she do her job?'

The woman answered.

'She was exemplary,' she said. 'We haven't had such a good au pair since she left.'

She swallowed before going on. 'My husband and I aren't

naïve people. We know what a drug addict looks like. And Sara ... she wasn't like that. She was better than that.'

I breathed something that felt like a sigh of relief.

We had finally met someone who had something good to say about Sara.

33

The woman didn't share her husband's fiery temperament. Her whole being exuded calm reflection. I could tell just by looking at her that she wasn't the sort of woman who would have left her children with an au pair she had the slightest reason to distrust.

'I believe you,' I said. 'But try to understand my curiosity. How could Sara hide who she was from the family she saw every day, and even went on holiday with?'

The man looked sad all of a sudden. He was harder to read than his wife, but seemed a fundamentally sympathetic character.

'That's something we've given a lot of thought to,' he said in a calmer tone of voice than before. 'How could we not have known, not have realised? To be honest, we've even wondered if the police might have made a mistake. That all the bad qualities that Sara was supposed to have had were made up. But . . .'

He threw his arms out helplessly and fell silent.

'That doesn't sound very likely,' Lucy concluded.

'No, it doesn't.'

His wife fiddled with her car-keys.

'Don't misunderstand us,' she said. 'Of course we could see that Sara was troubled, almost haunted. But she seemed incredibly grateful for the chance to be part of our family. She was happy. And she did a good job. So we never questioned keeping her on. She was far keener to do a good job than any of the girls we've had from better families.'

I heard what they were saying, and saw before me the cornerstone of American society that says there's nothing better than a 'self-made man'. Sara had all the trappings of someone who had dragged herself up from the bottom and was fighting to get on in life. Yet she still hadn't managed it. Why had she been such a devoted au pair if she was simultaneously being dragged back into the gutter? Had she just been an unusually confused young woman? Or had she made a serious attempt to break away from her old life but failed?

God knows, many more than her had tried and failed.

Frustrated, I wiped away the beads of sweat that were starting to appear on my forehead.

'I've already met Jenny,' I said. 'Do you know if she had other friends here in Houston I could go and see? To get a better idea of Sara, I mean.'

The Browns looked at each other.

'There were two other au pairs she used to spend time with,' the woman said. 'Both Americans. But they don't live here any more. I don't even think they're still in Texas.'

'What about in Galveston?' Lucy said. 'We understand that you used to go there quite often.'

'We still do,' the man said. 'But I'm not aware that Sara had any friends there.'

A mobile phone rang. The man pulled it from his inside jacket pocket and excused himself.

'Now I come to think of it, there was someone,' his wife said. 'I remember Sara mentioning a Denise in Galveston. I never met her, but I know she used to work at our favourite hotel back then, the Carlton. Who knows, maybe she still works there?'

Denise. I made a mental note of the name.

I wondered with wry amusement what the Browns' current favourite hotel was. They had evidently tired of the Carlton.

'How come Sara stopped working for you if it was all going so well?' Lucy said.

Sara's former au pair mother let out a sigh.

'We wondered that too,' she said. 'Some time during the spring of 2008 she changed. She spent almost all her free time in her room, she never went out in the city. Then came the news that she wanted to leave. Two weeks later she was gone. In hindsight we figured out that her behaviour changed when the taxi driver was murdered. At least the timing seemed to fit, anyway. My husband and I didn't recognise Sara in that picture the police released after the murder. But she recognised herself, of course.'

I was thinking out loud: 'Strange that she wasn't in more of a hurry to leave the country after the murder. If I'd killed someone, I wouldn't be cool enough to wait several weeks before getting to safety.'

The woman nodded eagerly.

'That's exactly what we thought. Because she was taking a huge risk. But if she was such a hardened criminal as the police say, perhaps it wasn't so strange. And it would have attracted more attention if she'd upped and left us overnight.'

I put my hands in my trouser pockets and looked the woman right in the eyes.

'Tell me,' I said. 'What do you and your husband think? Did Sara murder all those people she was accused of killing?'

There was a pause before she answered. Her husband finished his phone call and came back.

'I don't know,' she said. 'I'm not a police officer, and I'm not a lawyer. But I've been forced to realise that it can sometimes be hard to know someone as well as you might wish. However much I might want Sara to have been innocent, there are still certain facts that I can't close my eyes to. Why didn't she get in touch with the police when they started looking for her? And if she was so desperate to have a normal life, what was it that drew her to circles where drugs and prostitution were commonplace?'

Sara Tell was becoming more and more of a paradox. And in my world such things lack all credibility. A paradox is based upon something having two contradictory sides. But I'm of the firm opinion that these two sides are never equally valid. There's always one that has the upper hand. The contradiction is therefore only superficial, more like a façade hiding a well-concealed truth. Often an uncomfortable one, at that.

I remembered something else I had been thinking about.

'Were you ever questioned by the police about the murder in Galveston?'

'Sorry?' the man said, starting to look angry again.

I hurried to reassure him.

'As witnesses, not suspects. Sara had a long weekend off. Did the police ever ask you where she told you she was going?'

'No,' the man said. 'But they didn't need to. One of the

police officers recognised her. He questioned her at the scene that night.'

'We could never have said with any certainty where Sara went that weekend,' the woman said. 'But we both remember her talking about Galveston. And not San Antonio. We offered to help book the hotel but Sara declined our help. She said she already had a place to stay.'

Of course she did. But in San Antonio, not Galveston.

'Was there anything else you wondered about?' I said. 'Anyone she knew who seemed a bit suspicious, anyone causing trouble for her?'

I know you're not supposed to ask leading questions but sometimes I do anyway. Particularly when I haven't got time to wait for the correct answer.

The Browns looked thoughtful.

'I know she had problems with an ex-boyfriend from Sweden,' the wife said. 'But I suppose you already know about him?'

Yes, we did.

'You never heard anything about a boyfriend in San Antonio?' Lucy said.

They just shook their heads in response. That bothered me.

'Really?' I said. 'Would it surprise you if I told you that Sara wasn't in Galveston when the girl was murdered there, but in San Antonio instead? With Jenny. To see a guy she'd just got together with.'

The woman looked like she didn't know whether to laugh or cry.

'By now there's very little that would surprise us,' she said. 'You must appreciate that yourself. But we never heard anything about a boyfriend in San Antonio.'

The man looked at his watch and grimaced.

'I wish we could be of more help, but we both need to get off to work now.'

'I understand,' I said. 'Thanks very much for your time.'

I gave them a card on which I had scribbled my new contact details.

'Call me,' I said. 'If you think of anything else. Anything at all.'

It was the woman who took the card. She blurted out: 'There was one more thing. That peculiar tattoo she got in Galveston.'

'What?' I said.

'Yes,' the man said. 'Out of the blue Sara suddenly had a name tattooed on the back of her neck. It got infected, took weeks to heal.'

'She was so secretive about what the name meant,' the woman said. 'She claimed it was a nickname she'd been given in Sweden, but I never heard anyone use it. She didn't either, come to that.'

The sun was burning my back.

'What was the name?' Lucy said.

Lucifer, I thought. Say Lucifer, so I've got something to go on.

But that wasn't it.

'The name was Lotus.'

'Lotus?'

'Yes. Just that. Lotus.'

And with that, the field of play expanded to include yet another name.

Lotus.

A name that someone had branded onto the back of Sara Texas's neck.

34

We left the au pair family when they couldn't spare us any more time. And the hunt went on. The hunt for the truth about Sara Texas, and the hunt for proof of my own innocence. Tirelessly we went on fighting for a story that so many people seemed keen to conceal and forget.

New leads were falling out of the sky like confetti.

Sara's diary featured someone called Lucifer.

The name Lotus was tattooed on the back of her neck.

But no one was either able or willing to help us understand the whole picture. We knew a lot, but our overall understanding of what was going on was extremely limited.

'The most highly populated ghost-town in the world,' Lucy said when we were back downtown.

It was a fitting description of what claimed to be the fourth largest city in the USA, but which seemed as deserted as if someone had let off an atom bomb.

'It's the heat,' I said. 'People prefer to be underground in hot weather like this.'

'Underground?' Lucy echoed.

I parked the car at the hotel and took her for a short walk. I showed her the extensive network of tunnels that links a large number of places in the centre of Houston. The Americans know no boundaries in their attempts to make life more comfortable. On some level I find that deeply admirable. I'm a lazy bastard myself.

Hand in hand we spent an hour exploring subterranean Houston. Lucy said very little. I was starting to detect a change in her. She was losing the spark. I squeezed her hand and tried a smile. She didn't return it.

Under different circumstances I would have been more attentive. But not this time. We weren't just running out of time – it felt like it had already run out, as if I had been on borrowed time right from the start. I no longer checked my watch, it was as if I had an inbuilt clock inside me. And I felt I couldn't waste any more time sightseeing.

'We need to hurry,' I said when Lucy stopped to buy two croissants for breakfast.

She didn't answer. I knew what she was thinking. If we didn't have time to eat, we might as well lie down and die there and then.

I had managed to get hold of Larry the policeman as we were driving away from the Brown family's house. His name cropped up in a number of newspaper articles online. But I hadn't seen any pictures of him.

To my surprise, he wasn't as uncooperative as I had assumed he would be. Wary, but not impossible. He wasn't averse to dropping by our hotel to talk about the police work that led to him recognising Sara from Galveston, and thus being able to identify her as a murder suspect.

It only served to increase the pressure I felt.

'We need to figure out if she really was in Galveston that night,' I said to Lucy when she had paid for the croissants. 'Or if that's just something our friend Larry made up.'

'And you think he's going to admit that to two strangers in a hotel lobby?' Lucy said.

She was radiating deep scepticism as she snuck a bite of her croissant. I followed her example and ended up with crumbs all over my shirt.

'Of course not,' I said irritably. 'But he might let something slip.'

When we got back, the hotel lobby was empty. We may not have known what Larry looked like, but I imagined we'd be able to recognise each other. We sat down in a couple of armchairs and waited. Businessmen came and went. No sign of a policeman.

Just as I pulled out my mobile and was about to call him the doors slid open. A uniformed man in his thirties appeared. He had ruddy cheeks and was wearing sunglasses. He didn't remove them until he reached our chairs.

'Martin Benner?'

I hurried to stand up.

He held his hand out.

'Good to meet you.'

We couldn't thank him enough for taking the time to see us. He settled down warily on a sofa that was slightly too far away from us.

'I don't honestly see how I can help you,' he said. 'I mean, I can't see that there's anything that isn't clear.'

A lot of people seemed to share that opinion. I decided not to waste time. In a few simple sentences I described my dilemma. That I was unwilling to doubt the word of a police officer, but that I didn't see how it was compatible with Jenny Woods's testimony saying that she and Sara had been in San Antonio on the night of the murder. I didn't mention the fact that Jenny had told me Larry had hit on Sara and been rejected with a cup of hot coffee in the face.

Larry Benson listened impassively.

'I'll answer your question,' he said when I had finished. 'Not because I have to, but because I want you to learn a lesson. It's not a smart move to set more store in a whore than a police officer. Someone of your background ought to realise that, but okay, let's play this by your rules.'

I responded by mimicking his own expression. I didn't move so much as a muscle in my face. Without looking at Lucy I knew she was doing the same. But inside me the question marks were growing and multiplying.

Whore?

Jenny too?

Objections were piling up in my throat. But Larry Benson hurried on.

'It's not my fault you haven't done your homework,' he said. 'Just so I understand this right – and please don't waste time by not answering honestly – you're wondering if I made up the fact that Sara was at the hotel in Galveston the night one of the cleaners was murdered there?'

I didn't hesitate.

'Yes,' I said. 'That's exactly what I'm wondering.'

'How come?'

'Because we, or rather I, met Jenny Woods before she died. And she told me she had been with Sara in San Antonio that night.'

Larry's eyes grew wider.

'Sorry, Jenny Woods is dead?'

His surprise was genuine. So he hadn't heard that we'd met Sheriff Stiller the previous evening.

'She was run down and killed on a pedestrian crossing. The police think it was murder.'

I'm not sure if I saw correctly, but a twitch seemed to flit across Larry's face. What I'd just told him had unsettled him.

Then he pulled himself together, and as if to reinforce his strength, spread himself even further across the sofa.

'But she wasn't the one who dragged you into all this?' he said. 'That was Sara's brother Bobby?'

'Correct,' I said. 'And he's dead too, by the way. Murdered, same way as Jenny.'

Larry turned pale. Too much unsettling news in one go. The murders said something about Sara Texas's case that he would prefer not to have to deal with.

'Then let's take it from the start,' he said in a sharp voice. 'Jenny was lying. Why, I don't know, but she was. Sara was at the hotel in Galveston the night of the murder. I know that because I was the one who questioned her. We spoke to everyone staying there. Sara didn't stand out. Not back then. I realise it was pretty damn stupid not to write up a proper report of the interview, but that sort of thing happens. Her name was on the list of people who were questioned, though.'

He looked like he wanted to apologise to me personally for neglecting to write the report. That was entirely the wrong conclusion. I didn't need an apology – Sara did.

'A list like that must contain hundreds of names,' I said. 'The Carlton's a big hotel, after all. You couldn't have got Sara mixed up with someone else?'

'No. Do you want to see the list?'

'Thanks, but there's no need. What about Sara's au pair family? Did you question them about Sara's activities on the night in question?'

'No, that wasn't necessary, seeing as I'd spoken to her myself.'

I let out a laugh.

'Of course,' I said.

Larry Benson flared up. His face turned even redder.

'You little shit,' he said, loudly enough to make the hotel receptionist glance over at us. 'Do your homework before coming over here to cause trouble! Did Sara say she was in San Antonio on the night of the murder when she was questioned in Sweden?'

His question took me by surprise. She must have done, surely? Larry interrupted my thoughts.

'I see you're not sure. So let me help you. The answer's no, she never claimed she was in San Antonio when the woman was murdered in Galveston. In the first interview she claimed she couldn't remember what she was doing the night of the murder, and in the second one she confessed, as we all know.'

He sank deeper on the sofa.

'You just think she mentioned San Antonio, and you think that because you've seen that damn train ticket. Why Jenny Woods went to the effort of coming up with something like that I can't say. I just know what I saw with my own eyes: Sara Tell was in Galveston the night of the murder.'

I clenched my teeth while I considered how strongly to go on the counterattack. I had ended up at a disadvantage, and that wasn't good.

'How do you explain that Jenny Woods was murdered in Stockholm after telling me about her and Sara's trip?'

'I don't honestly feel I need to explain that. Mistaken identity, maybe?'

'And Bobby?' Lucy said, speaking for the first time. 'He was the other person fighting on Sara's behalf. Was it a coincidence that he was murdered at the same time as Jenny?'

'Another question I don't have to take responsibility for.'

Larry Benson got to his feet.

'You're digging for oil but getting nothing but sand. Let this shit go. Leave the past alone.'

It evidently wasn't a friendly piece of advice. There was something else hidden in his words. An unspoken threat.

Lucy and I stood up as well.

'The rumours about Sara being a prostitute and a drug addict,' I said. 'Was there any substance to them?'

'That was the whole reason why she was in Galveston without her au pair family,' Larry said. 'To meet as many clients as she wanted without being seen. There were others doing the same thing at that hotel. As well as the drugs. But we put a stop to that after the murder.'

'What do you think the motive was for the woman's murder in Galveston?' I said.

'Competition,' Larry said, with complete certainty in his voice. 'The women clashed over how to divide the clients. One of them had to go. Sara won that battle.'

I shook my head slowly. That was both too simple and too weak. It didn't make sense. If Sara had had a better lawyer, it wouldn't have held up in court either.

'Think whatever the hell you like,' Larry said. 'I have to get back to work.'

He got ready to leave.

'The tattoo,' Lucy said. 'We heard that Sara had the word

"Lotus" tattooed on the back of her neck. Do you have any idea what that means?'

'Not a clue,' Larry said. 'It doesn't feel particularly interesting either. Most people seem to have tattoos these days.'

Not Lucy, I thought. Nor me.

'Lucifer,' I said, and Larry stopped mid-stride. 'Do you know about him?'

Larry stood still, breathing heavily. Then he turned slowly towards me.

'Let me give you a final warning,' he said. 'Stay away from Sara Tell's story. Stay away from Lucifer. Otherwise you'll find yourself in a shitload of trouble. Is that understood?'

I nodded curtly and Larry looked happy. He marched out of the hotel without shaking hands.

'What do we do now?' Lucy said.

'Now we find someone who's willing to talk to us about Lucifer,' I said.

35

Across all the ages and in every culture, people have taught their children to beware of fire. If you get too close, you get burnt. And you never lose the scars. They stay on your body as a permanent reminder that you once broke one of life's most basic rules. The one about taking care not to try to resist forces that are bound to destroy us if we get too close.

I keep asking myself over and over if I ought to have known. If I, or we, ought to have realised. The answer is obvious. Of course we should have. But in my defence I have to point out that we had no choice. I can't see how I could have extricated myself. Not once I was faced with being charged with two murders I hadn't committed. The potential consequences of having walked into a trap like that were impossible to live with. So I kept going. Heedless and blinkered. Bit by bit things were being dismantled. Without knowing it, I was heading at speed towards my own private Pompeii.

I had plenty of help getting there. Amongst others from the individual known as Lucifer, a man at the forefront of one of the biggest criminal networks in Texas. Its tentacles reached both north, far into the American continent, and south to the furthest reaches of Mexico. Sheriff Stiller had said the network had been broken and all the main players put in prison. They even managed to get Lucifer. Lucy and I managed to confirm what Stiller had said in countless newspaper articles online. The press seemed to share Stiller's enthusiasm about the police investigation and its results. Neither Lucy nor I could understand that.

Because just as Stiller had said, Lucifer had only been convicted of a single offence. One feeble count of assault. For that he got less than a year in prison. He had been sentenced a few months after Sara left Texas. What Lucifer was doing now was unclear. But from the newspapers we did manage to learn his real name: Lucas Lorenzo.

'Exactly what did they achieve by putting a guy like him in prison for six months?' I said. 'He's hardly likely to have emerged a reformed character.'

Lucy agreed with me.

'Unless the other inmates taught him a lesson,' she said.

I thought that unlikely. A man like Lucifer was bound to have people inside every prison in Texas. He would never have had any reason to worry about his physical safety.

Lucy pushed the computer from her lap. We had shut ourselves away in our hotel room and only opened the door for room-service.

'Can we be certain this is the guy Sara meant when she wrote about Lucifer in her diary?'

I had been asking myself the same thing. But now that we had found out who Lucifer was, and with the suggestion that Sara had been involved in both drugs and prostitution, my doubts were starting to shrink.

The only thing that seemed utterly incomprehensible was how surprised Stiller had looked when we asked about Lucifer. He didn't seem to have had a clue about Sara's connection to the famous drug baron. How could that be the case? Lucifer wasn't the sort of guy you caught overnight. Destroying a network like his took years of work. The police must have spent thousands of hours documenting his contacts through surveillance and phone-taps, bugging and internet monitoring. And they were bound to have had access to a large number of physical sources too. How could Sara's name not have cropped up at least once? Even if she, as Sheriff Stiller had suggested, had been on the periphery?

'Lotus,' Lucy said.

'You're wondering if that was her alias?'

'Yes.'

That would explain a lot. Sara only lived in Texas for eighteen months. Being drawn into a network like Lucifer's probably took time. So it was reasonable to conclude that Sara had only become involved in his activities relatively late in relation to the police operation.

'There must have been loads of people in that network who were never identified,' I said. 'People the police assumed they could ignore because they were too low down in the hierarchy to pose any real danger to others.'

'You don't think we could risk asking Stiller if anyone called Lotus had cropped up in the investigation?' Lucy said.

'We could try. But I don't think he'll be very forthcoming.'

I got Sara's diary out of my suitcase. I had marked the pages where Lucifer was mentioned. Considering that there wasn't much writing in the book, and that the entries were undated, it wasn't possible to say exactly when Lucifer first appeared in

Sara's life. And he appeared a grand total of three times in the book. When I read them more carefully, I was embarrassed that I had at first believed that the name Lucifer referred to Sara's own father.

I read them out loud to Lucy.

'The first time she mentions him is here: "Lucifer is still being a problem. Why does he keep bothering me?" A bit later she writes: "I've told Lucifer to leave me alone. His whole fucking attitude scares me. Hope he doesn't contact me again." And the last mention: "Lucifer is talking about favours given and debts repaid. Don't know how I'm going to get out of this."'

Lucy took the diary and read for herself.

'This tells us far too little,' she said. 'Was she working for Lucifer? Or did they have a personal relationship?'

'Or both?' I said. 'Bloody hell, Lucy, we're not getting anywhere with this. We need to find someone who can help us interpret what Sara wrote.'

'The friend in Galveston. The one the Browns mentioned.'

'Denise.'

'Exactly.'

I leaned back against the tall, padded headboard. It looked like something from a porn film.

'We've got other reasons to go to Galveston,' I said. 'I just want to finish things off properly here in Houston first.'

'Who else do you want to see?'

I took my time replying.

'Well, I haven't given up hope of talking to one of the police officers who worked on the Lucifer investigation. And obviously I'd like to meet Jenny Woods's husband. I also want to try to meet our mafia boss in person.'

Lucy stared at me.

'Lucifer?'

'Yes. What the hell was his name again? Lucas Lorenzo.'

She got up abruptly from the bed.

'You'll have to do that one without me, then.'

'Baby, listen . . .'

'Like hell I will! Martin, people keep warning us off looking for Lucifer. We're not even supposed to talk to anyone else in the police about him. Don't you realise how dangerous this could be?'

No, I didn't. And nor did Lucy. But her gut feeling was better, and more reliable, than mine. Feelings are what they are. Soft and malleable and made by nature to be overridden by our more logical brains. So I got my way.

We didn't leave Houston until we had taken more steps towards Lucifer.

Belle's grandfather answered on the second ring.

'Everything's fine here,' he said. 'How are you getting on?'

I had no good answer to that.

'Okay,' I said. 'It's hot. Can I talk to Belle? Or has she already gone to bed?'

She hadn't. It was eight o'clock in Sweden, and Belle was playing with her cousins in her grandparents' garden. It struck me that if I ever had biological children, they'd be Belle's cousins and not her siblings. On paper, anyway.

She was soon on the phone.

'Martin?'

I had never encouraged Belle to call me Dad. She already had a dad. A dead one, admittedly, but that wasn't the point.

'Hi, Belle, how are things?'

'Wonderful!'

I don't know what I'd have done if she'd said anything else. I'd probably have started crying or something else stupid.

'That's good to hear. I hope you're not wearing out Grandma and Granddad?'

She laughed down the phone. In long, rambling sentences she started to tell me what they'd been doing since we parted. The line was distorted by the fact that she was outdoors and it was windy. But from what I could make out, she was telling me excitedly that she had been in a boat, had had ice cream, had cooked sausages on a fire, and had been swimming.

'Swimming?' I said. 'Isn't it cold?'

Stupid question. Children would be only too happy to swim in holes in the ice if we grown-ups didn't hold them back.

'It's really warm!' Belle said. 'And rainy.'

So things were much the same. Even the weather. That was good. But I didn't feel completely confident until I spoke to Boris a bit later.

'I've put two of my best guys onto it,' Boris said. 'Everything's fine. They had nothing to report last time I spoke to them. Other than the fact that you've given them a hell of a difficult job, keeping an eye on a kid out on an island in the archipelago.'

He laughed. I wasn't having any trouble keeping serious.

'How are you getting on?' Boris said.

'Two steps forward, two steps back,' I said.

Lucy had gone out to do something and I was on my own in our room.

'Anything I can do to help?' Boris said.

It struck me that there probably was. Not just one thing, but several.

'If a young woman caught up in drugs and prostitution suddenly gets a tattoo on the back of her neck, what would you think was going on?'

'That someone had marked her, of course. So that other people could see who she belonged to.'

It sounded like the most natural thing in the world. I felt slightly sick. I wanted never to have a full picture of what Boris was involved in. But what he said fitted what we'd already guessed. Getting the tattoo hadn't necessarily been Sara's idea. It could just as easily have been someone else's.

There were other things I needed help to understand.

'I'm looking for a particular person here in Texas,' I said. 'Someone whose background is a bit like yours.'

'What do you mean, a background like mine?' Boris said.

His voice sounded wary. Why did you have to be so fucking diplomatic the whole time? I didn't have time for that crap.

'I mean someone who knows an awful lot of people, and earns an insane amount of money from criminal activity.'

Boris started laughing again.

'You're a blunt bastard,' he said. 'Cocky. That's one of the things I like about you, always have done. Do I know the person in question? The person you're looking for, I mean?'

'I don't think so. But suppose someone wanted to get hold of you in Stockholm. Someone who knew who you were and what you do, but not where to find you. How would they get hold of you?'

Boris became serious.

'I know you're under pressure, but don't get careless. People like me don't want to be found. Not by you, and not by anyone else. Think about it. What do you think someone like me would say to someone like you if you turned up at my house uninvited?'

I retreated at once.

'Not a shit,' I said.

'So what do you have to do?'

'Give up. It was a stupid idea from the start. I'll have to revert to my original plan, which was to get information about the man I'm looking for from the police.'

Boris interrupted me.

'Sorry, you're going to get information about someone in my position from the police? In the USA? With all due respect, but have you gone stupid?'

I could see him before me. Shaking his shaved head and looking up at the ceiling. His voice exuded contempt, and that wasn't particularly flattering to my powers of analysis.

'I'm afraid I don't understand what you're getting at,' I said.

'People like me don't survive in the USA, and definitely not in Texas, without the protection of the police. So you won't get anything out of them. There's far too great a risk that you'll end up in the clutches of some corrupt bastard who'll tell his boss a dumb Swede is running round asking loads of stupid questions.'

Even if I thought Boris was exaggerating about how many police officers might have been bought off by someone like Lucifer, I realised that he was making an important point.

'Let me see if I understand you correctly,' I said. 'I shouldn't try to contact Lucifer directly. And I shouldn't try to find out anything about him from the police. Have you got any better suggestions? Or should I just give up?'

There was a scraping sound down the phone.

'Lucifer? He calls himself Lucifer? What a joke.'

'Agreed. But I didn't want to discuss Lucifer's alias, just how to get hold of him.'

'You're not hearing well today,' Boris said. 'What I said was that someone like me wouldn't see someone like you without an invitation.'

'Meaning?'

'Meaning that you need to switch roles. You're not going to look for Lucifer. Give him a reason to look for you instead. And pray that he listens to what you've got to say before he shoots you.'

36

The last but one time I had sex with Lucy in Texas it was raining. If we'd been in Stockholm we would never have remembered the weather, because of course it rains there most of the time. But in Houston every summer shower of rain is a miracle. The light drops fell like a blessing from God against the window of our hotel room as I, with all the strength I could muster, was guiding Lucy towards an orgasm that made her let out a short, hoarse scream. I think I was fifteen when I realised that girls who scream the whole time, or just unnecessarily often, when they're having sex have watched too much porn. Men basically never scream when they come. It's a myth that women's orgasms are so much more intense that they have to be celebrated by a two-minute-long operatic howl.

Afterwards we lay back on the bed, breathless. I don't really like too much proximity. But with Lucy it's different. I like to feel her sweaty skin stick to mine.

'That was a very good fuck,' Lucy said.

'Agreed,' I said.

She smiled and took my hand in hers. She pulled it slowly towards her and kissed it.

We'd been having an argument just before we had sex. I hadn't been able to resist, and told her about my conversation with Boris.

'Boris,' Lucy said, with unusual sharpness in her voice. 'We're not taking advice from him, surely?'

'Then think of something better yourself, then!' I said. 'Because time is running out and we aren't getting anywhere.'

I hated having nothing to do but wait. For the phone to ring with information about a fresh catastrophe. Telling us to hurry back to Sweden because they wanted to question me again. Waiting for Didrik to realise I'd lied about why I had to come to the States, then telling his American colleagues to be on the alert, or, alternatively, to throw me out of the country. Or – worst of all – that, in spite of all my precautions, something had happened to Belle.

When I thought about Belle my heart started to race with terror. Anything else could happen, just not that. However this struggle ended, Belle had to make it. And included in that thought was the idea that no one but me would raise her. If Belle ended up with foster parents I didn't know what I would do.

I squeezed Lucy's hand.

'If anything happens to me,' I said. 'Would you look after Belle?'

Lucy raised herself on one elbow.

'Don't talk like that.'

'Can't you just answer the question?'

She ran one finger across my forehead.

'If anything happens to you, Martin Benner, I'll look after Belle,' she whispered.

In the end I got my way. We decided to make an attempt to get Lucifer to come to us instead of vice versa, and then we would leave Houston. I usually like to sleep for a bit after I've had sex. This time I got out of bed and prepared for full-scale war. It was hard to know how we were going to attract Lucifer's attention, but I figured that Boris had given me more ideas to work with than I had at the outset. Seeing as we only had a limited amount of time we were going to have to be creative. And noisy.

I passed Lucy her laptop.

'Here's what we do: we dig out all the big articles we can find about the police operation against Lucifer's network,' I said. 'Make a list of police officers quoted in the media. Then we contact them.'

'Seriously? That's going to be a lot of people. The investigation seems to have been organised on both a local and federal level, in all the major cities in Texas. As things stand, we don't even know if Lucifer still lives in Houston.'

'We won't bother with the FBI,' I said. 'We'll just focus on local police officers. The important thing is to get the jungle drums working. If Boris is right, then at least one or two of the people we contact will be working for Lucifer.'

Lucy looked sceptical, but opened the laptop and began systematically going through the articles the way I had suggested.

'You don't think Didrik has contacted any of his colleagues here in Houston to warn them about us? What are the odds of him letting a suspect in a double murder run around as he likes in Texas?'

'Pretty big,' I said honestly, and looked up from the computer on my lap. 'I mean, think about it. It must be clear to Didrik that even if I lied about the reason for this trip, I haven't actually fled the country. If that were the case, I'd hardly have come to the USA of all places. If I seriously believe I can get myself off the hook by conducting my own private investigation here in Texas, I don't think Didrik would have a problem with that. I mean, it would evidently never occur to the Swedish police to try to get to the bottom of this case. They're probably so confused that they're just grateful we're giving them a hand.'

Lucy grinned.

'Grateful? You're very funny, you know that?' she said.

But I was convinced I was right. Didrik and I had known each other for a long time. Deep down he must realise that I hadn't driven into Bobby Tell and Jenny Woods. If he did, I was sure he would have remanded me in custody rather than let me go after questioning. But, on the other hand, he didn't have any other leads to go on. He wasn't prepared to re-examine the truth of the Sara Tell case, which meant he couldn't see why anyone would subject me to a conspiracy. So I would have to help him understand what had happened. Especially as I had a nagging feeling that someone else might want to do the same. Possibly the same person who had got Sara Tell to confess to five murders she hadn't committed. If that was true, then I stood a high chance of drowning in the shit that surrounded me.

The discussion with Lucy died away. We made a list of local police officers who had taken part in the operation against Lucifer's network, then started to call round. You could say we phoned like lunatics. Call after call. This probably wasn't exactly what Boris had in mind, but we didn't have time to be delicate and cautious. It was all or nothing. Because right then we were both the hunters and the hunted.

It was late afternoon, and we managed to get hold of a surprising number of them. Together we concocted a story that we stuck to in our phone calls. We said we were lawyers and that we were from Sweden. Curiosity had brought us to Houston. We thought we could see connections between a murder trial in Sweden and a character by the name of Lucifer. Was that by any chance the same Lucifer whom the Texas police had tracked down?

And had they encountered the name Lotus during the investigation?

Over and over again we trotted out the same story. None of the calls generated any particularly interesting information. No one we spoke to was willing to concede any link between Lucifer and Stockholm. And no one recognised the name Lotus.

Fuck.

My thoughts began to race again. They were like wild horses, impossible to catch. New ideas took shape, each one more time-consuming than the last.

'We ought to go to San Antonio as well,' I said, quickly and intensely. 'Try to find the guy Sara was going to see there when everyone seems to think she was in Galveston.'

Lucy leaned her head against my shoulder. I detected a silent plea in the gesture.

'Martin, you're probably going to have to accept that she wasn't in San Antonio that weekend.'

I closed my eyes and saw Jenny Woods in front of me. I remembered how she had looked when we were sitting opposite each other in Xoko, when she told me about her trip with Sara. She had been able to explain everything, even why she, rather than Sara, had the ticket and diary.

Lucy rubbed her cheek against my shirt.

'Think about what Larry told us,' she said. 'Why didn't Sara mention the trip to San Antonio as her alibi?'

I opened my eyes. My body was throbbing with irritation.

'You mean during the first interview, before she made all those confessions? It's hardly that strange. Five years had passed since the murder in Galveston. Besides, she did remember later – she called Jenny and asked for help proving her alibi.'

Lucy shook her head tiredly. She stretched and reached for the diary. Her long fingers closed round its covers and opened it.

'It's not really a literary masterpiece, is it?' she said. 'Half-written pages and bits rubbed out. Almost as if its writer had censored her own work.'

'Sara doesn't seem to have been in a good place,' I said. 'I suppose she wrote things she later regretted.'

Lucy didn't answer, just gently stroked the rough pages of the diary with her fingers, as if she were playing a silent piano. Then she reached for her handbag and took out a pencil.

'What are you going to do? Finish the masterpiece?'

Very carefully Lucy began to move the blunt end of the pencil back and forth across the erased sections. The diary's writer had pressed hard with the pen; the letters were almost imprinted on the paper. When the pencil traced over them they became visible again. White letters stood out against the grey.

'Lucy, you're a genius.'

I kissed her on the cheek. God knows, I'm not good at giving praise, but I recognise a brilliant idea when I see it. And I also know that you must never, ever steal them.

We weren't lucky enough for Lucy's trick to work everywhere that any text had been erased, but that didn't seem to matter. The words that did appear were more than enough to show us what a bad misjudgement we had made.

With our heads close together we started to read.

I don't know what I would have done without Sara. She's my only friend right now.

'Sara?' Lucy said. 'Did she used to refer to herself in the third person?'

I didn't answer. The more I read, the more obvious our mistake became.

Sara fucked up badly this weekend. Neither of us can sleep. I think she'll be going home to Sweden soon.

'Martin, do you understand this?'

I read the last fragment of text we had found.

Sara's trapped. I don't think Lucifer's going to let her go. Does he know she's pregnant?

'Fucking hell,' I whispered.

I looked at Lucy and saw that she had drawn the same conclusion as me.

It wasn't Sara's diary that Jenny Woods had sent to Sweden with the train ticket.

It was her own.

PART V

'Forgive me'

**TRANSCRIPT OF INTERVIEW WITH
MARTIN BENNER (MB).**

INTERVIEWER: FREDRIK OHLANDER (FO),
freelance journalist.

LOCATION:
Room 714, Grand Hôtel, Stockholm.

FO: You started this conversation by saying that this was the most clichéd story I'd ever hear. I'm wondering if you shouldn't have said it was the most complicated and fascinating.

MB: Fascinating? Maybe. Misery has always had a peculiar attraction to people who aren't affected by it.

FO: I didn't mean to sound insensitive or patronising.

MB: Of course not. So far you haven't said anything to shake my faith in you.

FO: How much longer did you stay in Houston?

MB: Not long. Just one more day. Then we got in the car and drove down to Galveston.

FO: You mentioned wanting to go to San Antonio as well?

MB: Not after we figured out the diary was Jenny's. After that there was obviously no point going to San Antonio.

FO: You were completely sure the diary wasn't Sara's?

MB: That was the only logical interpretation.

FO: How did that affect your thoughts on the question of Sara's guilt? Did you think she really had committed the murders she had confessed to?

MB: We carried on differentiating between the Swedish murders and the two that had been committed in the USA. As far as the Texas murders were concerned, we decided to withhold judgement until we'd been to Galveston.

FO: You must have reflected over the strange turn the story had taken? Seeing as you said back at the start that you weren't running a detective agency.

MB: Of course I thought about that. Day and night. But it never felt like it was a conscious decision on my part. Circumstances were forcing me to act in a particular way. At the start I was driven by nothing but my own curiosity. But towards the end the survival instinct was the only thing motivating me.

(Silence)

FO: You keep coming back to the fact that you
couldn't understand why you got mixed up
in this story. When did you realise just
how bad it was?

MB: You want the honest answer to that?

FO: Please.

MB: I'm afraid I still haven't realised just
how bad it is. I'm not even close to the
end of this drama.

FO: It's still going on?

MB: Day after day.

FO: What's your biggest regret?

(Silence)

MB: Regret implies that you had a choice when
you made your decision. And that never
applied to me.

FO: So what happened after you discovered that
the diary belonged to Jenny?

MB: The worst.

FO: Sorry?

MB: You asked what happened and I replied the
worst. The very, very worst thing of all.

37

'Where are we going?' Lucy asked as I turned off the freeway.

We had been driving aimlessly around Houston. After discovering that the diary had belonged to Jenny we both needed a break. So we got in the car. We had been past the alleyway where the taxi driver was beaten to death, and the club where Sara had been photographed getting out of the taxi. Stiller had said there had been a lot of drugs and prostitution going on in the club's basement. There was no trace of that now. The basement had been renovated and turned into a bar and restaurant. The maître d' told us that the club had changed hands a few years before, and that things were very different now.

Neither of us felt like lingering so we were soon back in the car. At first I said I wanted to go back to the hotel, but on the way I changed my mind.

'We're going to drive past the house where my dad lived,' I said.

'You said you didn't want to go anywhere near ...'

'I've changed my mind. I want to now.'

I've never known what to call him. I call my mother Marianne, but I only ever refer to my dad as my dad. On the few occasions when we actually met and talked, neither of us used names or titles. Just an exchange of terse remarks.

Lucy put her hand on my arm as I pulled up in front of the house where the man who had been my father used to live. I don't know what had taken me there. It was as if I had to do something else apart from chasing Sara's ghost. Something I had a bit of distance from, something that belonged to the past rather than the present.

'Has your dad's wife moved or does she still live here?' she said.

'I think she's still here,' I said. 'But I don't know her.'

I could barely remember what she looked like. We only met once while I was living in Texas. It hadn't been a good meeting. Not good at all.

I tore my eyes away from the house and smiled at Lucy.

'So we won't be going in for a cup of coffee.'

Lucy smiled back.

'Shame,' she said. 'That could have been pretty memorable.'

Just as we were pulling away a car turned into the drive of the house. Automatically I slowed to a crawl and looked at the car to see who got out of it.

It was a tall black man in his thirties. Sunglasses made his face anonymous, but he was neatly dressed in jeans and a white shirt with the sleeves rolled up. He was carrying a blue jacket. A metal bracelet hung from his wrist. Like a lot of American men, his clothes were too big for him. Why they chose to look like that was beyond me.

'Do you recognise him?' Lucy said.

I shook my head. He was darker than me, but I couldn't

help noticing that we had a similar walk. Lucy had demonstrated it to me once when we were in the first flush of infatuation.

'You walk like a cowboy,' she had said, then showed me. 'Like someone with a ridiculously low centre of gravity. You're only a hair's breadth from looking like you've shat yourself.'

She only said that last bit to wind me up, but ever since that day I've tried to walk with my legs straighter. It's impossible.

I felt a pang in my stomach. The guy disappearing into the house could well have been my brother. It felt odd not to recognise him.

'Have you ever met your American siblings?' Lucy said.

'Never,' I said. 'Not remotely interested.'

As if to underline the point, I put my foot down and drove away. Neither of us said anything until we were back at the hotel.

'Are we going to Galveston tomorrow?' Lucy said.

I reached out to her, wanted to have her close to me. I couldn't bear to think of the next step, the next trip.

Lucy pulled away.

'Sorry, I'm being boring, but I'm so damn tired.'

She had nothing to apologise for. I did, though. I just kept on making demands and never giving anything back. One day, when all this crap was over, I'd find a way of compensating for all the misery I'd brought into her life.

I yawned. I was tired as well. Totally fucking exhausted.

'I'm so knackered I can't even summon up the energy to feel horny,' I said as a dry statement of fact.

Lucy burst out laughing.

'But at least you're honest,' she said.

She kicked her shoes off and went into the bathroom. I sank

onto the edge of the bed. It was starting to get dark outside and the sound of traffic was quieter.

'We've only got one thing left to do in Houston,' I said. 'We can do that first thing tomorrow morning. Then we can take off for Galveston.'

'What are we doing tomorrow?' Lucy said from the bathroom.

I pulled the diary out from where we'd hidden it under the mattress.

'We're going to see Jenny Woods's husband.'

Evening turned to night and I lay awake in the cool hotel room. From a distance we probably looked like a couple of kids at summer-camp. We were fishing for sharks with a tiny fishing rod. Any fool could see that if we did get a bite, the entire jetty we were standing on would quake and the fishing rod would shatter into a thousand pieces.

I could hear from Lucy's breathing that she had fallen asleep, and waited to follow suit. It was a long wait. I didn't fall asleep until three. I'd be lying if I said I felt rested when the alarm clock went off at seven. We packed our bags and threw them in the car. By eight o'clock we were on our way to where Jenny's husband worked.

I had tracked him down with Eivor's help. She had been surprisingly helpful considering I called her in the middle of the night.

'You don't happen to have Sara's friend Jenny's address in Houston?' I said.

It was a wild guess, but because I knew they'd been in touch it wasn't impossible. My gamble paid off. I managed to get the name and phone number of where Jenny had worked.

'I know she works at the same place as her husband,' Eivor said. 'If you want to talk to him as well.'

I registered the fact that she said works, not worked. So Eivor didn't know Jenny was dead. I decided not to tell her what had happened, it would only prompt too many questions. But I was grateful for the information. Paying a visit to Jenny Woods's husband when I myself was the police's main suspect for her murder was a pretty bold move, even for me. But the fact remained: I hadn't killed her, and I needed to prove it.

The company was located less than twenty minutes from downtown Houston. We were there before half past eight. A receptionist sitting in the lobby told us Dennis Woods was there.

'Do you have an appointment?'

'No,' I said. 'But I'm pretty sure he'll want to see us. We knew his wife.'

Saying we knew her was a bit of an exaggeration, but the receptionist didn't need to know that.

I could see from the look on her face that she had been informed of what had befallen Dennis Woods. The colour drained from her cheeks when I mentioned his wife.

'Please, take a seat and I'll call him,' she said.

We sat down and waited on one of the ugliest, most uncomfortable sofas in the world. If the circumstances had been different I would have started laughing, but the way things looked just then it was easy not to. I held Lucy's hand while we waited. I never used to do that sort of thing. Not even when we were a couple. After a brief internal argument with myself I decided not to pull my hand away. We had crossed so many boundaries together in the past few days. This was the least dangerous of them.

The lift pinged and the doors slid open. A man with greying hair and a poorly knotted tie emerged. He looked like he hadn't slept a wink for at least a week. To my surprise, he was in his fifties. Jenny Woods had been twenty-seven when she died.

He stopped a metre away from the sofa and we stood up.

'I hear you knew my wife,' he said. 'But I don't think we've ever met before?'

I explained why we were there. I told him almost the whole story, only leaving out the embarrassing part about the police's suspicions regarding my own involvement. When I had finished, Jenny's husband considered what he had just heard. Then he held out his hand.

'Dennis Woods,' he said. 'Come up to my office with me. But you can't stay long.'

In the end I don't think we were there more than ten minutes. But that was all we needed.

Dennis Woods's office was furnished in a way that made you think of an aquarium.

'Jenny told me you met in San Antonio,' I said.

'Is this an interrogation?' Dennis said.

'No, definitely not.'

'Then we'll leave my private life out of this conversation.'

This posed a problematic limitation on the discussion for Lucy and me. We were hardly there to talk business, after all.

I tried to explain why I had asked about where Dennis and Jenny first met.

'When Jenny came to my office, she told me several things which were of great interest regarding Sara Tell's case,' I said. 'But to be able to make any further use of them, it would be very helpful if you could just confirm them.'

Because it looks like she was lying about certain things, I might have added. But didn't.

Dennis Woods had turned away and was looking out of the window. His office was on the thirty-fourth floor. The view was vast. The heat made the horizon quiver.

'Jenny never stopped talking about Sara,' he said quietly.

'What did she say?' Lucy said.

'That Sara had had such a tough life and had been so brave, trying to break with the past. That she was an incredibly loyal friend, the best you could imagine.'

'What was their relationship like after Sara left Texas?' I said.

'They were in touch less and less often, until finally it faded away altogether. Until Sara got into trouble a few years later and contacted Jenny, asking for help. At first I didn't know what it was about, but then the papers started writing about it. I pleaded with Jenny to stay out if it; it was nothing to do with her. But she refused to listen.'

So at least that part of Jenny's story had been true. Sara really had got in touch asking for help.

'Did Jenny ever say if she thought Sara was guilty?' I said. 'Or did she think she was innocent of the murders she was accused of?'

Finally Dennis Woods took his eyes off the window. He looked distraught.

'That was what I never understood,' he said. 'The question of guilt didn't seem to matter to Jenny. She just kept repeating that Sara needed her help and deserved to get it. She said there were things I couldn't possibly understand, and that I just had to accept that Sara was important to her. I'll admit I felt frustrated, but she wouldn't tell me more than that. I had no desire to get dragged into a murder trial, and I didn't like the fact that Jenny seemed to be heading that way.'

'But that didn't happen in the end,' I said. 'And it wouldn't have done, even if the trial had taken place. Sara refused to accept Jenny's help. Were you aware that she had a diary and a train ticket couriered to Sweden?'

Dennis sat down at his desk. I had already noticed two framed photographs on the windowsill. One was of Jenny, the other a young boy.

'My son,' Dennis said, nodding towards the photograph. 'We adopted him six months ago. How am I going to explain to him that his mum's gone?'

I almost expected him to start crying, but he didn't. The question was rhetorical rather than emotional.

'I have an adopted child myself,' I said. 'They can deal with more than we think.'

Dennis gave me a look that was hard to read.

'Really,' he said.

Lucy was looking intently at the boy's picture.

'Why did you choose to adopt?'

Dennis Woods's face turned bright red.

'You've crossed the line now,' he said. 'How dare you come here and ask a question like that?'

Lucy backed down quickly and apologised. I stared at the boy, trying to memorise what he looked like. I had a feeling I knew why Lucy had asked that question.

To change the subject I reminded Dennis of the earlier question he still hadn't answered. Had he known about the train ticket and diary?

'No,' he said. 'I didn't know they were what Jenny took with her when she went to Sweden.'

I stiffened on the uncomfortable visitor's chair.

'She sent them by courier,' I said. 'What do you mean, went to Sweden?'

Dennis looked surprised.

'She may have sent them by courier, but she certainly went to Sweden. Sara couldn't make her mind up. First she was desperate for Jenny's help, then she said she didn't want it.'

'At what point did Jenny travel to see Sara?' I said, thinking about what Jenny had told me. 'Was it before Sara was arrested?'

'After,' Dennis said. 'Just before the trial. As I understand it, they never actually met. Then when Sara managed to escape and commit suicide, Jenny came back to the US. She was in a terrible state, I might add.'

This was information Jenny had withheld from me. And from Bobby and Eivor. Unless perhaps they had met her then?

'I really am quite pressed for time,' Dennis said. 'So if you haven't got any more questions . . .'

'Just two more,' I said quickly. 'Three, actually. Did Jenny have any tattoos?'

Dennis grimaced. Tattoos evidently weren't his thing.

'One,' he said. 'On the back of her neck.'

My heart started to beat faster and I could feel the adrenalin kick in.

'What was it of?'

'It was a word, not an image. It said Venus.'

Venus and Lotus. I started to see a pattern that I'd been blind to before. And I remembered what the policeman Larry had called her: whore.

'Did Jenny ever mention anyone called Lucifer?'

'No.'

Of course not.

It was becoming more and more obvious that Sara and Jenny had made the same mistake while they were au pairs, and ended up in Lucifer's clutches. Then they spent the following years trying to extricate themselves from the past.

Neither of them had succeeded terribly well on that score.

'You said you had one more question?' Dennis said.

I had two, really, but I didn't say that.

'What was the reason for Jenny's trip to Sweden last week?'

'I presume she wanted to see you. She had been in touch with Sara's lawyer's secretary about getting her things back. Don't ask me why, maybe she just wanted to draw a line under everything. But then she heard that the case was being looked at again, this time by you. And suddenly her old obsession seemed to come back to life. She was impossible to reason with. Even though Sara was dead and buried, she was adamant that she had to travel to Sweden and make one last attempt to clear her name.'

For the first time in our conversation his eyes clouded over.

'I hope it was worth it,' he said in a low voice. 'Because now she's no longer here. My only hope is that the police find whoever did it, but that doesn't seem very likely, does it?'

I opted to stay silent. Lucy and I thanked him and got ready to leave. But I wasn't prepared to give up so easily. I wanted an answer to the question I had asked at the start.

'With all due respect for your private life,' I said cautiously. 'There's no way you could tell us if you and Jenny first met in San Antonio the weekend when Sara was accused of having murdered a woman in Galveston?'

Dennis Woods's expression didn't change.

'My wife and I met here in Houston,' he said. 'Here at

work. She was a trainee in my department. Where she was the weekend a woman was murdered in a hotel in Galveston I don't know. But I can tell you I haven't set foot in San Antonio since I buried my mother there almost ten years ago.'

38

According to the thermometer in the car it was almost forty degrees when we drove out of the car park and set off towards Galveston.

'We could have been in Nice now,' Lucy said.

I didn't answer. My sunglasses were pressing against my temples and I took them off.

'Or we could have stayed at home,' Lucy said. 'We could have gone to Dad's place in the country and picked berries. Made juice and gone for walks in the forest.'

She took one hand off the wheel and put it on my arm.

'Please, go on,' I said. 'Tell me about berries and juice.'

People are often surprised when I tell them about my hidden talent. I'm a demon when it comes to making juice and jam. Who I inherited that skill from is a little unclear. Marianne isn't remotely practical, and my dad can't have spent many minutes in the kitchen during the course of his entire life. But of course not everything needs a genetic explanation. Blind chance can have a violent impact on any bloodline.

I opened my eyes in time to see a road sign that confirmed

we were on our way to Galveston. I was trying to put on a brave face, but inside I was in pieces. Self-control was another thing I was usually good at in professional contexts, but this time I wasn't sure how much longer I could keep it up.

Everyone has their limit. You just have to be able to figure out where it is.

'She killed the taxi driver,' I heard myself say. 'Possibly in self-defence, but she did kill him.'

Lucy took several deep breaths.

'I think she killed the woman in Galveston too,' she said quietly.

'So why was Jenny Woods so keen to give her an alibi for that murder in particular?'

'Because she felt sorry for her? Because she believed she was innocent?'

I shook my head.

'That doesn't make sense,' I said. 'Jenny went to great lengths to try to get Sara off. Not only did she construct evidence which was clearly false, she also travelled to Sweden to help. Twice. I can't understand what was driving her. She must have felt personally affected by what was happening to Sara. Otherwise her actions seem completely illogical.'

A car pulled up behind us. Far too close. For far too long. I watched it in the rear-view mirror. It wouldn't be strange if we were being tailed. Impractical, though.

'The child,' Lucy said. 'Jenny's child. The one they adopted at more or less the time that Sara died. I could see you were thinking the same as me.'

I took my eyes off the mirror.

'That it could be Mio?'

'Yes.'

The car behind accelerated and drove past. Not following us, then. I couldn't help breathing a sigh of relief.

'But how could something like that have happened?' I said. 'How could she have got Mio out of Sweden? Without leaving any trace of what she'd done?'

Lucy shrugged.

'I don't know,' she said. 'But Jenny went to Stockholm without telling anyone except her husband. If she'd met up with Bobby or Eivor – or Sara – then we'd have known about it. There must have been some purpose to that trip.'

I thought so too. Perhaps Sara had called in desperation and asked her friend to come to Sweden. Asked her to take care of Mio. But that didn't feel like a particularly safe plan for the boy. Because Jenny had a tattoo at the back of her neck as well. If Lucifer was behind the threats against Sara, it seemed odd that she would entrust her son to someone who had previously been part of Lucifer's network.

'Maybe not,' Lucy said when I aired my thoughts. 'Maybe it felt safe to entrust the boy to someone who had the sense to appreciate the threat against him. And who could give him a decent upbringing. Think about the people Sara had around her – gangsters and thugs.'

'That was before she became a mother,' I pointed out. 'We still know very little about Sara's social circle during her last years in Sweden.'

The fake Bobby's words about everything being connected were ringing in my head. He had said I wouldn't be able to ignore Mio's fate. That it formed part of the whole picture. If Jenny had ended up looking after Mio, then fake Bobby was most definitely right.

Even so, I said, 'We mustn't get stuck on in-depth analysis

of what happened to Mio. That's not the priority. Not as much as the murders Sara was accused of committing, anyway.'

'But if he's right in front of our eyes it would be stupid to ignore him,' Lucy said.

'We can look into that once we're back in Stockholm,' I said. 'Right now I can't actually remember what Mio looks like.'

A thought came and went in my head. There was something wrong about the fact that I couldn't remember how Mio looked.

Lucy took out a bottle of water.

'You can always call Boris and see what he thinks,' she said.

I ignored the sharp tone of voice she used to talk about Boris. But it reminded me that I hadn't heard from him for twelve hours. I got out my mobile and sent a text.

Everything okay?

Then I called Belle's grandfather. The phone rang forever before I finally reached an answer-machine. I tried calling Belle's grandmother, but her mobile was switched off. There was no landline out to the island.

'No answer?' Lucy said.

'They're probably out in the boat,' I said.

Only in Sweden would anyone get it into their head to go out in an open motorboat when it's only fifteen degrees and cloudy.

I kept my mobile in my hand, waiting for one of them to call me back.

'Those tattoos,' I said. 'We'll have to see if Sara's friend Denise has got one as well.'

Denise was the only one of Sara's friends whose name her au pair family knew. That bothered me.

'You mean she ought to have had more friends than that?' Lucy said. 'More friends that the Browns would have met enough times to remember them?'

'Exactly.'

Those damn tattoos. The Texas police could think what they liked. I was still convinced that Sara – and probably Jenny too – had been working for Lucifer. Lucifer. The demonic shadow I hadn't managed to get an inch closer to, despite my best efforts.

I remembered something my old professor at university had said, and swallowed hard. He had said I mustn't be so hasty, so quick to draw conclusions. But in Texas I had no choice. If they were wrong, I'd just have to go back and adjust them later. Even if that meant I was taking risks. The sort of risk that could end up getting me and Lucy killed.

In that respect Sara Tell was rather surprising. What had she been up to? Hadn't she learned anything on the streets of Stockholm? Didn't she realise that she had to keep a guy like Lucifer at arm's length?

A new thought took root. So quickly that it made me sit bolt upright in the car seat.

Lucy started.

'What is it?' she said.

'Do we have any idea how Sara ended up with the Brown family in the Heights? Did she find them through some agency, or answer an advert?'

'I don't know,' Lucy said. 'What difference does it make?'

I didn't reply. A suspicion was starting to develop, and I didn't have time to wait for it to be confirmed. The thought was as crazy as it was unlikely, but if it was true then it would explain several things which had thus far seemed inexplicable.

It didn't take long to find Mr Brown's contact details on the internet. Victor Brown's name and photograph appeared on his company's website, along with a phone number. It would have been better to talk to his wife but I didn't have time to be fussy.

I could hear how disgruntled he was when he realised who was calling him.

'I really can't apologise enough for bothering you,' I said. 'I'd just like to know one important thing. How did you first come into contact with Sara?'

'How do you mean?'

'I mean how did you find her? How did she end up being your au pair?'

It sounded like Brown was talking to someone next to him. He sounded stressed when he answered.

'We like Swedish au pairs and usually advertise in the larger Swedish morning papers.'

'And how come you chose Sara? You must have had a lot of responses to your advert.'

'If I remember rightly, she sent a very persuasive application letter. Then we interviewed her over the phone, and after that it was a done deal. One worry we always have is that we'll get an au pair who quickly realises that Houston isn't really much of a fun place to be. In that sense Sara stood out, because she made it very clear that she wasn't interested in any other American city, she only wanted to come to Houston.'

'Did she say why?'

'She said some friends of hers had lived here before and loved it. And she'd always wanted to go to a famous riding school just outside Houston. That was where she was planning on spending her wages.'

I tried rather half-heartedly to kill a fly that was buzzing against the window.

'A riding school?' I repeated.

'Didn't I mention that when we met? It was one of the things that attracted her to Houston. Preston's Riding School, that's the name. It's just off the road to Galveston.'

I started looking around for signs beside the freeway.

'Are you sure Sara spent her time at the riding school?' I said.

'I don't know how sure I am really. The way things developed, I'm not actually sure of anything at all. But she used to say that was where she was going when she was gone for a while.'

Victor Brown broke off to talk to someone else again.

'I'm really sorry,' he said to me. 'But I'm afraid I'm going to have to go.'

And with that he was gone. Slowly I lowered the phone and let it rest in my lap.

'What was that all about?' Lucy said.

My mobile buzzed. A new text from Boris.

Everything fine. Getting another report from the guys in a few hours.

I felt relief spread through my chest. Never mind the fact that Belle's grandparents didn't have their mobiles on. Boris was the one who really mattered.

At that moment I caught sight of a modest sign by the side of the road.

Preston's Riding School.

'Turn off here,' I said. 'Follow the signs to the riding school.'

Lucy did as I said.

'Do you want to tell me what exciting things you've figured out?'

'I don't think Sara first came into contact with Lucifer when she arrived in Houston,' I said. 'I think she was part of his network before she left Sweden. And that was why she decided to come to Texas.'

39

If Belle ever comes home and announces that she wants to start horse-riding, I shall say no at once. Horses are big, clumsy, and smelly. A small part of me also thinks they're lethal. But there were no horses visible at Preston's Riding School. I may have detected a faint whiff of them, but that was all. Presumably that was what posh riding schools were like. Too clean for real animals.

Lucy didn't share my views on horses. To my surprise she exclaimed: 'What a wonderful place! I'd have loved to go riding here.'

'No way, you were a horsey girl?' I said.

'God, yes. I practically lived in a stable until I turned fifteen.'

I didn't like to be reminded that I didn't know all there was to know about Lucy. In my world we had always known each other, and that was the way things were going to stay. Which was obviously incredibly naïve. We don't even know our own children as well as we'd like.

As far as Preston's Riding School was concerned, even I could see that it was high class. I found myself thinking of the Spanish Riding School in Vienna, where horse-riding shows were performed in a huge, castle-like facility. How the hell could Sara's au pair parents have thought she could afford to ride here?

The same thought occurred to Lucy.

'They're hardly going to offer impoverished au pairs subsidised riding lessons,' she said.

The spacious school was surprisingly calm and quiet. I realised we must have come in the wrong way. There was no one in sight. It felt like we were in some sort of large practice hall.

'There must be a reception area or information desk,' I said.

We went out into the heat again. The three-metre tall door swung shut behind us. The sunlight hurt my eyes and I fumbled for my shades.

'Over there,' Lucy said, pointing to a much smaller door in a much smaller building.

'Administration,' a discreet sign said.

'Good job we didn't go straight there,' I said. 'Then we wouldn't have seen the lovely school.'

We hurried over to the other door. The heat was oppressive, and in combination with the high humidity was soon unbearable.

Indoors an Alaskan chill reigned. The Yanks love their airconditioning, but don't seem to have the faintest idea of how to use it. It's either too hot or too cold, and if the difference between them is too great you end up catching a cold.

'Can I help you?' said an elderly woman with grey hair, round glasses and a blouse so tightly buttoned at the neck that I wondered how she could breathe.

By this point we had become practised liars. This time we gave a minimalist background explanation for our visit.

'What we'd like to know is if you've ever had a Sara Tell registered with you,' I said.

'Or a Jenny Woods,' Lucy said.

'Woods is her husband's name,' I said quietly in Swedish. 'What was she called before she got married?'

Lucy thought.

'Eriksson,' she said. 'Jenny Eriksson.'

The old lady hesitated.

'We take care to protect our members' confidentiality and we don't hand out their details to anyone,' she said.

I was trying to make as reassuring an impression as possible. It wasn't easy when beads of sweat kept appearing on my forehead. My shirt was sticking to my back and I kept shuffling to avoid contact with the damp fabric. Lucy looked like she was about to start laughing but managed to stop herself. I had no idea how she was able to stand there looking so cool and unperturbed by the heat.

'I had hoped you might be able to make an exception,' I said. 'For Sara Tell's brother's sake. You see, Sara is dead.'

To keep the woman on side I neglected to mention that the woman I wanted information about was a suspected serial killer. It worked. Somewhat reluctantly she tapped at the keyboard in front of her. After a while she looked up.

'Both of the women you mentioned are in our register,' she said.

I started with surprise.

'Are you sure?'

'Absolutely. They joined at the same time, early in 2007. They left in May and August respectively the following year.'

I glanced at Lucy. She was as surprised as me.

'Can you see how often they came riding?' I said.

The woman raised an eyebrow.

'Sorry, how often they were here riding?' she said brusquely.

I looked around, bewildered.

'Yes, what else would they be doing here? This is a riding school, isn't it?'

The woman laughed, and it wasn't a friendly laugh.

'I could see at once that you and your friend weren't aware of what sort of establishment this is. This isn't a riding school for girls who dream of horses. Our riders are among the best in the country, and all our training is aimed at dressage competitions at national or international level.'

She pointed a bony finger at a series of diplomas and trophies lined up in a locked glass cabinet behind her.

'One of our riders won gold in the World Championship just two years ago.'

'Really,' I said. 'So if Sara and Jenny weren't here to ride, would you mind telling us what they were doing here?'

'Hard work,' the woman said, stretching her already straight back. 'They were among the many volunteers who come to our school to participate in an extraordinary equestrian environment.'

'So they worked for free?' Lucy said.

'Yes, but from what I can see, not terribly often,' the woman said. 'They worked here on a total of three occasions. Now that I come to look at it, I can't honestly understand how they were allowed to remain on the register for so long. We're usually very quick to get rid of girls and boys who aren't prepared to give their all.'

I kept my opinion of the woman's attitude to unpaid labour and the exploitation of young people to myself. I had one further question.

'Would you mind looking to see if any other young women registered at the same time as Jenny and Sara?' I said.

The woman looked hesitant again.

'You're on rather thin ice now,' she said.

'You don't have to say what their names are,' Lucy said. 'A yes or no would be fine.'

Further hesitation, then finally an answer to the question.

'Another two girls were registered at the same time,' the woman said. 'One of them was Swedish, just like your girls, and one was American. They seem to have followed the same pattern. They don't come and work very often at all.'

'Come and work?' I repeated. 'So they're still registered?'

'Yes. But it's been six months since the last time either of them was here.'

I leaned heavily against the reception desk. I was prepared to go to great lengths to learn the names of those two girls.

'I can see what you're thinking, and the answer's no,' the woman said firmly. 'And that's not negotiable.'

'We understand,' Lucy said quickly. 'We're very grateful for the information you've given us.'

'Yes, truly,' I said, nodding in agreement. 'I won't press you for further details. You don't by any chance have any printed material about the school that we could have? It would be interesting to learn about the background to the school, who's on the committee, that sort of thing.'

A moment later I had a heavy brochure in my hands.

'I hope this will be of some use,' the woman said, evidently eager to be rid of us.

'I'm sure it will be,' I said.

We thanked her for her help and prepared to leave. At least Lucy did. I couldn't move from the spot. Because I knew I hadn't done all I could to get the names of the other girls. And like hell was some miserable old cow in the middle of a baking hot Texas going to get in my way.

I looked her right in the eyes.

'Just answer this one question,' I said. 'Was one of the girls who was registered at the same time as Jenny and Sara called Denise?'

Time stood still while I waited for the woman to make her mind up.

'Yes,' she said. 'One of them was called Denise Barton. According to our records, you'll find her in Galveston.'

40

In a lot of ways cities are like people. When one is fashion-able, it's really fucking fashionable. And for one that used to be cool and fashionable but no longer is, there's no way back. Barcelona is the clearest example of this. People who go there today can never get the magical first impression as those who went for the first time in the eighties and nineties. Time can be merciless. I've no idea how that can be prevented.

Galveston is far more tragic than Barcelona. Galveston's age of greatness is so far back in time that there's no one left alive who can remember it. Lucy was steering the car through areas where colourful wooden houses stood side by side with abandoned hovels.

'Exciting,' she said. 'They've done a great job of integrating the disadvantaged into society. Every second house looks like it's about to fall down, while the others look like something designed by Alice in Wonderland.'

I saw a chance to occupy my mind with something new, and gave a brief explanation of why the city looked the way it did. I told her about the hurricanes which sweep in to torment

Galveston each year, tearing apart any buildings that aren't strong enough. With my eyes half-closed behind my shades I talked about American society's lack of solidarity and how much I actually like that, because it makes reasonable demands of individuals, as long as it doesn't go too far. When a hurricane blows down the homes of hardworking people, I think it would be acceptable for society as a whole to help repair them.

'Do most people have home insurance here?' Lucy said.

'Yes, but that doesn't cover extreme weather conditions. They get defined as force majeure.'

'So people don't get financial compensation?'

'Exactly.'

Force majeure. I tried out the expression, and decided it was magnificent. Force majeure was why I couldn't take Lucy to Nice as we had planned. Exceptional circumstances had forced me to take drastic decisions. Force majeure was also the reason I had left Sweden even though the police had told me to stay in Stockholm. If I had felt confident that they were doing their job I would have acted differently. I would have felt secure in the knowledge that they had reached the only reasonable and acceptable conclusion: that I was innocent. But things didn't seem to be moving in that direction, which was why I had, as the stupid phrase goes, taken the law into my own hands.

We checked into the Carlton Hotel. I paid for two nights but hoped we would be able to leave after just one. In spite of strenuous efforts to attract Lucifer's attention we still hadn't heard from him. All that remained of our plan was to meet Denise. We had come to the end of the road in Texas. It was almost time to go home.

While we were waiting for the key to our room I pulled my mobile out of my pocket again. Still no messages or calls from Belle's grandparents. Irritated, I tried calling again. Still no answer. Hopeless people. I'd been through this before. They would disappear on an outing all day, and I would break out in nerve-induced eczema when I couldn't get hold of them. I had reluctantly learned to appreciate that, because it taught me how much Belle meant to me.

I wondered what my sister would have thought if she could see me now. All sweaty palms and eyes red with tiredness. She'd have said she was disappointed. She would have wondered how I could leave Belle alone when I was in such a dangerous situation.

But that's not what I had done, I thought. I hid her away in the archipelago with Boris to watch over her. She wouldn't have been any safer if I'd hidden her in the Pope's wardrobe in the Vatican.

The thought of Boris made me feel calmer for a while. He had promised to give me an update in a few hours. If Belle's grandparents didn't bother to get in touch in the meantime, at least Boris would let me know that everything was okay.

At last the receptionist was ready.

'You're on the top floor,' she said. 'The elevator's over there.'

I thanked her and then asked the question that contained the entire purpose of our trip to Galveston.

'Denise Barton,' I said. 'Does she work here?'

The receptionist's smile faded.

'I'm afraid not.'

'But she used to work here, didn't she?'

'Yes, but that was several years ago.'

'You don't know where she's working now?'

'I'm afraid not.'

I smiled my most ingratiating smile.

'It would be a huge help if you could ask around,' I said. 'Lucy and I would really like to get in touch with her. It's urgent, really very important.'

The receptionist was more malleable than the old woman at the riding school.

'I'll see what I can do,' she said. 'I'll get back to you.'

We left it at that and squeezed into the lift.

Lucy let out a whistle when we walked into our room. I had booked a mini-suite with a view of the Gulf of Mexico. Perhaps the magnificent view would help Lucy relax.

'Have we got anything planned here, apart from seeing Denise?' Lucy said.

'Not that I know of,' I said.

'Good,' Lucy said. 'Then I'm going to take a long bath.'

She shut herself in the bathroom and I sat down on the bed with my eyes fixed on the big picture window. The view was magnificent. The water was clear blue, the beach endless. Unfortunately it was also packed to bursting with people. Presumably that was why Lucy would rather lie in a bath indoors than on a sun-lounger outside. Best to stay inside until the sun went down or the receptionist got in touch to say where we could find Denise Barton.

Exhausted, I gave in to tiredness and lay back on the bed. The whitewashed ceiling with its little spotlights had an almost hypnotic effect on me. I pretended the lights were tiny stars and that I was drifting weightless in space, out of reach of anyone trying to catch me.

I believed I had solved a large part of the mystery that had made Sara Tell so hard to understand at first. The whole story was more logical if there was a link between her involvement in Lucifer's network and her decision to come specifically to Houston. As far as we were aware, Sara had never even sat on a horse before she left Sweden. Something else must have enticed her to Texas. I thought about what her sister, Marion, had said. That Sara had belonged to a gang who wreaked havoc on the streets of Stockholm. Could that have been where she got her contacts?

To say I had doubts about my own theory was putting it mildly. If Lucifer's network extended all the way to Sweden, then I wouldn't have been the only one who knew about it. The police in Texas and Stockholm would have known. But perhaps Sheriff Stiller had been right: if Sara had been part of Lucifer's network, she was so far from the centre that she hadn't shown up on the police's radar.

All that linked Sara to Lucifer were some sporadic mentions in a diary that turned out to belong to someone else. How much significance could I place on something like that? When we weren't even sure that the Lucifer mentioned in the diary was actually the mafia boss and not someone completely different?

'Baby?' I said in a loud voice.

'Mmm,' Lucy said from the bathroom.

'Why did Jenny send Bobby her diary?'

'To get Sara exonerated.'

'But what specifically in the diary would do that? There was nothing in there that could help Sara. The entries weren't dated, and there was nothing that gave her an alibi for either of the murders.'

Silence from the bathroom. The only sound was the lapping of the water, as if Lucy were splashing it with her fingers.

I got up from the bed abruptly and ran over to the bathroom.

'Are you okay?' I said, pushing at the half-open door.

Lucy was lying in the bath with water up to her chin and her hair in a knot on top of her head. She looked at me with wide eyes.

'Yes. Are you?'

I laughed and leaned against the edge of the door.

'Sorry, I'm getting paranoid.'

'Martin, no one could blame you if you were. You've got far too much on your mind right now. What did you think had happened?'

I shook my head. I refused to talk about the images that had flitted through my overloaded brain. Visions of someone sneaking into the bathroom and holding Lucy's head underwater. Or cutting her with a knife and turning the bathwater red.

'Are you getting out soon?' I said.

'I've only just got in,' Lucy said. 'Feels like you could do with relaxing as well.'

I didn't respond, and walked back out into the room again. My pulse was too high and I was sweating even though the air-conditioning was doing its best to turn our room into a fridge. I had to make sure I didn't lose my grip. There was no time for that.

'The diary,' I said, loudly enough for Lucy to hear. 'It proves nothing. Jenny must have realised that.'

'Possibly,' Lucy said. 'But I can't think what she meant with it if not to help Sara.'

'Yes, I'm sure that's what she wanted, I just don't understand how it ...'

I broke off abruptly.

Because I did understand.

Without any hesitation, I expanded my theory with yet another supposition.

'The diary was never about giving Sara an alibi or revealing anything revolutionary about her life,' I said. 'It was about one single thing, and that was to make sure that the link to Lucifer was made visible in the investigation. That was why she removed the passages showing that it was her diary.'

'Because she didn't want to be linked to Lucifer?'

'Exactly. But she failed. The police had nothing else to indicate that Sara had anything to do with Lucifer, and therefore no one reacted to the contents of the diary. It's not even certain anyone bothered to read it. Sara herself didn't want anything to do with it, after all.'

I heard Lucy knock over what sounded like a plastic bottle, and resisted the urge to dash to her rescue again.

'Or else Boris was right when he guessed that Lucifer had friends in the police. Which means it isn't impossible that someone actually read the diary but made sure it got discounted from the investigation. The fact that no one in Sweden reacted to the name isn't so strange, but Jenny took it to the police in Houston first. Regardless of the fact that they can't read Swedish, the name Lucifer ought to have jumped out at anyone in the know.'

Everything she said was right, but the idea was still pretty damn difficult to accept. The suggestion that Lucifer's network was so extensive that it even included police officers working on their investigation into him. But maybe that was why they failed to get him for more than assault.

Lucy continued her analysis from the bath.

'One thing that contradicts Boris's guess about Lucifer's

connections to the police is the fact that we haven't had the slightest response to our attempts to get his attention.'

The same thought had occurred to me. I wasn't happy about that. We had gone over the top and had called far too many people. There was a serious risk that we had attracted the attention of police officers who were merely doing their job. It would be unfortunate if another police force started to regard me as a potential criminal.

Then the phone on the bedside table rang. It was the receptionist.

She had found Denise Barton.

41

The Hotel Royal where Denise Barton worked was only three blocks away. I realised at once that I'd made a mistake booking a room at the Carlton. The Royal was considerably fancier.

We hadn't arranged a meeting with Denise Barton. From the receptionist we had learned that she was expected to show up for work before two o'clock. So we set off to the Royal, making sure we'd be there half an hour before then. Lucy's hair was still wet and I hadn't had time to shave.

'You look good with a beard,' Lucy said, stroking my cheek.

'I look old with hair on my face,' I said.

'Not old,' Lucy said. 'Just a little older. Like someone with more experience of life.'

How much experience of life can anyone really want? I felt like asking. I thought I'd managed to get through more than most people my age.

We settled down in the bar at the Royal. It struck me that I had pretty much been with Lucy twenty-four hours a day for the past week. We each ordered a glass of iced water and tried to look cool and relaxed. Considering how cold it was indoors, it would have made more sense to order a cup of hot coffee or chocolate. Belle loved hot chocolate when she was younger. Then came the day when she declared out of the blue that she was too old for chocolate and would rather drink tea like Lucy and Grandma.

Thinking about Belle wasn't a good idea. Frustrated, I pulled my mobile from the chest pocket of my shirt. Still not a word from either Boris or Belle's grandparents.

'Martin, listen to me now,' Lucy said, taking the phone out of my hand. 'They've gone on an outing, that's all. They haven't got any mobile coverage. They'll call you tomorrow.'

But I couldn't relax. In Sweden it was getting towards nine o'clock in the evening. They weren't usually gone that long.

'Maybe they decided to spend the night somewhere else,' Lucy said. 'The archipelago's full of great places.'

I interrupted her.

'I was very clear about the rules,' I said. 'They were only allowed to leave the island for brief periods.'

To both of our surprise my mobile started to ring. My normal phone, the one I'd avoided using from the moment I realised I was in trouble with the police.

I recognised the number. Didrik.

'Don't answer,' Lucy said. 'Not now. Because I think we're about to have company.'

She nodded towards a young girl with her black hair cut in a simple bob who was heading in our direction. We had asked the doorman to look out for Denise Barton when she arrived for work. He had agreed to tell her we were waiting in the bar.

Denise had the longest legs I've ever seen on a woman. Together with her high-heeled shoes and fairly short skirt, they formed a perfection so beautiful it made my eyes sting. Some idiots think you're objectifying women if you point out and notice their external qualities. Few things annoy me more than that. Gifts are gifts, talents are talents. Of course they should be praised.

'Denise?' I said, slipping off the bar stool as she reached us. The time was ten minutes to two. We didn't have long.

'Who wants to know?'

Some replies are as classic as they are appropriate. I introduced myself and Lucy, and said why we were there. Denise Barton received what was without doubt the most honest explanation. But still not completely honest. Just as before, I left out the fact that the police thought I was involved in the murders of Jenny Woods and Bobby Tell.

Denise's face turned pale when I told her Jenny was dead.

'Out of all of us, I always thought she was the most likely to get away,' she said quietly.

I decided not to waste any time.

'Which "us"?' I said.

She shook her head.

'I don't know you,' she said. 'You have no idea what you're asking me to tell you. But I'll do you a favour and give you a warning, if you haven't already heard it. Get out, while you still can. Even in your wildest imagination, you have no idea what forces you're going up against.'

I lost my temper.

'Thank you, we've lost count of the number of people we've heard that from. I'm starting to get seriously fed up of it. Warning after warning, but no substance whatsoever. So far seven people – eight if we count Sara – have died here in Texas and in Stockholm, and there'll probably be more unless someone summons up a bit of courage and starts talking.'

My voice was far too loud, and several heads turned to look at me.

Denise looked me straight in the eye. Hers were almond-shaped, her irises shimmered between green and brown.

'Can you actually hear what you're saying?' she said. 'Seven people have died. Seven. Doesn't that tell you all you need to know?'

My anger drained away and was replaced by something else. Desperation.

'Believe me, I wouldn't be here now if I had a choice,' I said. 'I'm begging you – if you think you know anything that could help us understand how this whole mess fits together, please, just tell us. Because there aren't many other people we can turn to.'

That last bit was unnecessary but true. It would be more damaging not to tell her. I wanted Denise to know that she was hurting us if she chose not to cooperate. That she was responsible for our fates, whether she liked it or not. It worked.

'You say you made a serious effort to contact Lucifer?' she said.

'Yes. Not him personally, we haven't been able to do that, but by contacting people we think are part of his network.'

'Then you'll have realised that the so-called police operation and all the raids and trials were just playing to the gallery? That Lucifer and his partners were left untouched by the big clear-out.'

In all honesty we hadn't realised that, but I chose not to say anything. I nodded silently.

'Good,' Denise said. 'But it's funny that hasn't told you all you need to know. Did you say you were at Preston's Riding School today?'

'Yes. Very smart, for a riding school.'

'That's because it isn't a proper riding school. The whole damn thing's just a façade.'

Really? I knew what façades looked like. They rarely, if ever, consisted of smart buildings that were easily accessible. Besides, the riding school could boast a considerable number of successes.

But I didn't say that to Denise. If she wanted to believe that no horse riding took place at the school, she was perfectly entitled to do so.

'A façade? Interesting,' I said instead. 'Intended to cover up what, exactly?'

Denise lowered her eyes.

'Not here,' she said. 'We'll have to meet somewhere else to talk. You never know who's listening here.'

I shuffled nervously from one foot to the other. My nervousness stemmed from the fact that she was about to go, the woman we'd set such high hopes on.

'Okay,' I said. 'Where and when?'

'When are you leaving?'

'Tomorrow, ideally.'

She thought for a moment.

'Okay, how about this? The back of the Carlton. Do you know where I mean? It used to be fenced in, but these days it's a big car park.'

Lucy and I nodded like children. Yes, we knew where she meant.

'Good, let's meet there at eight o'clock this evening. I can't get away before then.'

She lowered her gaze, then looked up once more. She seemed genuinely frightened.

'You say you've got a lot to lose by not talking to me. I could lose everything if I say too much. So I need to know I can trust you. One hundred per cent.'

I looked her straight in the eye.

'In less than twenty-four hours we'll be leaving this country. You'll never hear from us again, and we'll never let on that you were our source.'

My words evidently hit home. When Denise walked away I knew she would show up behind the Carlton a few hours later.

When she turned her back on us and walked off, I caught a glimpse of the back of her neck. She was wearing a top that was cut fairly low at the back. The tattoo was right at the top of her back.

Vega.

Lucy saw it too.

'Bloody hell,' she said, turning pale.

She took hold of her water glass and I could see her hand was trembling slightly. Had the reality of the story not struck her until then?

'How do we know we can trust her?' she said. 'What guarantee do we have? I mean, she still lives in Galveston, in spite of everything that's happened. And she still works in a hotel. Who knows who she reports to? Maybe she still belongs to Lucifer's gang.'

'I'd be inclined to agree with you if we had a choice,' I said. 'But for God's sake, Lucy, we haven't. We have to dare to tug at the few threads we've got left. Otherwise we'll end up going home just as empty-handed as we arrived. And, as she made very clear, she's got just as much reason to be frightened. I think that's our biggest guarantee, that we're equally exposed and on our own.'

'I just hope we're doing the right thing,' Lucy said.

'We are,' I said firmly.

And then I uttered a phrase that I've never said again since that day:

'Either way, things can hardly get any worse than they already are.'

It was meant as a joke. What I meant was: what could be worse than being accused of two murders you didn't commit?

I received the answer to that question thirty seconds later when Lucy had gone to the toilet and I sat at the bar and called Didrik back.

'Sorry I didn't pick up in time,' I said. 'We were stuck in a load of traffic.'

'No problem,' Didrik said. 'Martin, where are you?'

For some reason I got the impression it didn't matter what I answered. So I chose to be honest.

'I'm in Galveston, Didrik. Hopefully I'll be home in forty-eight hours.'

I heard Didrik breathing heavily down the line.

'You can't get back any sooner?'

I thought about it. We could catch a flight from Houston the following morning. With a transfer in Chicago or New York we ought to be able to get home in twenty-four to thirty hours.

'What's this about?' I said, trying to suppress the anxiety in my voice. 'Has something happened? I mean, I've promised to cooperate, and of course I am, but ...'

Didrik interrupted me.

'Martin, it's about your parents-in-law.'

Taken aback, I put my glass down. I didn't have a steady relationship, I didn't have any parents-in-law.

Then I realised.

'Oh, dear God,' I whispered. 'Lucy's mum and dad. Please, tell me they're okay.'

It was Didrik's turn to be surprised.

'Lucy's?' he said first. Then, 'No, bloody hell, sorry, Martin. My brain short-circuited. I didn't mean your parents-in-law. I meant your sister's.'

It was as if the hotel bar disappeared. All sounds stopped, all sensory impressions dissolved into nothingness.

'My sister's?'

'Your brother-in-law's parents. Belle's grandparents. The ones with the summerhouse in the archipelago.'

As if in a trance I pulled out my other mobile. No news, no missed calls from Stockholm. I began to realise that there weren't going to be any either. At least not from Belle's grandparents.

'What's happened?' I said.

Or did I shout?

I don't remember.

Didrik's voice sounded brittle when he replied.

'Martin, it feels terrible to have to tell you over the phone. At first I didn't realise who they were, but when the penny dropped I swear we did everything we could. But we got there too late. Well, maybe not we. There was nothing the fire brigade could do when they got there.'

The fire brigade?

The fire brigade?

'Our first thought is that it was an accident,' Didrik said. 'We believe that a gas stove in the kitchen caught alight, probably early this morning. As you know, they don't have any close neighbours who could see the smoke and fire in time. The alarm was raised by someone who happened to be passing as they walked their dog. But by then it was already too late.'

I couldn't take in what he was telling me. It was impossible. Didrik himself must have been in shock, because he didn't notice my silence and just went on talking.

'Christ, Martin, I'm so sorry, for Belle's sake. And yours. I know you liked Belle's grandfather after all that business about who was going to look after Belle. They're both gone. They died of smoke inhalation; they were badly burned by the time we got them out.'

The room started to spin.

They died of smoke inhalation.

Both of them.

Both?

'Belle,' I said in a voice so hoarse it was barely audible. 'How's Belle?'

'Belle?' Didrik said. 'I don't know. I assumed you'd want to tell her yourself.'

I shook my head so hard it hurt.

'You don't understand,' I said. 'Belle was staying with her grandparents. They were looking after her.'

Didrik fell silent.

'For Christ's sake, talk to me!'

I'm sure I was yelling now. Lucy still wasn't back. Where had she got to? I needed her. More than ever.

'I don't know what to say, Martin,' Didrik said. 'The bodies of four adults were found in the house. It looks like they had guests staying the night. Two men we haven't been able to identify. But no child has been found. Not inside the house, anyway. I'll contact the patrol out on the island. Maybe she managed to get out of the house, Martin. Because she wasn't in there. Maybe she's frightened and hiding somewhere. I swear – forget everything that happened before you left. You have my word that I'm going to find her.'

I could no longer hear what he was saying. Four adults had died in the house. Belle was missing. You didn't have to be a genius to work out that the unidentified men must be Boris's guys, and that whoever had lit the fire had taken Belle away from there with them.

I sank to my knees in the bar.

I prayed to a god I didn't know I believed in, begging him to spare her.

'Take me instead,' I whispered. 'Take me.'

Didrik was calling to me down the phone but I pressed the button to get rid of him. My fingers were slippery with sweat as I pulled out my other mobile. I got to my feet, my legs shaking badly. An elderly couple sitting nearby made an attempt to help me. I backed away from them.

Stay away, I thought. For your own sakes.

Boris answered on the second ring.

'Martin,' he said.

It sounded like he was crying.

I don't know how I got out of the bar, but suddenly I was standing in the blazing sun on the scorching hot pavement.

'Forgive me,' Boris said down the phone. 'Forgive me. I've failed. She's gone, Martin. Belle's missing.'

42

We think we know how we'd react when life takes us by surprise. We think we know how we'd behave if we suddenly won three million on the lottery, if we found out we only had a year to live, if someone we love were to die. But we don't. There are some scenarios that are so unthinkable that any attempt to predict how we might react to them becomes absurd. Yet we still try, over and over again. We conjure up the worst things we can imagine, and then the most wonderful things, and we utter the most mendacious words any human being can say: 'If that happened to me, I'd ...'

Standing on a pavement in Galveston I learned that a child I had come to think of as my own had been snatched away from me. I didn't know why. I didn't know if she was alive. All I knew with any degree of certainty was that I would die if anything were to happen to her. Part of me died there and then, on that pavement. Because we're born with a belief that we and our nearest and dearest are immortal. The terrible things, as well as the most wonderful ones, always happen to someone else. That gives us a false sense of security. By generously signalling a willingness to forego the greatest of successes we believe that we've entered into a pact with both God and the devil. We will never see the greatest riches, but neither will we be afflicted by the greatest trials.

Then something happens to prove that no such pact ever existed except in our imagination. And then everything collapses. The world changes in front of our eyes, becomes less predictable and thus more dangerous. What was once dark becomes pitch black. What was once as white as snow becomes dirty grey. The fear that squeezes our hearts when we look death in the eye never lets go.

Lucy came running out from the hotel. She had returned to the bar and been told what the other guests had seen.

His phone rang.

He sank to his knees.

He shouted.

Then he disappeared.

'What's happened?'

Her voice was shrill with fear. I couldn't stop shaking. I stood there with a phone in each hand, not knowing how to make time start moving again.

'They've taken her,' I whispered. 'Belle's missing.'

Words that could barely be spoken. Only when they had left my mouth did I fully understand that they were true. I had failed in my duty of care to Belle. I had failed as a parent. Utterly failed.

Lucy put her arms round me and stroked my back as if I were a child. I told her what I knew. That Belle's grandparents had been killed in their summerhouse along with two other adults I assumed must be Boris's men.

'How the hell did they manage it?' I said. 'How could they

knock out Boris's gorillas? Have you seen those guys? Built like fridges and armed to the teeth.'

I could hear how I sounded, and what conclusions could be drawn from what I was saying. Either our adversary had infiltrated Boris's team, which I was almost certain we could discount, or something infinitely worse: our adversary was so powerful that even a protector of Boris's standing could be crushed with a swat of the hand.

I don't remember how we got back to our hotel. All I have left of the short walk are fleeting impressions of intense heat, blaring cars and the sound of laughter and yelling from the beach. It could have been idyllic. But for me and Lucy, Galveston had turned into something reminiscent of Dante's inferno.

'We have to go home,' I said when we were back in our room. 'Tonight.'

'What about Denise?' Lucy said tentatively.

'Fuck her!' I roared.

Lucy got her laptop out and started looking for flights. I felt sick and went into the bathroom. I spent a long time kneeling in front of the toilet staring down at the white porcelain. Lucy came in and sat behind me. Her tears wet my shirt.

'What's going on?' she said. 'How have we ended up in the middle of this?'

I was wondering the same thing. The more I thought about it, the clearer it seemed to me that I wasn't going to find Belle unless I found an answer to that particular question.

Someone had come to my office with a plea. A young man wanted justice for his dead sister, and to find his missing nephew. I had reluctantly and then with growing enthusiasm embarked upon the job.

Now I was up to my ears in shit. I didn't know who the man who had come to my office was, and all I had to show for my weeks on the case was getting myself accused of two murders and losing my daughter.

I leaned back against Lucy who went on holding me.

One of her hands reached round to my chest. Maybe she thought I had no energy left, that I was on the point of giving up.

'We're not done yet,' she said, and I felt her breath on my ear. 'This isn't over yet. We'll never stop looking for Belle. Never. And we're going to get her back. I promise.'

How Lucy could make a promise like that was beyond me, but I let her empty words bring new life to my paralysed heart.

I stroked her arm and pressed myself even closer to her warm body.

'You never said anything to me,' I said.

'About what, darling?'

'You never said you wanted a child. I didn't realise until we were sitting in Bebe with Belle and I made that bad joke. I'm sorry.'

She held her cheek against mine. Fresh tears wet my skin. Unless I was the one crying.

'I think you probably knew,' Lucy said. 'But you chose not to say anything about it, because you also knew that the only man I've ever wanted to have a child with is you. And you don't want any.'

I turned my head so I could kiss her. The desire that overwhelmed me took nourishment from the grief and despair that were threatening to shatter my chest. I'm very good at pretending to be romantic, but I rarely genuinely feel anything. This time I felt everything. From the moment I took hold of Lucy's head with one hand as the other felt for her breast.

I felt everything and I heard everything. Lucy's laboured breathing against my neck, my own eagerness to be released for a few brief moments from the nightmare that my life was evidently going to resemble from now on.

Hands and fingers fumbling. Shirt buttons and zips. The knot in the scarf that Lucy used as a belt on her skirt. Finally the underwear that was the last barrier in our struggle for temporary respite. In the middle of the cold tiled floor of the bathroom.

Was it comfortable?

No.

Was it good?

God, yes. The best ever.

And I promised myself that if we both made it out of the chaos in which we found ourselves, I would seriously consider fathering a child with Lucy.

The sun went down just after half past seven. At five to eight we were standing at the rear of the hotel looking out across the illuminated car park. That was where the first murder victim had died.

The second-hand on my watch ticked inexorably onward. We waited ten minutes. We waited another five.

'She's not coming,' I said. 'Bloody hell.'

'She could just have got held up on the way,' Lucy said. 'Give her a bit of time.'

I clenched my fists in my pockets. The last few hours in the hotel room had been a fusillade of agitated phone calls. Belle's father's sister called, in tears. She believed her parents had died in an accident and I let her go on thinking that.

'Where's Belle?' she sobbed. 'I can't understand why it should be so hard to find Belle.'

Which was pretty much what Didrik said when he phoned.

'Martin, we've searched every last bush on that island,' he said. 'I'm sorry, but she isn't there.'

'I already knew that,' I said.

But Didrik wasn't listening.

'We're dragging the water round the island,' he said. 'We're going to find her. At any cost. You have my word on that.'

As if there wasn't one hell of a difference between looking for Belle on land and at the bottom of the sea.

'When are you coming home?' he said.

'We've checked the flights and we can't get away from here until first thing tomorrow morning,' I said.

That was how we came to be in Galveston that evening. That was why we decided to go ahead with our meeting with Denise Barton, in spite of everything. I was a long way from being finished with my thoughts about everything that had happened, but I did know I wasn't going to stop looking for Belle until I found her.

Dead or alive.

In order to do that successfully, I needed someone like Denise. Someone with the mark of evil branded on the back of her neck and her name inscribed in the register of Preston's Riding School.

While we waited for Denise to turn up, I received another phone call from Boris. I'd already spoken to him twice more since he confirmed what I had heard from Didrik. The Boris who had broken down in his shame at having failed, sobbing down the phone, was gone. This time I was speaking to a man who, like me, believed he had been dragged into a full-scale war.

'I'm not giving up until I know who's behind this,' Boris said. 'My informers will work day and night to dig out information about who we're after. It might take a bit of time, but believe me, I'm not going to let this go as long as I live. Never.'

'It's to your honour that you want to do the right thing,' I said. 'But I want you to know that I don't hold you responsible for anything, Boris. You did your best. What happened is my fault, and mine alone. I thought I understood what I was going up against. I didn't.'

My voice started to get hoarse as I concluded my speech.

'I can only say how seriously fucking sorry I am for dragging you into this. I'll do all I can to keep the police away from you.'

I said that for my own benefit as well as Boris's. Didrik was already wondering what I was involved in. It wouldn't look good if it came out that I had links to the mafia on top of everything else.

'We both know you can't do this on your own,' Boris said. 'Martin, promise me that you won't try to get out of this on your own. Because you'll never manage it. We made the mistake of underestimating our opponent. We won't do that again. Okay?'

That was when I caught sight of her. She was standing in the shadow of some large bushes, out of reach of the lights in the car park. Denise was shuffling nervously on the spot, glancing at her watch.

I nudged Lucy and nodded in Denise's direction.

'I have to go,' I said into the phone. 'Speak later.'

'You're not hanging up until you promise not to do anything stupid on your own,' Boris said.

I couldn't promise that.

'Look after yourself,' I said, and switched my mobile off.
We hurried towards Denise Barton. Boris was wrong. He
couldn't help me to get out of this. And nor could Didrik.
I've never felt so alone.

43

'It isn't a riding school,' Denise Barton said. 'Not only that, anyway. It's mainly a brothel. Or rather the head office of the business.'

We had moved away from the streetlights and were standing behind a large van that was parked beside a high wall. The sky was black and studded with stars. A beautiful backdrop to a life that otherwise resembled hell on earth.

'I don't know how they recruit other girls. They found me at the hotel.'

'Who are "they"?' I said.

'I don't know. They seem to exist all over Texas.'

'What do they do? Other than pimping?'

'Drugs, mainly. But I don't know anything about that side of it.'

'Are they active in other countries?'

'Mexico.'

'Europe?'

'I don't know. I think someone in the network has links to Sweden. Well . . . I know they have.'

'Sara Tell and Jenny Woods were from Sweden.'

Denise looked away and felt for something in her pocket. She took out a crumpled pack of cigarettes and pulled one out, along with a lighter. Her hands were shaking as she tried to light it.

'Did you know Sara and Jenny well?' Lucy said.

Denise nodded.

'We were friends. Proper friends. But we didn't see each other often. Only when Sara was in Galveston with her stuck-up family. I saw Jenny even less. She sometimes came to visit Sara.'

'There were rumours that Sara worked as a prostitute here in Galveston,' I said.

'We all did. Not just in Galveston. We worked wherever we got gigs.'

'So you no longer work for Lucifer's network?' I said.

I noticed her flinch when I mentioned Lucifer's name.

She shook her head and took a deep drag on the cigarette.

'No,' she said. 'Well . . . I'm not sure you can actually stop. Ever. But I'm taking a break.'

'How did you manage that?' Lucy said.

Denise blew smoke over her shoulder.

'I got pregnant and things got all fucked up when I got rid of the kid. Infections and stuff.'

My stomach churned and I put my hand on the wall to help keep my balance.

'I'm sorry,' I said.

'Don't be. Worse things have happened to others. Sara, for instance.'

'Did you ever talk about how she came to start working for Lucifer?' I said, trying to get back to the question of how a

Swedish girl would have come into contact with a pimp and drug baron in Texas.

Denise sucked greedily on her cigarette. It was a habit I've never understood. How some people can make themselves feel better by breathing in substances that damage their bodies for years afterwards.

'Lucifer works with what you could call talent scouts,' she said. 'They do a lot of their work on the internet, but also out on the streets. If they find a girl who would fit in Lucifer's stable they conduct an evaluation. If she fits the bill she gets offered a place. Most girls say yes. The ones who say no run for their lives. But you don't know that until you have to do it. Mind you, it was different with Sara. She was recruited straight from the streets in Stockholm.'

This was new. We hadn't been aware that Sara had been involved in prostitution in Stockholm.

'What's the attraction?' Lucy said. 'Why would a girl want to be part of Lucifer's network?'

Denise looked up at the sky with a sigh.

'No one tells you it's Lucifer's network. Not to start with. And they pay really well. Much better than other people. And ... like I said, they make it clear that it's possible to turn them down. But that anything might happen if you do. They're not good with rejection.'

Practical, I thought. Making sure there's an element of fear right from the start.

'So who pays to have sex with Lucifer's girls?' I said.

'Rich guys who demand discretion.'

'And the connection to the riding school?'

'The riding school is like the mother ship. I don't understand how the police missed it in their investigation. That's where the whole operation is administered from. Sometimes you meet clients there, but usually somewhere else. Hotels and so on. It's important that you don't have to travel too far, because otherwise it would be impossible to combine it with another job.'

'So the girls don't see enough clients to make a living from prostitution?' Lucy said.

Ash tumbled from Denise's cigarette, falling like grey rain to the tarmac.

'Oh yes, they sure do. But you're not allowed to do it if you haven't got another job. It's important that you're not turning tricks the whole time. You need a cover story; that helps protect the organisation.'

I was starting to feel properly sick now. I've paid for a lot of things with my money, but never a fuck.

'Like we said, we paid a visit to the riding school,' I said. 'You and the other girls are registered to look after the horses. Why?'

Denise shrugged.

'Maybe to explain our connection to the riding school if the cops or anyone else ever asks?'

I bought that explanation.

'We've heard that Sara was involved with drugs,' Lucy said.

'That's not true. Lucifer's girls aren't allowed to do stuff like that; they have to keep themselves clean.'

A car drove past with its lights dipped. It parked a few spaces away from us. We stood in silence as the driver locked the car and walked off.

'The tattoos you all have at the back of your necks,' I said. 'What do they mean?'

Denise's hand went automatically to her neck.

'They're our aliases,' she said, and the shame she exuded as she touched her own skin was painful to witness. 'I refused to let them do it, but in the end I realised I didn't have a choice. The tattoos are also a signal to other people that we belong to Lucifer and should therefore be left alone if there's ever any trouble.'

'Dear God,' Lucy said. 'Just how big is this network?'

Denise looked at her through narrowed eyes.

'Haven't you figured that out yet? It's huge. You can't escape it.'

That was one thing I couldn't buy. Evil international empires only exist in bad films and the fevered fantasies of sick minds. But I could accept that there was a large criminal network in Texas that was able to influence the police. But the notion that 'you can't escape it' seemed a bit far-fetched. I wished Denise could be a bit more specific, but I was starting to understand that she was far too far down the food-chain to be able to give us any detailed information.

And I could tell she was starting to get stressed. She'd have to go soon and we'd be left standing there with our unanswered questions.

'Sara's son,' I said, in a sharper voice than I intended. 'Did you know she got pregnant and had a son?'

She turned pale at my question.

'What do you mean, "got pregnant"? She was already pregnant when she left the US.'

I held my breath and glanced at Lucy. Had we realised Sara was already expecting Mio when she returned to Sweden? Lucy looked as surprised as me. I did some quick calculations.

'She can't have been very far into the pregnancy when she left Texas,' I said.

'Six weeks, maybe,' Denise said.

'Did she get pregnant because she was working as a prostitute?'

Denise took a deep breath.

'Sorry, but I daren't talk about this. Sorry.'

She put the packet of cigarettes back in her pocket and started to walk away. But that was more than I could deal with just then.

Furious, I stepped in front of her and forced her into the corner between the van and the wall.

'Let me go, for fuck's sake!'

'Not until you tell us what you know,' I said.

Lucy was standing behind me, watching out anxiously in case anyone could see what was going on. I was horrified by my own anger. If the van had been alarmed it would have been blaring out across the car park, because it rocked as Denise banged into it.

'Those bastards have taken my daughter,' I said with my face so close to hers that she could have bitten me if she wanted to. 'I've got very little left to lose.'

I waited until what I'd said had sunk in and I felt her relax in my grip.

'I've got no fucking idea why I've been dragged into this, but now my little girl's missing and I've got to find her. Get it?'

I was talking like a self-obsessed bastard. Just because I didn't have anything left to lose didn't mean that Denise didn't.

She began to cry softly.

'You'll never find her,' she said.

'How the hell can that be possible? She disappeared in Sweden. Don't try to tell me some bullshit about Lucifer being everywhere, because no one's capable of that.'

Denise just shook her head and I let go of her arms. She stood motionless beside the van with her arms folded over her chest and her head bowed. I decided not to mention Sara's pregnancy again until she had calmed down.

I stroked her arm gently.

'I can see you're scared. Do bad things happen to the girls?'

She nodded in silence.

'You obviously know that Sara was accused of two murders here in Texas. Do you know if she committed either of them?'

Denise stiffened once more.

'That's one hell of a direct question.'

'I'm a man with one hell of a big problem.'

'Yes.'

'Yes?'

'Yes, she did commit one of the murders. The one in Houston.'

I have to admit that it stung to hear her say that. I was shocked too, even though her reply wasn't unexpected.

'Did she talk about it?'

'Yes. The taxi driver was behaving like a real pig. She got pissed and yelled at him when she got out of the car. I think she was going to some nightclub in Houston. Completely the wrong place for her. One of Lucifer's competitors ran his own operation in the basement. Drugs and women. Sara figured out she needed to get out of there at once. And she ended up back in the same taxi. He recognised her, of course. He drove her into a dark, rundown alleyway and told her to get out of the car. At first she didn't realise he'd opened the trunk and taken out a golf club. He started waving it around and said he was going to fuck her with it.'

Denise stopped talking.

'And then she managed to take the club off him and hit him with it?'

'She didn't mean to kill him.'

I didn't know what to say. I was standing under a starlit night sky in Texas, listening to the saddest story I'd ever heard.

'And the murder in the hotel here in Galveston?'

'That wasn't Sara. She was here that night, and she was staying in the hotel where the girl died. But she didn't kill her. It was one of Lucifer's guys.'

'Jenny went to great lengths to give Sara an alibi for the murder here in Galveston,' Lucy said.

'I know,' Denise said. 'She contacted me as well, wanted me to help. Apparently she had been in San Antonio with a friend that weekend, and she still had the tickets. She thought they could help Sara. But I refused to get involved.'

'Because you were still caught up in Lucifer's network?'

'Because you can never escape. Jenny knew that. I mean, she'd tried to move on, she got married and everything. But she was just as scared as the rest of us that her past would come back and haunt her. I never really figured out how, but when Sara got into trouble with the police Jenny saw a chance to get Lucifer. The police would never had made the connection to him on their own, so she thought she'd help them along. But doesn't seem to have turned out so well ...'

No, you could certainly say that. For the first time I thought I had a better understanding of Jenny's motives. Her struggle to help Sara had been just as much about herself. If I compared Sara, Denise and Jenny, then Jenny was without any doubt the one who had done best for herself. Until she got killed. Denise said you could never escape. Jenny must have woken up with her stomach knotted with anxiety every morning, always aware that the life she had constructed with her husband and her job could be snatched away from her.

Husband, job ... and child.

'Jenny said she met her husband in San Antonio,' Lucy said.

I couldn't help feeling annoyed. Who cared where she'd met her husband?

'Did she, now?' Denise said. 'Maybe that's not so strange. I suppose she had to say something.'

Reluctantly I pricked up my ears.

'About what?'

'About how she met her husband. They've probably got several versions. But the truth is that he was one of her clients.'

'Oh, fucking hell,' Lucy said before she could stop herself.

As for me, I was on autopilot. I made no value judgement about how Jenny had met her husband. I didn't have the time or energy for that. Obviously her husband had lied to our faces. He had said they met at work. But in truth – what was he supposed to say to two strangers?

'The girl who died here at the hotel,' I said. 'Was she one of Lucifer's girls?'

Denise nodded wearily.

'Yep. One who wanted to get away.'

And that was that. Now I knew the truth about the two American murders. The mystery I had set out to solve was solved. Sara Texas was no monstrous serial killer, just as I had suspected all along. The man who had come to my office and said he was Bobby could be happy.

The job was finished, I had plenty of evidence to sow doubts about the matter of Sara's guilt.

But doubts were as far as it went. Because I still didn't know who had framed her. And me.

'I can't leave Texas without knowing who Mio's father is,' I said. 'Please, help us with that bit as well. Who is he?'

Denise was as pale as my grandmother's finest antique china. What would I do if she refused? Assault her? Hardly. She could go. And Lucy and I would be lost.

But Denise started to talk. Her voice was so quiet that it was almost impossible to hear what she said.

'Sara fell in love,' she said. 'Properly in love. By the time she realised who he was it was too late. It didn't matter that she fell out of love overnight. She was trapped. Jenny and I were the only people she told. We had no advice to offer. All three of us were just as horrified.'

'Who was he?' I said.

She pursed her lips and looked at me with blank eyes.

'Who do you think?'

'Can't even guess. We heard she had a guy in San Antonio, but ...'

'Forget it. Sara never had anyone in San Antonio. How would she have had time for something like that?'

'Fine, but she evidently had a boyfriend of some sort,' I said impatiently. 'Tell us. I can see you know.'

Then I heard the answer I had least expected to hear: 'Lucifer.'

Time stood still. All sound vanished. If the stars had come loose from the skies and fallen to the ground, I wouldn't have reacted.

I heard Lucy gasp for breath beside me, but couldn't bring myself to look at her. This was worse than we could ever have imagined.

'Sara had certain privileges right from the start. She worked much less, saw fewer clients. None of us could figure out why until she told us who her boyfriend was. She was the only one of us who knew who Lucifer really was. She wouldn't reveal so much as a syllable of his name, no matter how much we nagged her. She was that scared. Or ended up that scared, anyway. And then she found out that she was pregnant as well. That was the final straw, coming on top of the fight with the taxi driver that had gone so horribly wrong. She left the USA as fast as she could.'

'Did Lucifer know?'

'Not at first. Once the police operation against him kicked off she got a bit more time and was able to go home. After Sara left we didn't really stay in touch. But I understood that her problems continued when she was back in Sweden. When he heard about the pregnancy – obviously he found out – and realised that she'd indirectly stolen his child from him, he went crazy. He ... he made her life hell.'

'How? I mean, there was a whole ocean between them.'

Denise kicked the van.

'Just how stupid are you? Don't you get it, Lucifer is just like you.'

I started.

'Like me?'

'Almost, anyway. You asked if Lucifer's network extended outside the borders of the USA and I said it was in Mexico. And in Sweden. Don't ask me what the connection is. Sara said he could even speak a bit of Swedish.'

My head was spinning.

'Hang on a minute. Sara went home at the same time that Lucifer ended up in prison. How ...'

Another kick at the van's tyre.

'He was never in prison!'

I was momentarily lost for words.

'Yes he was.'

'No. No! Definitely not. That was the whole point. The guy who was identified as Lucifer was a total fucking nobody. Lucas Lorenzo, the man they wrote about in the papers, isn't Lucifer. The police knew, and Lucifer knew. Maybe they all managed to fool the FBI, but the rest of us knew that the real Lucifer had escaped unscathed. So he had no problem heading to Sweden to cause trouble for Sara. Over and over again.'

Over and over again. There we had the true culprit who had extinguished lives around Sara and then pinned the blame on her. All because she had left the network. Because she had taken the big mafia boss's son from him.

Denise lowered her eyes.

'She was so scared,' she said. 'So fucking scared.'

I heard Lucy sigh with frustration. She hated loose ends, not being able to see the whole picture.

'So Sara was the only one of you girls who knew who Lucifer was?' she said.

'Yes.'

'Jenny didn't know?'

A very good question, and one that I had forgotten to ask. If you read Jenny's diary properly, it was apparent that she had been in direct contact with Lucifer several times.

'I'm not sure, but I think he started to go after her when he started to have problems with Sara. He probably needed another way to get at her, so went for her friend.'

A way to get at her, or information. Something else that could help explain Jenny's desperate behaviour. Unlike the others who shared her background, she possessed the most top-secret piece of information: who Lucifer really was. The more I thought about it, the more unfathomable it seemed that Jenny had managed to break away. She must have been strong. And horribly lonely.

A fresh silence descended. An impotent silence. Because although I now knew much more, I still didn't know what my own role in the story was. Was it simply that the real murderer had feared I would do a good job and get too close to the truth? Was that why I had to be silenced? Anxiety and anger were tying my stomach in knots. Because Lucifer was still protected. I didn't have the faintest idea who he was. So why was he so worried?

I realised that Denise couldn't help me to understand that.

'Just one last thing,' Lucy said. 'Do you believe Sara killed her son? Or is he still alive?'

The question provoked an unexpected reaction. Denise stopped as if frozen to the spot.

'I don't know,' she said. 'I don't know.'

'We've been wondering if Jenny might have been looking after him,' Lucy said.

But Denise merely shook her head.

'Maybe,' she said. 'I don't know anything about that.'

'But you know that Jenny adopted a child at roughly the time Sara died?'

'No, I had no idea.'

She was lying.

She was lying, lying, lying.

But we still had to let her go. Because, as I reminded myself, Mio's fate wasn't our priority. Yet there was something about the boy that nagged at my ravaged brain. Something I should have reacted to, but hadn't yet done so.

Lucy saw me frowning.

'What is it?' she said in Swedish.

I didn't answer, just let my thoughts run free. The ghostly boy, Mio, what was it about him that I had missed? A thought that had struck me while we were in the car heading out of Houston.

Then it hit me.

'Why haven't we seen any pictures of Mio?' I said.

Lucy shook her head as if to sort her thoughts.

'We have, haven't we?'

'When? Not in the papers. Not even when he disappeared from preschool. And not in the material from the preliminary investigation. How can that be?'

I recalled the photograph of Jenny's son that I'd seen in her husband's office. And my own inability to say whether or not he resembled Sara's boy.

The fake Bobby's words came back to me: *You'll see. It's all part of the same story.* But I wasn't yet seeing what there was to see. Not in its entirety.

Denise had no interest in standing there listening while we had a conversation in Swedish. She was done with us, and wanted to go.

'If there's anything we can do for you . . .' I began.

She interrupted me with a sad smile.

'Forget it. You've got your hands full trying to save yourself. Don't worry about me, I'm always okay.'

'I feel sick just thinking about what could happen to you.'

She shrugged.

'Getting beaten up isn't the worst that can happen.'

She turned and started to walk away. Then she stopped and looked at us one last time.

'You know, we call it the blues.'

'What?' Lucy said.

'When we get beaten up by a client or one of Lucifer's guys. Blues, like when you're depressed. Your mood's in the gutter, then you pick yourself up. And we say that the blues have blown away.'

A surprisingly fresh evening breeze blew across the car park. Denise turned her face instinctively towards the cool air.

'One time I heard Sara scream when she was with a client. I was in the next room with one of Lucifer's men. You know what he said?'

I shook my head stiffly. I didn't know if I could bear to hear what she had to say.

'He grinned and said: "Do you hear that, Denise? That's this evening's blues. That's Lotus blues."'

PART VI

'I'm not a barbarian'

TRANSCRIPT OF INTERVIEW WITH
MARTIN BENNER (MB).

INTERVIEWER: FREDRIK OHLANDER (FO),
freelance journalist.

LOCATION:
Room 714, Grand Hôtel, Stockholm.

FO: I don't know what to say.

(Silence)

FO: So Belle disappeared and her grandparents died. And you and Lucy were drifting about in Galveston. And heard about Lotus blues. Christ, that's disgusting.

MB: Disgusting is a good word, but I'm afraid it's not strong enough in this context. It was worse than that. It was . . . indescribable.

FO: Yet we still haven't got to the end.

MB: The end? No, and we may not get there either. I'm still stuck in the middle of this story. Living it every damn day.

FO: I'm not sure I understand, but never mind. Perhaps you'd like to explain why you wanted to meet in this particular room?

MB: We're getting to that.

FO: So everything has an explanation?

(Silence)

MB: I hope so. I really do.

(Silence)

FO: So you don't know how this story is going to end?

MB: No one does.

FO: But I thought . . .

MB: Don't bother. It doesn't help.

FO: But Belle is okay? I mean, you found her?

(Silence)

44

There's an amusement park in Galveston. It's called the Pleasure Pier and, as the name implies, it's located on a pier. Lucy and I were walking along the beachfront watching the big wheel go round and round.

'We know almost all of it now,' Lucy said. 'Except what happened to Mio. And who it was who dragged you into all this.'

The wind from the Gulf made her hair billow. Her long, red curls looked almost like flames.

I stopped and looked out to sea. It could have been a perfect evening. But I had never been more unhappy. My brain had been transformed into an open-plan office staffed by ten thousand co-workers. I no longer had control of all the thoughts going round inside my head. One single word kept coming up again and again, with never-diminishing force.

Belle.

Belle.

Belle.

'Do we really not know what happened to Mio?' I said.

'You think Jenny took him? Because Sara asked her to?'

'I can't make sense of it otherwise,' I said. 'Why else would she have travelled to Sweden just before the trial?'

Lucy tried to catch her hair and hold it away from her face.

'You've seen what Lucifer is capable of,' she said. 'How can you even think Jenny could have managed to take his child without him finding out? Not just take him, but carry on with life as though nothing had happened. In Houston.'

She shook her head.

'Forget it,' she said. 'Just forget it. Maybe she wanted to and tried, but failed. Obviously we ought to check it out, but I bet all the money I've got that Jenny's adopted son isn't Mio.'

I tried to absorb her very sensible argument. Obviously, I knew she was right. It was impossible to imagine that Jenny could have made Mio her own without Lucifer finding out about it.

'You're probably right,' I said. 'She wanted to, she tried, and she failed.'

'And that could be why she didn't meet Bobby or Eivor when she was in Stockholm?'

'Exactly.'

We walked further away from the Pleasure Pier. Belle was as present in my thoughts as she would have been if she'd been running along in the sand beside us. Thinking about her made me want to cry, when I thought of how much she would have loved running on the evening-cool sand and paddling in the water.

'She said that Lucifer was like me,' I said, forcing myself to think about something other than Belle. 'What the hell was that supposed to mean?'

Lucy sat down on the sand.

'A lot of what she said didn't make much sense,' she said.

I followed Lucy's example and sank down beside her.

Her face shone pale against the darkness of the beach.

'I don't mean to sound flippant,' I said. 'But from what she told us, I have to say that Lucifer's network sounds like pretty much every other advanced criminal syndicate.'

Lucy stared at me.

'It's true,' I said. 'Girls being sold as prostitutes have a shit life all over the world. Not just here in Texas. What does seem to differentiate Lucifer's network is that it's so sophisticated. And that the links to the local police seem alarmingly extensive.'

'What she said about it not being the real Lucifer who served a prison sentence,' Lucy said. 'Could that be true?'

'It would explain a lot,' I said. 'A fair few police officers must have known they had the wrong guy. That was probably the whole point. That from the outside it would look as though they struck a hard blow against organised crime, while they were actually doing it a favour.'

A vague pain began to throb right at the back of my head. I was too tired to be awake, too worried to sleep. But I knew I needed rest. Otherwise my chances of helping Belle would shrink even further.

'We should go back to the hotel,' I said. 'Tomorrow's going to be a long day.'

We got to our feet and brushed the sand from our clothes. I found myself thinking of the day I decided Belle would grow up with me rather than with foster parents. And how much I cried then. I blinked several times. My eyes were dry, tears far away. Inside my head, along with the pain, a single mantra throbbed relentlessly.

Keep it together. For God's sake, keep it together.

'How would you summarise what we've found out so far?' Lucy said.

She averted her gaze as she asked the question.

'I think Sara was just as difficult and violent as her sister Marion said. I don't know how she came into contact with Lucifer's network, but if we're to believe Denise, then there's a branch of it in Sweden. Someone made Sara an offer she couldn't refuse. But she had to fulfil the requirement of having a normal job, and as a Swedish citizen with no qualifications there wasn't much she could do except get work as an au pair.'

We started to walk back to the hotel. My headache was slowly working its way forward through my head and I massaged my temples. It didn't help.

'Somehow Sara managed to get introduced to Lucifer. How that came about is beyond me, maybe they met by coincidence. I mean, we have no idea who Lucifer is. Presumably he has a proper job as well, to hide the sordid side of his life. Maybe he didn't even know Sara was one of his girls. Either way, the two became a couple, if we're to believe Denise. According to Sara's au pair family, the rumours about her taking drugs are without foundation. I think we can agree with them on that point. Denise says Lucifer's girls need to be clean, and the same must have applied to Sara as well.'

'Do you think she was in love with Lucifer, or did she only stay because she was too frightened to leave him?'

'According to Denise, Sara fell out of love when she realised who her boyfriend was,' I said. 'If she really did love him I suppose she would have stayed in the US. But she didn't. Her biggest problems were presumably the murder of the taxi driver and her pregnancy. It seems incredible that she didn't opt to have an abortion. By having Lucifer's child she was creating another link to him, one she'd never be able to escape from.'

'So she went back to Sweden,' Lucy said. 'Lucifer may not have been caught when the police tried to destroy his network, but he was forced to keep a lower profile. It's hard to imagine a better chance for Sara to make her escape.'

'Exactly,' I said.

We had almost reached our hotel. Sand fell from our feet as we walked towards the road we needed to cross. Lucy pointed at the pedestrian crossing and we headed for it. I carried on talking. If I stopped I would become irrational. Nothing scared me more than the idea that worrying about Belle would make me lose my grip. If that happened, she would be lost for good.

'On paper it looks like Sara kept it together in Sweden,' I said. 'She got a job, had her child, found somewhere to live. But another three people died. That's one hell of a cynical way to get control over someone else's life.'

I added silently to myself that it was evidently a method worth repeating. Against me. Two murders had been carried out using my car. Four people had been murdered to get at Belle. I had never been given any opportunity to back out. The same applied to Mio. The child without a face.

'Good evening,' a voice said behind me and Lucy. 'Lovely evening, isn't it?'

We turned round. Sheriff Esteban Stiller was standing less than half a metre from us. I barely recognised him. In his pale blue shirt, sleeves rolled up, his khaki trousers and open sandals he looked like any other holidaymaker. He was smiling so broadly it must have been hurting his face.

Neither Lucy nor I managed to reply. We just stood there as the light turned from red to green, staring at him.

He nodded towards the crossing.

'Shall we?'

We started walking automatically.

'Because you are going back to your hotel, aren't you?'

'Yes,' I said.

My pulse-rate went up. How long had he been following us? Had he been in the car park and heard our conversation with Denise?

'You look worried, Benner,' Stiller said when we reached the other side of the road and were standing in front of our hotel. 'Anything I can do to help?'

I forced out a thin smile.

'I don't think so, but thanks for the offer.'

Stiller laughed and waved at a small child who was passing on the pavement. The child looked at him, wide-eyed.

'They're wonderful at that age, don't you think?' Stiller said to me.

I didn't understand what he was trying to say. The child was roughly the same age as Belle. Had I ever mentioned her to Stiller?

And, even more importantly: did he know what had happened?

'You look surprised,' he said, nudging my arm with a force that signalled that his intentions were not merely friendly.

'I didn't know you were going to show up here,' I said, unnecessarily quietly.

'I can imagine,' he said. 'I didn't actually know myself. I was planning a quiet evening at home with my family, but that didn't happen. Do you know why?'

I was getting fed up of people with hidden agendas.

'No, but obviously I'd love to hear about it.'

Sheriff Stiller's face switched from friendly to angry so quickly that it was impossible to measure the time between them.

'You need to watch yourself, Benner,' he said. 'You've been asking a lot of questions recently. Way too many, in fact. I've had phone calls from colleagues wondering what's going on. They're wondering who you are and what you're up to.'

I kept quiet. As did Lucy.

'In the end I found myself thinking the same thing myself. I started asking myself if it made sense that someone like you had travelled all the way from Stockholm just to give a dead tart a helping hand. And do you know what I did?'

Keep it together. Keep it together. Don't go mad, don't lose your grip.

Stiller came closer.

'I called a contact of mine at the Stockholm Police. A man I got to know when we worked together to catch Sara Tell. I don't mind telling you that I was pretty shocked when I realised why you'd left Sweden.'

I began to suspect who Stiller had spoken to and what he'd been told.

'You're suspected of two murders, Benner. Didn't you think I'd find out?'

Cops stick together. I'd learned that much during my brief career with the Houston Police. Evidently the ties of loyalty also applied between police forces in different parts of the world.

'I haven't killed anyone,' I said. 'And if you and Didrik were decent police officers you'd have realised that.'

Stiller's eyebrows knitted together.

'We would, now? Well, seeing as you're so brilliant, maybe you could help us out? If you're not the murderer, who is?'

'Someone who has a reason to silence both Sara Tell's brother and her friend Jenny Woods. Which I didn't have. The fact that you can't see that these two murders are connected to the five others that Sara was accused of is utterly absurd.'

'It's possible that I'm both an idiot and going senile,' Stiller said. 'But didn't Sara confess to all those other murders? And seeing as she's dead, it seems a little unlikely that she's committed two more.'

'Quite,' I said. 'So perhaps it might be possible to contemplate the possibility that someone else was the perpetrator? Someone who's still alive and carried out all the murders?'

Except the one in Houston, I thought.

'And how do you think that theory sounds?' Stiller said. 'Most smart ideas lose some of their gloss when you say them out loud.'

'I think this one stands up,' I said.

Stiller let out a deep sigh. In profile he looked very similar to an American actor whose name I couldn't remember.

'Sara was part of Lucifer's network,' I said. 'How the hell could you miss that?'

Stiller switched to the sort of silent response I'd just been demonstrating.

'He's probably the father of her child as well,' I said. 'What does that say to you?'

I'd been expecting a violent reaction from Stiller, but it didn't come. His expression didn't change.

'Your investigation stinks,' I said. 'Completely fucking incompetent. The question is, how did you get away with it?

If I were you, I'd do the whole damn thing again. Go back to square one. Take another look at Sara's network of contacts. Talk to her au pair family. They can tell you she wasn't on drugs. Analyse the tattoo she had at the back of her neck and why she was known as Lotus. When you drive home tonight, you can start by turning off the freeway when you see the sign for Preston's Riding School. Get out of the car and take a look around at the impressive grounds. And ask yourself how someone like Sara could afford to register there.'

My blood was boiling by the time I finished. I prayed to God that I was going to have time to continue the investigation when I got back to Stockholm. If Didrik pulled me in at the airport and held me in custody, it would all be over. Didrik would never manage to find Belle, I was convinced of that.

Stiller cleared his throat.

'Listen, Benner,' he said. 'It's not that I don't like you, because I do. But I think you've lost your grip on reality. Maybe that's what happens when you kill two people, I don't know. Anyway, who gives a damn, I've had a nice evening here in Galveston. So I'll be generous and give you one final warning. Leave. I expect you to be gone first thing tomorrow morning. Please don't disappoint me. It would be a shame if we parted on bad terms. Because we are going to part. And you're never going to come back to Texas.'

He came closer and took a firm grip of the back of my neck. He was shorter than me, but I still felt much smaller.

'You understand? Never, ever. Not as long as I have any say in the matter.'

His grip on my neck tightened, making my eyes water.

'I understand,' I said.

'Sure?'

'Yes.'

I tried to nod but it hurt too much.

Then he let go and stepped back.

'Good,' he said.

He gave Lucy's hand a brief squeeze.

'Look after him,' he said, and looked at me. 'I shall pray for you next time I'm in church with my wife. Because neither of you is going to get through the time ahead without the help of higher powers.'

45

With Stiller's curse hanging over us, we flew home the next day. The flight took us from Houston to New York, where we changed planes. From there we flew direct to Stockholm. We slept through the entire journey. It was as if my body couldn't remember how to relax until it left the ground. It wasn't just about relaxing. It was more a matter of conscience. If I closed my eyes for more than ten minutes, if I allowed myself to sleep, I felt like I was actively trying to kill Belle. I needed to stay awake and strong. I needed to be ready to pounce at any moment.

Sheriff Stiller's words echoed through my head as the sound of the engine made me drowsy. What did he know about the difficulties Lucy and I had ahead of us? Not a damn thing. At one point I woke up with a start and sat bolt upright in my seat. Lucy was fast asleep beside me. The sight of her chest rising and falling in time with her breathing soothed me. I wasn't alone. I had one single person I could cling to. It would take a nuclear strike to prise me away from her.

We landed at three o'clock in the afternoon, Swedish time.

Stockholm welcomed us with heavy rain. I thought about Lucy's sun-creams and realised sadly that she had barely had to use them at all. When this was all over, when we had got our lives back, I'd take her to a beautiful beach at the other end of the world. I whispered that in her ear as we stood and waited for our luggage.

'I don't care what it costs. We'll close the office and go. You, me and Belle. No one else.'

Lucy smiled weakly but said nothing. I was talking like a man who still thought life always kept its promises of a happy ending.

I'm a changed man these days. One who now doubts that.

Our hire car was still in the long-stay car park. It felt almost surreal to get in it and drive back towards the city. I realised I had lost track of the days. How long had we been gone? Three nights. Four? No more. And then the flights on top of that.

'Where are we going?' Lucy said as we were approaching the centre of Stockholm.

It took me a few moments to realise what she meant.

'I thought we could drive back to mine,' I said. 'Unless you'd rather go to yours?'

Lucy was exhausted. I had spent days trying to understand what had driven her to follow someone like me all the way to Texas. A man who would fuck anything on two legs, and who was rarely much of a support for her when she was having a rough time. Had I, in spite of all my inadequacies, somehow managed to convey the fact that I loved her? Because I did. Beyond reckoning. If I hadn't known that before, I did now. And actually, now that I came to think about it, I wasn't sure I was particularly attracted by the lifestyle that had seemed completely natural just one week before. If I managed to get Belle out of this nightmare in one piece I felt I was going to be a changed man.

Someone who was whole.

'Let's go home to yours,' Lucy said. 'That'll be fine.'

She switched our mobile phones on. Soon the messages we had received while we were in the air began to pour in. Boris had called. Didrik too. Belle's aunt, my mother.

I called Didrik first.

'Are you home now?'

'Yes. Thanks a fucking bunch for being so open with Esteban Stiller.'

'What the hell did you expect? I have to act professionally even if you and I do happen to know each other. When a colleague phones from the USA and asks questions about you, I can't just neglect to mention something as significant as the fact that you're a suspect in two murder cases.'

I tried to divide my attention between driving on the drenched road and listening to what Didrik was saying.

'So nothing has changed on that score in my absence?' I said. 'You still think I ran down Bobby and Jenny?'

'I refuse to discuss this over the phone,' Didrik said curtly.

'Then I suggest we arrange to meet,' I said. 'Preferably today. Because even if I suspect that you're going to ignore what I'm going to say, I want to make sure the information gets fed into the system. In case anything happens to me.'

Didrik answered in a voice that was supposed to sound trustworthy. 'We can do that. When can you be here?'

'Lucy and I will be with you within the next hour and a half.'

'If you can make it by then. If not, I'll wait for you.'

He didn't need to. Prioritisation is only a problem for someone with too much time. When every minute counts, it also becomes very obvious what you should be spending your time doing. During the drive home from the airport we worked our way through all the calls that needed to be made. Boris had nothing new to report, not that I had expected anything different. Belle's aunt was still distraught, and started to sound genuinely hysterical over the phone.

The conversation with Marianne was the hardest. She had read about the fire in the archipelago in the paper but hadn't realised who had died in it. Nor had she realised that Belle was missing.

'Oh, Martin,' was all she said before she started to cry.

'I'm going to find her,' I said. 'Don't worry, I'm going to find her.'

We didn't get much further than that. When I put my mobile down I was in tears as well. What would happen to my mum if anything happened to Belle? I was hardly a source of joy to her, and her only daughter was already dead.

Frustrated, I wiped the tears from my cheeks. Real fighters don't cry. They arm themselves.

We slipped into Police Headquarters after stopping off at the flat to dump our bags and change clothes. Didrik himself came down to fetch us. The grief in his voice was genuine when he said how sorry he was about what had happened to Belle. But I didn't want his sympathy. I wanted an apology, and I wanted my daughter back.

Once again we sat in one of the interview rooms rather than Didrik's office. But a number of things were different this time. One of Didrik's colleagues was present, but remained almost ridiculously passive during the meeting. We were offered coffee and sandwiches, and said yes to both. A weak man is a weak man. And everyone needs to eat.

Didrik gave a brief summary of what they had found out about the fire. If it weren't for the fact that Belle was missing they'd probably have written it off as an accident. Now they were leaning more towards arson.

'Have you done any toxicology analysis of the bodies?' I said.

The sandwich was surprisingly good. There was no way it had been made in Police Headquarters. Everything prepared there tastes of rubber.

There was something wary about Didrik's expression that I would have reacted to under different circumstances. But the warning sign passed me by.

'Why do you ask?' he said.

'Because I think it's odd that four people should be sleeping so soundly in the same house that none of them managed to escape the fire. I've been in that house. They can't all have been sleeping upstairs. The ones sleeping downstairs ought to have had time to get out.'

Didrik folded his hands behind his head. It was a gesture I associated with my grandfather, usually when he was about to say something patronising to my mother.

'So what you're trying to say is that you think one or more of the victims was sedated or given tranquillisers so that they couldn't get out of the house?'

I took another bite of the sandwich.

'Either that or they were knocked unconscious before the fire was started,' I said when I had swallowed my mouthful.

'Interesting,' Didrik said. 'Very interesting.'

'How so?' Lucy said.

Didrik lowered his hands.

'Because that's quite correct. The two men who were found on the ground floor both had injuries to their skulls which indicate that they were already unconscious when the fire broke out.'

He fell silent and looked at me.

I let go of the sandwich and it fell onto the plate it had been served on.

'Oh, for fuck's sake!' I said, doing my best not to raise my voice. 'You're seriously sitting there implying that there's something suspicious about me questioning the fact that none of the adults got out of the house?'

'Not at all,' Didrik said calmly. 'You're a smart man. That sort of thing is easy to work out. No, what surprises me is that you haven't shown the slightest interest in who the men are, or what they were doing in Belle's grandparents' home.'

Damn.

As I struggled not to look like I'd been rumbled, Didrik went on.

'But perhaps there were four adults in the summerhouse when you dropped Belle off?'

He answered his own question.

'It's probably hard for you to know. Bearing in mind that you handed Belle over to her grandfather at the quayside.'

I thought about coming up with a lie. Something that could explain why I hadn't been curious about the number of adults in the little summerhouse. I could have said I'd spoken to Belle over the phone and that she had said that Grandma and Granddad had guests. But I knew that wouldn't sound believable.

'Come on, Martin,' Didrik said. 'I don't hold you responsible for the arson attack. So tell me. Who were the guys we found on the ground floor?'

I took my eyes off Didrik and looked out of the window. Where were all the clouds coming from? And all the damn rain? It was as if the weather gods had decided not to give up until they had drowned the whole city.

I had no idea how easy or difficult it would be for the police to identify the bodies. And I had no idea if the police might then be able to link the men to Boris. But I realised it would hardly help my case if it came out that I'd had dealings with the Russian mafia. So I needed to distract Didrik's attention, and regain the initiative in the conversation.

'What were Jenny and Bobby doing out in the middle of the night? As late as, what, two o'clock, half past two?'

Didrik's eyes narrowed.

'We have our theories.'

'They were lured outside?'

'Maybe.'

'What do you mean maybe? It's perfectly obvious that it wasn't a coincidence that—'

'I can't discuss this with you. You have to understand that.'

Of course I did. I realised that the police had no more than theories, and that they couldn't prove anything. I welcomed every gap of that sort in the investigation. Every gap was a point of weakness. Every weakness hindered them from remanding me in custody. My fingers drummed silently on the armrest of my chair.

'Do you know what Lucy and I were doing in Texas?' I said.

Didrik threw his hands out.

'We visited a magnificent riding school.'

Didrik looked at me suspiciously.

'A riding school?'

'Yep. We made a little detour on the way down to Galveston.'

'I see. And what did you find there?'

'A place where you can be struck by a very particular form of the blues.'

46

Why was I still a free man?

That question was tormenting me as I left Police Headquarters. I kept comparing my situation to the one Sara had found herself in. Whoever it was who had framed Sara for five murders had done a thorough job of it. In the end she had even been forced to join in by delivering a number of bizarre confessions. No similar demands had been made of me. But my daughter was missing and no one had been in touch with either an explanation or any demands of what I had to do in order to get her back. Whoever had decided to blast my life and my honour into little pieces was taking a break. The question was: what were they waiting for?

I hated the feeling that my future was in someone else's hands. I had been turned into a puppet. Of all the roles I had played in my life, this was by far the one I loathed most.

My Porsche was waiting for us outside the main entrance. Didrik handed me the keys.

'Drive carefully,' he said.

I drove the Porsche and Lucy the hire car. Once we had

dropped it off at the rental firm she jumped in and sat beside me.

'What now?' she said.

I was itching all over. The car felt dirty after having been with the police. Obviously they must have bugged it. Otherwise they would almost certainly have kept it. Even though Didrik hadn't mentioned a word about it, I knew they had been in my home and conducted an invisible search of the property. Nothing illegal about that, and it's obviously nicer if they can do it in such a way that isn't visible. I'd been struck by a number of odd things the moment we opened the door when we got back from the airport. The very thought of Didrik's goons creeping about playing cops and robbers in my home made me feel sick.

'I'll tell you in a bit,' I said in response to Lucy's question.

We drove through Stockholm in silence. The countless dull buildings stretched up to the sky. Stockholm is so predictable, so simple. Beautiful but feeble. Like a woman in some chivalrous tale from the 1300s.

We lack substance, I thought. Sweden hasn't become impoverished, the way people keep saying. It's become insubstantial, and that's worse.

I pulled up outside the front door. When we were in the stairwell I stopped.

'There's a good chance we're being both bugged and followed,' I said. 'So I don't want us to stay in the flat. Let's grab a few clothes and get a taxi to a hotel. Or walk, that almost makes it easier to shake anyone following us. We pay for the hotel in cash. We don't speak more than necessary in the flat. Okay?'

Lucy nodded.

'Okay.'

But I could see hesitation in her face. She was saying that everything was okay, but it wasn't, and it hadn't been for several days. Lucy was losing her enthusiasm at an accelerating rate, and I didn't know how to handle that. I barely had enough energy to keep myself going.

I held her tight in the lift.

'This will be over soon,' I said. 'I promise.'

It would be difficult to find a more empty promise, but just then I had nothing but meaningless words to offer. It worked. Lucy found the strength to repack the case she had taken to the States, and soon we were on our way back out.

'I didn't like the fact that Didrik asked about the men who died out at Belle's grandparents' house,' Lucy said when we thought we had probably shaken anyone following us.

'Believe me,' I said. 'Neither did I.'

We were half-running along the pavement. It had stopped raining, but there was thunder rumbling rather too close for comfort. We must have been walking for at least ten minutes before I noticed that Lucy was crying.

'Baby, what is it?'

She kept walking and I followed her.

'I'm so fucking knackered. And terrified. How are we going to find Belle? How, Martin?'

I swallowed hard. I was in a pretty manic state. The only thing – the *only* thing – that was stopping me from falling apart was the thought that to do so would be as good as signing Belle's death warrant. And that was an impossible thought. I had already let Belle down in so many ways. It couldn't end with me killing her by giving up.

We turned another corner. Soon we reached Blasieholmen, heading for the Grand Hôtel.

'We'll be seeing Boris later this evening,' I said.

Lucy stopped dead.

'Boris? Come off it, we can hardly trust him again?'

I stopped too.

'Look, it's not his fault Belle is missing.'

'No, and it's not his fault we didn't manage to get hold of Lucifer, even though we followed his excellent advice. "Don't look for Lucifer. Let him look for you instead." What a fucking joke.'

Angrily she started to walk again.

'We're not seeing Boris because he's got some incredible master plan to share with us,' I said.

'Really? So what's the point of seeing him, then?' Lucy said.

Sarcasm seemed to have become a permanent feature of her voice.

'You'll see,' I said curtly. 'He's managed to find some interesting material that he wants to show us.'

'What?'

We had reached Stallgatan. The Grand Hôtel was less than two hundred metres away.

'He's not entirely unlike Lucifer,' I said. 'He's got contacts in the police as well. It looks like he's managed to get hold of a list of people who were in the same gang as Sara here in Stockholm. You know, the one she belonged to before she left for the States.'

Lucy clutched the shoulder-strap of her handbag.

'And what do we want that for?' Lucy said.

'We need more names, Lucy,' I said. 'Names and faces. I'm not saying Boris can give us all the answers, but we need to start looking somewhere. Because we have to find the link to Lucifer's network in Texas. And we desperately need to find the guy who came to the office and dragged me into this whole circus.'

Obviously it was a gamble. Maybe bad, maybe good. The only person who had mentioned the terrible company Sara used to keep was her sister Marion. There wasn't a word about it in the file from the preliminary investigation, which was odd. It would have been an advantage for the prosecutor if he could have pointed to a history of violence. Didrik had said they had chosen not to include that information because it couldn't be proven. So there was information, but it had ended up in what was known as the dump. Surplus material from preliminary investigations that couldn't be included in the final files. Material I had requested but hadn't had time to read.

I was thinking that there might be someone in Sara's network of thugs who stuck out from the crowd. Someone who could explain how she managed to find out about Lucifer's network in Texas and what it could offer her while she was still in Stockholm. It was a big step to go from beating people up on the streets to selling her own body, so what had persuaded Sara to take that decision?

I reminded myself that Sara could hardly be counted as one of the more rational people I had ever come across. She was damaged. Her own father had sold her to his friends. Perhaps Sara saw the journey to Texas as a chance to get revenge. She could sell herself on her own terms, and make a lot of money at the same time. In her naivety she probably hadn't counted on getting beaten up.

Lotus blues.

Bloody hell.

Lucy refused to meet Boris so I went on my own.

'I won't be long,' I said to her back.

She was standing looking out of the window with her arms folded. Her hair was loose and hung like a cloak down her back. She didn't turn round.

I left Lucy in the hotel room and walked quickly through the long corridors of the Grand. It's a strange feeling, staying in a hotel in your home town. You become a visitor to your own reality and everyday life. I wasn't at all sure I was happy with the experience, not that it really mattered. We weren't going to be staying at the Grand Hôtel for the rest of our lives. Just until everything calmed down. Until we had got Belle back.

It was pouring with rain when I left the hotel. I opened a large umbrella and set off towards Skeppsholmen, where I had arranged to meet Boris. But my ordinary mobile was switched off. If the police wanted to find me now they would have a hard time. That was also the point. I wanted to avoid being taken by surprise by them while I was with Boris. Partly for his sake, but mostly for my own.

We met at the back of the Måsen restaurant. He was standing beneath a raised veranda sheltering from the rain. I closed the umbrella and went and stood beside him.

'I know I've already said this, but I really am so damn sorry about what happened,' he said.

I knew he was. I would have been too if I were him.

'My mistake was far worse than yours,' I said. 'I should have known better than to leave her behind.'

'I could never have imagined ...'

'None of us could.'

I had no defence against the pain. The violent force of the anxiety I felt genuinely surprised me. Without Belle, the rest of my life looked like a pitch-black road stretching ahead of me, and there was no way I'd be able to handle that.

'The police say the men who were found on the ground floor of the house had head injuries which suggest they'd been knocked unconscious before the fire started. Or before they managed to get out of the building, anyway,' I said.

'Yes, I heard that from one of my sources,' Boris said. 'My lads must have gone into the house for some reason. After all, they were watching Belle from outside, not inside. Close enough to have a good overview, but far enough away not to be seen.'

I had trouble finding words.

'Perhaps the fire wasn't part of the original plan,' I said. 'Perhaps your guys saw someone break into the house to snatch Belle and decided to catch them unawares. And then it all went wrong. God knows how, but they ended up unconscious.'

'Looks that way,' Boris said. 'Once my lads were knocked out, torching the whole house probably looked like the best option. That's what I'd have done. Fire is a good way of destroying unnecessary evidence.'

'Seriously?' I said sharply. 'You'd have set fire to two innocent elderly people like Belle's grandparents just to get rid of evidence?'

Boris started to wave his hands.

'Stop it,' he said. 'I didn't phrase that very well. I . . . I don't actually know what I would have done.'

Neither of us felt like continuing that particular debate. He pulled out a folded envelope from the inside pocket of his jacket. In spite of his shaved head and bushy eyebrows, he had one of the kindest faces I have ever seen on a man.

'This is what I've got for you,' he said, handing me the envelope.

'Thanks,' I said, and took it.

'Take care of the contents. It cost quite a bit to get hold of.'

'Forgive me, but I'd rather not know how you got hold of this information,' I said.

It was best if I didn't even hear that Boris had bribed individual police officers in order to help me, even though I realised that was what must have happened.

'Your contact,' I said. 'Was he or she absolutely certain that the names mentioned in this envelope are the people Sara Tell used to hang around the city with?'

'Pretty much,' Boris said. 'Everything fits. The time when they were active, their ages, and how many of them there were. Sara's name is mentioned in one memo, where an anonymous source identifies her as a gang member, but because the police didn't have anything else on her they left her alone when they went for the rest of the group. They probably thought she'd sort herself out if the gang was broken up.'

Maybe it was a sensible supposition. The police could hardly have known that the unthinkable would happen. That Sara would use her contacts to get herself into an even worse situation.

I clutched the envelope tightly in my hand.

'Did you manage to get pictures too?' I said.

'No problem. Passport photographs of all of them. Some of them are probably a few years old now, but with a bit of luck they'll do, well enough.'

I was inclined to agree. As I'd said to Lucy, I didn't know what to expect. I just knew I had to start somewhere. And I was hoping I might recognise one of the members of Sara's gang. Someone who could explain a few of the many things I couldn't get my head round.

'Thanks, Boris,' I said.

He shook his head, his mouth tense.

'You don't have to thank me,' he said. 'Not for anything.'

I didn't have the energy to offer him any comfort. It was as simple as that. I'd already said he shouldn't blame himself for what had happened, and that was all I could do for him. If that wasn't enough he'd have to turn to someone else for help to come to terms with his own shortcomings.

'You'll be in touch if you want help talking to any of those jokers?'

He nodded towards the envelope.

'Of course,' I said, hoping that wouldn't be necessary.

Boris glanced at an abandoned wheelbarrow a short distance from us. It was full of rotten apples. The sight of the sodden windfalls made me feel even more miserable.

'So what's your plan now, Martin?' Boris said.

'I need to understand how Sara ended up in Lucifer's stable. And I want to find the man who came to my office and figure out who sent him. Because I still haven't worked out why I was asked to do what I was, nor who was indirectly responsible for the commission.'

Boris coughed into the crook of his arm.

'You haven't?' he said slowly.

I looked at him warily.

'No,' I said. 'I haven't.'

Boris hesitated. A bird landed on the pile of apples and started pecking at the dark flesh.

'Can I hazard a guess, or have you had enough of those?'

I held back a sigh.

'It didn't turn out too well when you tipped me off about how to make contact with Lucifer,' I said, remembering the

way Lucy and I had sat in a hotel room in Houston calling
police officers whose names we had found in various newspaper articles.

Boris twisted his head and looked me in the eye.

'How do you know it didn't?'

'Sorry?'

'It would be a shame to declare that project dead,' Boris
said. 'How long did you stay in Texas after making those
calls? One day? Two?'

When I opened my mouth to protest he went on.

'How do you know you haven't already met him, Martin?
It sounds like you met a whole load of weird people you didn't
know over the past few days, so you wouldn't actually be able
to tell. And besides, your daughter's gone missing. I hope and
pray that she's been kidnapped, but we obviously can't be
entirely sure of that.'

I needed to digest what he had said before I replied.

'Okay,' I said. 'Go ahead, Boris. Let's hear your guess as to
what this is all about. Because I haven't got a fucking clue.'

Boris laughed.

'You're underestimating yourself, and it doesn't suit you. If
you give it a bit of thought, you can probably figure out what
this is about.'

His mobile buzzed discreetly and he pulled it out of his
jacket pocket.

'You're wondering why someone came to your office and
asked you to help a dead woman and find her missing son. So
my question is: who in the whole world would care about a
serial killer's kid? Answer: the kid's father. Or someone else
with a strong connection to the child.'

I'd got that far myself.

'Lucifer was the child's father,' I said.

'Are you kidding?'

'Nope. At least not if we're to believe what Sara told her friend in Galveston.'

'Fucking hell. Well, then. What else are you wondering about?'

I jabbed the point of the umbrella at the ground.

'I made it very clear to the guy who came to my office that I wasn't going to look for the kid. He replied that everything was connected, and that I wouldn't be able to prove Sara's innocence unless I understood the child's role in the story. But I stuck to my guns. I also said I had no intention of going to Texas. Despite that, I still got the job. He didn't take it to someone else.'

'Which makes you think that there was another purpose, beyond exonerating Sara and finding Mio, because they picked you specifically? A hidden purpose that you're only now understanding the consequences of?'

'Exactly. Because if the real purpose was just for me to find the child, why frame me for two murders I didn't commit before I'd even started looking?'

'Maybe because the person who asked you to look for the boy isn't the same one who has put such effort into ruining you?'

I opened my mouth, then shut it again. What Boris was describing was a double nightmare. One that couldn't be true.

Boris shook his head.

'Now you're thinking all wrong again,' he said. 'You're assuming both of these forces have sought your attention out of sheer malice alone. But that isn't necessarily the case. The one who came to see you first, the one who said he was Bobby, might well have been genuine. He wanted nothing more than for you to clear Sara's name and find her son, if he's still alive. But the other one, the one who's trying to wreck your life. Maybe you'd never have crossed his path if it hadn't been for the fake Bobby.'

'So who is this second person, then? Who doesn't want me to get justice for Sara and find Mio?'

More rain had started to fall, harder this time.

I already knew the answer before Boris said it.

'The real murderer, Martin. Remember, Sara was never actually convicted of any crimes. Her case never even made it to court. Most of the evidence suggests she was forced to confess, for reasons we still don't know. So who would get seriously fucked off when you start pulling at loose ends and poking about in the shit? The person who's been feeling nice and safe since Sara's death, seeing as he's been able to hide in the shadow of her pathetic confessions.'

A cold wind gusted off the water. In the distance I could hear a man talking German very loudly.

I pondered what Boris had just said. It wasn't remotely implausible. Far from it.

'And Belle?' I said.

'You get her back once you've given the murderer the guarantees he needs to feel safe long-term.'

Upset, I started to pace up and down, like a badly drawn cartoon.

'But I hardly know anything,' I said. 'And what I do know, I've already told the police.'

'You're a right idiot, aren't you?' Boris said with a deep sigh. 'You've got to stop that at once. No more contact with the police. Got that? No more contact.'

'That's not so easy when you're being investigated about two murders.'

'I don't give a damn. It's one thing if the police pick you up. Then it's obvious that it isn't voluntary. But you need to break off all other contact. Otherwise you'll never get Belle back. Do you understand?'

I understood. But not everything.

'Mio,' I said.

'You want to talk some more about him?' Boris said drily.

'There aren't any pictures of him.'

'What do you mean, no pictures?'

'Nothing in the papers, nothing with the police. Doesn't that seem weird?'

Boris shrugged his shoulders.

'Not necessarily. Maybe you could tell who his father was by looking at him. In which case his mother probably didn't want there to be any pictures of him.'

'But Lucifer already knew. That's why he was pursuing her, and committed murders that he then pinned on her.'

I had no better explanation, but I knew there was one important detail that was missing.

'Go back to your hotel,' Boris said, putting his hand on my shoulder. 'Don't keep yourself so isolated that you become difficult to trace. Be a bit more patient this time. You can be certain of being contacted in the near future. Even the most hardened bastards would be reluctant to kill a four-year-old girl.'

I gave him a long glance.

Was it enough that they were reluctant to kill her? Being reluctant to do something wasn't the same as refusing or ruling it out.

Even so, Boris's final sentence gave me the strength to leave him on Skeppsholmen and walk back to the hotel. The envelope Boris had given me contained the promise of fresh leads to follow, and I was no longer oppressed by the crushing conviction that Belle was gone for good.

But all the renewed energy drained away from me when I opened the door to the hotel room and discovered that it was empty. Lucy was gone. She had left a message for me on my pillow.

Martin, forgive me, but I can't do any more of this right now.

I'm not abandoning you. I just need to be on my own this evening.

I'll call tomorrow.

Love you,

Lucy

47

As the summer night closed around Stockholm I sat awake in my hotel room. Loneliness has so many different dimensions. Most of them I only know because I've had them described to me by other people. From a personal point of view, I barely know what loneliness is. I don't like it, and I avoid it whenever I can.

But that particular evening I had nowhere to go. Lucy had left, and I didn't want to pester her. Nothing must be allowed to increase the distance between us. It was bad enough as it was. If I gave her a chance to catch her breath she'd get in touch the following day, just as she'd promised.

And Belle was gone. I hardly dared to think about her. Panic threatened to consume me entirely. I knew Boris was right. Belle was worth nothing to her kidnapper if she was dead. And even bastards didn't want a child's blood on their hands. That was scant solace, the notion that the only thing that could save Belle was if the perpetrator had a functioning conscience and a scrap of morality.

I opened the envelope Boris had given me. I remembered

what I had said to fake Bobby the first time he came to see me.

'Look around you. This isn't a film studio, this is real.'

I almost burst out laughing. Loud, nervous laughter. Because the sense of unreality that was eating me up was so overwhelming that nothing felt real any more. My hands were shaking. I daren't allow myself to have any expectations about the contents of the envelope. Just hopes. And vague ones at that. I couldn't handle any more disappointments.

The envelope contained two documents and a number of photographs. One of the documents was an account given to the police by a so-called protected source. That was the one which mentioned Sara Tell's name. The informant had no first-hand information, but rumour had it that Sara was a member of a violent gang that was going round the centre of Stockholm beating people up.

The other document was a brief summary of the members of the group the police had chosen to focus on. Four names: three guys and one girl, the same age as Sara. There was no mention of Sara. The only name I recognised was Edvard Svensson, Sara's ex-boyfriend. His photograph was also at the top of the pile. I recognised him from the picture Sara's mother had shown me. A shiver ran through me as I recalled my meeting with Sara's mother. It felt so long ago. As if it had taken place in another age.

With clumsy fingers I went through the pile of photographs. The next picture was a girl. She had three rings through her nose and a horrible amount of make-up on her face. I had never seen her before.

The third picture was of a young man I didn't recognise either. I looked at his face for a long time to see if I could see anything familiar about it, but I couldn't. I was feeling frustrated. I just wanted to make some progress, to get closer to Belle.

And in the end that was what happened. With a sense of having closed the circle and come nearer to a solution. Because the last photograph was of the guy who had come to my office claiming to be Bobby Tell.

I couldn't take my eyes off his face. It was him, yet it wasn't. The young man staring out of the photograph had laser-like eyes and features that exuded force and decisiveness. That was hardly the impression he had made when he was pretending to be Bobby. My hand trembled slightly as I held the picture up in front of me.

Finally, a fucking breakthrough. A far better one than I had dared to hope for.

At last.

My first instinct was to call Didrik. Now I had something to show him. A picture of the fake Bobby. But how would I explain where I got it? Didrik could never force me to answer that question, but the fact that I didn't actually have an answer was a problem. After further consideration I decided not to involve the police. I would try to find the guy on my own.

His name was written on the back of the photograph. Elias Krom. I picked up the list of gang members, which also gave their official addresses and last-known telephone numbers. Elias lived on Södermalm, close to Tantolunden Park. I sat for a long while with the sheet of paper in my hand. Everything would have felt much easier if I'd had someone to discuss it with. I actually got as far as reaching for my phone to call Lucy. But in the end I put it down again. She had asked to be left in peace that night. I risked losing more than I could imagine if I didn't respect her wishes.

I must have run through my options a hundred times before I reached a decision. I didn't have that many choices, but the factors affecting them were practically infinite. Time had dissolved and lost its normally solid structure. The darkness told me it was night, but my brain felt ready for action.

In the end I left the hotel room. Armed with nothing but my intellect and battered judgement, I headed out into the streets to find a man who, in spite of his stated intentions, had helped to ruin my life.

That sort of thing couldn't go unpunished.

Fate solves a lot of things for us. Elias Krom wasn't home when I got there. But his girlfriend was. It was after one o'clock at night when I rang the doorbell. Answering the door at that time ought to have been an unusual occurrence. But she still did so.

I had evidently woken her up. And it was just as evident that she wasn't expecting anyone.

'What do you want?' she said.

I couldn't help thinking that society hadn't yet become utterly racist. There were still women who would open the door in the middle of the night to an unknown black man who looked like shit.

'I'm looking for Elias.'

'He's not home.'

'I'm a lawyer, I need to see him as a matter of urgency. When are you expecting him back?'

'What do you want?' she repeated.

'I don't know if you've seen the news in the past few days,

but four people were killed recently in a fire in the archipelago. That's one of the things I want to talk to him about.'

The girlfriend fell silent. Ordinarily I ask myself if I want to sleep with women I meet as a matter of course. Not because it's important, but because it's an entertaining diversion. But I couldn't say what Elias's girlfriend looked like, even at gunpoint.

'Elias drives a taxi. He ought to be home in an hour or so. He should have been home by midnight but his shift got extended.'

I had spotted an all-night café on the other side of the street. I could sit and wait there until he got home.

'Tell Elias I'm in the café over the road,' I said. 'Thanks.'

The café smelled of cigarette smoke. Maybe the owner smoked in the kitchen in spite of the ban. I certainly didn't see any lit cigarettes among the few customers sitting there.

I took a seat by the window and ordered a black coffee, then was left alone. My life was no longer my own. It had been torn apart by forces I couldn't even name. Now I was trying to put the pieces back together in a squalid little café on Södermalm, a part of the city that I otherwise try to avoid as much as possible.

I hadn't dared leave any of the material at the hotel, so was carrying everything with me in a shoulder-bag. The coffee was steaming in its cup. It looked more like tar when I took a closer look. Whether or not it was drinkable was unclear.

The zip on the bag made a noise as I opened it. I put the pile of papers on the table and started to look through them. They included the notes from our trip to Texas, as well as 'Sara's' diary and the wretched train ticket from Houston to San Antonio. And the envelope Boris had given me.

At the bottom of the pile was the brochure we had been given at Preston's Riding School. I hadn't known that Lucy had been a horsey girl before. I hated knowing that there were things in her past that I would never know about. Either you've lived your whole lives together or you haven't. If you meet later in life you can spend thousands of hours talking about yourself and still not manage to cover everything.

I glanced through the brochure while I kept an eye on the door to Elias Krom's building. I assumed his girlfriend would phone and warn him that I'd been. It didn't matter. Elias could run away to the moon if he liked, I would still find him. If he had any sense at all he'd realise that.

Preston's Riding School. It was easy to understand that someone from Sara's background had been drawn to that sort of environment. Denise Barton in Galveston hadn't said much about the conditions. How much did the girls earn? Did they earn more if they got beaten up? I felt my frustration mounting inside me, and I felt like throwing the cup of coffee at the wall.

I forced myself to focus my energy on the material I had in front of me rather than on all the gaps in my knowledge. I had tipped off Sheriff Stiller about the riding school. It was laughable to think that he'd care. He hadn't cared so far, and he wasn't likely to care in the future either. It was one of the things I had reacted to most strongly. That no one we had met had been willing to admit that they could have linked Sara Tell to Lucifer's activities.

I leafed quickly through the brochure from the riding school. Glossy pictures of horses and smart buildings interspersed with tedious, boastful information about the facilities on offer. It wasn't until I reached the back of the brochure that something caught my eye. A brief historical summary. The riding school was ten years old. To mark its fifth anniversary a former American President who was mad about horses had joined in the celebrations. One of the President's nephews had also sat on the school's inaugural committee. Impressive. I had to admit that as a front for prostitution and drug dealing, the school was convincing. From a distance there was no reason to suspect anything. Not if a relative of a former president had been on the committee. It seemed obvious to me that anyone with that sort of public profile would be unaware of the true purpose of the organisation. It was important to show that they had nothing to hide. In that respect they had succeeded admirably. The riding school had remained unscathed when Lucifer's network was broken up a few years ago.

Out of curiosity I read the names of the people who had been on the riding school's committee. Almost all men from what I could see. A few women. Each name was followed by a single sentence describing the person's background, and I soon realised that most of the committee members came from the business community. All apart from one woman who was a doctor, and a man who was a prison governor.

My eyes froze on the paper. I didn't hear the door to the café open as someone came in. Nor did I notice when that person walked determinedly in my direction.

The only thing I had eyes for was the name of the former prison governor who had sat on the very first committee of the riding school. A man who had gone on to become a sheriff in Houston.

Esteban Stiller.

48

'I heard you were trying to get hold of me.'

I recognised the voice immediately and flew up from my chair. But I didn't get more than halfway before I felt unexpectedly strong hands and arms pushing me back down again.

'Okay, okay. Don't let's get overexcited here. Or we might have to go somewhere else and talk, and I don't think you want that.'

Elias Krom let go of me and sat down on the other side of the table.

The café owner padded over to us.

'Everything okay?'

It wasn't clear which of us he was addressing, but I took the initiative and replied.

'Everything's fine. Sorry if we disturbed you.'

'I don't want any trouble.'

'No trouble,' Elias said. 'We're just going to have a chat.'

The owner withdrew doubtfully.

Elias sat with his legs apart, leaning back in his chair. I had to give him credit for his acting skills. He'd done a good job of embodying Bobby. I'd swallowed the whole story, hook, line and sinker. I hadn't doubted that he was who he said he was for a second.

'I don't know if you've been trying to reach me before,' he said, and turned away to cough. 'Sorry if you've had trouble getting hold of me. Things have been a bit hectic lately.'

Only then did I see that hidden beneath the superficial toughness was a hint of fear. I wasn't the only person at that table under a lot of strain.

'Three questions,' I said as calmly as I could, holding up three fingers.

'You can ask as many as you like, but I'll only answer if I feel like it and am able to.'

I could have said the same, but kept quiet about that.

'First question. Who asked you to come to my office and pretend to be Bobby Tell?'

One corner of Elias's mouth twitched. If the idiot was about to grin he was making a grave mistake.

'Who says I didn't come of my own initiative?' he said.

'I do,' I said. 'And please don't insult my intelligence with cheap jokes. I haven't got the time for that right now. Just answer the question. Who was it?'

Elias's expression didn't change.

'Do you remember what you said to me?' he said. '"In this room you have no equal, just a man who is superior to you in every respect." How does that feel now? I presume you're not so superior any more?'

I forced myself to drink some coffee. It would be a disaster if I beat the guy to death before he'd even answered the first question.

'Sorry,' I said. 'I was born arrogant and there's no changing that. Let me ask again: *who sent you?*'

Elias leaned so far across the table that he was almost lying on his arms.

'What makes you think it wasn't Bobby?'

'Bobby's dead.'

Something dark came into his eyes.

'I know.'

'So tell me. Before you meet the same fate. Who told you to come and see me and plead on Sara Tell's behalf?'

Elias sat up. His face was different now. There was something more relaxed, something sadder about it.

'Fuck it,' he said. 'It *was* Bobby who first dragged me into this.'

The air in the café was thick with sour coffee and old food smells. It seemed to catch in my nose when I breathed it in.

'Prove it,' I said.

I clenched one fist on my lap. Surely that couldn't be true? That Bobby had got in touch with one of Sara's old friends and asked for help?

'I can't,' Elias said. 'But I can tell you he wasn't the one who first contacted me. That was Ed, Sara's ex. Bobby didn't know me that well, so he called Ed. He'd heard you on the radio – Bobby, I mean. Thought you sounded okay. Because, you know, Bobby never got over what happened to Sara. The rest of us didn't really know what to think, but it hit Bobby so hard it almost killed him. He moved abroad and ended up in all sorts of shit. Then he decided to make one last try. Mostly to find out what had happened to the kid, Mio. That was how you came into the picture.'

The hand in my lap kept opening and closing, opening and

closing. I believed what Elias was telling me. There was something liberating about his story. So distant from everything that came later, nocturnal death rides in my car and burning houses.

'Go on,' I said.

'Bobby was so used to being rejected. After all, he'd tried going to Sara's lawyer and the police. But no one would listen to him. They didn't even want to see him when he got hold of new evidence from Sara's friend in Texas. That's why he didn't dare turn up in person and asked one of us to do it instead. Ed didn't want to, so I ended up doing it. Once you'd taken the bait and a bit of time had passed, we were going to explain what was really going on.'

'I would have been allowed to meet the real Bobby?'

'Yes. Bobby had come home from Switzerland and was involved from the start. He was here for something like three weeks before he died.'

I thought through what I'd just been told. Put the pieces of information together. Belle loved doing jigsaws. I didn't have the patience.

'When Bobby died he had the mobile phone I'd tried to reach you on in his pocket.'

'Because it was his phone,' Elias said. 'I only used it to communicate with you. And we only did that by text, too.'

'That's not true,' I said. 'We spoke on the phone before we met on the Sunday when I accepted the job.'

'Yeah,' Elias said. 'Bobby was staying at mine for a few nights.'

I sat without saying anything, trying to understand. So it really had been Bobby who had set the whole thing rolling, even if he hadn't dared do it in person. But what about everything that had happened since? Bobby obviously had nothing to do with any of that.

'I don't know anything about that,' Elias said quickly when I broached the subject with him.

Far too quickly.

'Believe me, I've been lying seriously bloody low since Bobby died,' he said. 'I've been totally fucking terrified. I have no idea why Bobby had to die, and I don't want to know either. I'm really sorry if we've messed things up for you, that wasn't the intention at all. But keep me out of this battle, I don't belong there.'

It was only then that I realised. Whoever had murdered Bobby had no idea that it was one of Sara's friends who had come to see me. Whoever killed Bobby had done it to shut him up, which from the killer's point of view would probably still have been deemed necessary even if he had known about Elias's role in the story.

'Bloody hell,' I whispered. 'Bloody hell.'

Elias squirmed on his chair.

'My girlfriend said you mentioned that fire out in the archipelago. What's that got to do with anything?'

I was no longer in any doubt. Elias looked genuinely bewildered and stressed. He didn't have a thing to do with anything that had happened later.

I felt like bursting into tears at my impotence. Fucking bastard bollocks ... How do you find your way out of a labyrinth? You don't. You get directed the way its designer wants you to go. And in this instance that wasn't Elias, and it wasn't Bobby. It was a shady character from Texas who went by the name of Lucifer.

'You need to be careful,' I told Elias. 'Do you hear? If

whoever killed Bobby finds out that both you and Ed knew about Bobby's plan, you'll have serious problems.'

Suddenly our roles were reversed. I had the upper hand and Elias was at a disadvantage. That had been the case all along, but I hadn't realised before now.

Elias rubbed his face with his hands to wake himself up. He was tired. Considerably more tired than I was.

'Who burned down the house in the archipelago?' he said.

'I don't know,' I said. 'But I'm going to find out.'

Esteban Stiller's name came into my mind. The man who had been on the riding school's committee and pretended he didn't know that Sara had belonged to Texas's biggest drug baron's stable of prostitutes.

Stiller is Lucifer, a ghostly voice whispered inside my head.

I tried to stay calm. Denise Barton had said that Lucifer had some sort of link to Sweden. That was how he had been able to recruit prostitutes from here. If I could find a link between Stiller and Sweden, I'd have an explanation that actually held water.

Elias cleared his throat.

'I get it if you're angry with me,' he said. 'But ... fuck it, my girlfriend and I are getting married. Don't torch me if you can avoid it, okay?'

He was as pale as freshly fallen winter snow.

'Don't worry,' I said. 'I'm capable of a lot of things, but I don't kill people. But I'd really like you to answer another question, if you've got time?'

He nodded.

'When Sara left for Houston, did she say what she was going to do there?'

'She may have done, but not to me. I was in prison. Only

six months, but all the same. We didn't have any contact at the time.'

Shit. But I tried all the same.

'When you were in the same gang as Sara ... Did she ever talk about prostitution? To be blunt, was that something she was involved in?'

Elias hesitated, as if he didn't want to reveal Sara's secrets even though she was dead.

'Look, her dad was caught up in all that. He used to sell her. So she had it in her, somehow. She used to do it from time to time, fuck people for money.'

'I can understand that these questions might seem a bit weird, but do you know if she had any particular contact who helped her find clients?'

'Like a pimp, you mean? No, she didn't. She wanted to be independent, that was the whole point.'

No matter how I tried, I wasn't getting any closer to the truth. How on earth had she managed to find – or be found by – Lucifer's network?

Elias looked thoughtful.

'Although there was actually one guy she used to talk about,' he said slowly.

I held my breath, felt my heart hammering against my ribs.

'She met some American guy, an older bloke. I don't know how old the bastard was. But I know she fucked him at least once. When she started talking about Texas, Bobby told me she'd mentioned him. Said he was going to help her. I don't know how. But Bobby was really fucking worried.'

I swallowed.

'Why?'

'Because he thought she was acting like she was in love.

And that's not smart. Falling in love with someone who's paid for you.'

Finally some important pieces fell into place. Denise had been wrongly informed. Sara hadn't got to know Lucifer by chance in Texas. He had recruited her in person.

My stomach knotted. This was worse than I could have imagined.

'I think I'm going to have to go now.'

Elias stood up. The feet of his chair scraped on the floor. He held his hand out feebly across the table.

Without hesitation I stood up and took it.

'Thank you for coming,' I said. 'Good luck.'

Relieved, he shook my hand hard, with feeling.

'Thanks,' he said. 'You too.'

Then he disappeared from the café, out of my universe. The man who had never really had any interest in helping Sara, who had just agreed to help Bobby. I sat down again. I watched him as he crossed the street and vanished into the building where he lived. The pressure in my chest felt immense, relentless. The story looked pretty clear now. Sara had been the exception. She had been Lucifer's very own find. And she ended up pregnant with his child. Then, when she decided to run, the eventual consequences were worse than she could ever have imagined.

Five premeditated murders. She had been framed for five premeditated murders. When she had actually only committed one. And that was unpremeditated. It was self-defence, and could never have been classified as anything but manslaughter, at the very worst. In all likelihood she would have been found not guilty as long as she could prove that she had feared for her life.

I pulled out my mobile and started searching aimlessly for information about Sheriff Stiller on the internet. I had limited expectations, but it did no harm to look. I knew that American sheriffs were elected by the people. So there had to be quite a lot written about them.

The first search results led me to various Texan newspapers that had published articles about Stiller in various contexts. I went onto the sheriff's office's own website. It featured a picture of a smiling Stiller. An untroubled man with happy eyes and deep dimples.

Sheriff Stiller liked playing chess, according to the brief biographical note. He had been married to his wife for fifteen years, and they had four children. They went to church regularly. The family had two dogs and lived in a beautiful house in one of the more prestigious suburbs. I was about to close the page when I read the last lines:

'The Stiller family love travelling, and do as much of it as they can. They particularly like visiting Europe. Sheriff Stiller's wife Pamela's parents are Swedish, and they love to see their grandchildren as much as possible.'

Nausea rose up out of nowhere. I rushed through the café and to the toilet, only pausing to grab all my papers under my arm. They fell to the floor as I leaned over the edge of the bowl and threw up so violently that it splashed the white porcelain.

He had been right under my nose the whole time. The man who had managed to escape the Texas Police's big operation against his network. The man everyone knew as Lucifer, but whom no one seemed to have met.

Esteban Stiller was Lucifer.

Of course. How the hell could we have missed that? The fact that Lucifer not only had contacts inside the police but actually belonged to the force himself.

I vomited until only bile came out. With my legs trembling I straightened up and leaned on the washbasin. My eyes were bloodshot when I looked at my reflection in the mirror.

My brain was working at top speed. Could Belle be hidden away with Stiller's Swedish parents-in-law? Or had she been smuggled out of the country? I didn't think so. Belle was still in Sweden, I was convinced of that.

So why hadn't I got her back? Why hadn't anyone been in touch?

Then, as if in answer to my musings and prayers, my mobile phone rang. A voice I knew I'd never heard before said: 'I've got something that belongs to you.'

49

My first impulse was to roar down the phone. Which is what I did.

'You fucking bastard, where is she?'

There are limits to the polished manners of a lawyer.

'Bastard? Listen, if I can be civilised then so can you.'

He was speaking English with a heavy Southern States dialect. But he wasn't Sheriff Stiller. I knew that much.

The man went on, 'It's a damn shame it's ended up this way, but I believe we have a solution that we could both live with.'

'Okay,' I said.

I waited, unable to breathe.

'You see,' the voice said, 'things have got a little complicated. What with you managing to become a suspect in two murders and all.'

'Yes, thanks very much for that,' I said. 'It's good for a lawyer to see what life is like as the accused.'

A dramatic pause followed. The line hissed and it struck me that I had no idea where the man was calling from. I yanked open the toilet door and peered out into the café. No one was behaving suspiciously.

'Oh,' the man said. 'You think I'm the one trying to frame you for two homicides as well?'

'Er, yes?'

The man clicked his tongue.

'Then I can understand that you're confused. Sadly I cannot claim the honour for that.'

'Yeah, right.'

I walked out of the toilet and over to my table. I stuffed my paperwork into the bag and left the café.

The man sounded noticeably irritated when he replied.

'It's a shame to hear you use such a sarcastic tone of voice,' he said. 'Now listen to me, because, strange though it may sound, you have more problems than the ones I have caused for you.'

I stopped on the pavement a metre or so from the café. The street was dark and it was pouring with rain. The feeling of being utterly exposed was so strong that I almost turned and went back inside again. The cool summer's night gave me goose-bumps.

'There's only one problem I care about,' I said. 'Belle. Where is she?'

'She's two hundred metres from the Grand Hôtel,' the voice said calmly.

The bag slid from my grasp and landed on the ground with a thud. I crouched down to pick it up, then found that I didn't have the energy to get back up again.

'Sorry?' I said.

'You heard what I said. And best of all is that she can be at your room within ten minutes. So she could be there waiting for you when you get back. How does that sound?'

My throat stung when I breathed. I clutched the bag to my chest.

'That sounds good,' I said. 'I'll do anything. Anything at all.'

'I don't doubt it,' the voice said. 'I'd do the same if I were you.'

'I don't care about anything that's happened,' I said. 'I don't even care if I get convicted of those murders. Just give Belle back to me. Please.'

Up to that moment I was a man who hadn't used the word please in that sense since I was seven years old and learned that it didn't work. Pleading seemed to work for other kids, but never for me.

'Okay, for the last time. I'm not responsible for the fact that you're suspected of two homicides. Admittedly, I was planning to silence Bobby and Jenny, but using different methods. The less blood, the better the agreement. Like the one we're looking at here, for instance.'

An alarm started to sound in my head.

Like the one we were looking at now.

Exactly what had we agreed on?

I felt sick again. Fear is an unpleasant thing, it can assume a million different colours and shapes. Beyond the fear of any agreement I might be forced to accept was an entirely different terror. If Lucifer wasn't trying to frame me for two murders, who was?

'It was both entertaining and disquieting to follow in your footsteps in Texas,' the voice said. 'You would have made a good policeman, Martin. You could have gone far.'

I tried to think rationally. How much could he really know about what I knew? If he had spoken to Denise then it was all over. But if not . . .

'I don't know that much,' I said. 'We tried, Lucy and I. We tried like hell. But you were always one step ahead of us. No one was willing to talk to us.'

'Apart from the au pair parents,' the voice said. 'And Jenny's husband. And ... Denise.'

Fuck. Fuck, fuck, fuck.

'I still don't know who you are,' I said. 'And I've got no proof. Of anything. Not for Belle's kidnapping, not for the murders in Stockholm that Sara was accused of.'

'No, you haven't,' the voice said. 'And for that we are of course very grateful. But I'm afraid that isn't enough.'

We?

My legs would no longer carry me. I sank to my knees, ready to be shot in the temple. I didn't know where the conversation was going, and fear had drained me of all energy.

'Get to the point,' I said. 'Tell me what you want so I can have Belle back.'

I heard him take a deep breath.

'I'm not a barbarian. I basically have zero interest in harming your child. But I need a promise that your investigation into my activities stops here and now. And by that I mean right here and right now. Do I have that promise?'

At that moment I didn't give a damn who the hell he was. I wasn't curious, I never wanted to know. The only thing I wanted was to get my daughter back.

'I promise,' I said. 'You have my word of honour. I swear by all that is holy – I shall never take another step in your direction.'

'Excellent,' the man said. 'That's the first part done, then. But do us both a favour and bear in mind the lengths I was prepared to go to in order to get hold of Belle. You know that if I really want something, nothing can stop me. I think that ought to suffice. Don't waste time trying to hide Belle. Or Lucy, for that matter. Just stick to what we agree tonight. Then I'll let you live. All three of you.'

Hearing him mention Lucy and Belle's names in the same context left me in free-fall. *What we agree.* Did he seriously think I had any other choice than to do exactly as I had been told?

'Then we have a mutual dilemma to deal with,' the man said matter-of-factly. 'I would very much like to know who's trying to frame you for those two homicides. But on that point I assume you don't need any further motivation to realise how important it is to discover the identity of the person who would go to such lengths to be rid of you. Drag the bastard into the open. Using whatever means necessary. Find out who is pursuing you. So that we can get a bit of peace and quiet.'

I sat there as though I'd fallen from the heavens, incapable of thinking of anything to say.

'Why should you care who's trying to frame me for two murders?'

'How hard can it be to understand? I want to leave this story behind me. Stop it causing trouble. But it won't let go of me, just keeps coming back. First when Larry Benson recognised Sara and kicked off the murder investigation. And now you've started digging about in the same mess. Naturally I shall conduct my own research to find out who is after you, I need to ascertain what the individual in question knows. But my resources in Scandinavia are limited. Which leads us neatly to the last point I want to discuss with you before we hang up.'

But I didn't want to hear the last point. Not yet. A glimmer of rationality broke through all the panic. What the hell was he saying?

'It was you who framed Sara for those murders, no one else,' I said.

'Correct. But that wasn't the plan back at the start. That was something I had to come up with once things had started to move. It didn't strike me as even remotely possible that a police officer would recognise Sara from a picture that was several years old. Naïve of me, perhaps, but such is life.'

My thoughts were swirling faster now. Too fast.

'So what *was* your plan? If you weren't trying to get Sara arrested?'

The man took a deep breath.

'She was supposed to get arrested. But just for the murders in Stockholm. And only if she didn't do what I wanted. It was never about anything but the kid. But she didn't want to surrender him voluntarily.'

'Why didn't you take him when you had the chance? After all, you had several years in which to do it.'

'You mean I should have just snatched him away from Sara. That would have let her off the hook in a way she didn't deserve. Besides, it's dangerous to deprive a vulnerable person like Sara of the only thing she holds dear. There was a risk that she'd go to the police and lay all her cards on the table. So I needed some kind of hold over her. To make sure I could control her.'

'So you threatened her?' I said. 'To make her surrender the boy to you of her own volition?'

'Well, maybe not quite of her own volition. Once a year I went to Sweden and asked her to come back to the States

with me. And every time she said no, I made sure I got rid of
another person she could be linked to.'

'All that, just to force her to capitulate one day? Did she
know about the murders?'

'Of course she did. That was the whole point. It was a
simple choice. Either she and the child came back to the
States with me. Or she stayed in Stockholm and lived with
the consequences. Every time she said no, an innocent person
died. Someone whose murder she risked being accused of.
But I honestly never thought we'd get to that point. I assumed
she would soften. And I also knew that she wouldn't be able
to keep quiet, and would tell the friends she still had in the
US. Which was fine. It's important to make an example of
someone.'

'And you did all this yourself? Or did you send an
underling?'

'This was and is personal. I did everything myself.'

'How did you choose the victims? How did you know
which people Sara knew or had been in contact with?'

'You ask far too many questions. I let her choose. Which
was nice of me, don't you think?'

The awareness of what I was up against was paralysing. It
was screwed up beyond belief.

'So what happened?' I said quietly. 'The Americans suspected Sara of the murders in Galveston and Houston and
contacted the Swedish police. She was called to an initial
interview and denied everything. Then what?'

'I realised that she actually risked being convicted of those
two murders. And I was concerned that her defence would be
based upon her links to me. That she would try to bargain
for her freedom by volunteering crucial information about my

network and activities to the police. So I went in and sorted things out. I made sure the police found out about the three murders in Sweden as well, making Sara look like a serial killer who had run amuck in two continents.'

'All to make yourself invisible,' I mumbled.

'Exactly. But Sara needed something in exchange, of course. So I promised that if she confessed to the five murders, I would leave the child alone.'

The irony stung like disinfectant in an open wound. Because there I was, in possession of the whole truth. And the man who had asked for it, Bobby, was dead. I had no one to share my tragic triumph with.

My fingers moved over the wet wall behind me. The bricks were cold and slippery.

'You've told me everything else, so tell me where Mio is now,' I said. 'Don't try to claim that you abandoned your efforts to make him your child just because you'd made a promise to Sara. I don't believe that.'

Nor had Sara, I realised. That was why she had escaped. To save Mio.

'Of course I had no intention of letting Mio go,' the voice said. 'But I was planning to wait until after the trial. That was a big mistake.'

'You didn't have time to take him,' I said. 'Sara got there first. She . . .'

'She tried,' the voice interrupted. 'God knows, she tried. But she wasn't sure she could do it on her own. And her escape plan had to succeed, of course. So she asked Jenny for help.'

I nodded slowly. The picture was getting clearer and clearer. But not in the way I had expected.

'But Jenny didn't succeed with her mission either,' the voice said. 'According to their plan, Jenny was going to take Mio to safety. It wasn't a particularly good plan. It was based on such improbable factors as Sara managing to escape and then joining them. Really, what place on earth could be so remote that they would never be discovered?'

My stomach was cramping. Images of Belle in her grand-parents' summerhouse brought tears to my eyes. I knew better than anyone that there were no safe places to hide if it happened to be Lucifer you were running from.

'Where is he?' I said. 'Where's Mio?'

'That's precisely what I don't know,' the voice said. 'Do I have to point out that I find that really fucking annoying?'

I didn't understand. Sara hadn't killed Mio, as the police thought. And he wasn't with Jenny, as Lucy and I had guessed. And now Lucifer was saying that he didn't know where the child was either.

'I thought you said there were no safe places to hide?' I said.

The brick wall took the weight of my body as I leaned back against it. Rainwater streamed down my face. I didn't care. Cold or warm, wet or dry. Nothing mattered.

'Not for anyone whose identity I know. Like Sara. And you. But that's the problem. I don't know who took the boy.'

So you don't know where to start looking, I thought.

'How do you know he isn't dead?' I said.

It was a terrible question, but I didn't think I owed the man on the phone any great sensitivity.

'I spoke to Sara after she escaped,' the voice said. 'She was utterly hysterical. The boy had gone missing from his preschool and she was sure I'd taken him. Later, once things had calmed down, I contacted Jenny. She said that was why

Sara had jumped from the bridge that night. Because she was certain I had Mio, even though I denied it.'

'But you hadn't?'

'No.'

I didn't know what to think or say. Mio wasn't my boy. Everyone who had ever wished him well was dead. Yet I still couldn't help wondering. If neither Sara, Jenny nor Lucifer had taken him, where was he?

'I want you to find him for me, Martin. That was the last point we needed to discuss. I want Mio.'

I stood up. My whole body was shaking. With fear, cold and anger. It evidently didn't make any difference how much effort I put into moving on, moving forward. It was as if I was caught in a huge spider's web. Impossible to escape.

'I won't be able to find him,' I said. 'Believe me, if I had even the weakest clue to go on ...'

'You'll just have to do your best,' the voice said. 'Someone's got Mio, and you're going to find out who. That's all there is to it.'

'You just want a name?'

'Exactly. Then I'll fetch the boy myself.'

I stood in silence on the pavement. So fucking alone. So beside myself with anxiety and objections.

'And if I fail?' I said.

My voice was weak, and I hated the inferiority it betrayed.

'I think the situation is as follows, Martin: you won't be able to let go of this story without finding Mio. Ultimately the whole thing is about him. Whether we like it or not. So it's in your own interests to track him down. Obviously I shall take a number of measures to locate him, but, let me repeat, I have limited resources. I need someone in Stockholm who can help me. I want that person to be you. And, for the sake of clarity – this is a non-negotiable wish.'

Problems the size of icebergs loomed up ahead of me, joining those that were already there.

'I'm already in the shit,' I said. 'I can't afford to start running errands for the mafia.'

'You aren't going to be running errands,' the voice said angrily. 'You're going to help me find the boy. No more, no less.'

I swallowed hard.

'And when do I get Belle?'

The moment I said my child's name, the dark blue summer's night was split by a bolt of lightning. It lit up the street I was standing on. A taxi was waiting some distance away. There was no one but the driver in it.

The rain that followed was like nothing I had experienced before. I ended up as wet as if someone had thrown buckets of water at me. Even so, I couldn't bring myself to move.

That business of time standing still – I know it's true now. I held my breath and waited for what he would say next.

Give her to me, I thought. Let me have her back and I'll do anything.

'According to the original plan, Belle was kidnapped to make you stop. To put a stop to everything, really. Both you and we needed a break. The fire made you go home from Texas quick as hell, and gave you a certain respite from the police. And I wanted to give you a warning. So that you would end up as willing to cooperate as you say you are now.

'I'll do anything,' I said hoarsely.

I scraped my fingers against the bricks.

Say it, for God's sake. Say I can have her back.

'Belle will be in your hotel room when you get back.'

I slid down towards the gutter. My back scraped the wall as the water from above did its best to drown me. I no longer knew what was rain and what were tears on my cheeks.

'Thank you,' I whispered. 'Thank you.'

As if I owed the man on the phone a huge favour. I suppose I did. But not the way you usually imagine someone to express gratitude.

All the cold and wet had numbed me, left me impotent. I was an incompetent wreck who had got caught in the gutter. The rain would wash me away at any moment. I was going to get Belle back. Everything else was secondary. And in truth – I didn't need any warnings. I had already understood that I had nothing to gain from hiding my nearest and dearest away.

'How do we stay in contact?' I said.

'I'll be in touch,' the voice said curtly. 'Two more things. Firstly, if it hasn't already been made clear enough: from now on you stop telling the police what you do and don't know. I assume you appreciate that?'

I did. I had already told Didrik everything I had found out in Texas. Even if he probably wouldn't do a damn thing with the information. And he wasn't going to get any further details.

'Absolutely,' I said. 'And secondly?'

'Secondly: I'm not Lucifer.'

I almost dropped the phone. Quarter of an hour ago I had been certain Sheriff Stiller was Lucifer. Then my mobile had rung and I hadn't recognised the voice. So Lucifer had to be someone else. Now I was suddenly back with the same thought I had had a short while before.

'I realise that I let you believe I was Lucifer throughout this conversation, but that isn't the case. I am merely an associate. An assistant. A very senior assistant. You can think of me as a deputy. Lucifer sends his best wishes.'

I opened my mouth, then closed it again.

'Take care of yourself, now, Martin,' the voice said. 'We'll be in touch. And don't forget what I said. It's all about Mio.'

Then he was gone.

I looked at my phone as if I'd never seen it before. As if I didn't understand how it worked. Then I managed to make my clumsy fingers work. I called the only person who could confirm that Lucy was still there. As the call went through I thought how ironic it was that in spite of the fact that I'd taken a hundred steps forward, I was back standing where it had all begun. With someone telling me that I couldn't ignore Mio's fate.

Eventually Lucy answered. Despite the note she had left at the hotel, despite wanting to be alone.

'Are you okay?' I said.

Or did I sob?

'Of course I am,' she said.

Then, with a little more doubt than before: 'I always am, Martin.'

50

There was never any hope of restraint. I tried to stop myself, but of course it was impossible. I ran over to the taxi that was parked up a short distance away. It was busy, the driver was waiting for a customer. I turned and ran on. I ran so fast it felt like my lungs were on fire. Because I wanted proof that I hadn't been tricked. That I hadn't managed to lose Belle by being clumsy or naïve.

I hadn't. The next taxi I hailed was free.

Exactly as promised, Belle was in my room waiting for me. She was sound asleep, but there was nothing wrong with her breathing. Belle was alive, and she was in my room.

And Lucy was on her way.

I kicked my shoes off, shrugged off my jacket and climbed onto the bed. Carefully I lay down beside Belle and held her. Not too hard, I was still soaked after all that rain. Her hair smelled faintly of smoke, which brought tears to my eyes and made me clutch her tighter.

I'm never going to let you go, I thought.

That lightness I had dreamed of. Which had existed as a

mirage in my mind the whole time. It wasn't quite there yet. I was still stuck in the same purgatory. And I still had the sense that I was living on borrowed time.

One silent minute followed the other. My heart was thudding so hard it felt like it was growing with each beat. I couldn't help thinking that there was a limit to what a human being could tolerate. And that I had come dangerously close to my own limit.

Then Belle woke up. With a start and a hoarse cry. She struggled to get out of my arms.

I hurried to turn her round so she could see my face.

'It's only me, Belle,' I said. 'Only me. Martin.'

Softly, as I didn't want to disturb her.

She looked at me with eyes wide as saucers, simultaneously horrified and relieved.

'Where's Lucy?' she whispered.

Her voice was hoarse. Did she need to go to a hospital? Could she have been harmed by the fire?

I stroked her hair.

'She's just gone out for a little while,' I said quietly. 'But she'll soon be here.'

Belle relaxed and rested her head against my chest. With something akin to fascination I realised that I was crying. My new self was evidently a softer character.

I lay down on the bed and waited. For Lucy to arrive, for my daughter to become herself. Belle nudged closer to me again.

'Daddy,' she whispered. 'Daddy.'

TRANSCRIPT OF INTERVIEW WITH
MARTIN BENNER (MB).

INTERVIEWER: FREDRIK OHLANDER (FO),
freelance journalist.

LOCATION:
Room 714, Grand Hôtel, Stockholm.

FO: Sorry, but I'm almost in tears as well. So this was the room you stayed in? Is that why we had to meet here at the Grand?

MB: Yes. I didn't move back home until I was sure Boris's guys had checked the flat for bugs. There weren't any.

FO: Bloody hell. Sorry to swear, but what a hideous fucking nightmare. And, sorry again, what a ridiculously unlikely story.

MB: You don't believe me?

FO: I do. But the question is, will anyone else?

(Silence)

FO: And Lucy?

MB: She came to the hotel. She's okay.

FO: But I mean, what the fuck? You're really not going to the police with this?

MB: The police?

FO: So you get some protection!

MB: Protection? Against what? Against someone who found and snatched Belle even though she had Boris's men looking out for her? That's a ridiculous idea. The police can't help me. Only I can do that. And the rules are simple enough. As long as I stick to them, I can feel safe.

FO: What does Lucy say about all this?

MB: She's staying with me and Belle. She says she's already far too involved to back out. Besides, Lucifer knows who she is. She won't be properly safe until I am.

FO: So what are the two of you doing now?

MB: Well, I don't know about the two of us. I'm attempting to find the person who's still trying to frame me for murder. And, one way or another, I'm supposed to be trying to find Mio. Unless the two things are actually one and the same. That seems to be what some people think.

FO: What about the police, then? Do they still believe you murdered Bobby and Jenny?

MB: I'm sure they do. But the arson attack in the archipelago which killed Belle's grandparents has messed things up for them. Because I obviously wasn't

responsible for that. At least that's what
they seem to believe at the moment.

FO: But they do know that Belle is back?

MB: Yes, but not where she's been. And that
bothers them. Above all because I'm not
being particularly cooperative. I've said I
have no idea who took her. The same way I
have no idea who's trying to frame me for
two murders.

FO: I understand. But perhaps you'll have to
tell them in the end? So it doesn't look
like you were guilty of kidnapping Belle as
well?

MB: Maybe. Right now the police seem to be
divided. Their suspicions against me
are weaker after the fire. But that's not
enough. It's only a matter of time before
whoever wants me out of the way makes
their next move. The reason I called you
was to make sure there's a secure record of
my version of events. I hope you don't feel
you've been deceived? I think I gave you a
fairly accurate description of the task.

FO: Absolutely. And, like I said on the phone
the first time you called, I've worked on
sensitive stories before. Nothing quite
like this, mind you.

MB: I can imagine.

(Silence)

FO: Lucifer. Who is he? Sheriff Stiller?

MB: For a short while I was absolutely certain.
Now I don't know. And I don't know how much
I dare investigate that question either.
And, to be crass about it, it doesn't
really make any difference if he does
remain anonymous.

FO: I'm thinking about what you found out in
that phone call. That it was never the
intention for Sara to be charged with
murder in the USA. That Lucifer got worried
when that cop, Benson, recognised her in
a photograph and started a preliminary
investigation against her. If Stiller
is Lucifer, that shouldn't have been a
problem. As sheriff, surely he could have
just sat on the investigation?

MB: Not without seeming weird or appearing
to have poor judgement. And, on the other
hand, he had easy access to the information
and could make his countermoves quickly. If
Stiller is Lucifer, of course . . . we just
don't know for certain.

(Silence)

MB: I'm trying to view everything that's
happened as a stage play. Sara Texas was
the first act. Now the second act is about
to start, and I've got the lead role in
that. I've got two murders to solve. One

missing child to find. And a family to take care of. God knows how I'm going to manage all that. But it has to work. One way or another.